Chasing Twilight

By Molly Brogan

Chasing Twilight

By Molly Brogan

ALSO BY MOLLY BROGAN

- Without a Word
- Remember Me
- Shadow Dancing

Chasing Twilight Published By Molly Brogan Enterprises

Copyright © 2007 Molly Brogan

ISBN 978 0 6151 4216 6

Cover photography by Gerald Klida

Cover Design By Molly Brogan Enterprises

For Information:

mbrogan@mc.net

MONTH ONE

THE BEGINNING

From: mbrogan@mbc.web
Sent: Monday May 6, 2002 9:16 AM
To: JAZMAN@mbc.web
Subject: Jake?

Found your name on my high school web page. Lawrence Bryant Jacobs. How nice they have the device that puts us in touch. Are phones becoming a thing of the past? Do I have the right guy? Are you the Jake I once knew? I don't think I ever knew your full name!

Do you remember sitting at the beach with a bonfire blazing like the sun and having to run like hell because the police were coming? Must have been in '71. I think you were with your friend Jim Nolan. I was with my friend from high school times, Viv Thomas. Christ, it's fun to remember those times.

Molly Brogan

From: JAZMAN@mbc.web
Sent: Monday May 6, 2002 2:22 PM
To: mbrogan@mbc.web
Subject: Molly?

Hi,

Yes, it is me! It is great to hear from you. I just
recently put my name on that web page. Almost didn't.
Jim actually convinced me to! We see each other or
talk every couple of years. Guess he was right. Look
who found me! He lives in Pennsylvania now and
works for the History Channel, filming all over the
world. Do you remember those little films he made in
high school? I remember the three of us acting for him.
Quite an imagination he had back then!

How is Viv? It has been a long time. But I remember
you both. And the times at the beach. Amazing that we
never were actually caught. Please tell me what you are
doing now. Are you still in the Chicago area? I am
living in the San Francisco area now but have business
and family in Chicago so I return once a month or so.
My kids are still there.

Phones a thing of the past? We carry them in our
pockets now! I wish I could get away from mine
sometimes.

Good to hear from you. Fill me in...

Jake

From: mbrogan@mbc.web
Sent: Tuesday May 7, 2002 10:14 AM
To: JAZMAN@mbc.web
Subject: Filling in

Good job clearing out the memory cobwebs. Those films of Jim's were great fun! I still see Viv every so often. I will have to remind her. Are you still into Scientology? I remember some long and lively talks at the beach that got me home quite late! Glad I didn't have a phone in my pocket then or my parents might have been able to pull me away.

I moved back to Northbrook after college and then moved up to the Gurnee area after my wedding to raise my children. They grew up in Wildwood, a little lakeside community on Gages Lake.

After my divorce in '95, I bought a townhouse not too far from the house the kids grew up in, across from Warren Township in Gurnee. It was a good spot for my children who used the Township for their backyard with all the ball fields, tennis courts, basketball courts, youth center, sledding and skating. I can always take a walk over there in the spring or fall and catch a friend watching one of their children's ball games. Stay until the sky becomes like lapis, then head home before dark.

My oldest son, Jack (Christopher John,) plays football at Augustana College. Just finishing his sophomore year. He has lived with me since the divorce. My youngest, Jamie (James, Jamie,) is a freshman at the high school, playing football also. He lives with his dad. That is it, two boys.

I don't know that I ever became deeply involved in any spiritual practice. I take my children to the local community church to be a good mom. I meditate daily, but never belonged to any group. Just tried to do what works best for me. Quiet myself between light and dark and consider it all. Scientology continues to fascinate me though. I am always glad to see faith (any) working for people.

I just finished my first novel. Pretty much stopped writing when my children were born and gave my life over to motherhood. I think it paid off. I have two wonderful sons. I picked up writing again when they became independent teen agers and I had the time to devout. I am glad to be writing again. Didn't know how much I missed it.

I also work for the local cable company. Hopping from project to project, what ever they need me to do. Pays the bills.

Please tell me more of your story. This is fun.

mb

From: JAZMAN@mbc.web
Sent: Tuesday, May 7, 2002 5:01 PM
To: mbrogan@mbc.web
Subject: RE: filling in

You still write. That's fantastic. I remember you and Viv laughing and reciting Shakespeare at the beach. Starry nights when we were all wrapped up in blankets to keep the cold off. Every so often, she would recite one of your poems and encourage you to give us more. You were so shy about your writing back then. But I kept asking you to show it to me. Do you remember?

We had that creative writing class together. Someone read your poem on Viet Nam aloud. It blew the whole class away. I think that is when I began to pay attention to you and Viv. You both had so much to offer. Still do, undoubtedly. What is she doing now?

So you live in Gurnee. I had a night club there for a few years. Between 80-98 I had twelve all over the Chicago area. When the economy soured (and my marriage) I sold all but two and got into the brokerage business out here. The clubs bring in decent money for the two or three days a month I put into them. A good place to see old friends too! Do you ever go out downtown?

I have two children. They are in Glenview with their mom. My daughter Grace, 15, and son Michael, 20. Sounds like our oldest kids are the same age. I wonder if they played each other in sports. Mike didn't play football, but did wrestle and play basketball. I've been having a hard time with him since high school. He's been in and out of college. Hope to get him out here and back into school soon.

I have been into scientology consistently over the years. Sounds like you have also been doing some soul searching.

Tell me more about your scene. Do you still write poetry? Would love to read some.

Jake

From: mbrogan@mbc.web
Sent: Monday May 13, 2002 10:23 AM
To: JAZMAN@mbc.web
Subject: small world

Hi Jake,

I've been out of the office for a few days at the Mount Prospect office. Yes, I work for the cable company. My current project is administering 1-3M a month in contract labor for the North Chicago Market. It was new position so I suppose they wanted me to come in and put processes in place. I had to learn to swear again and kick contractor ass.

I don't know how I got here. Just accepting opportunities as they arrived I suppose. When I divorced in 95, work became all about the money. It took a lot of interesting and very different jobs to get here. Put many miles on several cars.

Our oldest sons may have played each other in basketball. I can't remember if Warren played Glenbrook South in a non conference game. Sports seemed to be a good way to keep them involved and out of trouble.

Wouldn't it be great to have your son out there going to school near you? Fall is wonderful, watching the college football games. I spoil myself and get a room at my favorite B&B in Rock Island so that I can spend more time with Jack after his home games. All we seem to do is eat and shop for a couple of days. Such fun just bummin'! He's not one to talk on the phone so I go down there when I can to keep the home fires burning.

My youngest is rebelling like your oldest did. At a much more tender age. He was a freshman in high school this year. Decided to live with dad where he can come and go as he pleases. The courts allow children to choose here in Lake County once they are in high school. Every morning over coffee, I watch the birds fly in and out of the bird house he built and hung in a tree in my front yard, and think about him. Sure do hope he twigs soon. Well, I guess I was a handful myself. Payback.

I started the book a couple of years ago and recently finished it. I hope I will finish editing it soon so that I can begin the process of finding a publisher (took Anne Rice over 10 years to get Vampire published.) I just

can't seem to let go of it. It is a part of me. Very
different than writing a short piece or a play or poem. I
suppose I will know when the time is right.

Viv is teaching at NYU. She got her Masters in Art at
Yale and shows her work quite a bit in the Manhattan
galleries. I try to get out there to see her amap.

So good to hear you are enjoying this crazy ride....tell
more when you can.

From: JAZMAN@mbc.web
Sent: Wednesday, May 15, 2002 9:13 PM
To: mbrogan@mbc.web
Subject: RE: small world

Hi Molly,

Your job sounds big. 1-3M a month is quite a lot of
labor costs. What do the contractors do? Where is your
primary office? Do you travel in the Chi area a lot?
Travel anywhere else in the country?

Tell me about your book. Anyone I know in it?

I think Glenbrook South did play Warren in basketball
their junior year, the year Warren took second in state.
Must have been exciting for you to see those games in
Peoria. I loved coaching the little league sports. And
miss the high school games. My daughter is an artist
(like you and Viv!) not an athlete. She plays the guitar
and flute. She is really quite good and has played with
different local orchestras.

Where is the boys' father? Still in the area? Was he
from Northbrook or Glenview? I don't remember your
married name listed on the web page. If you don't want
to talk about it, I will understand.

Had a martini with dinner and now I am tired, but still have work to do.

Write soon and take care,

Jake

From: mbrogan@mbc.web
Sent: Thursday May 16, 2002 8:52 AM
To: JAZMAN@mbc.web
Subject: small world

I sat and watched the sunrise before heading off to work this morning. I could have lingered in that moment all day...

How funny we shared a game with our children and didn't know it. I wonder how many other affinities I miss each day...

That was such a great basketball year for Warren. They did take second in state.

My ex, Luke, lives in Wildwood and is very involved with the children. Still has not forgiven me for the divorce, fought it every inch of the way. But even our Catholic Priest told me it was the right thing to do. The tension has been hard on the children. I think that has a lot to do with my second son's rebellion. It is so much easier for children of divorce to rebel. They have 2 homes to bounce between. But rebellion isn't all bad in the end. Look at us!

The book is about love and loss. About how children have a wonderful way of accepting life as it comes to them. And about what happens to adults when they continue to do the same, and can't process it consciously. It is also about how the current Family Court system exacerbates family problems because of its lack of understanding on some very basic human issues and ineffective laws.

I guess the book originated out of my frustration with the court system and the feeling that there were things that should be brought to light. I have some friends who are Judges in the county that agree! I don't think they should see change as an impossibility when it comes to the welfare of children.

I did a lot of research into the workings of the court, and the frustration of the men and women trying to get some help from an antiquated and overburdened system. Also a lot of reading of contemporary women authors to get a feel for their voice, structure and what is being published. It is written in the vein of Goethe. By that I mean as an examination of the effects of character and relationship on experience.

I believe it is good and that I can get it published. It will take some time is all.

It's not hard to tell I like to write is it? Better get back to work.

mb

From: JAZMAN@mbc.web
Sent: Thursday May 16, 2002 9:17 AM
To: mbrogan@mbc.web
Subject: RE: small world

Good morning. Your book sounds interesting. Like you draw from a great deal of personal experience. And use it to try to change. Good for you. You were always like that. I have a friend going through a rough divorce out here. Courts here are very different. More family friendly. I think it varies from state to state.

Warren did have a great year that year. Beat Zion in the sectionals. St. Joseph actually won the state championship didn't they? Mike and I went to as many play off games as possible, even though Glenbrook South did not make it into the playoffs that year. Exciting games. Too bad I didn't see you.

It's great that Luke is an active dad, but why is he still mad at you? It has been over a long time. Is he stuck in the divorce? Has he found someone else?

What do you do these days for fun? Go to clubs, parties, movies?

Off to work now. Can't wait to hear from you again.

Jake

From: mbrogan@mbc.web
Sent: Thursday May 16, 2002   3:48 PM
To: JAZMAN@mbc.web
Subject: small world

OK, but now you are going to have to give up some more of your own story.

Where are you living in CA? Do you like it?   How about telling me your divorce story? Believe me, I have heard many, many divorce stories researching this book.

Well, I guess that is enough questioning for now.

My ex - I don't really talk about him much. Something people have always had to drag out of me. And lots of people have been curious. I can't say if he has moved on or not. But he is still very angry with me. Probably always will be. But he became angry before I filed, it just intensified afterward. Something happened to him in midlife that I have stopped trying to understand. But

I did give it my best shot before I filed. We were in different varieties of counseling together for 3 years before I filed. What I learned was this. His anger has little to do with me. I am just the target. There seemed to be something that caused a great deal of pain that he was unwilling to face.

I don't think he is stuck in the divorce. I think he is stuck there. He became someone very different than the man I married. And I can honestly say that he did not know me at all by the time I filed for divorce. He saw me as someone completely different than who I am and who he fell in love with.

I am not a psychologist, but it seems intense pain can do strange things to people.

I watched several people that I grew up with not make it out of adolescence without stunting addictions or mental health problems. Midlife was the same. Some make it through - some get stuck. For some people, human psychology is as mysterious as Mythology. To others, it comes as naturally as spiritual breathing. I suppose there are very good reasons for this that people like Carl Jung or the Dali Lama spend a life time explaining. But for me, there comes a time to let go and move on. Raising more questions in a story or a poem is the best I can make of it.

I have dated a bit since then. But honestly, I am really enjoying my independence. Especially now that the boys are more independent. It takes someone extraordinary to draw me out of my comfortable singleness. More than a flash fire. Have not found anyone to keep me out of it. And I am not really planning on it. My love flows like a river in so many other ways. I love writing when I want to, sleeping when I want to, eating what I want to, going out when I want to. The darn job can get in the way of all that though!

The contractors that I administrate do cable installation and repair in customer homes. Cable, high speed Internet and telephony (local phone over the cable.) Contractors make up 5-25% of the workforce. The work fluctuates in volume with the market and company staffing levels. In the cowboy cable days contractors made money hand over fist. Now days, since the broadband companies have clustered in large metropolitan areas it is easier to establish uniform contracts, procedures and administrative tools. A year ago, none of that was in place. I am glad to say that we have established processes that make it more efficient, cost effective and just plain easier to kick ass when necessary. In a very blue collar culture, that is necessary on occasion. I am not sure if they put me here because I am good at developing processes, or kicking ass, or both. Probably both. I have learned a lot about communication and people over the years.

OK. I've written a short story here. Your turn.

Smile,
mb

From: JAZMAN@mbc.web
Sent: Wednesday, May 22, 2002 8:43 AM
To: mbrogan@mbc.web
Subject: RE: small world

OK. You want to hear my story. After all the stories that you have already heard.

Well, I suppose I can say that I married for the wrong reasons. At the time, I thought they were the right reasons. I was in my late twenties, wanted a family. Knew it was time to settle down. Made my best choice. But we were never really friends to begin with. Social companions, is a better description I suppose. None of those long talks on the beach that help you figure things out and grow close.

I stayed for the sake of my kids until '00, when I made the blanket decision to change direction with my business. Told her it was over and moved out here to get into the stock market. When the economy is bad, there is money to be made there with all of the fluctuation. We managed to get through the separation process with the church but I have been waiting to file for divorce until she is more agreeable. I would like to spare my kids the blood bath.

I currently live in Mill Valley, just off of Highway 1, not too far from the ocean. , north of the city. Very pretty and close enough to the office in downtown SF. Much better climate than Chicago. Have you seen it? Have any (other) friends out here?

I know I have the best of both worlds. A business here and there. I go back to Chi for three or four days a month to see my friends there, handle the clubs, see my kids. Gives me the time I need to get this business off the ground here and enjoy the California culture, which always fit me like a glove.

What do you think of that?

Jake

From: mbrogan@mbc.web
Sent: Wednesday May 22, 2002 1:41 PM
To: JAZMAN@mbc.web
Subject: small world

I think I have more questions!

Two years is a long time to be separated. Although divorce can be more expensive if two people can agree on financial terms of separation, but not financial terms of divorce! Divorce is very expensive if people can't agree. Or it can cost as little as $600 and only require one attorney if two people agree. Every story is as different as the people involved. Any future plans there? The whole process sucks no matter how it is done, especially when children are involved.

Chgo to SF once a month is a lot of traveling! Two different homes, two different cultures. Don't you feel torn? Do you like flying that much or need to throw down a few martinis before takeoff?

I did spend time in CA in the 70s. San Francisco and Sonoma where I had two dear friends. While I was in college I would go out there every spring break. Also LA where my brother Ned lived for awhile. I thought about settling in Sonoma in the late 70s, but decided instead to come back to Chicago and have a go at my relationship with my then future husband who is now my X. A turning point I suppose. Miss the beaches and sunsets out there.

I am not sure why, but after my first son was born in '81, I only traveled east. I don't think I realized that until now. New York, Vermont, Florida and places in between. Haven't been west since. I do have close friends currently living in SF, Denver and Las Vegas. Now that I am more on my own, I may begin travel more. With Jack in college, I have a hard time justifying spending much on fun. He plans to go on for a Masters, so finances will be tight for awhile. He is a great guy and I don't think twice about doing what I can to give him a good start in life.

Tell me some more about your California home. I will be doing a little local business traveling for the rest of this week - won't be able to get my email until Monday. In the car a great deal, not near the computer at all.

Take care,
mb

From: JAZMAN@mbc.web
Sent: Monday, May 27, 2002 11:22 AM
To: mbrogan@mbc.web
Subject: RE: small world

It's Monday. Are you back, or off, because it is
Memorial Day? You might get this tomorrow instead.

I have been separated for almost two years. She is not
happy about it and I think she keeps hoping I will
change my mind, although I tell her that won't happen.
When I am back there next week we will go over it
again. She is thinking of moving to North Carolina
where she has some family. That may settle things
once and for all.

I hope that Mike will be out here this fall for school. It
is MUCH less money out here as a resident. He will
need to bring his grades up before I will spend much
more. Grace wants to move out here but that won't
happen unless her mom does. It is all very confused
now. But we will have to make some decisions soon.

Hope you had some fun this weekend. I do remember
that you were very good at having fun. I always had
fun when you were around. Do you have certain things
that you do in your spare time? Do you ever date?

Later,

Jake

From: mbrogan@mbc.web
Sent: Tuesday May 28, 2002 8:52 AM
To: JAZMAN@mbc.web
Subject: small world

Do I date? Speaking from experience, there were many
more choices in the dating world the last time I was
without a partner - in late teens early twenties. I have

had some very bizarre offers, most of them with questionable intentions. It did not take me long to remember why I hated dating.

I do have a friend in SF that might be good company for you. She is bouncing in and out of a relationship currently. Margaret O'Brien. She was my roommate for two years at SIU before she transferred to Chicago Academy of Fine Arts. We made quite a pair. We both have the map of Ireland written on our faces. We were sometimes called "those sisters," although I have to say, she has and always will far outshine me.

She has an Interior Design company in Berkley, O'Brien and Associates. She has traveled the world, her work has been in the industry magazines and she has projects to her credit like U2's castle in Ireland. Our lives have been very different. But when we get together, it is like we have never been apart - the inside jokes, the abstract conversations. I've always thought her to be amazing. Might be date worthy. Or just a good break for both of you.

I must say that you seem to be handling the end of a marriage admirably. Waiting until she is ready may be the best you can do. It will be hard for her to be separated from the children. For a mom, it is an almost physical reaction. Taking it slowly may be the best course. Kenny Logins would say that you are on the "precipice" headed to the point of no return. It may be easier to accept the change after living some of it already. One of the hardest things about divorce for the children and adults is not understanding how life can possibly be lived differently. Maybe once everyone gains more of their independence and knows they will make it through, the legal process will be easier. I envy your ability to take this course. The courts are full of people who, for whatever reason, could not.

Spare time? Well, I have more to do than time to do it, that's for sure! Most of my spare time is spent reading and writing. I am still cleaning up the novel. And have started a collection of poems to help me cope with the separation from my youngest. I work on the townhouse or go out with friends - clubs, concerts, plays. The term "reclusive writer" has its allure. My friends keep pulling me back to the world though.

Hope things go well for you next weekend. I'll send out a prayer...

mb

From: JAZMAN@mbc.web
Sent: Wednesday, May 29, 2002 8:52 AM
To: mbrogan@mbc.web
Subject: RE: small world

Good morning Molly. Hope you had a nice holiday weekend. Mine was relaxing, but not much fun. Did go out with some girls from the office Friday after work. Five girls. Had a few martinis. Still got home by eleven. Don't usually go out much. Don't know many single people out here, and I am still married I suppose.

Do you go out? Have a boyfriend? Must be strange to go back to dating after so many years. Found anything serious since you divorced? Is your ex remarried? OK, enough being nosy.

I can't imagine myself dating again. Going out with people you don't know very well. And what if one begins to feel more than the other. Is it my imagination, or was it easier in high school?. We just hung out with friends more.

Your friend sounds great. But a total stranger. I had a blind date once. Swore I would never do it again. Disaster. What are your thoughts?

I went down to the ocean shore here this morning, remembering nights in the past on the shores of Lake Michigan. The color of the water is a deeper blue here. Lapis, as you say. It was quite windy, an ocean mist wet my face. I thought of you. Come down to the club some night, will you?

Look forward to your next letter,

Jake

From: mbrogan@mbc.web
Sent: Wednesday May 29, 2002 4:02 PM
To: JAZMAN@mbc.web
Subject: small world

Good Morning Jake, you Big Fat Baby! Don't think of it as a blind date. Think of it as an adventure. What is the worst that could happen? You meet someone that you won't meet again. You could start exchanging thoughts by email! I can assure you she is not fatal attraction material. If it turns out that you are, I can assure you, that I will come out there and kick your ass (I protect my friends.)

I would love to see you while you are here. But let's not call it a date. How about getting reacquainted with an old friend.
I have reservations about going out with everyone. The Jerry Seinfeld school of dating. I do much better having fun with friends in a group. Which shouldn't surprise me - it is where I felt the most comfortable earlier in life.

I really didn't "date" much then! I went out with Patrick Thompson through most of High School (how I

met so many Lake Forest folks.) And dated my X
while I was in college. Actually, he was from
Northbrook. My brother introduced us when I was in
high school.

Anyway, I am not the person to advise anyone on
dating. Although 5 girls after work sounds like a good
start! But I know what you mean. There were so many
more choices in my 20's! I think the key is being what
Seinfeld called "a good breaker upper." Don't expect
anything deep, say thanks, move on! I am sure it
sounds easier than it actually is. I have been saying no
thank you to dates a lot. It is easier to keep friends that
way. I'm pretty good at it now. I try to get a smile
before I go. I have gathered some very good
confidantes on the way. It is really just getting to know
people.

And I am not really actively seeking dates. I hope you
don't think that is why I am looking up old class mates.
I am fascinated by people's stories. Must be the writer
in me. It has been great fun finding people and hearing
their stories. I really am happy being independent right
now. After so many years of compromise it feels great
just being me.

And your story...why do you stay in California? What
gets you up in the morning? What do you think about
before sleep? What are your dreams?

You are a wonderful communicator! Not everyone is.
Viv can't write an email worth a damn. But every once
and awhile she sends something short and sweet to keep
me up to date. I am hoping that when I stop paying
college expenses my finances will free me up to travel
more and reconnect.

I made plans with Peg to go out there in the fall
sometime. I have to work it around the football
schedule. I am hoping she can make it here at least

once before then. Those frequent flyer benefits of hers come in handy.

I look forward to your emails too. Keep 'em comin.'

mb

From: JAZMAN@mbc.web
Sent: Thursday, May 30, 2002 9:06 AM
To: mbrogan@mbc.web
Subject: RE: small world

Wish I was staying longer for my next trip to Chi. Would love to see you too. I will have to book an extra day or two on the next trip. Between being needed at the clubs and kid time, I don't think I can swing it. But you have me thinking now. If I can't work it out, I will be back in a few weeks.

Those five women were not what you are thinking. They all have husbands. And I wouldn't date anyone from work - too dicey. But I guess if you don't take blind dates to seriously, it might be OK. Being a friend of yours, I am sure she is a blast. Actually, when I think of the girls I saw you with in high school, I don't remember a bad looking or weird one among them. You had a great group of friends. People from a few different groups actually. Do you ever see any of those folks from so long ago? I don't, so I feel out of touch.

You are coming out here in the fall? Why not sooner? Guess Jack has a bye weekend during football season. Do you go to all the games? If Mike were playing college ball I would attend any within a few hundred miles.

You say no a lot? Do you ever say yes? What would it take?

Have to run, will answer your personal questions next time around. Can you imagine depending on the postal service for this kind of talk? I really look forward to hearing from you.

Take care,

Jake

From: mbrogan@mbc.web
Sent: Thursday May 30, 2002 2:13 PM
To: JAZMAN@mbc.web
Subject: small world

With Jack home for the summer, I hate to take a trip and miss out on any time with him. I miss him so during the school year.

Luckily, most of his away games are closer to me than Augustana! Many are in the Chgo area. It is really the home games that take up my entire weekend because I get a room in town and spend time with Jack after the game and the next day before I leave town. For his away games, I show up, get a hug and some conversation after the game and off he goes so that he is on the bus on time. I don't miss too many of them.

What does it take for me to say yes...now there is the Jake I remember! Huge flirt. You and Jim both. You were quite a pair.

Spend as much time with your kids as you can. If anyone knows the importance of that, it's me. I just like you for your emails anyway (just kidding.)

All of those books that are all about letters between famous people...I wonder if email will change the face of them. A kind of Marshall McLuhan Understanding Media thing. That media is an extension of man. The more we access it, the more immediate information becomes. The more immediate the information, the higher the collective consciousness...Are we in for a leap in spiritual growth? And what will the effects be on relationship? Letters will be immediately delivered. Communications more immediate. All so interesting.

All I know is, that I have found many more people willing to send emails than write letters. A good thing...I do see folks from high school from time to time. Any one in particular?

The California trip...I will stay as long as I can. It may be a long weekend. I had a job offer today that I am seriously considering from one of the contracting companies in the north Chicago market. If I stay in the position, it will definitely be a long weekend so that I have time off around Christmas. If I can negotiate more vacation time....who knows. The fall is a long way off.

But I would like to spend as much time with Peg as possible. I miss her presence in my life. We met on my first day at SIU met while I was standing in line to get my ID picture taken. It was an incredibly long line and I was alone. Peg and a couple of her friends were in front of me. For about an hour I was thoroughly amused and fascinated by her – her humor, her relationship with her friends, her entire being. When it came time for her picture to be taken she freaked out, because there was a $1 charge and she did not have it. I gave her a dollar and told her not to worry about returning it. Her company for the past hour was well worth a buck. I remember walking back to my dorm and feeling the sun on m face. I knew then that something significant had just happened.

She returned the dollar that afternoon and we have been fast friends ever since. Best investment I ever made.

Take care - mb

From: JAZMAN@mbc.web
Sent: Friday, May 31, 2002 4:29 AM
To: mbrogan@mbc.web
Subject: RE: small world

Jim and I will always be friends, although years have gone by since I saw him last. When we do get together, it is like no time has passed. Probably like you and Peg. Friends we make in our teens and twenties are more deeply burned into our minds than friends developed at a later time. Maybe because we are still developing. I do regret not keeping up more with folks from that time.

Who was that guy you dated in high school? Patrick. Ever see him anymore? Anyone else from Lake Forest? I can't remember which of your friends were from where.

Being married for 20 years, my kids, businesses took up so much time. Do you think you can get some of those old friends to come down to the club with you some night when I am in town? I should drop a line to Jim and see if he has any plans to travel that way soon.

This job offer. Is the job better than the one you have now? More money? What do they want you to do? Well, it's Friday. Did you say "yes" for tonight? What would you like to do if I ever get the opportunity?
lbj

From: mbrogan@mbc.web
Sent: Friday, May 31, 2002 2:13 PM
To: JAZMAN@mbc.web
Subject: small world

Your email was a welcome diversion from an otherwise CRAZY morning. So nonsense much goes on in large corporations.

I am glad that you and Jim have made your friendship lifelong. I smile every time I think of you two together. I think that we are blessed with so few people in our life that make us "more" than we are without them. That wonderfully deep connection that can only be experienced with two. Whether it is children, friends, family....

I have not said yes in so long, I can't remember what it takes to get me there. But I like to do the simple things. Sit on the beach and have a very long talk (remember?) Walk in the woods. You are welcome to tag along to an Auggie game this fall!

I did not keep up with Patrick Thompson since he broke my heart at 17. I did see him a couple of times in my 20s. We spent some time together and caught up a little. But it was hard to get past the disappointment I guess. I couldn't help but wonder if his new love knew we were together... He was two years ahead of me in school. Turns out his second year in college he had two of us in tow. He tried to work it out after I found out but I could not get past that. He saw her for almost an entire school year before I figured it out. He began to kiss me differently. When I questioned it, he confessed. I don't know why kids think that a high school/college romance can work. It rarely does.

But I have kept up with some of his group. Sue Bissett (now Burchall) married Jack Burchall from Highland Park. I actually got married at their home in Libertyville all those years ago. Sue, Peg and Viv were my bridesmaids. Sue's high school sweetheart, Jeff Black married money and is living in the Bahamas. Ken Gustafson teaches at a University in Missouri. His high school sweetheart, went on to become a major heroine user. I saw her in 79, very incoherent. I would be very surprised if she was still with us. Lots of very different stories!

The job offer is about 10,000 more and much less stress. I would be the Finance Manager for one of the contracting firms that does business with the cable company. Wild because numbers were always my weak point. I am so much better with people, programs, processes, training, leadership, writing (even grant writing.) I have done many very different things since I rejoined the workforce. But the finance person? If someone had told me 10 years ago I would have laughed. But the offer is interesting because I know all of the needed processes and have probably more detail on how these companies need to be accounting than most of them do, having seen it from the customer's standpoint. I utilize financial reports to track the contractor's performance and have even developed some reporting tools of my own that are being used market wide. I guess I could do it. I would rather work with children. Too bad it doesn't pay.

I really would like to move west soon. I had planned to move out of state when Jamie went off to college, but I see him so seldom now, and spend so much time alone, it might be sooner. I got offers for jobs in DC and Vegas, but my sons were not happy at the news. I don't know what I will do. But I have time to consider.

What about those personal questions?

Have a great weekend.

mb

M ONTH TWO

From: JAZMAN@mbc.web
Sent: Saturday, June 1, 2002 9:42 AM
To: mbrogan@mbc.web
Subject: RE: small world

You probably won't get this until Monday, unless you can get your email at home. Guess I will find out!

An Auggie game sounds like a great time. I miss the high school games. The players play because they love the game. What position does Jack play? Is he on special teams?

I have some hometown friends living out here. Do you remember Sam Young, the Storyteller's son? Remember that PBS show? He is out here with his high school sweetheart. Been married 26 years and still going strong. Would that qualify as a solid relationship?

I remember those guys from Lake Forest. Can't place Sue though. You were married at her home. Do you still see her? Does she like Jazz? For that matter, do you?

Sounds like the job change is a good one, unless the company is too small to be solid. Don't know much about contracting for cable companies. How long have they been in business? Your mind is so well organized I imagine that you are just fine in finance.

You asked why I ended up in California. My parents moved out here after I was out of high school. My dad was transferred. I moved out and attended UCLA. Decided to move back to Chi afterward because so many of my friends settled there. The nightclub business began with a little club in Evanston and just grew. At first the hours were crazy. After a few years I had enough staff to cover the night hours. Met a lot of great people and don't regret it at all. Still love it actually. Which is why I hang on to the two clubs downtown? Each a little different. The one in the loop is a strictly jazz venue. The north side club mixes it up more: jazz, blues and occasionally swing. As long as they bring in decent money I will keep them.   It is nice to have my own place to bring friends and kick back. Do you dance?

When I needed to make a break, I moved out here near my mom and bought a seat on the stock exchange. Have a small firm now that does quite well. Lots of work though. Very different than the clubs. But I really needed a total change. Change in profession. Change in climate, culture and relationship.

Your questions finally. What gets me up in the morning? Well, your emails! I go on line first thing. Building this business. The need to breathe (just kidding.) Think about before sleep? Your emails. The future. My children. I wish I could see into the future. We need to put our postulates out there and make them reality, know what I mean? How about you?

I would really like to see you.

Jake

From: mbrogan@mbc.web
Sent: Monday, June 3, 2002 8:43 AM
To: JAZMAN@mbc.web
Subject: small world getting larger

Do you know of a way to expedite those postulates? I
would now be living above my bookstore/coffee house
strategically positioned near a University if I did! May
just have to wait for the paperback and movie deal for
my book. Patience seems to be one of my greatest
lessons here.

I love jazz and blues and swing. Sue's husband was in
several different bands that Luke and I followed around
and danced to for years before children. Sounds like
you started your clubs after the kids came along.
Funny, the parallels in our lives. We still have music in
common. And the love of good conversation.

Jack is a running back. I have a very hard time
containing myself when he is running with the ball. We
have run into a roadblock this summer. His MD and I
suspect he has not recovered from the acute mono that
he developed at the end of his freshman year football
season. There was one night that I almost called the
ambulance because his spleen was so enlarged that he
was in a lot of pain. I will never forget driving him
back to school after Christmas break at his insistence,
and the helpless mom feeling it left me. I admired his
determination but worried about his health.

Well, he is exhibiting the same symptoms, although
they are not near as severe. Inability to stay awake after
a night of 14-16 hrs. sleep. Loss of appetite. Feeling ill
after working out. He is reluctant to take a blood test
because he is worried about not being able to play in
the fall. Although he is not all that broken hearted that
I am insisting he not get a job this summer. He needs to
be in the best shape of his life in mid August when he

returns to the football program. Not to mention get over this mono once and for all.

He hopes to start this fall. I suppose his health will set the perimeters for his performance. I know that worries him too. It is wonderful to see him live his dream so early in life. And I have seen him bear great disappointment with total grace already. He had an ankle injury that kept him out of four games his senior year. The orthopedist told him it would be an eight week recovery, but he worked his way back to the playoffs and really starred.

Although that injury really kept his stats down and probably kept him from Division One recruitment, I think I did convince him that he was better off in 1AA or Division 3 because an injury would not mean the loss of his financial aid package. He was disappointed.

Anyway, that has become the goal for the summer. Regain health, optimum fitness, enjoy each other's company and have mom foot the bill. An increase in salary is probably a god send. Or maybe a postulate working.

Don't get me started telling you about my children....

I was very disappointed that I missed out on a relationship and family experience like your friends the Young's. Were you? That WAS the postulate. I think sometimes, the primal gets in the way.

You mentioned your mom lives in SF. Is your dad still alive? My dad flew bombers in the Pacific during the war. He was a Marine Corps Colonel when he retired. Irish Catholic Marine Corps Colonel...maybe that's why I say no thank you so much! But that war experience haunted him all his life. I can't imagine living it, can you?

I very much enjoy our emails. You are a terrific communicator. I think about the same things between dreaming and awake. That is when I do most of my prayer/mediation. There is a place somewhere in there that feels so right, where postulates are not only posited but inspired. I love that place. But usually, I fall asleep before I find it.

Have I overworked that postulate thing?

Before you see me, you should know that since my late teens, I have gained 150 lbs, lost half my teeth and most of my hair. (Smile.)

mb

From: JAZMAN@mbc.web
Sent: Tuesday, June 4, 2002 9:07 AM
To: mbrogan@mbc.web
Subject: RE: small world

You might be at work now. What is your work schedule? When will you be making the job change? If you postulated finding a job with more income, that one seems to be working.

I hope Jack regains his health soon. Young adults really run their bodies down trying to get so much out of life, wanting it all at once. Knowing that good health takes effort and attention comes with maturity and experience. Mono is a common illness on college campuses. I know it was rampant at UCLA in the Freshman dorms. Juniors and Seniors learn to pace themselves a little better. Meningitis is now a problem also isn't it?

I perused the Augustana web page. Jack is about the same size as Mike! Did he play JV freshman year? Does JV work the same way in college as in high school?

I would really like to see a game with you. An away game in September sounds good. Won't be too cold by then for a guy from California.

Your dad flew for the Marine Corps. I am surprised to hear they had pilots. I can imagine it, but would not want to be up there doing it. My dad was an Army medic. He would not talk much about his war experiences. Had three purple hearts and various scars though.

We can find you a wig, and a good dentist. Have you considered Metabolife? We may have to address those 150 lbs. I need to start working out again myself. Could stand to lose 20 lbs. Just need to put the postulate out there and find a handy club, on the way home from work probably.

Watch out for those negative postulates. The ones you don't realize you are making. They can destroy the creative ones.

I love your emails. Take good care of yourself.

lbj

From: mbrogan@mbc.web
Sent: Tuesday, June 4, 2002   10:32 AM
To: JAZMAN@mbc.web
Subject: you

I work from 7-4. Nice for me because I am an early riser. Lately, I can sometimes catch my nocturnal son as I get up at 4:30 AM to start my day. On those days I watch MTV instead of the news over morning coffee and get much less housework done but enjoy myself much more. I think he understands that he will be enduring my healthy lifestyle lectures until he goes back to school. I did admit to him that I tried surviving on minimal sleep in college, only to have a health service doctor tell me that I would not live to see 40 if I kept it up! Kids...

As you can see, the Auggie team is bigger than the Chicago Bears. JV played Monday games with local non conference colleges. Jack did play in some of those his Freshman year, but I don't think last year at all. I hope next year is everything he wants it to be. He appeases me by staying on the Dean's list. A smoke screen for his true priority. Any Auggie game you choose in Sept. would be just fine.

My stupid joke about my appearance was just to check expectation. I imagine a guy like you can easily find a Hollywood hard body 20 years younger. And that is not me. Like you, I play with the 20lbs up and down on the heavy side. After Jack was born, I struggled being 20 lbs underweight because he changed my metabolism. I like the padding better. Could you really handle a person with only half of their teeth? And by the way, my pounds moved and left no forwarding address a long time ago. Age may be hard on the body, but it has such a lovely effect on self concept.

My Buddhist influenced philosophy of no attachment, no aversion, makes it a lot easier to not worry so much about appearance or public perception. I suppose that is easy for me to say because I have been blessed with a pretty good gene pool. But time stops for no man, or woman. Taking good care of myself helps.

Yep, my dad flew bombers that were like tin cans with toggle switches. He had nightmares all his life, yelling at his wing men to cover him. I don't remember the names of his planes but he used to take me to the Glenview Naval Air Base with him where he reported to his reserve unit and show me the planes that he flew. And tell me stories about him and his buddies making the Amtrak engineers mad by bouncing their wheels off of the train engines.

I just had a major DeJaVu about this email. Chilling. Anyway, you take care of yourself also.

mb

From: JAZMAN@mbc.web
Sent: Wednesday, June 5, 2002 8:52 AM
To: mbrogan@mbc.web
Subject: RE: you

A bit sleepy this morning after oversleeping a bit. I usually only sleep 6. Last night 7. Harder to wake up.

Your joke about the new you – I liked it. The teeth – I would like to see 80% but like I said, they are replaceable. A Hollywood hard body? You must not know any of those. Not at all my style. And the difference in age, why would I do that to myself? Hard to keep up the conversation. Values so different. Different view points.

I have been thinking lately, next time, I would like to start as close friends. Someone that I can communicate with, share key points, am physically attracted to. Once you have fallen in love, which is the easy part, you need to keep creating it every day. Not put it on automatic pilot. Have to commit to each other at that point too or it won't work. This isn't the third world where multiple wives are possible. How does 7 husbands sound?

What do you think it takes to make a relationship work?

I think I made the mistake marrying someone who was not a close friend. Before long, our fundamental differences created barriers. Once we put it on auto pilot, the barriers created too much distance.

Communication died. Affinity dimmed. Reality became stagnant.

I miss my children when I am not in Chicago. That is the part that is hard to get past. I wish there was some way for me to be in their lives more. I am sure you understand.

Buddhists say no attachments. You will need to explain that. And that chilling DeJaVu. Intriguing. Please tell me more about it.

Your dad must have had some real emotional scars from his war experiences. Killing people for a couple of years has to have some major effects. My dad wouldn't talk about it but watched a lot of war movies. Those old movies didn't have the blood and guts that the new ones do. Are your folks still alive? My mom is, but my dad passed away 14 years ago. Doesn't seem like that long ago, really. Strange.

Take care,

lbj

From: mbrogan@mbc.web
Sent: Wednesday, June 5, 2002 11:22 AM
To: JAZMAN@mbc.web
Subject: really me

Good morning. These emails are a wonderful way to begin the day. You do have more than 80% of your teeth don't you? (Smile.) Over the past few years I have learned to take each relationship as it unfolds. My instincts about people are great. I keep my expectations in check. I have always enjoyed people and that will probably never change. Each relationship, no matter the duration, is a gift. I venture as deeply as time and other constraints of reality will allow.

I am not sure why I have not settled down with anyone. I can say that I have such a strong idea of who I am that it may put guys off. Lots of guys seem to need to me fit into a particular, pre slotted place in their lives. Not enough freedom there. I guess starting with deep mutual respect and friendship is good. Somewhere common visions and postulates need to be formed. Agreements about the future. That seems to be where things have stalled out for me. I will have to think about that more. I seem to have just been taking it as it comes and not thinking too much about it. I am happy being on my own right now so I guess I have not felt the need to analyze that. But I think if the right guy came along, it would be a no brainier. 7 husbands? I have had some interesting offers but that has not been one. Might need to approach it as a team. Wait - my dad's image is blocking the idea of the sexual aspect of marriage to 7 guys. No can do, I guess.

If you missed out on the depths of respect, trust, support, self discovery found especially in marriage then you probably did need to move on. I have seen marriages go there and the children see it. Even if they don't understand it, they understand that other parents share something that theirs do not. Or they grow up with a limited idea of what love can be.

My relationship was very close and very deep. When we were at our best, his company totaled 1.5M in revenue for the year, we were designing our dream home on Gages Lake and our children were gloriously happy. I was lucky enough to stay home with them for 12 years and I will never regret that. Something happened in mid life that I have stopped trying to figure out. I suspect that Luke was predisposed to problems (they sometimes come on for guys at that time in life cleverly disguised as a mid life crisis.) Looking back, I wish that I understood how his family problems forewarned our family problems.

Now I tell all children, individually and in groups, that it is important to pay attention to the relationships in a person's life. If you want have an idea about how your relationship will work out, look at the quality of the relationships currently and in the past, for that person. Not everyone understands how their relationships with their families create internal formulas for behavior. If they don't understand it, they are destine to repeat those patterns until they do. The world is full of people who are not self aware. At a certain point, we are not responsible for others difficult behavior. But knowing how a person handles difficult behavior can tell you a lot about them. Am I rambling? Anyway, I learned a lot surviving the end of that relationship. I hope that my children fare as well. I worry about the little one.

The Buddhists say no attachments, no aversions. I think the idea is that pain of any kind is a matter of perception and response. It only hurts if you let it kind of thing. What keeps us returning to the wheel of life is desire (attachments and aversions.) The less you have through exercising compassion, the more peace you have and the closer you are to god. Being an emotional creature...I struggle with this. But I think it does make sense. I love the current theories on Consilience. Because I think there is some truth to all of these ideas. No attachments I struggle with more than no aversions.

I think my dad's aversion to being shot out of the sky is what haunted him. Not talking about war experiences must be a military man thing. One of the Admirals at Great Lakes Naval Training Center was a very good friend to me before he moved from the area. He would never admit that the military taught men not to talk about it. But I teased him about it all the time. My dad passed on in 1979 and my mom in 1999.

Don't you have DeJaVu? For me it is always the same. Come to think of it, I have never tried to explain this before so forgive me if I fail to deliver clarity.

When DeJaVu comes on, there is a trigger. This time it was our email. I had written to you before, many times. There was a mathematician around the turn of the century named Oupensky. He wrote a book called In Search of the Miraculous. Later, he became a follower of the Russian philosopher Gurdjieff who led groups of some of Europe's greatest minds in today what would probably be called workshops.

Anyway - Oupensky had a theory about time before he met Gurdjieff. He believed that time was vertical, as well as horizontal as most people perceive it to be. And he thought that in each moment, we are experiencing that same moment in an infinite number of other realities. Simultaneous time.

I think this could be true, and also think that the strength of our affinities in each reality determines the number of realities that we share. In other words, I probably share the most number of realities with my son Jack with whom I share my strongest affinity. I think the Buddhists also have an explanation like this in that complicated level of consciousness thing they have.

For me, DeJaVu is like vertical time opening up. And I get a glimpse of the trigger (the letter) in many other realities at once. The stronger and longer lasting the DeJaVu, the wider and more profound the glimpse. I probably have an incredibly vacant look on my face while it is happening. My body becomes extremely passive. After reading up on other people's ideas, I think it might be something that happens briefly while we are awake, that people can achieve through meditation. The knowing of lifetimes nesting in time through a thought or point of space. Well, that is my best guess. I do enjoy the visual part of a DeJaVu. Being able to actually SEE into those other realities. I hope that made some kind of sense. Who knows, it could have been the taco I had for breakfast. Like I

said, I just try to enjoy life as it unfolds. I think it all
may be true - or none of it may be true. Or something
in between. Sometimes I get tired of looking for
explanations. Other times, not.

I am taking Friday off because the weather should be
fabulous this weekend. Time to be good to myself. I
will miss our exchange over the long weekend! In the
mean time, here is a poem for you:

Hello

You are
So familiar to me.
As we reveal
Our stories
To each other
Your words
Your phrasing
Your rhythms
Your images
Are all so familiar.

They create a stirring inside
That compels me
To keep reaching for you,
Keep writing you.
My curiosity
Grows with every letter.
Excitement fills
Each morning and evening
As I rediscover myself
While writing to you.

Your words
Tell your story
And explain your character
And touch me
In ways I can't explain.
And I now look forward

To each and every day.
Look forward to taking you
Farther inside me
So that I can know
And remember
Who you are.
And who I am.

Take care,

mb

From: JAZMAN@mbc.web
Sent: Thursday, June 6, 2002 8:22 AM
To: mbrogan@mbc.web
Subject: really you too

Hi Molly,

Thank you so much for your beautiful poem. It is as
amazing as I remembered your poems to be. The
surprising part is that you have expressed my thoughts!
How did you do that? Or is that part of the Art?

You are taking off tomorrow. I can't remember the last
time I took a day off. I could use one. Been working
long days and weekends for quite some time. A long
Vegas weekend sounds really good. Do you ever go to
Las Vegas? I am not much of a gambler but have a
couple of friends who try to teach me occasionally.

Seven wives - now that would be expensive! I think
polygamy was accepted during war time, when
repopulation was needed. If women had multiple
husbands, how would children know their fathers?
Would sure be different!

Sounds like your ex changed. Did something happen
he couldn't handle? Some transgression against his
moral code? Might be buried under what he thinks is

wrong, if he thinks about it. At least you experienced a deep relationship. And you know what they say. An ending is really just a new beginning.

I have had DeJaVu before. Like seeing a ghost or uncovering a buried memory. Do you think we have been around before? Not our bodies, but our beings? Maybe a DeJaVu is just one of those memories. A clue to the spiritual past.

I will be flying into Chicago Saturday and out Tuesday. Wish I had more time, but one of these days we will have to get together. I look forward to seeing your email after the weekend.

lbj

From: mbrogan@mbc.web
Sent: Thursday, June 6, 2002 2:01 PM
To: JAZMAN@mbc.web
Subject: RE: really you too

Actually I have a dear friend in Las Vegas who has been asking me for sometime to pay a visit. He and his wife just bought a small ranch outside of Summerlin. He is president of a company that sets up and runs telecommunications for several of the big convention centers across the USA. I think they just cut a deal with Disney. Anyway, I am sure that I could stay with them. You should meet him. What a great guy. I don't drink much or gamble at all but I love those little comedy clubs in the hotels. I have stolen some of my best comedic lines from those shows.

Are you thinking about moving to Utah? The Mormons won't admit to polygamy but it may be accepted! I don't know if you would find much cultural diversity there so you might just have to struggle with telling your children apart.

I corresponded with a professor at Western Illinois University for awhile while I was researching "visual imagery" for my major at Southern. He specialized in past life regression and really tried to persuade me to do it. I just never found the time. He uses a lot of visualization techniques for it. I have always been fascinated with past life regression and would love to find someone to take me through it.

This weekend, I am going to read in the sun, catch up on housework and with friends, and enjoy my son. That's the plan.

Before you think about meeting me for a football game, or a Vegas excursion, there are a few things that you should know, might bother you about me:

I sometimes listen to jazz vocal blends or classical music. This bugs my kids who are endlessly trying to educate me on contemporary music. Those facts stick about as much as details about the game of football.

I sometimes don't take my mail from the mailbox for a few days. Junk mail and bills anyway. This bugs my postman.

I spend much of the month of December baking and decorating gingerbread houses for Christmas. I have so many friends who like to get them and help decorate that I haven't had the heart to stop even though my own boys have long outgrown their enthusiasm. This may sound strange but I have had one date actually come into my home and tell me the smell of gingerbread made him sick. He didn't call back (although this may not be why!)

I let go of the need to have a perfectly clean home, since my kids are gone so much and I spend so little time there myself. I think this only bothers me.

I can be outspoken when I see someone being hurt or used badly. I try to start out compassionately but sometimes can only end up with that firm go to your room and think about what you've done, tone. This can put people off. But I can't stand by and watch (especially children) people or any creature being hurt.

When I was not working, I was VERY good at gardening, cooking and entertaining and community service. I do very little of that nowadays. Relaxing at home is what suits me. Some of my old friends aren't too happy about my change of focus. I think they liked my parties.

I can be embarrassing to sit next to during a football game. Although I will say, I have never had to sit alone. There are some compassionate souls in the world.

I can often be absent minded. This bothers everyone. I remind them that Einstein was self admittedly absent minded.

I can take a very long time decision making. Earlier in life, I made quick decisions that failed because they needed more thought. I might be taking a little too much time now because people around me sometimes become frustrated. But, they are my decisions...

My occasional prophetic dreams can sometimes give people the creeps.

I read too much. Usually books that no one else is reading so that I really have nothing to contribute during a book discussion.

I watch Shakespeare movies when I am alone and need cheering up. Actually, this doesn't bother anyone because no one is around. I just don't know anyone else that does that.

I have a way of challenging my friends in ways that are sometimes welcome, sometimes not. But my diplomacy skills have improved over the years so this gets me into trouble less.

I think that companies that focus on results might find better results if they focused more on process. This can frustrate people at work. But it is true!

My lack of desire to find a mate has bothered some people. Why do people think that I have to be "in love" to be happy? That bothers me! But it is nothing new. After I broke up with Patrick Thompson, and before I hooked up with Luke, I met the same public perception.

My Christian friends (I include Catholics, Protestants etc. in this category. I don't really have any reborn again friends.) question my lack of dedication to the church. My agnostic and atheistic friends question my (one of a kind) ideas on faith. I just do the best I can. I know this leaves my dad rolling in his grave in the Catholic cemetery. And I know he would forgive me if I could sit beside him and smile again.

I make it a practice to treat everyone with respect and kindness. This can aggravate my friends who like to fight. I prefer to negotiate.

I give things away a lot. This bothers my children. My gift giving used to bother my X.

I don't rescue anyone and don't let anyone rescue me. This bothers rescuers.

I only date men. This has occasionally bothered women who date other women.

My breath is bad in the morning. I spend too long in the shower. I need more sleep than most people. I like my fingernails short. I have been known to cut my own hair. I haven't had any plastic surgery, even though it might be an improvement. I use whole, not refined sugar. And whole wheat, not white flour. I stopped making my own pasta. I let my car get a little dirty before washing. I talk to strangers. I make friends too easily. I don't like pantyhose. My wardrobe isn't what it used to be. I hate to shop. I have a little dog (a gift.) I let my filing at home go. And my garage (summer job when the muscle is home.) I don't do anything that I wouldn't want everyone to know about. I can keep a confidence but not a secret. I am not sexually liberated. I like Ozzy Osborne, especially after Sharon publicly complained about what she was served at the white house for dinner. Good stuff.

Well, I think this thing with Peg might still work for you...

Enjoy your children! Take care,

mb

From: mbrogan@mbc.web
Sent: Friday, June 7, 2002 6:33 AM
To: JAZMAN@mbc.web
Subject: to ME

I finally set up my home computer to access all my emails. It wasn't that hard, I don't know why I didn't do it sooner.

Found out that this weekend is the Wells Street Art Fair (well, that's what they used to call it.) If I can convince Jack, I might have to put aside some of my plans for reading in the sun and head down there.

Have a terrific trip.
mb

From: JAZMAN@mbc.web
Sent: Friday, June 7, 2002 8:13 AM
To: mbrogan@mbc.web
Subject: to you

Good morning Molly. My day became much brighter
after reading that we can now exchange emails over the
weekends. They have become part of my morning
routine. Sip coffee, write, think, stare out the window
remembering, sip, write, think. The day is just not the
same without it.

Those comedy clubs sound great! And a martini now
and then is about all I drink. I work too damn much for
anything more. And driving after a couple of those can
be risky.

Gambling isn't something I do much. Occasionally
with friends in Vegas. Won $2,500 on a roulette spin
once. Then lost it on Black Jack. I would love to have
the opportunity to teach you. That would be fun.

This professor at Western sounds interesting. What did
he teach? Do you have any thoughts about living past
lives? Sudden memories popping up that don't fit this
life? Buddhism teaches that we are more than our
bodies, doesn't it?

OK. I looked over your list. Your music preferences
sound fine, but I hope you don't listen to your kids
music when they are not around. Rap is like nails on a
chalkboard for me. The postman needs to shut up and
do his job. I can do my own cleaning and don't mind
helping at all. Being outspoken and compassionate is a
plus, not minus. I love to make crowd noises at
sporting events, especially when my kids are in the
game. Tell me more about those dreams. I really want
to hear about those. Can someone read too much?
Unless it interferes with other parts of your life, I don't
think so. Probably what gives you all those interesting

and charming ideas of yours. What do you give away? Respect and kindness are rare qualities these days. Just make you more of a treasure. Don't stop that. Ozzy Oborne was a surprise. Interesting guy.

My list would be WAY too long. I am hoping that as you discover the contents for yourself, you still like me. How is the job search going? Need to get ready for work. Hope I hear from you before I leave. Have a great weekend.

lbj

From: mbrogan@mbc.web
Sent: Friday, June 7, 2002 9:12 AM
To: JAZMAN@mbc.web
SUBJECT: you too

Well, you are just too damn sweet. There has to be a catch!

I showed my friend Meg my list of things that might bother you. She claims to be able to lengthen that list by volumes, if you are ever so inclined! I am glad that I found your email before you left. I have been waiting for an email from my boss, who has not been very accessible lately. I plan to meet with him next week and let him know that I will be looking outside the company. He may see it coming. He knows that I have been looking inside the company already. And he knows that my current position is not meeting my financial needs.

When I gave the opportunity with a contracting company more thought, I realized that I really need to let my bosses know prior to submitting my resume anywhere else in the industry. The cable company is the primary customer to these contracting companies. So much diplomacy will be needed here. I spent the past week undercover, getting the support I will need from the top. I think that I have done what I can there, so telling my supervisor is the next step. After that, I plan to get my resume out to many companies and let the bidding begin.

There is one company in Grayslake, 5 minutes from home. One of my friends just took it over so that the owner could go back into retirement. Really just exploring opportunities right now. I hope to have this wrapped up in a month. But who knows.

The Western Illinois professor was in the psychology department. Very interesting guy. I have had random feelings that could have been from other lives. The Buddhists do believe that we all live many lives, and our body is our vehicle for this one.

I think I smell my brownies burning. Gotta go.

Enjoy this great weekend!

mb

From: JAZMAN@mbc.web
Sent: Saturday, June 8, 2002 6:24 AM
To: mbrogan@mbc.web
Subject: to you

It's 4:30 AM and I'm on my way to the airport. Wanted to sent you a note before I left. With all the craziness after 9-11, you never know what can happen in the air.

I went on line and found Old Town Art Fair site. Only $5 admission. Are you going today? Grace might like to go but it would have to be tomorrow.

Now why would Meg say that? Unless she shares your sense of humor.

I am so glad that we can email each other from home-thank you. Almost as if you have allowed me into your private life. Invited me into your home.

The Grayslake job is a better location and would save travel time. 252 hours a year! Cut it out.

Well, better go. SF traffic can be unpredictable. Maybe I will see you at the fair.

lbj

From: JAZMAN@mbc.web
Sent: Tuesday, June 11, 2002 7:15 PM
To: mbrogan@mbc.web
Subject: quick hi

Hi Molly,

I am back in town. Can't write now but will email you later. Have a meeting to run to. Just wanted you to know I am thinking of you. Have a nice night.

Jake

From: JAZMAN@mbc.web
Sent: Wednesday, June 12, 2002 8:16 AM
To: mbrogan@mbc.web
Subject: safe return

Hi. Home now. That was a fast three days. Grace had a school project to work on so we did not make the fair. I helped her with it in between minor home repair projects. She called me today to tell me she aced it. Need a reference for your job search? I would be glad to give you one.

The flight home was turbulent. The seat belt sign stayed on the entire flight. There were several fellows of Middle Eastern descent with turbans that caused some discomfort among the passengers. Crazy times.

Past lives. I suppose we need to decide if we are just
our bodies, conglomerate cells, or more, a spirit. When
you see memories in your mind, you see pictures. The
question is, what looks at those pictures? The answer is
- you. The real you. Not your body, but you.

What happens to "you" after death? The body is gone,
but where are you and your memories? Too deep?
Well, just remember, you are not just that cute body.

Time to get ready for work. Have a good day. Hope
you're feeling good.

lbj

From: mbrogan@mbc.web
Sent: Wednesday. June 12, 2002 9:15 AM
To: JAZMAN@mbc.web
SUBJECT: RE: safe return

QUOTE OF THE DAY - We do not stop playing
because we grow old, we grow old because we stop
playing.

Hope you had some time for that this weekend. I love
these quotes. I send them to Jack as they come in from
the company newsletter when he is in school. He is not
very communicative otherwise through email. But he
can be very chatty on the phone.

You and your daughter seem to adore each other. That
is so important for her. It will set the tone for all of her
love relationships to come. My son went to the fair to
please me, I am sure. But he did enjoy the fact that
after getting an understanding and history of Old Town,
he saw it on the show "Insomniac" on MTV that very
night. He spotted a place for us to eat dinner across
from Second City. That seemed to amuse him. I just

bought tickets on line for the July 13 Second City show. He is going to love it!

My friend Meg has a way of saying the most surprising things. But her diplomacy skills are so exquisite that she always pulls it off. She probably knows me better than any of my friends currently. We have been the lean on person for each other for the past ten years.

I met her after she had an unsuccessful run for the Mayor of Gurnee against the 20 year incumbent. I admired the fact that after the much talked about race, she was able to establish a solid friendship with the Mayor and his strongest political backer, the County Board Chairman. I knew both men well because at the time I was working for the county board chairman.

She approached me and told me that she heard I was going through a difficult divorce and followed that up with the fact that she was too. Turns out that both of our Xs went off the deep end in mid life. I found myself turning to her more and more because she always understood.

She is one of those attachments. She is currently at the top of the list for a double lung transplant at Loyola Medical Center. It would break my heart if we lost her. She is one of those people I give things to. You asked me what I give away and I apologize for forgetting to answer. I give things away that would have more meaning for someone else. There are things that I won't give away... things from the nursery that I want my children to have - their keepsakes and the things that make them comfortable. But if I have something that I don't use, and I know someone whose life it might improve, I would rather give it away than sell it. I think that you always get back more than you give.

For example, Meg needed a washer and dryer for her apartment when she split from her X. I gave her my old set because my new townhouse had a new set. At the time, she could not afford to buy one. When she remarried, she insisted on giving them back and I just put an ad in the paper and sold them. When I divorced, I had two sewing machines. One old pedal singer that was easy to use. I really only made toys and blankets and stuff for the kids when they were little. I don't sew. But my X decided that I SHOULD sew because his mom (who sews) convinced him of that. So I also had a new, fancy, can do just about anything Singer portable machine that I used once or twice because, duh, I don't sew.

The antique machine went to the antique dealer after the divorce. I kept the new machine but never really used it. Meg told me one day that her girls had asked her to teach them to sew. She said she knew how because her mom taught her and all of her sisters. But she couldn't afford a machine and felt terrible about it. She didn't know I had a machine because she knows me and makes fun of the fact that I take all of my sewing to the tailor at the cleaner's. (They do great work!) She cried when I gave it to her. She and her daughters make Christmas presents each year with it. I probably could have put an ad in the paper and sold it, but their smiles (and presents!) are so much better.

My boys have a hard time letting go of stuff. I installed a dishwasher into my town home. In the garage I have the box that the dishwasher came in filled with all kinds of balls. We have been collecting them since Jack was born. His first ball might be in that box. Tennis, baseballs, basketballs, footballs, mad balls, nerf balls, kush balls - that have not been played with in at least two years. The boys have their favorite NFL or NCAA or NBA standard balls that they use. So I started giving those balls away to other kids. The (abused) boy down the street.

Meg's kids got a ream paper box full and were so excited they told everyone about them. I took some flack from my boys though. They need to learn to give and LET GO. Too much to store or move (when the time comes again.)

OK, enough . I have the feeling she could have a lot of fun with creating a list for you.

QUOTE OF THE DAY - Electric communication will never be a substitute for the face of someone who with their soul encourages another person to be brave and true.
-Charles Dickens

Do you see a Mars/Venus thing developing in our emails here? I go on and on, you are to the point. It is a wonderful way to get to know someone. I haven't had another pen pal more consistent or interesting than you. And there is something so safe about using only the written word. You can't hear me sip my coffee or swear when I get up and stub my toe. I find myself really looking forward to your responses.

QUOTE OF THE DAY - The longest journey is the journey inward.
- Dag Hammarskjold, former Secretary-General of the United Nations

I understand completely about the "me" that sees the visual imagery inside my head. That is the me who meditates as well. I think that it is the seat of the mind (the intelligence of the spirit, soul and body) the spirit (that part of the mind and soul that is shared with the world) and the soul (that part of the mind and spirit that continues on when we are through here.)

I had a moment of crisis when my mom passed away. I didn't know what she needed me to do. Stay and pray? Puerto Ricans keep vigil by a body for three days and pray to help the soul pass. Should I stay and help the nurse wash and prepare the body? The Jews have a wonderful tradition around that.

It turned out that my youngest sister broke down and needed help home. I knew that was what my mom would have wanted me to do.

But when I got home, I read the "Tibetan Book of the Dead" for the gazillionth time. Very interesting stuff. It is what the Buddhists think happens when we pass away. Don't get me wrong. I am not a Buddhist, nor do I know one. I just think it is fascinating.
Thanks for the reference offer. Are you sure you know what you are getting into?
Take care,
mb

From: JAZMAN@mbc.web
Sent: Thursday, June 13, 2002 9:06 AM
To: mbrogan@mbc.web
Subject: RE: safe return

Good morning Molly. The first quote was great. (Good for you too?) (smile)

My daughter and I have always been very close. Not quite the same as it was when she was little now that I have been gone so much the past two years. I worry that I am missing so much. We get back into each other the longer I stay. But if I stay away too long, she becomes so distant.

Your friend Meg. A tough situation. How long will her lungs hold out before she needs the transplant? Is she your age? Running for Mayor takes a lot of energy. Has her health declined recently?

I would love to be there to hear you swear when you stub your toe. And giggle when your coffee sipping makes a noise. I clearly remember your giggle. It always made me smile. You weren't sipping coffee back then. Wine I think. What kind of wine do you like now? Do people give you things too? With all that giving you must be getting in return, or you soon will be. Seems to work that way. Is that what Buddhists call Karma?

What do Buddhists think happen when we die? Many TV shows now days on near death experience or spirits on the other side communicating to us. And people remembering and verifying a previous life time. Not easy to do, depending on how long ago the life was.

Do I know what I am getting into? No - but that's fine! You don't seem dangerous to me either. In fact, intriguing. Again, thanks for the quotes and take care. Lbj

From: mbrogan@mbc.web
Sent: Thursday, June 13, 2002 10:05 AM
To: JAZMAN@mbc.web
SUBJECT: Friday

FYI - I will be in my home office tomorrow (Friday) but in Schaumburg all next week. I am not sure if I will have access to my business email much during the day. But I will write you from home.

Do I detect a hint of remorse or regret in your changing relationship with Grace? I know just what you mean. I miss Jamie and struggle to find my place with him.

Meg will make it to the transplant. She was born with a hereditary condition that causes the tissues of her lungs to harden. Two or three of her siblings have it also. And I think her parents lost one or two young children to it. Her health has rapidly declined in the past two years. No she is always on oxygen and struggles for breath after walking. But she is a tall woman, the easiest kind of person to fit with lungs. The hospital almost called her twice, but the lungs turned out to be not viable. The medical team has four hours from the time they take a set of lungs from one body until they have to have them into the next. There is a field next to Meg's home where the fire department helicopter will land to get her. Her second husband is a paramedic/firefighter. Handy.

My taste in wine has migrated from the dry, full bodied red variety to the dry white...a Sauvignon Blanc or Pinot Grigio. My problem with wine is that I am such a brat. I don't enjoy cheap wine, it usually gives me a headache. And while my friends like to drink my selections, I have learned to remove the price tags because I always get flack. It is a good thing that I don't drink much because I am too damn picky. When I go to Pops (not often, but I like it there) I will get a half bottle of Mums and be happy all night. Was that too much information? How bout you? What are your preferences in coffee, wine, women, friends, family, home, entertainment, etc?

I think I will speed read "The Tibetan Book of the Dead" over the weekend so that my synopsis is accurate. They spell out a very detailed description about phases that a soul goes through before it is released to the next life or next level. But what I liked most of all is the idea that the stronger a person's faith (and it doesn't matter what the faith is, as long as it is strong) the more easily the soul passes through the phases.

I like that non denominational approach. And I like the importance they place on strong faith. I think that faith is like exercise for the soul. And in the way that there are many different forms of physical exercise one can use to attain physical fitness - the exercising of faith can result in heath for the soul, and hence, the mind and spirit. I don't think it can be neglected for a person to be healthy. Strong faith can change perception, and thus, the world or a person's life. Like feeling the miracle of a sunrise.

Well, anyway, let me do a little digging and come up with a little more for you.

By the way - this psychologist at Western was doing just what you suggest with his graduate students 30 years ago. Recording their past life regression sessions and then having them research the validity of them. They found solid evidence in the public records. Very amazing stuff.

mb

From: JAZMAN@mbc.web
Sent: Friday, June 14, 2002 8:25 AM
To: mbrogan@mbc.web
Subject: RE: Friday

Good Morning my friend. It is so great to begin each day with you.

Sorry about Meg. It puts our small problems into perspective doesn't it? I will postulate health for her. Would be more effective if I actually knew her. But knowing her through you helps because of our closeness.

Too much information? Not a chance. Just keep it coming. MY tastes? I like my coffee strong and black. Women? I don't have any specific physical traits in mind, but I would need to feel an attraction. Her attraction to ME would be key. Massive weight would turn me off, not sure how many extra pounds would be OK. Some, I certainly have a few. Age, close to mine. Maturity and experience are important. As far as her being, I would not want someone to try to change me. But introducing me to new ideas and things would be great. Without pushing them on me, I don't like to be pushed or harassed. Reminded or nudged can be good sometimes. I love music and like to go out sometimes. But with the right person, I also like to kick back at home and just enjoy being together. Intelligence is important. Sex is fine, but romance and love making are essential. I look forward to being in love again. Such an empowering feeling. It has been a very long time.

This time around, affinity will be important. How much spiritual reality do we share? That will be a primary question. I made the mistake of not investigating that enough before my marriage. It wasn't long before I found out that we just did not have enough in common in that arena. A solid foundation there is a must next time around. Do you think about that at all?

OK - now you.

lbj

From: mbrogan@mbc.web
Sent: Friday, June 14 June 13, 2002 8:43 PM
To: JAZMAN@mbc.web
SUBJECT: Someday

I was thinking about you and Grace. It reminded me of how Jack and I missed each other his freshman year. He was wonderful that year with emails. He discovered all of the songs, video clips and wave files that the students post on the network. Wild and wacky. He would send some to me that I passed around the office, and my office mates would send me things that I could pass back to him. Good fun. Do you think that Grace could get into a daily email? It really helped to keep us feeling close.

Keep postulating for Meg. She is important to me.
That is certain.

Well, my plan was to send out several resume packets
(with cover letters and letters of reference) this
weekend. I may only send out a few and wait a little
while for the rest.

So you like the: what kind of woman question....I have
to admit, that I did not consider an answer for myself. I
may need to give this more thought. Let's see.
Certainly his looks would need to tug on my heart
strings. But coming from someone who considers Dan
Ackroyd to be the sexiest man alive, that field is wide
open.

As far as what kind of person in what kind of
relationship......I have so much going on in my life right
now I have not taken the time to pursue anything
superficial. I suppose the only thing that would make
me stop and look would be the promise of a relationship
with depth again. Like you, I loved to be in love. And
I loved being part of a partnership. The first few
weddings after my separation were very rough. Now I
can go just about anywhere alone and it doesn't bother
me. But I do remember sharing it all and loving that.

Some people say that we negotiate ourselves through
other people. That may be true at work. But I think in
our personal relationships, we discover ourselves. Next
time, he will need to be willing to take me farther into
myself that I have ever been. I think it would be
important to have enough respect and trust so that
mistakes can be made and forgiven. I wouldn't want
someone trying to change me. But I would want the
opportunity and freedom to change through my
relationship. Someone who could challenge me, but
take no for an answer. And learning from past
disasters, someone faithful, sober and stable. Someone
to laugh with. To hold me when I cry. To remind me

of who I am when I forget. To open doors, not close them. Compassionate,
adventurous.......

Well, until this guy comes along, I would rather be on my own than in a difficult or tedious relationship. I can wait for the something real. Every once in awhile, someone peaks my interest for just long enough to remind me of how nice it could be!

Thanks for reminding me.

mb

From: JAZMAN@mbc.web
Sent: Saturday, June 15, 2002 11:22 AM
To: mbrogan@mbc.web
Subject: RE: Someday

Will you send me a resume too? I know people, you never know what can happen! I loved reading what you had to say about yourself when you were trying to put me off. Would be VERY interested in what you say about yourself when you are trying to generate interest.

You got me thinking lately. I went back to my Scientology roots at the process for forming a postulate on a life partner. Not something I have ever done. Interest was always spontaneous, not given any thought ahead of an encounter. Deciding what kind of person I want to share my life might just bring her to me. If she isn't here already. Like you, I thought that I didn't have enough time for a relationship. But it might not take as much time as we think. Might have to try it someday and see. Doing anything tonight? (smile) It would be great to be able to look at each other and not have to wait a day for a response.

I am at work now, need to run to a meeting. Hope I hear from you. Have more to say but need to go. Until later.

lbj

From: mbrogan@mbc.web
Sent: Saturday, June 15, 2002 1:14 PM
To: JAZMAN@mbc.web
SUBJECT: RE: Someday

Very perceptive. I have never been good as self promotion. It is a personal politics isn't it. Never good at competition or politics. I just do the best I can and let my work speak for itself. My boss? I had 3 different bosses in 2000, three different bosses in 2001 and 3 different bosses already this year. The telecommunications industry is and extremely high change industry. Corporations cannot keep up with the demand for technology. I seem to do well in a climate of rapid change. Everybody wins negotiation comes in handy. Although I have been telling everyone I am going to kick their ass lately. Not the boss though. I kick ass for the boss. Probably something my military dad taught me while I wasn't looking.

I was thinking the exact thing today that you described. Why have I not given some focus to creating the vision of a partner. So busy with the book and the career and the son in college and the friends and the prodigal son postulates. Better get to work on that one. You have given me great material for inspiration. Thank you. But you are right. An email relationship is far from spontaneous.

Tonight, Jack and I are just hanging out. Tomorrow he will be with his dad and Meg has asked me to hang pictures at her home. I have the family history in pictures going up my stairs here. She has gathered and framed hers and wants some help grouping them on the wall.

I will look for an email from time to time though.

Well, I just got the "me so hungry" line from my baby bird.

Gotta go,

mb

From: JAZMAN@mbc.web
Sent: Saturday, June 15, 2002 2:22 PM
To: mbrogan@mbc.web
Subject: RE: Someday

What's with all the boss changes? What position are you applying for? I can write a reference letter for you.

Personal public relations. You do it without knowing it. You have such a way of revealing yourself to me, exciting actually. I have not been this interested in another being in quite some time. Are you doing it consciously? Or do you just naturally reveal yourself, like breathing in and out?

Hope you enjoy your evening with Jack. Are you cooking dinner? I will need to think along those lines shortly so I'd better get on the phone and see what's going on. Wish you were here. We could grab a couple of bottles of Pinot and head to the beach. Talk long into the night like the old days. Maybe stay until sunrise, since your folks won't be looking for you.

lbj

From: mbrogan@mbc.web
Sent: Saturday, June 15, 2002 6:00 PM
To: JAZMAN@mbc.web
SUBJECT: RE: Someday

Many thanks for your offer to connect me. And while I
do believe that every healthy relationship provides
connections (unhealthy ones destroy them) you need to
know that I am not looking forward to your emails
every day because I think that you can "do" something
for me. I want to tread very carefully there. It took me
a long time to understand that I needed to stop letting
guys rescue me. My dad and three older brothers did
such a good job for so many years. And while I like
that protected feeling (being female and all) I curse
myself for not learning all the things I relied on a guy to
for me the first 40 years of my life.

The cable company has been restructuring for the past
several years in many different ways. I have only been
with the company 5 years and had several
administrative roles. But it is a complicated business
and takes much technical knowledge so the learning
curve is extensive. When we launched telephony a
couple of years ago, several middle managers from
Ameritech were brought over and the company was
restructured to operate like a phone company. The
cable side faltered because it is much more labor and
product intensive, so another restructuring. I have been
neither too high up the ladder, nor too close to the front
line in my positions so I have managed to avoid the
workforce reductions. But I have enough industry
knowledge under my belt that I think I can find a pretty
good job in the telecommunications industry.

In five years, the company has experienced 4 corporate
mergers. Each brought change, restructuring, culture
blends. In those 5 years, the company also went from
being strictly cable to adding telephony and high speed
internet and a wave of high tech products into the

customers' homes to support those services. The plant has been changed from cable to fiber optics, the head-end technology has advanced by leaps and bounds. The cost of the upgrades slows the availability of high tech products to the customer. All very technical and quite frankly, beyond me. I am a good administrator. And while I can understand it in the broad brush stroke, the engineers drive me a little crazy. I did let them coach me on swearing skills though.

The boss changes are just a result of the next wave of restructuring. We have had 3 Chicago market leaders in the past three years. Each time a new one comes in, the faces change. And so do the shape of the departments.

But I think it is a good enough place to be for the next couple of years until Jack decides on a graduate school. I would like to move west after that. (you live somewhere out there don't you?) A book store near a University is the current postulate. Could be anywhere.

Thank you for your generosity and confidence. It is nice to know that I have good people in my corner. Sooner or later, the bell rings. Say, you don't know Dan Ackroyd do you? (smile)

Talking until sunrise on a California beach sounds heavenly. Would make me feel 20 or so again. But I will be cooking every couple of hours instead. Jack is on the weight gain program. The only one gaining weight is the cook.

Be good to yourself this weekend.

mb

From: JAZMAN@mbc.web
Sent: Sunday, June 16, 2002 10:02 AM
To: mbrogan@mbc.web
Subject: RE: Someday

Hope your evening with Jack was enjoyable. Mine was
short. Dinner with folks from work and home early.
You know, it would be OK to let me help you.
Exchange is important. The flow doesn't just go one
way, with all that giving you do. Giving is a great
morale boost for people. Could be the problem with
out of control kids and criminals. They expect
everything for nothing and learned that somewhere.

I just wanted to do something for you if I can. Besides,
I would be doing whatever company you worked for
the favor, I'm sure.

You said you wanted to move west. How far west
(smile?) Chicago winters are easily left behind. Nice
around the holidays but that's about it. Not as hot and
humid here. In the winter, it is in the 50s or 60s,
sometimes gets into the 70s.

I have decided to start looking for that health club next
week. Get rid of the little aches and pains that come
with age. I have also been thinking about traveling
overseas. I have never been. Where would you go, if
you could?
lbj

From: mbrogan@mbc.web
Sent: Sunday, June 16, 2002 11:13 AM
To: JAZMAN@mbc.web
SUBJECT: RE: Someday

Have you updated your resume lately? Tell you what, I
will send you mine if you send me yours. It would
certainly make it easier for you to see my diverse
professional history. And who knows, I might be able

to pass yours along to a friend for you!

You are right about letting people help me. I can get carried away with my new found "independence." Probably just being hard on myself.

During my second year of working for the cable company, I confessed to one of the engineers that when I fix things around the house, I usually end up crying. Home repair was new to me after the divorce but I was determined to master it. My confession stopped him cold, and after a long look at me he said very quietly, "Why do you cry?"

I told him that I reach a certain point in frustration and I just can't help it. The tears start to flow. Makes it hard to see what you are trying to fix! Then he said "Well Mary, that's what swearing is for! I don't think I have ever heard you swear have I?"

The next time I saw him, he asked me how I was that day and I answered, "Shitty." We had a good laugh. Twenty minutes later, I left the Manager's floor and went down to the technical offices where everyone asked me how I was today.

This began my swearing lessons with the technicians and engineers. It has been a wonderful relationship building tool at work. And I don't cry as much when I fix things. But I am still doing my own home repair.

After several attempts and failures, I will break down and borrow a husband. But I always have to exhaust myself trying to do it first. Maybe I should have added this to the things about me that might bother you.

I can be cuddly though. That might make up for it.

And I can spot and appreciate a generous spirit. Don't think I can't! Thank you.

How far west? Somewhere with the right people, drier air and mountains close by. I am glad to hear you struggling with the same limitations of age. I used to be able to stop drinking Coke and drop five pounds. While I Don't gain much when I'm gaining, it is much harder to loose those unwanted pounds. But I don't stop trying. For the first time in my life I am watching calories.

I think I would like to see Ireland first. What do you say?

Well, now I will grab my book and head for the sun. Jack will be up soon and then it is off to Meg's.

Take care,

mb

From: JAZMAN@mbc.web
Sent: Sunday, June 16, 2002 12:31 PM
To: mbrogan@mbc.web
Subject: RE: Someday

You're probably outside with your book right now. Jack sure knows how to sleep in. I haven't done that since I was young. Even if I stay up late, I get up at the same time. Then I just have to power through the day with coffee. No time for naps. Now, if I had someone to nap with, it might be a different story.

Do you want to exchange pictures with our resumes? Promise to keep writing me afterward? I think I look completely different than I did in high school. Hair is much shorter. Tummy needs a diet. Mustache is a bit gray, but not too much gray up top. Still have hair all over the head, but not as thick as it once was. Would you want me to shave?

Ireland first? I actually have some ancestors there. I can bring along the lineage books and we can look up both our families. I have frequent flyer miles on two different airlines. We can upgrade our tickets to first class so I can easily get you drunk (smile.)

You like to cuddle? That more than makes up for any shortcomings (although I really haven't heard any yet!)

Have a terrific day.

lbj

From: mbrogan@mbc.web
Sent: Sunday, June 16, 2002 1:23 PM
To: JAZMAN@mbc.web
SUBJECT: Today

Well, I think I have picked out just the pic to send with my resume. It was taken at Meg's second wedding. My weight was on the upside then, before going down and then back up so it will be the most realistic picture. It is a head shot though. To be honest, while the face could use some cosmetic work, the body could use much more. So don't worry about your own picture. Sounds like we are in the same boat.

You have my solemn vow, I will be your pen pal as long as you like.

And save your money on those first class tickets. It only takes two drinks to get me drunk. After the silliness, the headaches mean a totally unproductive day following. Another warning! Could be a good time to cuddle though.

More than one email a day is nice. Too bad the work week will interfere with the fun.

Here is a poem for you:

Discovery

Beyond the excitement
And the flirtation
And the rhetoric
There is a hint
Of something soulful.
Something as familiar
As a mother's touch
Or coming home
Or a favorite song.

The problem with hints
Is that we aren't sure:
How much of what we see
Actually comes
From desire and hope
And how much
Is really there
Waiting
Like an unopened gift
On a coming-of-age
Birthday.

We won't know for sure
Until the opening
The revelation
The moment of discovery
Until then
We set our course
To that destination
By touching
With words
Thoughts
And desires.

Until then
We wait breathlessly
Cultivating hope
With prayer

Making ready
Ourselves
And our lives
For the time
When we can
Receive eachother
And give eachother
Everything saved
For the moment
When our two souls
Meet again
And remember
The sacred place
We always share.

mb

From: JAZMAN@mbc.web
Sent: Sunday, June 16, 2002 3:12 PM
To: mbrogan@mbc.web
Subject: RE: Today

Again, your poem blew me away. I read it again,
imagining myself in front of the fire, hearing Viv's
voice recite it. I remember the excitement and extreme
attention I felt then. I have the same feeling now when
I read your poems. I can't express what I feel when I
think that they are written for me. I am not sure that I
deserve them. That is the awe I feel. They express the
thoughts that I have not been able to articulate myself.
As if you are reading my mind, or my heart. You are
incredible.

I will have to ask anyone here if they have a picture of
me. I think I remember seeing one or two at the office.

Those headaches are caused by dehydration, lack of B-
1 and possibly low sodium and/or potassium. So take
your vitamins with a big glass of water before bed and
you should be fine. Something else you may be pleased

to know is that sex releases natural pain killers into the system. A little added bonus.

It's nice to know you won't blow me off after seeing my picture. OK, over to my friend Ron's to help him with planning for his new business. I hope to hear from you before the end of the day! Would like to think of you before sleep. Even though I don't remember my dreams usually, I would like them to be of you. I always wake up feeling like they are. You are my first thought of the morning, each morning. That is a very good thing.

lbj

From: mbrogan@mbc.web
Sent: Sunday, June 16, 2002 7:53 PM
To: JAZMAN@mbc.web
SUBJECT: When

Hey now, what happened to "do you think WE should exchange pictures with
those resumeS." Now it seems, you have neither a picture, nor a resume!
Hmmmmmm.......

After spending the afternoon with Meg, she brought to my attention that the
picture taken at her wedding was 5 years old. I can't believe it was that long ago. But she did agree that I was just as chubby then as I am now and advised me to buy new clothes. I think she just wants a pal a little overweight so that when she blows up from the steroids after the surgery, she won't feel so bad. She fed me pizza and coke while I was there. Not her usual chicken breast or salad. I hope those lungs come along soon. I didn't understand before that she was the talker and I was the listener in our relationship. We have had to reverse those roles now because she is so short of breath, and frankly, I suck as the talker.

Well, I am glad to know that you have perfected the cure for the alcohol induced headache. It may be awhile before I can test your pain killer theory. It been so long that memory will not serve. I hope that is not just another addition to the ever growing list of things that might bother you about me.

If you ever get me your resume and get a chance to read mine you will see that my first job back in the workforce was working with children in Prevention programs. The schools recruited me to work for them because of the volunteer work that I was doing for them. I did not drink at all for at least ten years because I thought that the kids that I was working with should have a role model who could say that she doesn't drink and still has fun. It was easy enough to give up for a good cause.

After I stopped working with children and started working for the cable company, I began to have a drink once in awhile. Actually, the same time I started practicing my swearing skills at work, I had a stout or two at dinner with work buddies. To this day they will proudly take credit for this total corruption. But I don't drink much so it doesn't take much to effect me.

As for the picture - what no scanner? No digital camera? What kind of company are you running? Sounds like you can use some help entering the twenty first century. Actually, my scanner and camera are at the office so I won't be able to send you mine until next week. That gives you one week to get your materials together boyo. How are you with deadlines? (smile)

These weekdays coming up just won't be the same without multiple emails. Well, I guess it just means we can look forward the weekends.

Thanks for your kind words on my poems and sweet dreams,

mb

From: mbrogan@mbc.web
Sent: Sunday, June 16, 2002 7:53 PM
To: JAZMAN@mbc.web
Attach: Resume with references in word02.doc
SUBJECT: Tomorrow

Good Morning Jake,

After reading this in the morning, I decided that extra calories was not the only thing I brought home from Meg's last night. A smart ass attitude to hide the worry seems to be showing.

I dreamt that I was on a beach at sunset talking to you. I don't know what we were talking about but I woke up suddenly remembering that I did not read "The Tibetan Book of the Dead" over the weekend. Seems deadlines are MY challenge!

Well, to make it up to you here is a glimpse at the successes and risks that did not pay off for me in the past 20 years.

Have a terrific week.

Still your pal, mb
From: JAZMAN@mbc.web
Sent: Monday, June 17, 2002 8:22 AM
To: mbrogan@mbc.web
Subject: RE: When

Now hang on honey, you'll get your pictures. But I have never needed a resume so that will be tough. Having the clubs, and then starting my own firm - I haven't ever applied for a job. Even in high school, I was part owner in the record store. Never filled out a job application, though I have reviewed my share! It has been very different for me.

I don't believe for a minute that you are "chubby." So you will have to prove that one to me. In person or with a picture, whatever you like. In person would be nice.

The pain killer "theory" I saw on one of those cable channels - the Science channel or something. A scientific FACT, not something I just made up to circumvent the age old headache excuse. I haven't tested it though. Someday...

Sounds like romance has not been part of your life for quite awhile. Mine either - I have been trying to get out of this marriage quietly for so long. But you have been out there, working to support your children, being there for your friends, putting your son through college. All that takes an incredible amount of hard work and energy. Admirable, not anything to put on any list. You might even have five extra minutes a day to read (smile.)

By the way, your resume is excellent. Thanks. An interesting past twenty years for you. We have very different business histories but would make a great team, don't you think? You handling the daily operations details. Me raising capital, negotiating deals, starting companies.

Time to get to work. Take care.

lbj

From: JAZMAN@mbc.web
Sent: Monday, June 17, 2002 9:06 AM
To: mbrogan@mbc.web
Subject: RE: tomorrow

Hi. Got ready so fast I have a few minutes to spare.
What do I do? Go back on the computer and reach for
you. What is this? Well, I didn't answer everything
from that last email.

I don't understand why you worry. Just be who you are.
Be you. Your resume is terrific. As is your beingness.

Want to do lunch today? How about taking the day off
and heading for the beach? We have a great beach not
far from my home here that might be as good as the one
in your dream. We would need to stay about a year to
finish this conversation we are having. Even then, it
would be a "to be continued" pause in conversation.
After a year, we may have to get back to work.

Well, now I do have to go. Take care.

lbj

From: mbrogan@mbc.web
Sent: Monday, June 17, 2002 7:53 PM
To: JAZMAN@mbc.web
SUBJECT: When

Thanks for both emails. A nice treat. What a long day
with the additional 2 hrs. drive time. I could not do 3
hrs on the highway everyday. This week will be quite
enough.

Does it really only take five minutes to kill that pain?
Wow, that is a scientific achievement. But I suppose if
we were in first class working on a mile high club
record, five minutes would be courteous to the other
passengers.

I worry about Meg. I sure do hope she gets her new lungs soon. Strange, to be waiting for someone else's ending so that your loved one has a new beginning. But it pains me to see her struggling for breath.

It is true. I have been ferociously independent since my divorce. I suppose the downside to that would be the ferocious part. I do to try to ask for help when needed. I probably wait too long. And I suppose that another downside would be the lack of romance.

Although I have dabbled a couple of times more in romance than in a relationship, the romance vanished when the reality set in. I think it is much harder when you are older to match your plans and visions and postulates to another's. Last time around I completely gave myself over to my husband's dreams. While I am not ruling it out, if fell in love with the dreams, I would rather keep some of my own next time. Haven't found that yet. Each person granted their own "beingness" as you so beautifully put it. Romance without it seems such a waste. I suppose if I didn't work, or have children and had more time...but that is not the reality. And I am OK with that.

I think that when you look back on your life and remember the romance, it will have great clarity and meaning if it is real and deep. That takes time, lots of work and the right guy. I'll get there some day. Right now, the only guy I see is 2000 miles across the country and hasn't held a steady job in 30 years. Well, there was that guy in the butcher shop last weekend that I said no thank you to. But he kind of scared me.

Thank you for your compliments on my resume. You did not even say anything like "What the hell is a community partnership?" or "why would anyone in their right mind agree to manage something called the "Teen Parent Program." Now we can schedule that interview.

OK, maybe we have a different definition of chubby. For me, if I can't fit into my favorite clothes, I am chubby. Mind you, I have had a few of these pieces since before I was married. Irreplaceable. I just can't give them up. So I do what I must to loose the weight instead. Just takes much longer nowadays. I am the all American size 10-12. And since I am 5' 8" (my god, I hope I am not shrinking yet!) I can pull it off. So put your mind at ease. A chubby, not a fatty.

What about you? What is your five year plan? Your ten year plan? Every business man without a resume has those.

So that was your record store we hid in after running off the beach! I always wondered if whoever worked there kept his job. Guess so, if you owned it. Handy little hide out. Much warmer than the beach that night too. I sure did get in trouble for staying out so late. But I do remember having so much fun and not wanting to leave.

Sweet dreams,

mb

From: JAZMAN@mbc.web
Sent: Tuesday, June 18, 2002 9:33 AM
To: mbrogan@mbc.web
Subject: RE: whenever

We will need to test that pain killer theory to see how long it really takes. You be the patient. It's only fair after all. I am sure the side effects are all positive. Better schedule the entire afternoon.

You want to know my business plan? Big profits for the company and our clients. That's moving right along. I have friends who continue to ask me to start new ventures with them. Some are tempting. I would need to find more time. Romance. It has been a very long time since I plunged into that. Doesn't need to consume huge amounts of time. Long weekends here and there sound good. But if things got serious it wouldn't be long before the distance would need to be handled. Can you imagine being totally in love and not being able to spend each night with someone? Or see them when you wanted to? After awhile, that would just be too hard.

I would love to interview you in person. If only to look into your eyes while I was talking to you. Then again, it might be hard to keep my mind on business. How about that picture? I really need to see you one day soon.

lbj

From: mbrogan@mbc.web
Sent: Tuesday, June 18, 2002 8:07 PM
To: JAZMAN@mbc.web
SUBJECT: Toothless in Chicago

Well, I can honestly say that I am officially hooked on these emails. (Maybe it is the hint of romance.....) After spending an hour and a half in traffic on the way home from Schaumburg (yuck) I arrived home to discover that my son was out! So instead of catching up with him, starting dinner, doing Mom chores - I ran upstairs and got right into my email. Yep, hooked.

It has probably been 40+ years since anyone asked me to play doctor. We called it something else when we got to Jr. High. Certainly, the best offer that I have had in awhile. Well, there was that guy in Home Depot who offered to help around the house. He was a little vague about what he was offering to do. No thank you. Your offer is much better.

I can see that all that high level thinking is not just applied to work! Maybe we had postulates for each other out there and did not know it. Missing romance, travel, vacations, our spirits crashed into each other and fell to earth in the form of email. Sounds like you invent or facilitate the invention of whatever is necessary to stay ahead of the curve. When that kind of creativity is applied to all aspects of your life it can generate powerful change. Now I could probably use your financial advice somewhere along the line. I will eventually have to head for the shooting range and stop shooting from the hip. I lost my financial advisers when I walked away from my husband's business. Since then, it has been slow going one step at a time. Current step is the job change.

I agree with your ideas on romance. If romance became love, distance would need to be eliminated. Hard to share a life with all that distance. And depth can only be achieved with time together. It would be a true crime to walk away from something real just to resist change. Suddenly, I CAN imagine wanting to be more a part of someone's life but facing barriers. I have always been good at making barriers vanish when the stakes have value. When it happens, I think that both of us are determined and creative enough to make it work. Maybe this is what each of us needs right now. The email now, the weekends later, the rest when the time is right. And if we discover that it never will be right for us, I have the feeling that we will each find someone that fits. We both value ourselves, romance, love, life. All the right ingredients.

You better look at my picture next week. Those missing front teeth might not do it for you.
Smile,

mb

From: JAZMAN@mbc.web
Sent: Tuesday, June 18, 2002 9:44 PM
To: mbrogan@mbc.web
Subject: RE: Toothless in Chicago

In the very near future, we will arrange for new teeth. Molly, whatever is going on with you, it is happening to me too. I am constantly checking my email to see if I have something from you. After a few lovely thoughts of you first thing in the morning, I head to the computer to find you. I would probably have a breakdown if there wasn't anything. But there always is! You fill my day. I need to analyze this. Or do I? Maybe this time, I should just go with the flow. And the flow is all to you.

I have been developing a life partner postulate for awhile, but had no clue that something like this would happen. Or someone like you would appear in my life. I get a lot of emails from people. But there was something magnetic about yours. Something completely irresistible.

That was my record store that we used as a hide out when needed. It was a great place to meet and bring chicks back then. My partner was a few years older and knew the ropes. I was the one that did things like ran away from the cops with girls in hand. He was the more mature business man. But a bit of a womanizer. I learned what I did not want to become by watching him operate. Learned quite a bit about the music business too. Met lots of area musicians. Really laid the foundation for the clubs.

If this relationship gets intense (in a good way) distance will be a problem. I will be happy to solve THAT one though. You are amazing. I will probably look at your picture all day long.

I am still at the office and not done talking to you, but want you to get this before bed. Might just inspire another dream about me. I would like your nights to be filled with those. The way mine are filled with you.

lbj

From: JAZMAN@mbc.web
Sent: Tuesday, June 18, 2002 11:13 PM
To: mbrogan@mbc.web
Subject: Dreams

I know you are sleeping. I am thinking about you. Hope that you are having a really nice dream, one that is making you happy. When you wake up, I will be asleep. Like we are on opposite ends of the world. Sweet dreams, sleep well. I will be with you in the morning.

lbj

From: JAZMAN@mbc.web
Sent: Wednesday, June 19, 2002 9:07 AM
To: mbrogan@mbc.web
Subject: (no subject)

Are you okay?

From: mbrogan@mbc.web
Sent: Wednesday, June 19, 2002 5:10 PM
To: JAZMAN@mbc.web
SUBJECT: just fine

I think we just have our timing skewed. I have been writing to you at night, after work. Since I have been driving to Schaumburg, 3 hour drive time round trip, I am getting home at 6:30. If Jack is here, I focus on him and write to you about eight or so. If not, I RUSH upstairs to find your email. today, I had two from my friends the Hanlons that I skipped over to read your three. Three in one day. Well, two last night and one today.

By the weekend we will be back to normal. Monday, I will get your email usually by 9:30AM and think about it awhile, maybe take some time composing it, but certainly get it off before I leave the office.

The tall one just got home from the gym. Dinner time. I will write before bed.

Just fine,

mb

From: mbrogan@mbc.web
Sent: Wednesday, June 19, 2002 8:34 PM
To: JAZMAN@mbc.web
Attachment: finding Jacob
SUBJECT: finding Jacob

I have forwarded the Hanlons' touching email. The Hanlons are my friends (one of the all time great couples) that have gone to the Ukraine this summer to adopt a son. Tell me if you are not interested in this story. I won't send another installment. I just think it is so fascinating, like reading a story as it is being written. Don't get me wrong, I could not start another family. But I clearly remember those wonderful feelings of a family beginning. The enthusiasm. Holding that little hand while they ask a million questions.

Do you think the name they have chosen for their son is a good omen?

Tears came to my eyes when I read Debra's email. But you need to know, that tears came to my eyes when I read your Dreams email too. Pillow talk. Stirring up memories of how wonderful it can be.

I am a little worried that we are putting a lot of pressure on ourselves that we will feel at our first meeting. I looked around the room today at the 25 or so people in my meeting and wondered what it would be like to be able to watch you from across a room. I have never had a flirtation through the email before nor had feelings for someone grow that I could not lay eyes on.

So here are some questions that will tell me some of the things I might know about you if I were near to see you:

Do you smoke?

Do you like to hold hands, or do you need your personal space?

Do you need time alone, or do you not like being alone?

Do you watch the sun rise or set? When was the last time?

Do you drive a truck or a motorcycle? (Not that there's anything wrong with that!)

Do you ever go barefoot?

What is your favorite food?

What kind of flower did you last smell and where?

What was the last sound that made you stop and listen closely?

What does your favorite chair look like?

Do you ever talk to yourself?

OK, enough for now.

Well, we already share such a rich, significant history. Suburban fugitives at a tender age. The illegal beach bonfires. The underage drinking. Cutting class on spring days to head to our Lake Michigan hide out and sing the afternoon away.

I liked your closing line "Have to run even though I'm not done talking to you yet." The ongoing dialogue that opens us up to eachother. Somewhere out there in cyberspace. Somewhere in here, deep inside. I suppose we should pace this so that we are opening to eachother as that time allows. Of course, that pace might be different for vertical time and horizontal time. My head tells me to stick to horizontal time and be cautious. Take it one email at a time, take it slow. My heart is telling me to fly with vertical time, and open this up in ways that disregard caution and all the other constraints of conventional reality. But I don't want either of us to be disappointed. I do so look forward to you.

Sweet dreams,
mb

From: JAZMAN@mbc.web
Sent: Thursday, June 20, 2002 12:21 AM
To: mbrogan@mbc.web
Subject: RE: finding Jacob

Yes! A good omen. I will take all I can get. Your friends are so happy. I was happy myself to hear from you again.

Molly, I don't have any experience to draw on here. I have never had such strong feelings develop in this way before. How cool it would be to watch you from across the room. When I finally do see you in person, I can't imagine what emotions will take over. But I know they will take over because they are a little wild right now. I have such a crush on you. Well, much deeper than a crush actually. Like something so familiar. I love your letters and ESPECIALLY your poems. Maybe it is the things you say and the way you say them. Your viewpoints remind me of a love in the distant past that I can't recall yet. One thing for sure, this evades all logic. Is it possible to feel such affinity through letters? But I will confess. I found your office number in the listings and called to hear your voice on the voice mail. I hope you don't mind. I just needed to hear your voice. Sooner or later, we will have to start talking by phone you know.

OK. To your questions. Smoke - I have off and on over the years. I currently do, but will quit totally for the right person, just so you know. How about just an occasional cigar outside?

Hold hands. When ever I can if I care deeply for the girl.

Time alone? I spend a lot of time alone when I am in SF. Didn't have much before then when raising the family. If you were out here, then no.

Sunrise and sunsets? Romantic with the right girl. Out here, the sun sets over the ocean. Can be quite spectacular. Been awhile since I watched one.

I have a car in SF and two SUVs in Chicago.

I do not go barefoot except on the beach. Remember those foot fights with bare feet? That just came back to me. One of the reasons I liked sitting next to you. I never did thank you for teaching me the fine art of foot fighting. Thank you Molly.

Favorite food? Not really picky. The seafood out here is terrific. I am sure if you are cooking, I will like anything

Flowers - this is amazing. I just had an office mate
bring my some agamanthas and jasmine to smell today.
Very timely of you. I don't go out of my way to smell
flowers.

The last sound that made me stop and listen closely.
Your voice on your voicemail. Fabulous. Before that,
an acoustic guitar at the club. The musician was
incredible.

Favorite chair? The one I sit in to write and read your
emails.

Talk to myself. Yes, but right now I can't remember
anything I've said. When I mess something up I say
"Good Jake."

Well, there you are. Hope you don't take me off your
email list now. The smoking question threw me. Non
smokers usually don't like the smoke. Do I need to quit
for good? Just say the word.

When I see you, I will NOT be disappointed. I know
that we can be great friends. I would love for it to be
more. I really needed to have these feelings awakened
in me. I can't wait to look into your eyes for a very
long time.

Are you going to answer those questions? I would love
to hear the answers. And I will try to think of some
questions for you.

lbj

From: mbrogan@mbc.web
Sent: Thursday, June 20, 2002 4:20 AM
To: JAZMAN@mbc.web
SUBJECT: RE: finding Jacob

A reply for you so that you can fire up this morning and touch me. I felt badly that yesterday, you didn't have that morning message to begin your day. But I have to warn you, my head is half in this world and half in my last dream that I cannot remember. You were in it though. I think that is why I can't let go.

Do you ever get an unexplained feeling of familiarity when you meet someone? I have learned to rely on my instincts about people and that particular feeling, if present, can tell me of the possibility of a strong relationship. Could it mean past life connection? Don't know. Sometimes those feelings do pan out into something meaningful. Sometimes the relationship doesn't develop for a long time, but does eventually. Now I have a confession, I had that feeling about you and Jim all those years ago. But you take the record for length of time for a relationship to develop.

Your confession made me laugh. Very sweet. I have been wondering about concrete evidence on you too. Is this guy for real? And I have wondered about your voice and if it has changed since high school. I think I can actually remember the sound of it from high school days.

Now is a good time to tell you that I was born with asthma. And while it is totally controlled with today's wonder drugs, one puff in the morning, one at night, living with a smoker would take a toll on my health. But I have friends that smoke. And can spend an evening in a smoky place and survive. And sit up wind but enjoy the aroma of a good cigar. (I suddenly remembered Viv and I smoking Swisher Sweets,

driving her mom's convertible Cutlass, age 17.) What a
sight we must have been.

A bonus:

Beginning

I feel a beginning
Within me
And all around me,
Like I am
Opening forward,
And you are
Wrapped around me
Like the soft
Summer air.

I find you
Each night
In one dream
After another
Always so welcoming.
Taking me into you
On the beach,
In the water,
In a cloud
Of desire,
Or a field
Of soft fresh flowers.
You always find me
And hold me
Until the next dream,
Until the next promise.

And so I wake
Each morning
With you
All over me
And a big smile
To greet the day.

It becomes so easy
To take on
The day's problems,
Knowing that in-between
You will be there
In word
And spirit
And invitation
Of the next encounter
Tomorrow
And yesterday,
Forever
In each moment
With you.

REEally have to start my day. Smile once or twice for
me today. And I will
do that for you.

mb

From: JAZMAN@mbc.web
Sent: Thursday, June 20, 2002 8:43 AM
To: mbrogan@mbc.web
Subject: RE: finding Jacob

I woke up feeling compelled to write to you whether or
not there was an answer from last night's email waiting
for me. I now need to write you before I go to bed and
as soon as I wake up. Did you cast a spell on me? I
feel like we are communicating while I am writing, not
like it will take hours for it to reach you. Like we are
connected in the spiritual universe and only 1,700 miles
apart in the physical universe. Distance is not the same
in the spiritual universe. My attention is on you,
completely. Amazing. I will figure out what is going
on here one of these days. And I just can't wait to hug
you. (smile)

We certainly have an unusual connection that we created outside the normal physical universe. But I don't expect anything other than to have you in the same space and enjoy your company and affection for awhile. I won't put any expectations out there besides looking forward to being together. Just wanted to tell you that. I have been thinking of some questions for you. You don't need to answer yours.

lbj

From: mbrogan@mbc.web
Sent: Thursday, June 20, 2002 6:00 PM
To: JAZMAN@mbc.web
SUBJECT: lost time

Did you get the message this morning? I sent it about 4:30 AM. Your reply (about 9:00 AM) mentioned that you had not received an answer from last night's message. Maybe you meant that you only got this quick message and not the novelette that I usually write. Just want to make sure that you are getting these, and there is not a problem with the mbc server. I have heard complaints from my friends about mbc email trouble.

I did decide this morning that I should probably write in the morning, and then (beginning next week) after I get yours at work. That way, I can always say good morning and hear your dreams. And leave room for pillow talk.

 I can assure you that I don't cast spells. (Although I would be open to winning the lottery that way if you know how.) But I do agree that there is much more to "us" than these emails. Maybe that was part of my DeJaVu.

You should probably know that I go barefoot whenever possible. Is that a deal breaker? My mom complained about that during her last days. (I could not keep shoes on that child.) I let that one fly and took it as a compliment. But when she told the story (for the zillionth) time that when I was born, she could not believe how big my feet were, I promptly asked my sisters what size shoes they wore. One of my sisters has a whole shoe size bigger. (mine are 8, again, the all American norm.) But my mom had tiny feet (5) that she was obviously proud of until her dying day.

Thank you for checking expectation. Whatever happens, I know that you are extraordinary. And if nothing else, you have a loving pen pal for as long as you want one.

mb

From: JAZMAN@mbc.web
Sent: Thursday, June 20, 2002 7:35 PM
To: mbrogan@mbc.web
Subject: this morning

I did not get your morning message until this afternoon, about two hours ago. Your beautiful poem was a wonderful surprise. Like a gift under the tree on Christmas morning. The same happiness hit me when I heard you woke up to leave a message for me in the morning. I really do love talking to you over morning coffee, even with the delayed response. I feel you here with me as I write to you.

OK. It is only fair that you call and listen to my voice mail. So to even things out, here are my numbers: cell 847-555-2213 and home 415-555-1142. Heck, let's throw in the office number just in case. 505-555-7001 is my direct line. So there you have it. Now you can listen to MY voicemail messages. What will you do if I answer? I have been told that I sound like Bruce Willis. I suppose if I looked like him you would be on the next plane out here.

I have had the feeling of knowing someone before. Which means I probably did. When previous lifetimes become as real as high school memories, you stop wondering whether they are real. If I know my car is blue, but if someone is telling me it is green, it doesn't change what I know.

You had those feelings for Jim and me? I can believe that we have a history beyond this life. We were very tight until I moved out of state. Stayed in touch for a few years until he married, then lost touch. We could find him though if you are so inclined. He may be single now! Or maybe I should be careful there. Wouldn't want to lose you so early in the game.

Looks like I will have to stop smoking for good. Or cure your asthma. I really don't believe all the hype about the connection between smoking and cancer. But if smoking bothers you, then it is gone! Who knows, you might be saving my life here.

Need to end here and go to Ron's for more business planning. If I get home at a decent hour, I will try to write again before sleep.

I am working on some questions for you. Until then, I would love to hear what you have to say about kissing.

lbj

From: mbrogan@mbc.web
Sent: Thursday, June 20, 2002 11:22 PM
To: JAZMAN@mbc.web
SUBJECT: RE: this morning

It is some ungodly hour and I woke from a vivid dream that I was searching an archive of photographs with the help of two women that I knew were standing behind me but I could not see. Photograph after photograph looking for yours. I hope this makes sense because I am still dreaming awake. Did not find that photo.

You have been one step ahead of my worry about silly things like revealing too much personal info without getting any....you having my phone numbers, I don't have yours. NOT that I am going to use it. Well, I may just have to hear that voice. I know just what to do if you answer. I am not sure that my heart knows, but I do. Would much rather cuddle at the beach and talk the night through. But I can wait. I think.

Well, I do remember you and Jim coming ON together, in a playful way of course. But I think you both knew and respected the fact that I was a virgin then. I remember seeing Jim around more than you – you were probably busy being a business man. I remember talking to Jim a lot about "relationships" and how we thought they worked. You both seemed so fascinated with my virginity which tickled me at the time. Probably lent itself to that feeling that you had one of those rare, eternal relationships. But the fact that I had that feeling for you both doesn't mean that I will necessarily have romantic feelings for both of you. Especially at once. Not in this lifetime. Better clarify that again. Hasn't changed in 30 years and I don't expect it will, thank you dad.

Rest assured that (probably dad to thank again) I have never been one to split my affections. Very singular in that respect. So I guess I will be saying no thank you in Gurnee for some time to come. Although no one here will notice a difference. This is all about you. And me. Until we change that. That is just how I was made (this time.)

I had a business associate die of lung cancer last year. A remarkable man. Extremely strong faith. Very gentle and firm personality. Left behind 5 children. If there is no other reason for us here, that one has meaning. Be glad to take ownership there. But if you could cure the asthma too, I am all for it. I'm told I was also born with a compromised immune system that goes with it. I have seen some improvements there with a divorce and some lifestyle changes. But a cure is a cure. You would be my all time hero.

If it bothers me, then it is gone huh? Wow. If I was not still dreaming I would probably have some smart ass comment. Those seem to be OK with you. I could try to give them up if they bother you. I developed them for survival in an Irish family of 7 children. May take awhile. But then again, I do enjoy them so on second thought, Nah. But I do appreciate your gesture about your smoking. I could not live with a smoker. I have some friends that smoke, it does limit our relationship. Don't be careful about Jim for any reason. You two are real. Some things you should not give up for anyone. That kind of familiarity of spirit right into the depths of the soul is one of those things. Might come back as a destructive resentment. I respect boundaries and can take no for an answer. Even in the throws of cyberspace passion.

I know I have rambled here and could continue to do so. I have so much to say to you. Damn time.....well maybe the mystery and the slow revelation is part of the spell.

Sweet dreams,
mb

From: mbrogan@mbc.web
Sent: Friday, June 21, 2002 4:56 AM
To: JAZMAN@mbc.web
Subject:

Well, the coffee hasn't completely pulled me out of the dreaming yet so it's probably a good time to talk about kissing.

I have always thought that kissing was essential. It communicates so much more than two mouths together because it can be extremely spiritual if the focus is not just on the mouth. I can always tell how far down into a heart or spirit a guy reaches with his kiss. Nervousness always comes through as does aggression and sometimes intent.

I have to say that a kiss revealed Patrick's infidelity to me. It wasn't anything that I could explain and Patrick was perplexed about it, believe me. But he did come clean.

I have also had a kiss reveal unequal intentions. At that point I put the relationship on cruise control until I figured out that this guy was, and always had been good at multiple relationships. Too bad too. He had such potential.

A kiss is the ultimate form of intimate communication because it is the beginning (and sometimes the end) of intimacy.

Do I like to kiss. Hell, yes. Or maybe that would be heavens, yes. I have been told that I am a good kisser, but that will be up to you to decide. I have never revealed this to anyone up front. But for me it starts at the mouth, explores both spirits as they combine, and then connects to the soul during the flight of passion. Any pressure there?

A kiss may reveal to us if we are "right." I love that scene in back to the future when Marty is kissing his mom back in time and she says "Ewe, that was like kissing my brother!" The spirit revealed. No lies can be told there.

Then there are so many varieties. Lightly brushing (to build desire.) the impassioned wrestle. The neck and shoulders. OK - here is the line. Cybersex I am not into. I prefer the real thing.

So I will sign off. As I try to focus my blurry eyes on the clock I can see that I have turned a short email into another long chapter of the book that is us.

Good morning. Thanks for this feeling that I have just plugged my torso into an electrical socket. Better than coffee.

Rub a flower petal between your fingers today and think of me.

Yours,
mb

From: JAZMAN@mbc.web
Sent: Friday, June 21, 2002 8:07 AM
To: mbrogan@mbc.web
Subject: RE: this morning

Good morning. It is a very good morning. Two of your letters waiting for me. Thank you. You were my first thought today. Who ARE you? I really need to look into those gorgeous eyes and be able to figure this out. Waking up with you on my mind is the best way to start the day.

Your viewpoints on kissing were fascinating. I am glad you see it like that. Quite an expression of affinity however you see it. Hard to kiss someone without having affinity for them. There is pure lust, but what a huge step down from what you are talking about. I'll bet you are a great kisser. I have been told the same, but will let you decide. Might have more to do with who you are kissing. Might need to give you more than a hug when I see you. What do you think?

I have always loved those romantic evenings when closeness is felt all night, but sex postponed to build desire. Can create some very intense feelings.

Are you worried that I have too much personal info on you? Whatever you want to know about me, just ask. And if you feel that I am asking too many personal questions, just say so. Like I said, I have no experience here. Just doing what comes naturally. In time, you will know I am perfectly safe.

OK. I have those questions for you. You won't be graded – although you did get an A++++ on the kissing answer.

Is it hard to make you laugh?

Are you suspicious of people or overly trusting?

Do you like dancing?

What are your thoughts on forgiveness? Do you hold grudges?

Can you make it to midnight on New Year's Eve?

Do you make New Year's resolutions? Do you make them that night?

What do you like to eat?

Where would you like to travel?

Describe the perfect weekend with someone you care about.

What is something you have always wanted to do?

Do you like foot message?

Describe your idea of the perfect kiss.

That's enough. I don't think I can wait all day for the answers. Did you call my numbers?

lbj

From: mbrogan@mbc.web
Sent: Friday, June 21, 2002 7:26 PM
To: JAZMAN@mbc.web
Subject: this evening

Good evening lbj. I will confess that when driving home from Schaumburg this afternoon, thinking of you of course, I did not realize that I missed my exit unit I hit the toll close to Wisconsin. I really need to get a grip here. I was absent minded enough before YOU.

When I got home, my son directed me to the kitchen, where I found a fabulous bouquet of flowers from you. With a card, instructing me to rub the petals between my fingers to my hearts content. A contented heart, thank you. It has been awhile. Your gift is deeply appreciated.

Who am I? You seem to know already, without seeing me. Reach deep within your self to know more. You are doing this already because you are anticipating my need, such as your phone numbers to create the balance I was needing. You seem to be sure that my eyes are not crossed and I really do have my teeth since there seems to be no scarring you. There is also the fact that when I was wondering about which questions you would ask, I found many of my guesses in your email. We are in tune. Although I did not guess some of the racier ones. There is the old Jake, way ahead of the virgin Molly in that category.

I would be much more comfortable letting the romance grow slowly. I have been the old married person ripping it all off and doing exactly what it takes to complete the moment quickly. I guess at the time, we thought it was passion. But once it became the routine, the romance was gone. I like the idea of allowing our romance to unfold. But I worry that we are creating expectations that I will not be able to fulfill. And I worry about your readiness for a serious relationship, with what you have going in your life.

I already thought about giving you my cell number 847-555-0312. This will probably change if I change jobs. I refuse to be one of those people that carry two or three cell phones around. I don't make enough personal calls on a cell phone to make that a problem.

I will also give you my emergency number (Meg) 847-555-5759 in case a sudden silence occurs. She always knows what is going on with me. A sudden silence will only occur if I physically cannot send an email because of some accident or illness. I would not want to leave you wondering.

So now I think I have given you complete accountability. Let me know if I slack. I am always open to feedback. Criticism is a big red flag, but feedback is always welcome. I like to be challenged.

Your answers:

I was in training on Employment Law Thursday and busted twice for laughing in class. But my classroom neighbors were very witty and when repeated, the teacher even laughed. I think I have one of those distinct laughs that can't be hidden. I was glad not to get the sense that it was an annoyance.

Is it hard to make me laugh? I don't understand dirty jokes. Hope that isn't a deal buster. My three older brothers used to tell them just to see the blank look on my face. I just don't think about that stuff. There are some things that other people think are funny that I don't. Jokes about violence or racism. Jokes that are disrespectful. Is it hard to make me laugh? You are a brilliant, intuitive guy with a sensitive humor. If we sat next to each other in class, I am sure I would be busted all day. (Don't you remember laughing until we cried at the beach?)

Suspicious of people? I think that I was probably overly trusting when I was younger but have learned to trust my instincts, figure out character pretty quickly and draw my boundaries accordingly. You don't need to trust someone to treat them with respect. Trust is a useful ingredient in all relationships that is established in a variety of ways. I am sure you've read the same Steven Covey books that I have. I use trust wisely.

The dance question I just knew you would ask. The only man that I have danced with in 15 years was the County Board Chairman. His tummy made it hard to get close to his ear to tell him that I had gotten a job offer and would be leaving his employment. (In his defense, he since lost a good deal of weight and has started running to keep himself healthy.)

I love dancing. I am not a good follower. But my X and I could clear a dance floor when swing dancing after a few years of learning each other's rhythms. I like to be held while dancing. Swing dancing is great for that. I am sure that if we started with the slow stuff, and you wore your steel toed shoes so I don't hurt your toes, we will be dancing in one rhythm in no time.

Do you agree that we already have discovered many of each other's natural rhythms through these emails? I think that is part of what tunes us into eachother.

I always forgive my friends. I try to forgive everyone. But that doesn't mean that trust can always be re-established. Or should always be re-established.

Friendships can cycle out that way and it is perfectly natural. I have not ended many friendships with hard feelings. When it has happened, I think it was because of their need to abandon. Some people just need to leave in a huff. We all have our lessons to learn. I don't hold a grudge.

With a nap, coffee and some wine closer to midnight, I can usually make it to the dawn of the New Year. I love New Year tradition. I spent most of the past 20 New Year's Eves with my children and we have developed a few yearly rituals that keep us up and busy until midnight. But as I transition into empty nester, I am being left home alone more on that holiday.

I had plans to go to some big party in Highland Park last year with Sue Burchall (Bisette) who has two college age daughters. I like making plans with her because she understands the child contingency. It turned out that we both had children stay home that night and cancelled those plans. I am, by the way, open to new traditions.

One of the family traditions that we have for the New Year is setting our goals for the coming year. My youngest got into this in a big way. So after we take a hammer to this year's gingerbread house and pour the hot chocolate, we look at last year's goals, talk about accomplishment and formulate new ones. We keep them in binders so that we can review them every year. I think that I had one that wasn't met that my kids saw me reformulate and accomplish next year. And yes, they begin with a verb and are measurable.

Without a need to coach the children, I guess I can do whatever the hell I want now, right? I will need to give some thought to actually what that is. Crossroads.

Foods? Right now, with my burning desire to become reacquainted with the bottom half of my wardrobe, I eat

for health. One piece of plain wheat bread in the
morning on the way to work to set the serotonin levels.
I mix a mean smoothie that has yogurt, natural
cranberry juice, blueberries (for memory,) black cherry
(for inflammation of any kind) etc. I freeze it and
if I need to nibble, I have some of that. I try to eat
several small meals instead of three larger ones to keep
my metabolism (naturally low) up.

I don't like cooking as much as I used to because really
good cooking takes time. I was totally into it as a stay at
home mom and learned some good tricks. Now, my
children have me trained to cook only their favorite
food and I comply to please and avoid waste. I have had
my disasters but for the most part I think consensus is
that my cooking is very good. Practice and creativity is
all it takes. Peg actually taught me that. I love a good
steak, fresh seafood, fresh veges, great Italian food –
lots of things. But they need to be well prepared.

Travel other than Ireland? Paris. Much of my reading is
centered around the artistic revolution at the turn of the
century. Paris, Florence, Berlin were the centers for
that. Those islands on the Spanish Rivera sound nice.
I am sure that there are zillions of places all over the
world that I could think of, but will never get to.

Perfect weekend? Walking, talking, cuddling, and
connecting. I usually let my partner tell me what they
want to "do" because the important part for me is
the being "with."

Something I have always wanted to do? Connect with
you.

Feet rubbed? I have already confessed that I have
always had this need to feel the world through my feet.
A foot rub would be heaven. Actually, one of my
favorite parts of a professional message, along with the
head.

The perfect kiss. There is only so much I can take feeling like someone has plugged my torso into a wall socket so I might have to think about that one later. Or maybe that is your answer.

Haven't called the cell yet. But I will so that in my dreams, your voice is real. Do you sleep in on the weekends? Would be nice to catch you first thing for pillow talk.

Sweet dreams,
mb

From: JAZMAN@mbc.web
Sent: Friday, June 21, 2002 8:34 PM
To: mbrogan@mbc.web
Subject: just hi

I got your letter and will answer later. Just wanted you to know that I am thinking of you. Needed to tell you that now. Just the way it is.

I think of you often. (smile)
Jake

From: mbrogan@mbc.web
Sent: Saturday, June 22, 2002 4:29 AM
To: JAZMAN@mbc.web
Subject: empty morning

No email this morning. I now know exactly how you felt. It is not easy to form a relationship on the cutting edge of technology is it? That mbc server may be messing us up.

Cloudy morning here. No sunrise to savor.

I plan to run into the office briefly this morning while I am out running Saturday errands. I am sure there is a mountain of invoices waiting for me. I would like to get organized before Monday. I am bringing some pictures to scan and send you.

Last night, after a pillow fight that really bothered the dog (he didn't know who to protect so he just gave up), I fired up the computer and got your quick hi. Smile.

Got three emails from the Hanlons yesterday. Mostly pictures. You are right. They look worn, but SO happy. One of the all time great couples are now a family. I will check for your email a little later. mb

From: JAZMAN@mbc.web
Sent: Saturday, June 22, 2002 9:15 AM
To: mbrogan@mbc.web
Subject: the visual you

Hi beautiful. Thank you so much. The pictures were great. I was wondering if your eyes were really crossed. Very glad to see those teeth. I am ready to hug you right now. Were you a child prodigy in high school? I was a year younger than everyone in my class. You look like you are in your 30s. Amazing. You have not changed at all except to get MUCH more beautiful. And since you were one of the hottest chicks in school that is really saying something. How the hell have you stayed single all these years? No wonder you say no thank you so much. You just keep doing that – OK? Except to me of course (smile.)

Do you want me to send you pictures or should I just surprise you? I should just buy a digital camera and get it over with. You are right, I need to move into the twenty first century. And I should take some of my kids and bring them back here.

So you made it to the office to send the pictures and are probably running errands now. I would love to hear about your errands – your day to day activities.

Sometimes I wonder how you fill your days and how I would fit into them.

I loved your answers. Especially the one about what you always wanted to do. The sweetest thing I've been told in quite awhile. Although that probably had more to do with the messenger than the message.

New Year's Eve hasn't been very exciting for me the past few years. What are you doing that night? I know I'm free.

I have never been to Paris and don't speak French. Do you? Your perfect weekend will be mine too. Especially if I can get you drunk on the plane. We will probably laugh for 12 hrs. all the way there. That is, between mile high club visits to the washroom.

Thinking of you,
lbj

From: mbrogan@mbc.web
Sent: Saturday, June 22, 2002 12:03 PM
To: JAZMAN@mbc.web
Subject: physical universe

Well, I guess if you have seen my picture and still want to go on here, we have taken a step. I re-read our past several emails and something definitely seems to be building up here. That might explain my adolescent inability to say anything coherent into your voice mail this morning.

After I sent the pictures I thought, what the heck, and called to hear your voice. It left me speechless as it did not occur to me that I would need to leave a message when I dialed. It was a very strange experience. Like that moment became every moment and there were no other moments.

When I came down from that and laughed because you do actually sound a bit like Bruce Willis in his Moonlighting years, I said "Good Molly," out loud and wondered to myself why the hell I did not think to leave a voicemail.

So the rational me called back and got so caught up in your voice that the emotional me took over and left me speechless again. I know that I said something, but I am not sure what.

Then I decided to listen to my outgoing message to hear what you heard when you called me. Did I sound like I just rolled out of bed with a cold? So I changed my message.

Then I got through the majority of my 137 emails, organized my workload for next week and went to the butcher. What do I do when I am running errands? Lots of food related errands when Jack is home because he eats an enormous amount of it. Then I take care of the car, the finances, the wardrobe, the house and my pals. Then I take care of me and read, write or nap. And think of you quite often in-between.

I realize that I am dodging your question about the hug and kiss. I don't mean to hold back. I do believe in transparency. I am just hoping to get a grip on this thing before I answer. Am I too careful? I guess in all honesty, this has become a bit confusing for me. Don't worry. I am a bright girl. I can handle it. Just give me a moment to think.

How have I stayed single since my divorce? I did forget what life without a wedding ring was like. While I was married and wore a wedding ring, I didn't get hit on (so much.) Nice to know that some things are sacred.

I think the fact that I am open and interested in people can be misinterpreted. I work very hard at sending clear signals. Sex doesn't motivate me like it does other people. It has a different place in my life. Less physical, more spiritual. And I think some people see any kind of interest or affection as sexual. I have gotten better at spotting those kinds of people. It is better than never looking at or talking to anyone.

You asked me in an earlier email to tell you about saying no thank you. I just threw in a couple of stories for you. Do they bother you? Believe me, my refusal skills are superb. But I guess you wouldn't know that since I have not used them on you. I am going purely on instinct here. And of course, what you have given me through your endearing correspondence. For the first time in a long time, no is not the right answer. I know that to my core. If that changes for you, let me know. And I promise to do the same.

At this point Jake, you would have to look like the elephant man to dissuade me. Unless you want to dissuade me after seeing my picture or hearing my voicemail. I hope you did open all three pictures! If you think I am the girl on the boat we may be doomed. I could never live up to that expectation. (I found that picture behind my picture in the frame. Thought it was so cute, I would send it first, just to get you interested.)

mb

From: JAZMAN@mbc.web
Sent: Saturday, June 22, 2002 12:03 PM
To: mbrogan@mbc.web
Subject: RE: physical universe

I was writing you the last email at the same time you called. Weird. I LOVED your voice. Very different than the voice on your recording. I had to listen a few times to find the resemblance. Thanks for leaving the message, like a gift. I saved it so I can listen to it again.

I have downloaded your pictures on my computer at home and the office. What do you think of that? You now fill my world. Your eyes are just as I remembered. What color are they exactly? You will never be able to keep me away from that neck!

I miss you,

Jake

From: mbrogan@mbc.web
Sent: Saturday, June 22, 2002 2:22 PM
To: JAZMAN@mbc.web
Subject: physical universe

This is strange, the crossing emails. but I like the weekends much more now because just two emails won't do.

Whew. You liked my voice and I was not as incoherent as I thought. Great relief. I add a little kick ass to my professional voice because those contractors can be a hard lot to work with. Rough and ready.

I won't be near a computer for awhile. Going to Libertyville to see Sue Burchall. Jack passed away suddenly a couple of years ago and she has been having trouble letting go of their home. Can't blame her. I have always loved that home. I also have many good memories of it.

Actually, I am trying to decide whether to sell this town house once the job is settled. I have about 50K in equity and need to restructure my debt. I am not really happy in Gurnee anymore with Jamie gone. The taxes are high. The traffic sucks. But, I won't take that step just yet.

After Sue's, I will be home. No plans to go out tonight.
I need some down time. And if my son will stop asking
me what I am smiling about, I will get it.

Something for you:

Promise

I see in you
Such promise
And possibility.
I feel in you
Excitement,
Hope,
And earnest desire
To come closer,
To explore together
This life,
Each other.

You suggest
We travel.
Place ourselves
In foreign surroundings
So that our adventure
Together
Can be
Inside/outside,
Complete.

You suggest
We search our souls
And choose
A place
Familiar
Yet unexplored
In this life.

A fabulous idea.
We can then unfold

On all levels
Simultaneously
From depth to detail,
Moment to eternity.

Is this by design,
Or by instinct?
Is it intention
Or natural curiosity
That compels you
To place us
Where the spark
Will instantly
Set our souls ablaze?

I hope
That you can stand
The heat
Of the extreme intimacy
You seek
But have not yet found
In this lifetime.

My answer to you
Is yes, please.
Bring on the heat
With your promise.
I know we
Can create it.
I hope we
Can sustain it.

mb

From: JAZMAN@mbc.web
Sent: Saturday, June 22, 2002 1:14 PM
To: mbrogan@mbc.web
Subject: RE: physical universe

Sorry to hear about Jack. They had been together since high school right? What did Sue look like. I am having a hard time placing her. Jack played guitar didn't he? I think I saw him play.

Your poem was amazing. With each new poem you reveal such keen insight and awareness. The ending made me wonder. I would really like to talk on the phone. Are you ready for that?

Property taxes in Illinois are MUCH higher than CA. Having places in both states I can tell you that the difference is incredible. Where are you thinking of relocating? Will it be in the near future?

Had a harried day at work today. The current fluctuations in the market are making customers extremely nervous. Takes a lot of counseling to get them to understand that this is the time money is made. Only risky if you don't know the market. That is what they pay us the big bucks for. The knowledge. Much communication is needed when the market is so volatile to convince people that our strategies will work. For the newer clients anyway. Once we make someone a fortune, they don't question us as much.

By the way, I didn't just like your voice. I LOVED your voice. And love it more every time I listen to it. So sultry. I will need to call you very soon, if that's OK. I love getting your emails, and writing to you. I would not want that to stop.

Wish we could have breakfast in the morning. Do you take your eggs scrambled or fertilized?
lbj

From: mbrogan@mbc.web
Sent: Saturday, June 22, 2002 5:01 PM
To: JAZMAN@mbc.web
Subject: risk free eggs

You will be encouraged to know that it is technically impossible to fertilize my eggs outside of a laboratory. Of course, that shouldn't stop you from trying. You are welcome to try all you want. And I encourage you to do so. Yes, my doctors relieved me of the monthly curse several years ago and dramatically improved the quality of my life (especially my romantic life.) And removed the possibility of a late life surprise.

You are welcome to call me whenever you get the urge. I crash early, get up early and usually have my cell phone with me. Those should be pretty good perimeters. If I am in a meeting, my cell phone has voice mail. Leave a good time to call back if you want me to. Am I ready to hear your voice? Judging from the effect that your voice mail recording had on me, I am not sure that I will have anything coherent to say. Your voice propels me. To where is uncertain. But my instincts tell me that this will be a huge step forward, or inward, or both. Too weird?

Do you remember a night in the record store when we talked until dawn about Scientology? I have been thinking about that night lately.

Time to cook dinner.
mb

From: mbrogan@mbc.web
Sent: Saturday, June 22, 2002 10:05 PM
To: JAZMAN@mbc.web
Subject: sweet dreams

It is getting late. So I will just say sweet dreams. Lots of them.

mb

From: JAZMAN@mbc.web
Sent: Sunday, June 23, 2002 1:14 AM
To: mbrogan@mbc.web
Subject: still here

Been several hours since my last email so I better get it together here. First thing I did when I got back to the house is fire up the computer. Had a late dinner with clients. Had a martini for the first time in a long time too. Missed you. I think now, I NEED to talk to you.

Have you ever had a martini? I would love to take you out and get you buzzed.

If we ever have a fight, we can go to separate computers and email each other until things are worked out. But I can't imagine us having a disagreement. Funny, us two peace hounds marrying two fighters. How does it work like that? Well, I did learn to look for someone who values peace. I haven't met anyone who understands it like you seem to.
Your ability to communicate is probably key.

My memory of those years at the end of high school and before I moved out here are very hazy. Too many drugs. It was the late 60s early 70s, after all. I quit all the drugs and moved out here shortly after our talk in the record store I think. Might have even been the next day. I guess I didn't interest you in pursuing Scientology. Or maybe you didn't trust me back then.

You have many of the same ideas. It feels like, although we have taken different roads, we have learned many of the same lessons.

Well, it is after 1 so I guess I will turn in. Are you coming? I'll be waiting for you in dreamland.

lbj

From: mbrogan@mbc.web
Sent: Sunday, June 23, 2002 4:11 AM
To: JAZMAN@mbc.web
Subject: RE: sweet dreams

Just woke up from this weird dream that I was in a basement. A lot of old people were sitting around desks waiting for some kind of service. I wasn't walking but kind of flying along, close to the floor. Everyone was very hot, but something I had done was cooling things off so I was happy about that.

Just as I reached the stairway, I saw a group of old people who were holding babies. They were waiting to adopt them. But one very old woman wanted to give hers back. I looked at the baby who was all stretched out on her tummy, smiling and kicking her legs. Then I woke up. Very weird. You have a different tone after a martini. I don't think I can articulate. Not bad, just different. Maybe closer to your speaking voice.

The more I think about our conversation in the record store, the more I remember the whole evening. The group broke up late at the beach because it was getting cold, even with the fire. Most everyone went home. But you and I had been having our own little conversation about Scientology that I did not want to end. So when you invited me to the store I was happy to say yes. I was fascinated by your scientology ideas because I was already meditating big time by then. As I drove away I felt as if I would never see you again.

And wondered why. I remember a feeling of great loss. I didn't see you again after that did I?

Those were strange days weren't they? I saw many lives wasted because of drugs. Sure am glad yours wasn't. I think that was why, when it came time to volunteer at my children's school, I chose the prevention programs. I really wanted to learn how to talk to my kids about that.

What was that great line from the movie Field of Dreams...if you remember the 60s, you didn't live through them. I am sure the early 70s are included.

I suppose we could figure out why we married who we did and then found each other. Let's do it after another martini. No, I have never had one. But I have seen the instant buzz of those who do. And, I will confess, had a little fun with it.

I am not sure if I trusted anyone back then, so soon after my break up with Patrick. I am much more trusting now. If anything, it can take too long for those instincts to kick in. Once trust is established, you will really have to hit me with a Mack truck to lose it. And then I would probably say, thank you, I have never seen the bottom of a truck before. But then I would open up awareness. Trusting doesn't mean stupid. If it is true, you were aiming for me, I would get the distance I need to avoid another crash and withdraw trust. And once again, take the time needed to mend. I have learned a lot from that mending process. But it doesn't seem to get easier.

I don't think I ever want to get so buzzed that I can't remember your touch. I want to take all of them with me always. Even if they are just words for now.

It would be so cool if we could figure out how to meet in our dreams. Sure would make dating easier. Keep working on that one. I think I am going back for more.

Well, with fair greeting, in she comes.
He's not the least surprised, it seems,
So good, so beautiful for sure,
He thinks, he's seen her off before.
   -   Goethe
   mb

From: JAZMAN@mbc.web
Sent: Sunday, June 23, 2002 8:52 AM
To: mbrogan@mbc.web
Subject: Sunday

Interesting dream. Odd. I usually don't remember my
dreams, or if I do, it is the one I am having when I wake
up. They seem to be just random images that
sometimes come together in a story, sometimes not. I
think of you first thing each morning, so I must be
dreaming about you! I will keep looking for you.

The late sixties, early seventies were amazing. LSD.
MLK and RFK assassinated. University riots. Kent
State. Viet Nam. Lots of change and turbulence.

Now how did you notice a difference in my tone after
one martini? Although alcohol can increase my sexual
urges. Your invitation to try for fertilized eggs thrown
on top of all the new emotions and a martini. Well, you
could be right.

What are you going to do today? Let's do something
together. (Would be so nice.) Guess we will just be
writing eachother. And maybe a call? I will be at work
for awhile. Running errands as you call it.

Sure do love talking to you.

lbj

From: mbrogan@mbc.web
Sent: Sunday, June 23, 2002 10:05 AM
To: JAZMAN@mbc.web
Subject: the coming week

I loved your third paragraph. Your hint about the emotional feeling that we are wrestling with. Yes, I suppose my first inclination when I finally do see you will be to wrap myself around you and not stop kissing for 24/7. There, now you know. I realize that these feelings do not balance with what is actually happened here so far. I have stopped trying to analyze it and begun trying to manage it. Hopefully, I will have it all managed by our first meeting. OK back to total transparency. Whew. Now I can stop dodging the "can I give you a hug and kiss" questions. Could we make that meeting sooner than later? Why don't you slip into town for a night. I know a private beach in Kenosha where we could talk the night away. The sun rises there. We can watch day turn to night, then dark to light. Build a fire. At night, the water is the color of lapis.

I will be in my office tomorrow at the time you leave for work - why don't you call me then? It will be nice to talk, instead of listening to your voice on a recording.

Today, home maintenance, with Jack's help.

The coming week will be very interesting for me. I took some risks last week that may or may not pay off but I was feeling confident and feisty.

I was asked to address a group of managers briefly on the direction of the company. Public speaking has always been anxiety producing for me. Something I did not find out until college, when I passed out during my first presentation on a comparison of the philosophies of Croce and Descartes. The feedback that I got Friday told me that I was cool and it didn't show.

Anyway, I started off by referencing a book (of course) called "The Structure of Scientific Revolutions" by Thomas Kuhn written in the 60s to introduce the concept of a paradigm and the idea of changing paradigms revolutionize scientific discovery. I asked if anyone had heard of the book (not read it mind you) or heard of a paradigm and got three nods. Hmmm.

Then I went on to say that a few years after writing the book Thomas Kuhn had it republished with an addendum because he discovered that American businesses were using this concept to reformulate their business strategies. His addendum illuminated the difference between businesses that simply formulate a new paradigm, and ones that actually put their new paradigm into practice.

After looking at some blank faces and feeling the anxiety rise I began walking around a bit and explained that the AT&T Broadband "Blueprint for Success" that was introduced to the Chicago market shortly after the change of command last year is our new paradigm. And it is a very good, thorough one. But the really good news was the new wave of training that was based on that paradigm that is now being implemented in the workforce. I explained that the fact that the company was giving us a process to implement the paradigm was very exciting and solid evidence of the company's commitment to excellence. I really do think all of that but think I caught some people by surprise.

But then I took the risk and suggested that the real proof of the company's commitment will be an evaluation piece to follow that will measure the company's practice of the paradigm. I ended my little ditty with a statement something like I hope to see that in the future and hope that you are all as excited as I am about this new direction.

I turned to walk back to my seat and saw our new market leader standing in the door way with a pretty good poker face. I smiled, sat down and did a little bio rhythm stuff to get my heart to stop pounding. Busted again. Oh well.

The corporate culture to date has not been too receptive to challenges. But when our fearless leader came in to follow up he did mention his commitment to measurement a couple of times. If they ever ask me to speak again, they will be wise to ask what I will say. And hopefully, tell me who will be listening in the doorway.

I will be meeting with one of the contractors to give them a resume packet Wed. The work days will be shorter because I won't have all that travel, missing my exit, taking the scenic route home.

More time with Jack. I have been too quiet lately. Trying to figure this thing with you out. He keeps looking at me and saying "What?" or "What are you smiling about?" Now that I have had a little time to process the last work week, I can probably share more with him. Since he is taking Business Management classes, he shows a real interest.

mb

From: JAZMAN@mbc.web
Sent: Sunday, June 23, 2002 1:20 PM
To: mbrogan@mbc.web
Subject: RE: the coming week

A hint you say? I'm not sure I can be more direct. But your offer of a night on the beach made me realize: I need to get my ex to accept the fact that it is over, and begin proceedings. I am afraid that you would not respect me if I didn't. We go over it and over it. Have had some counseling on it that turned out to be a dead end. I have encouraged her to begin her life again and see other people. Lived in California for the past two years! I just wanted to be able to agree on the terms and eliminate the lawyers and court scenes. I would feel much better with her finally accepting it so we can both move on.

I am going back the weekend of the 4th and will finalize things. If I can't, I will just have to move forward without agreement.

Keep your cell phone with you that weekend. I would love to see you, if only for a little while. Take a blanket to the beach.

Wish I could have been there to hear your talk to the managers. I would not have given you a poker face. You are so knowledgeable. Christ, I love to read your letters. I get this intense feeling in my chest. And a big smile on my face.

Today, I have several meetings with clients so I will be out for most of the day. I will look for you in between.

lbj

From: mbrogan@mbc.web
Sent: Sunday, June 23, 2002 2:40 PM
To: JAZMAN@mbc.web
Subject: step back

The cable company might be better off if you were the guy in the doorway. Oh well, I got raves on my schpiel on coaching employees on mistake recovery.

Listen Jake, I completely respect your approach to the end of your marriage. But I had the distinct impression that you were finished with the marriage except for the filing. Since you have taken a two year cooling of period 1500 miles away, I assumed that this would be happening soon. Did I misinterpret? And you have a way of stepping back that is disturbing. So I will say this. Don't take me anywhere that isn't real. This free fall is exciting. But make sure you are prepared to land where we will inevitably land here.

The character in my book, Remember Me, does not understand how her thoughts and intentions create reality. She has a vague notion at the end, that what she witnesses is created by her own internal workings, but never really "gets" the process. I mention this to say that I don't want us to fall into that ego trap. Let's not allow life to happen to us because we are so wrapped up in the emotion and illusion that we lose our grasp on what is real. Our affinity is real. The energy between us is real. The possibility we create is real. If we allow the daily strife to keep us from what is real, we might just watch it slip away...

I think your strategy for a peaceful resolution to your divorce is rare and courageous. But do what you need to do there because you need to do it. In your own time. Not because of me. It is important to keep it separate. I totally respect your privacy.

And I suppose we could tone down these emails. You are fun to play with. But now that I know that I have the schwing effect on you, maybe we should go back to exchanging ideas and creating history. Why ask why. We will just ride it out.

Smell a flower today for me.

mb

From: JAZMAN@mbc.web
Sent: Sunday, June 23, 2002 3:03 PM
To: mbrogan@mbc.web
Subject: RE: step back

Another mb classic. The schwing effect. Tone the
emails down? Can you stop a bird from flying? I am
hooked on the schwing effect. You are totally in my
universe, affecting me. A few words for you have more
impact than a stiff martini. It seems to come natural to
you, which is better for my sake I am sure.

Everything will be handled. We are on the right track.
Need to let this flow at its own speed. I am heading out
now to meet clients in Sonoma, but will be back. I will
think of you in the car every minute. I am glad that
Jack is there to help you.

And Molly – I am better looking than the Elephant
Man!

lbj

From: mbrogan@mbc.web
Sent: Sunday, June 23, 2002 4:11 PM
To: JAZMAN@mbc.web
Subject: our universe

We seem to be sharing a universe, wherever the hell it
is. I am glad you think that I know what I am doing.
Honestly, I am in the dark. New territory for me
also. I think we are doing it to eachother because I
haven't done this before! The fact that you make me
better than ever is a very good sign.

I moved a few plants around in my garden today.
Smelled a chrysanthemum for you. Yuck. Did not know
they smelled so bad. So I pinched some lavender. Sure
bet there. The sage and spearmint also came back
nicely. Chip ran into the spearmint looking for Dale.

Way too hot here to do too much outside. Even the mother bird worked slowly to feed her babies in Jamie's birdhouse.

I have enough of a memory left to know that you look nothing like the elephant man. And I am assuming that things could not have changed that drastically for you, given the life you are living. So sticking my neck out with that remark was not all that risky. I knew that. But the point is still valid. You don't have to worry about your looks, not in the universe that we have already created. And now that I know that I don't have to worry about mine, we can both relax.

How ever will I get by with only two emails a day during the weekdays. Spoiled brat that I have become. They keep that smile going.

"But passion lends them power, time means, to meet, Tempering extremity with extreme sweet." - WS

One question - are you sure that you have given yourself time to mend? I have had plenty of time. But you are not yet through the worst of it.

Smiling for you,

mb

From: JAZMAN@mbc.web
Sent: Monday, June 24, 2002 12:03 AM
To: mbrogan@mbc.web
Subject: RE: our universe

You're probably in the middle of the most romantic dream that you won't remember. I wish I was next to you, so that I could feel you. But then, a good night's sleep might not be possible.

Our universe is not a matter of where, like the physical universe. There is distance, but that is based on level of affinity – more affinity, less distance. We can be in each other's space because of the HUGE amount of affinity we share, in spite of the 1700 miles between us in the physical world. We are in both universes at once, physical and spiritual. But each responds differently to space, time, matter and energy. Definitely one of those all night discussions on the beach.

Have I given myself enough time to mend? During the past two years I have redirected my life and emotions. I do miss my children. But as far as the marriage, I am sure divorce will be a massive relief. I do know it is time to move on. That is my gut feeling, won't know for sure until it actually happens.

Very sweet dreams,

lbj

From: mbrogan@mbc.web
Sent: Monday, June 24, 2002 5:01 AM
To: JAZMAN@mbc.web
Subject: RE: our universe

I VERY much like that you are able to articulate the universe inside. Lots of people may be able to do that where you are, but I have not met many. While I have been adept since a teenager, at traveling around inside, there are many things about it I just do not have the language to explain (imagine that!)

When I want to look inside myself for you, I just conjure up that Jake feeling in my torso, move it up to my head, and dive right in. Right before sleep is the best time for that. I fall asleep quickly it relaxes me so. But then it is hard to remember. We flow like a river in the spiritual.

You can stop worrying about that less hair thing. My children seem to have inherited my dad's hairline. Hopefully, their mates will find it as attractive as I do. A very solid part of my animus. My dad's hairline receded very early. My mom still liked him! I think it's an Irish thing.

You are not only very tuned into me, but into yourself. I will trust your direction and readiness to move on. Just needed to ask. The healing is so important. If that changes, please let me know. It is also important that we continue to be clear about whatever comes up between us. Ignoring or looking away only makes the problems bigger.

What does your week look like? Same old moving and shaking? And hopefully,
emails.

Gloomy sunrise. Happy day. Think of me.
mb

From: mbrogan@mbc.web
Sent: Monday, June 24, 2002 8:07 AM
To: JAZMAN@mbc.web
Subject: careful tone

I had this great plan this morning to call your cell number and hear your voice before you turned it on for the day. Closed my office door so that the spiritual orgasm that your voice brings to me couldn't be witnessed. Wonder what THAT looks like. Then I realized, I wrote down your info this weekend but never transferred it into my planner. DRAGHT! Will wait for your call then. Popped in Anita Baker, Rapture again to see me through.

I would love to get to the place where I can hear your voice when I read your emails, instead of my own. That would be so grand.

Funny, a few months ago someone accused me of listening to "romantic" music. I laughed and told them that I was about as far away from romantic that a person could get. Now I listen to my music and see what he meant! Those songs have taken on a whole new meaning. Meaning colors our world doesn't it?

I don't think I am doing a good job of toning these emails down am I? I will have to keep working on that.

What then distinguishes
Gods from men?
That many waves
Before them move,
And eternal stream:
Us like the wave gathers
Us the wave swallows
And we sink.
 - Goethe

Enjoy that morning coffee.

mb

From: JAZMAN@mbc.web
Sent: Monday, June 24, 2002 8:52 AM
To: mbrogan@mbc.web
Subject: RE: careful tone

Hi, and thanks for the morning smile. Your first email was sent at 5:01. What time do you get up in the morning? What time to you go to sleep? Does it take you long to fall asleep? When do you leave for work? What time do you get home? What is your favorite TV show? What do you do in the evening? How do you feel about mid-night romance? Can you be roused for some while you sleep?

My week looks like another one of long work days that go into the evening. Soon, I am going to take more time for myself. Quit smoking, join the health club. I have been considering taking a Scientology course on ethics too. That will take up a couple of evenings a week.

You like Goethe? I can't say that I am familiar with his work.

I think you are right, I am tuned into myself more than most people, but I still have a lot to learn. And I have a lot to learn about you! And will thoroughly enjoy the learning. This is a new way to get to know someone. Exchanging words so many times a day. My need to reach out and hug you is continual. Especially when I am writing you, like now. I feel you so close, like I am talking to you and you can hear me now. Please don't change your tone. I love it.

I will call you in a bit, from the car on the way to work. But I don't want to lose our written communication once we start spending time on the phone. It's romantic – like so long ago – so familiar, without all the wait. Now what I wait for is to be able to hold you in person. The ultimate!

Bye for now Molly,

lbj

From: mbrogan@mbc.web
Sent: Monday, June 24, 2002 11:22 AM
To: JAZMAN@mbc.web
Attachment: pics
Subject: baby

Yes, I like Goethe very much. I especially love his fiction, his study of character and relationship as it effects experience...

Our phone call was great. I don't think I can describe what happened inside. I opened forward completely. I am sure my body was completely flushed. I really need to get a grip here. It was just a phone call. I feel like a teenager.

Something amazing happened Jake. Right before you hung up, you called me baby twice. I have always hated being called that. My X and I went round and round about it before I got him to stop. It felt demeaning and disrespectful before, like I was being placed beneath. I don't know. It was more of a gut reaction that I never really tried to explain before. But here is the amazing part. When the word came from you, in your voice, that voice that sends me into spiritual rapture, I LOVED IT! I am truly amazed by this. As much as I hated it before, I love it now. And there is nothing rational about it. But it comes from my core. WOW.

We better give me some time to get over this call before we have our next. I would like to become a reasonable person again. What the hell is going on here?

It might have been your question about mid-night affection that set the stage. Thanks Jake. Now what am I going to do with the image of reaching out for you in the night and falling into you completely? We would probably be making music in each others arms before even reaching consciousness. Just how am I going to get through the rest of the workday thinking about that? You tell me. I will be going to the river for lunch to let the sunlight carry me away with thoughts of you.

Smile,

mb

From: JAZMAN@mbc.web
Sent: Monday, June 24, 2002 12:12 PM
To: mbrogan@mbc.web
Subject: RE: baby

Thank you very much for the pictures. The one with
the pouty lip "no email," I have made my wall paper. I
really want to kiss that neck a few thousand times, if
you will allow it. We are going to laugh a whole
fucking lot aren't we?

You're 5'8" right? I am 6'2". A perfect fit for dancing
and many other things that we will be doing together
soon.

I truly meant nothing disrespectful when I called you
baby. The truth is, I don't even remember doing it.
And I have never been in the habit of calling anyone
baby. This is interesting. And so familiar. Like we are
becoming together, who we are meant to be.

Gotta make the rounds and check on productivity. Send
more. I love it.
lbj

From: JAZMAN@mbc.web
Sent: Monday, June 24, 2002 1:32 PM
To: mbrogan@mbc.web
Subject: quick hi

Hi baby,
I see what you mean about being all stirred up and not
being able to concentrate on work. I keep turning to my
computer to look for you, and at you. I suppose I could
stop, but don't want to. I am going to the house for
lunch. Will look for more playful emails from you
there. Maybe put another one of your pictures up as
wall paper.

Talk soon - lbj

From: mbrogan@mbc.web
Sent: Monday, June 24, 2002 2:22 PM
To: JAZMAN@mbc.web
Subject: lunch time schwing

OK. Hope you made it home for lunch and did not read this at the office (subject.) I thought about calling you on your cell but I did not want you to have an accident the way we are going today.

You don't remember calling me baby. That IS interesting. Especially since you did it twice. If it was once, I might think I heard you inaccurately. It did not feel at all disrespectful coming from you. Instant spiritual orgasm. Don't stop. (smile)

So here are some answers to your questions. New Year's Eve? (Did you think I forgot?) If you still have the schwing effect by then, I would love to.

I get up very early. Lately, I do not hit the snooze button so I can head straight for the lap top. It is good for me. Gets me going without caffeine. The alarm goes off at 4:30. This gives me time to do my housework while I have the energy for it before I leave about 6:30. Now a rational woman would not think to tell someone she has not set eyes on in 30 years her timetables. Big safety no - no. But I think that we know my reason flew out the window a couple of weeks ago when it comes to you.

At day's end I try to stay up and keep Jack company as long as I can. Once I hit the pillow, I dive into the dark and you, being immediately transported to wherever we are. I really like the night time now.

Haven't turned on a TV show of my own for awhile. Watched the movie Midsummer's Night Dream while Jack was working out the other day.

Thanks for making this a really nice day.

mb

From: JAZMAN@mbc.web
Sent: Monday, June 24, 2002 4:13 PM
To: mbrogan@mbc.web
Subject: RE: lunch time schwing

Well, I did not have time to look at the computer on my
trip home at lunch time. Traffic was a little heavier
than expected. What time do you leave work each day?
And how would knowing your timetables be risky? I
doubt that I will turn into a maniac stalker after all these
years. Never did understand that concept.

So you didn't call me to protect me. Hmmmm. Also
interesting. I know there are laws about driving while
talking on a cell phone. I wonder is there is a law about
driving while under the influence of the mb.

I think you're gone from work by now. I miss you.

lbj

From: mbrogan@mbc.web
Sent: Monday, June 24, 2002 4:20 PM
To: JAZMAN@mbc.web
Subject: lunch time schwing

OK you are right. After all of this fun with the written
word, I would not know what to say to a live you. I
was trying to come up with a clever voice message to
leave. I will need a written script because, well, you
know, my mind goes blank etc. I did consider it. But
then I got this goofy grin on my face and my heart
started beating like crazy and well, I thought it would
be better to save your life so you can corrupt me some
more.

So you are saying you can handle driving under the influence of the schwing? Good driver!

If you don't know how a daily itinerary could be used as a stalking tool, then it is safe to say you will never become a stalker. My workday is 7-4. Both tomorrow and Wednesday I am meeting with different contractors around mid day. So if there is a lapse in mischief, don't be discouraged. I will be back.

And I will be back tonight at least to say goodnight.

mb

From: JAZMAN@mbc.web
Sent: Monday, June 24, 2002 6:00 PM
To: mbrogan@mbc.web
Subject: RE: lunch time schwing

One of the brokers walked into my office as I was smiling intensely at my computer screen. She said "what are you looking at?" But then got a little embarrassed at being nosy. They are going to think I am using obscene web sites here! It is an extreme smile because of my extreme feelings. It is such a special thing we have, isn't it? What is going on here? Why this silly smile that won't go away? What is this? I will write later. Need to stop smiling awhile. But don't think it's possible. I would like to talk some more. Feel like I need an emotional fix. May I call tonight?

lbj

From: mbrogan@mbc.web
Sent: Monday, June 24, 2002 7:53 PM
To: JAZMAN@mbc.web
Subject: is it

Here is a good question for you. Give it some thought. What makes life worth living? Now, don't freak out. It is a question that was pivotal in my book. The philosopher William James wrote books about it. I really didn't like his ideas much - too trendy. But I very much like the question.

The main character in my book is based on me, but not me. I actually consulted with a therapist who helped me understand what the differences in character and behavior would be. And which of my experiences would apply, which would not. The character does not understand what makes life worth living. She has it all in front of her, but misses it. In order to put it all in front of her, I had to answer that question for myself.

But I would like to know your answer. Not exactly schwing producing. Although your answer could do it for me. I am continually amazed at how insightful and deeply thoughtful you are. I know it is a little different. But that does it for me. A gift for you. A secret about me. No one else knows. It turns the light on for me.

I need these emotional fixes more and more too. I am actually glad that you so beautifully described what I am going through because I don't want to be one crazy person all alone out here. I have gotten those looks and smiles all day too. And my son's "WHAT's" are not going away. I just tell him "I'm happy, that's all!" And I am. Gloriously so.

Yes, yes, yes. It is special, rare, splendid, fabulous, invaluable.....intense. I gave up analyzing it just before I spilled myself all over my answer to what I will do, or want to do, when I first see you. I don't have the language or the internal understanding to analyze it. And I thought I was pretty good at that. Until now.

All I can do is try to manage it. But I can't get that goon like expression off of my face. And I can't tone down the emails because it is all just too joyous. So what can I do? You tell me...

Can you write one more tonight? Call around nine. Jack will be off to the gym. I will be tucking myself into you.

mb

From: mbrogan@mbc.web
Sent: Monday, June 24, 2002 9:06 PM
To: JAZMAN@mbc.web
Subject:

I don't know where you went or if you received my emotional fix or if that did it for you.

But I called your cell phone because mine rang and I could not get downstairs in time to answer it. I thought about it for a minute. It could have been Meg. She was admitted to the hospital with a lung infection today and was complaining that she can not get through to me. It has been hard because I am on the computer so much. When I get the HSD over the cable next month life will be sweet.

Anyway, I called Meg but her line was busy. Then I thought that you might have gotten my email and just called. So I took the plunge and called again. But only left a message. Not a really good one. I still don't know who called. No message. Not many people call that number. If my computer is plugged in I can't answer the phone. And I usually leave my cell phone downstairs in my purse. And I suddenly felt like I had died and gone to techno hell. Guess I am just going to have to become one of those high end Broadband customers to facilitate the schwing. Lucky for me, the services are free while I work for the company. I can get local phone and HSD next month when they (finally) upgrade my area.

This doesn't sound anything like the last email. I realize that. I think the withdrawal has had a profound effect on the schwing. Oh no! What the hell are we going to do now?

Sweet dreams,
mb

From: JAZMAN@mbc.web
Sent: Monday, June 24, 2002 11:13 PM
To: mbrogan@mbc.web
Subject: RE: is it

Hello, my very special being. It is just past eleven where you are and I am sure you are dreaming. Sorry I couldn't write earlier so that you could have received this before sleep. I got tied up with clients so I could not call as planned.

What makes life worth living? Interesting analysis. Much more than just surviving. More than eating, sex and material things. I think it has to do with goals and purposes. Purpose gives meaning to life. Goals give you the means to move forward in them. Our feelings for each other may be the result of moving toward something that we both want, together. What was your answer?

Today I spent so much time writing you from the office. It brought intense happiness. I am usually an upbeat person, but I had several people comment today. Very cool. They knew something was different about me but didn't understand what. Or who.

I got your voice mail. Thanks for leaving it. Your voice is much better than the last message. I had to listen to it a few times. Sweet giggle. I did not call your cell. Doesn't it have a memory of numbers that call? Look in the menu. We will talk tomorrow. I have a busy day planned, but we can at least talk for a few minutes OK?

Tell me about Meg. Is she OK? What did you decide to do when we first get together? I will follow your lead. Whatever you decide. Ladies first.

Off to dreamland now. I hope to see you there. The more pictures you send, the more likely that will be. So thanks for all the pics.

lbj

From: JAZMAN@mbc.web
Sent: Tuesday, June 25, 2002 12:03 AM
To: mbrogan@mbc.web
Subject:

I just needed to say good night to you. I can't turn us off and wish you were here beside me as I wrap my blanket around me and I drift off. If I ever can control my dreams, I might just slip into a coma and never want to come out. Because you will always be there.

Good night baby. I'm still smiling.
lbj

From: mbrogan@mbc.web
Sent: Tuesday, June 25, 2002 3:03 AM
To: JAZMAN@mbc.web
Subject: dreams interrupted

Yes, it is way too early and I will have to get up in just a couple of hours. My son woke me up going to bed very late. How a person can be playful at 2 in the morning is beyond me. But there I was, giving into the moment and trying my best to run him down like a tackle dummy. I suppose that by the time I get used to the physical play of teenagers, mine will grow out of it.

(By the way, I could not budge him. Like trying to move a mountain.) The dog was even too tired to play.

Did I make a decision? Nice try Jake. I will do the best I can not to go crazy on you. No guarantees. If I was certain I could be acting on decision, I would not have a dilemma now would I? But you knew that, you fox. Well, it has become second nature to act on value and decision rather than condition and emotion, as Steven Covey would say. There is just so much emotion here. Hopefully, I will have learned by then how to manage it all. Can we have many more days like yesterday? Wild.

I am a little worried about Meg. She must have been calling. Her phone at the hospital was busy until 10 when I couldn't get through. I did not want to bother her husband. The lunatic just bought them a new home. It is beautiful but Jesus! I told Meg this would be a perfect time for that. She will not have to lift a finger. I hate moving. I have been on him about the possibility of mold toxins in that house. The timing here was astounding though.

The good news is that they can take their time selling the old house. They will move the family into the new before putting the old on the market. Reduce the stress there. But he might be a maniac before it is through. They hope to close mid July. It all went very quickly.

I am just wondering if she got the call last night for her transplant. And if she is eligible given the current infection.

Yes, you do not even have to be on the other line to make me giggle. Everything you do in my head creates enough of that. Or maybe it is my own delight at the us in my head. And my heart.

Were you smiling between 7:30 - 12:00 (5:30 - 10:00)
Where did you go? You had me all hooked in and
disappeared. The drawbacks or 21st century romance.

I think we need a night at the beach for my question. I
gave it real thought for almost a year before I began
writing the body of the book. But I think you are on to
something. Keep thinking. Might keep the schwing
from peaking.

Did you see the moon tonight? I wonder if you see the
same moon that I do. At 9 the color was very deep,
very bright. Very full. Inspiring.

This is real isn't? Sometimes I wonder how it could be.
Other times, I am so sure it is. Please Jake, don't take
me anywhere you can't make real. Promise.

Well, one thing for sure, when I ready myself for sleep
and conjure you up to fall into, it is real. And lovely.

More sweet dreams,
mb

From: JAZMAN@mbc.web
Sent: Tuesday, June 25, 2002 9:23 AM
To: mbrogan@mbc.web
Subject: RE: dreams interrupted

Wow, you were up early. Wrote all that and sent it by
3. Cutie. Out of curiosity, I checked to see how many
times I logged on to find an email from you yesterday.
13. This is why I had to work late last night. We do
spend a lot of time together in cyberspace. Yesterday
was great fun.

How do you do what you do to effect me the way you
do? I wonder if we lived in Salem together.(smile) It
feels like witchcraft, so unexplainable. I need to see
you so badly. What am I going to do? Calm down for

starters I suppose. Too early for a martini. Is it too soon to be falling in love? Is pure communication by itself the best way to build a solid foundation? Without the initial physical attraction and attention and social time? Can I just hold you for about an hour when I first see you? OK. Calm down. Change the subject. Yes, we will do it on the beach then. Talk about what makes life worth living, that is. What did you think I was talking about?

Missed the moon last night. But not the way that I missed you. I can't seem to stop my heart from talking. I will call you on the way to work.

Bye for now,
lbj

From: mbrogan@mbc.web
Sent: Tuesday, June 25, 2002 9:32 AM
To: JAZMAN@mbc.web
Subject: reports interrupted

A soothing interruption from productivity and financial reports. Why do I keep forgetting what I am doing today?

Thirteen is a power number for women, did you know that? In Salem, women got together every thirteenth to share herbal recipes and healing secrets. That's why the witch hunt began. Those men were jealous of the original girl's night out. Hmmmm…maybe I cast this spell in Salem all that time ago…

Smiling more now, mb

From: mbrogan@mbc.web
Sent: Tuesday, June 25, 2002 10:05 AM
To: JAZMAN@mbc.web
Subject: great morning

Thanks for calling. Your voice has an incredible effect
on me. Nothing rational. I am going to have to work
on a description of what happens to me when you call
me baby. Spiritual orgasm no longer covers it.

Now my palms are sweating and my skin is on fire.
How am I supposed to kick ass like this? You TELL
me...

mb

From: JAZMAN@mbc.web
Sent: Tuesday, June 25, 2002 10:14 AM
To: mbrogan@mbc.web
Subject: RE: great morning

Made it into my office with this huge smile of my face,
aftermath of our phone conversation. What is the first
thing I do? You got it. Find your emails.
Your Salem spell would be a reasonable explanation for
what is happening to me. Well, the most reasonable
that I can think of, which isn't saying much I know. We
may have reached a point where we are writing each
other at the same moment. An email just came in.

I have been thinking about things that we can do
together. How about a simple picnic, Little food,
Pinot, whatever else? No timetables. No cell phones.
Just us. We can refine our kissing skills. Start at lunch
and talk the night away. How does that sound?

lbj

From: mbrogan@mbc.web
Sent: Tuesday, June 25, 2002 10:14 AM
To: JAZMAN@mbc.web
Subject: great morning

I'm still smiling. My face is starting to hurt. Call at lunch if you can. mb

From: mbrogan@mbc.web
Sent: Tuesday, June 25, 2002 2:04 PM
To: JAZMAN@mbc.web
Subject: whew

Hope you made it back to the office again safely. I have not been able to open my door yet. Skin still on fire. Two phone calls in one day. My heart is full.

I reread some of your last emails and listened your voicemail messages again. Thank you. I think the more I hear your voice and laugh and listen to you search your soul for the words, I will hear your voice through your emails too.

It did not help that after I hung up, this damned romantic music was playing that three months ago, was not at all romantic: You came to me like the dawn through the night, just shining like the sun...how did this become so intense so quickly? By the way, I had one of those this moments turning to all moments moment when I heard you call me Baby. I may use that like a mantra to fall into sleep at night now. To fall into you.
OK, my smart ass remark that I could not say out loud on the phone. I told you that the warehouse techs gave me grief for going through so many batteries with my digital camera. They thought I was using them for something else. I was simply going to suggest that instead of buying batteries, as you so generously offered to do, I would rather you supplied the pleasuring tools. I would not have said that last week!

Actually, I couldn't say it out loud today could I? Not only do you make me better than I am, you corrupt me. I think I am in real trouble here.

And I have got to pull myself together. My door has been closed long enough and I have a meeting coming up.
Smiling eternally,
mb

From: JAZMAN@mbc.web
Sent: Tuesday, June 25, 2002 7:17 PM
To: mbrogan@mbc.web
Subject:

I laughed about your smart ass remark to myself all afternoon. My colleagues will think I am cracking up.

How is your evening going? What's for dinner? What is on the agenda after dinner? Details are appreciated. I think of you often. And wonder what you are doing.

Talk to me,
lbj

From: mbrogan@mbc.web
Sent: Tuesday, June 25, 2002 7:17 PM
To: JAZMAN@mbc.web
Subject: home again

Jack just left for the gym. So after dinner, dishes, a little gardening and laundry I am free to touch you. Again. You will be encouraged to know that although my appetite has been terrible lately, I did eat a little dinner. Sit down. Pork chops, O'Brien potatoes, fresh rolls, applesauce. One of the big guy's favorites.

I can hear the word baby in your voice echoing in my head. I think I will use it as a mantra and see where it takes me. Through the land of schwing and straight to you I hope. Tempering extremity with extreme sweet (thanks Will.) It really is nice to hear your voice, and your laugh, and your sigh on the phone. I feel like I know so much more of you. Why was that such a big fuckin deal? (no pun intended. I think)

So you are a Sagittarius. I am an Aries. Two fire signs might explain some of this heat between us. My brother Mike is a Sagittarius. He was in your graduating class. I am closest to him of all my brothers and sisters. I really did not do any more astrological investigating. But I can tell you that I always follow through, must be all the Virgo in all those other houses. And you are on the cusp so you have a little Scorpio in your sun. That is Jack. 11/2 is his birthday. Pensive. Quiet. Analytical. Intuitive. Secretive. Loyal. Any of that ring a bell?

I hope you got some work done tonight. That way, I can have some more of you by morning. My plan for the evening is to watch the sunset from my window, and think about you.

Sweet dreams,
mb

From: JAZMAN@mbc.web
Sent: Tuesday, June 25, 2002 8:34 PM
To: mbrogan@mbc.web
Subject: RE: home again

Are you going to bed already? So tired? Knowing that you didn't get much sleep last night, I really wish I was there to rub and caress you to sleep. Give you some lovin'. Now THAT would be pleasurable to do. Someday. Soon.

Let me know where your new mantra takes you. Keep in mind the conceptual intent - complete affection. I wouldn't want you to go to the wrong place with it.

I don't think I have been involved with an Aries before. Seems like a good match, doesn't it? I can take the heat. I know you can, since you are taking me there.

I LOVED talking to you today. Just more flow in the right direction. The caution and nervousness on the physical plane is just a result of the magnitude of emotion caused by our incredible affinity of the spiritual plane. As if we became acquainted as purely spiritual beings first, operating without bodies. Now we have them and it feels a bit clumsy. Or overwhelming. That's how it feels to me.

Do you realize that we sent each other emails at the exact same time. And that you answered my questions before you received them? What is between us is truly amazing.

I hope you get this before you fall asleep, baby. I miss you.

lbj

From: mbrogan@mbc.web
Sent: Tuesday, June 25, 2002 8:43 PM
To: JAZMAN@mbc.web
Subject: home again

Schwing. Haven't bailed yet but I didn't know how late you would be working.

Didn't know you were saying baby? So interesting. Because when you do, it goes right to my core. I could hardly say good by and hang up. Now when I read it, I can hear your voice and get that feeling all over again.

The amazing part is that it always had the opposite effect before. Like fingers on a chalk board. Always found a way to stop it I guess. I am not sure what is happening here, but please don't stop. Truthfully, my head was spinning so fast that I did not even think that there could have been anything but affection behind it. Did you know that you said it twice before hanging up? I wonder if we could do past life regression together. This feels like something that deep.

When you chuckled this afternoon and told me that you did not think that we would have a problem turning on to each other physically, well it grabbed me. Seems just right. Otherwise, why would we be thinking the same thoughts?

Thank you. For everything you have given me today. Especially this last email.

mb

From: JAZMAN@mbc.web
Sent: Tuesday, June 25, 2002 9:33 PM
To: mbrogan@mbc.web
Subject:

I am pulling up your pictures again before I leave for the night. You are just so damn cute. I may have to answer your letter when I get back to the house in a couple of hours. You will be asleep by then.

Enjoy your dreams. You are always in my thoughts, baby.

lbj

From: JAZMAN@mbc.web
Sent: Wednesday, June 26, 2002 12:12 AM
To: mbrogan@mbc.web
Subject:

Hope you are having an incredibly romantic dream right now, with yours truly in the starring role. It is midnight over there, the passion hour. And I am feeling such passion for you right now, can you feel it? What do you wear to bed? Does it change with the company you keep - or the seasons? I want very much to be there with you. Am trying to suppress this incredibly intense urge.

Past life regression together? We might not like everything we see. People forget past lives for a reason. It is not always easy to take responsibility for past identities. A strong curiosity does not always indicate that a person is willing or able to accept responsibility. Do you want me to review our past lives together? Would take some time and concentration. I wouldn't be able to talk about them until you remembered some. Your mind will only allow you to see what your being can handle. Being physically together and a lot of eye contact might bring some of it to the surface. I really need to see you in the now. With everything between us already, there is a good possibility that we have some common history. And some of it must have been wonderful to evoke this "long lost love found" feeling. I loved talking again today. Your voice seems to be getting more sensuous. Your laugh is unbelievably beautiful. Your being is so familiar and comfortable. I hope your mind is offering you very happy dreams as you sleep.

Good night sweet heart,

lbj

From: mbrogan@mbc.web
Sent: Wednesday, June 26, 2002 5:01 PM
To: JAZMAN@mbc.web
Subject: to day

You do like the details don't you? Well, you probably know by now that I work at bringing out detail, I am better at the bigger picture. So don't stop asking. And I will try to get better at providing it naturally.

Let's see, nightwear. Did not wear it for years. When
the children came along, I wore that pretty stuff, cotton
mostly, or satin. Now, I am sorry to tell you, it is
boxers and Ts. And although I am completely
comfortable in them, this is completely negotiable.

I haven't had any company at bedtime since my
marriage. Hope that isn't a shock or a let down. Just
never got that far. Suppose I could have easily
enough. But I never got to the point in a relationship
that I could see a future with another. I need to be there
to know its right. A step to the left of my catholic
upbringing. But I think that must have been the
spiritual intent. Commitment of the heart. I knew it
would come along someday. And was content to wait.
Working on those other "purposes."

The only pain I try to avoid is physical pain. This is
why I will probably never subject myself cosmetic
procedures. But in the spirit of no attachments, no
aversions, I have not walked away from psychological
pain or spiritual pain to avoid it. Probably why I have
seen so much of it. But I found that you have to get
through it, or it stays with you and can create other
kinds of pain. If there is some in there for us, we will
eventually need to get through it. I have no aversion to
that. I will let you lead. In your time.

In fact, I will let you lead this whole dance. You have
done a fabulous job so far. As I look through our
emails, we have come a long way in a very
short time. Was my resistance as much fun for you as it
was for me? I certainly revealed myself to you through
it. But Jake, if I step on your toes while we dance,
please forgive me. Just yell.

I dream with happiness mixed in with surrealism all
night long now. Sometimes the days are like that too
come to think of it. The baby mantra did not work. It

was energizing, not relaxing. It took me someplace, that's for sure. Can't quite articulate. Invigorating. A place of great release. But I have found that I cannot get a good night's sleep in places like that. So, I came back down, imagined you going crazy on my neck, and slipped right into dream. Worked like a charm. Everything else just melted away.

I am happy that our voices fit together. If you can't suppress the urge for pillow talk, call 847-555-9001. Did that sound like a sleazy ad? Sorry. I love pillow talk. Almost forgot it ever existed for me.

Great sunset here last night. This morning, the sun did not break the horizon yet. Should I wait to send this until it does so I can give you the details? I'll go make some coffee.

OK. No visible sun. A lot of gorgeous storm clouds not moving too quickly across the sky. Lots of depth, very billowy, shades of gray and blue. Oops, a little thunder. Should be an interesting commute. It is amazing that we share so much without sharing the same sky.

Is my voice getting hot, or you're getting hot listening to it. (Sometimes I wonder if what I am feeling comes from me or us.) Responding to you adds some sensuality I am sure of that. Thank goodness for that office door.

Long lost love finally found. You too have a way with words. And a sweet heart.

Smile,
mb

From: mbrogan@mbc.web
Sent: Wednesday, June 26, 2002 7:17 AM
To: JAZMAN@mbc.web
Subject: the rainbow

There was a big fat rainbow in the sky all the way to work this morning. What a great surprise. I don't know when I saw one last. While I was driving, it started at the top of the sky and fell to the earth, peaking in and out of the clouds with intense color. You could see the whole spectrum very clearly. Amazing. By the time I parked my car, it stretched clear across the sky but was beginning to fade. Closer to earth, it spread out wide. What a way to start the day. The only thing better would have been you sharing it. Someday. Too bad rainbows end. So cool to witness the cycle.

I think that good endings are so important. Must be the writer in me. I suspect you think so too. I am not afraid of endings. Have experienced some very beautiful and some very difficult, and lots in between. If we have an ending, let's make it as fabulous as the beginning shall we? I am at a place now though, that I hope there isn't one. Are you there with me? Such promise. Was that too bold? Inspired by that rainbow I guess.

Smiling now,
mb

From: JAZMAN@mbc.web
Sent: Wednesday, June 26, 2002 9:06 AM
To: mbrogan@mbc.web
Subject: you, of course

We both need to catch up in the romance department. I am there. When I read your words, it turns me on like a light switch. How do you do that? My affinity for you just soars as you communicate your ideas and share your life. Beautiful really. And new for me. Or buried so deeply it seems that way. A familiar feeling without memories. Rainbows, by the way, are good luck for lovers.

When I said your voice was sensuous, I meant that I liked it, it was having a positive effect on me. And yes, making me want to be with you in every way. Now, everything you say has an intense effect on me, but clean.

What you wear to bed won't matter as long as you have nothing on by morning. I want you in my arms when we wake up, feeling your soft skin on mine, with all of the emotion that I am feeling right now.

I did not know that I was leading here. From my viewpoint, you were leading. We have probably been taking turns. From here, it seems like you communicate, I melt. Now this may sound strange but when you told me you wore boxer and Ts, if affected me intensely. Like I am a fish being reeled in without resistance. As much as I would like to know what is going on here, I am also enjoying the mystery of it.

I do understand what you said about the mantra and where it takes you. I like what you were doing instead. Soon, you can do that in person. I can't look at your picture for long without wanting to be all over that incredible neck of yours. If this keeps growing like this, what will happen to us? It would be such an incredible waste if it didn't. Let's not consider an ending. It will be up to us to make sure one is not needed.

What is up with the ending talk? The only ending I want to see is the ending of our wild email relationship because we marry or move in together. We could handle any disagreement by writing to each other. Not that I can imagine having one with you.

I miss you baby. And will check the email before I leave for work. Gotta get ready now.
lbj

From: mbrogan@mbc.web
Sent: Wednesday, June 26, 2002 9:15 AM
To: JAZMAN@mbc.web
Subject: again

Whew. Now that was bold. And that baby thing never fails. Even in a letter. Quite the mystery.

I am struggling with the physical symptoms as well. It is as if my body is flooded with serotonin. I wonder if that is what happens. Skin tingles, like I can feel the blood moving through it. Heart beat is very strong. Guess I can give up the wheat bread in the morning until my body adjusts. I'll bet that is why emotions take a turn down in the absence of all of this.

The last thing I need to do is imagine you in my arms or in my bed. If I did, I don't think I would be able to breathe. I am still wondering if you are ready for where we have found ourselves.

What is this? Boy, we could spend hours there. I have been searching my past for something that compares and not coming up with much. Help me if I falter here. You will won't you?
mb

From: JAZMAN@mbc.web
Sent: Wednesday, June 26, 2002 9:15 AM
To: mbrogan@mbc.web
Subject: RE: again

I think we were writing at the same time again. I take much longer to compose my letters. A lot of editing. Staring out the window. I think we should take a trip to Salem. Some of your old powers may return. (smile) If nothing else, we could make love all day. Might have some ghosts around. Injustice can prevent spirits from moving on. They could still be holding that girl's night out in the spiritual universe. We will have to go on the thirteenth so you can pick up some good secrets.

I have always wanted to take a short vacation at a bed and breakfast somewhere. Have not been in a relationship that was romantic enough before. I would say I am there now. Most definitely there. And ready. But only for you. More than you know. How about a weekend during one of Jack's away games? I will call later. I miss you again.

lbj

From: mbrogan@mbc.web
Sent: Wednesday, June 26, 2002 10:14 AM
To: JAZMAN@mbc.web
Subject: again and again

Skin burning now. I kick ass on ghosts too. But I am sure the girls will welcome me and teach me all kinds of tricks to use on you. I am not sure I can take any more ability or emotion now. Although, every time I say that, you take me farther somehow. With every email. And every conversation. How do you do that? But you are right, it is not me or you - it is US. We do it. In rhythm. A beautiful, sensuous, spiritual rhythm.

I have a couple of meetings with contractors later. So I may drop off the screen for awhile.
I don't think I am managing this well. No appetite. Constant flush. No concentration. Any suggestions? God, your voice is great.

mb

From: JAZMAN@mbc.web
Sent: Wednesday, June 26, 2002 9:33 AM
To: mbrogan@mbc.web
Subject: RE: again

These contractors aren't good looking are they?

I know it isn't witchcraft, but you do seem to be
receiving my thoughts and intentions without my
expressing them. Very cool. The intensity of emotion
for both of us could be a result of that. We are just not
used to relating on this level.

You didn't answer my question about booking a bed
and breakfast for a weekend during Jack's game. What
do you think?

I think you are managing as well as I am, and I know
that might not be saying much. But we are in this
together, baby. I'll call you soon.

lbj

From: mbrogan@mbc.web
Sent: Wednesday, June 26, 2002 2:40 PM
To: JAZMAN@mbc.web
Subject: serious side effects

You brought my attention to another serious side effect
of my condition. All other men, are MUCH uglier than
before. And since there were none cute enough before,
I think you're safe. Besides, I have that tunnel vision
thing going this life time. It is only you. Those other
side effects I still don't have a handle on. HELP.
I think it will be dicey getting to know each others
children. We have plenty of time for that. Yes, I still
want you to come to a game with me. I just don't want
that to be on the weekend of our first time together. I
need some self control here. I can't imagine having any
that weekend. Or week. Or maybe month.

Did you call? Things were a flurry here. I will shut my door now.

mb

From: JAZMAN@mbc.web
Sent: Wednesday, June 26, 2002 3:21 PM
To: mbrogan@mbc.web
Subject:

I was just picking up the phone to call you when your last email came through. This is getting a bit weird. But good, so good. Like we are on the same frequency, in each other's space spiritually - and that puts us together although we are so far apart physically.

It was nice talking again, but now I MUST see you. Let me work on a plan.

I like the tunnel vision you have and am very glad those other guys have lost their looks. Nice to feel secure, although I can't understand how you have managed to stay unattached all of these years. Not that I am complaining. I couldn't be happier about the fact that you are available right now. I just hope that I don't end up a no thank you.

The kids can be later, you're right. No hurry. We need our time first. Maybe we should turn things around and just go to a movie our first night. You know, hold hands only. Sit inches apart and not say a word.

I was reading your poem Promise again. Are you having doubts that this will last? Do you wonder about yourself, or me? I intend to do everything in my power to make this work, Molly. I haven't ever felt anything so strongly. I am determined. And you?

Yours,
lbj

From: mbrogan@mbc.web
Sent: Wednesday, June 26, 2002 3:03 PM
To: JAZMAN@mbc.web
Subject: RE:

No turning back now bucko. You wouldn't do that to me would you? There is no chance for no thank you now either. God, I am so there. I am way out there. Gone. I wouldn't do that to you! My apprehension relates to the factors in our lives that may pull us apart. I suppose every new couple in mid life has them. Our ability to communicate and work together toward our goals will sustain us.

How have I managed to stay single? I am now convinced that I have been waiting for you. Does that sound trite? I don't know how else to explain it. We are just right. Why did it take 50 years?

You will still go to a game with me won't you?

mb

From: mbrogan@mbc.web
Sent: Wednesday, June 26, 2002 5:55 PM
To: JAZMAN@mbc.web
Subject: yes please

Home now. Jack was easy on me tonight. He took one look at me and said "how about pizza tonight." Sensitive child.
You are completely safe with me. I FEEL completely safe with you. Am I, or is there something I am missing? You will not be hearing no thank you from me. Only yes please:
meet me tonight: yes please
meet me this weekend: yes please
reinvent your life for me: yes please

But you know, not everyone likes me. What are you going to do if you find out there are things you just can't stand about me. Like, my feet look like Flintstone feet because of a lifetime of kicking off my shoes. Or the way I cry when I am happy. Or the way that I won't mind that you work so much because I always have something of my own to work on. Or the way other guys look at me, even though I never see it because my mind is on you. Or the way my check book doesn't always balance. Or the way my little dog barks. Or the way my kids can be brats at times because they are kids. Or the way I don't like to fight. (Are you a fighter?) Or the way I am going to hate to open up my arms and let you go when you have to. Or the way I like to be protected but not rescued? Or the way that most of my friends, like you, don't know why I have stayed single all these years and are probably going to be giving you the once over. What about all that? All you would ever have to do, is call me baby. And all that would melt away. Safe to say.

REALLY yours,
mb

From: JAZMAN@mbc.web
Sent: Wednesday, June 26, 2002 7:17 PM
To: mbrogan@mbc.web
Subject: RE: yes please

I will follow you anywhere. A game, a picnic, the beach - I have the feeling fun will be one of our favorite words.

50 years. May not have been that long. Or it may have been longer. All in how you look at it. This time around we had some chances about 30 years ago. I could kick myself for not recognizing them. Just not our time I guess. Now the feelings have surfaced, but the details of past lives might still be hidden. Are you interested in any areas of history in particular? Any

scenes or times in history that make you cringe? Any stars you find yourself staring at? What is the time and place of your birth?

My intention is to make this work. Why would I ever let it go?

Baby, I feel completely safe with you. And I want you to feel that way while you are in my arms. And my arms are always around you. Do you know that? Can you feel that? I send that flow your way every minute.

lbj

From: mbrogan@mbc.web
Sent: Wednesday, June 26, 2002 8:07 PM
To: JAZMAN@mbc.web
Subject: crazy

As crazy as all of this seems, it would be much crazier to let it go. True Crime. Have you seen the movie Field of Dreams? That's what this is like. Following with faith when nothing seems reasonable.

I was born in Highland Park, 3/28/53 5:08 PM. I have irrational fascination with Paris turn of the century and New Mexico, 1950's or so. The Georgia O'Keefe era. I have never been either place. I don't like to be in the inner city. That could be logical though. I don't really stare at the stars, but would start with you. I have done a bit of astral traveling, but can't really articulate the experiences. Familiar places and beings, but the form is not like here. Exchange of ideas without language. Can't explain it.

With my whole heart, I would like to see this work. (Smile)

mb

From: JAZMAN@mbc.web
Sent: Wednesday, June 26, 2002 8:25 PM
To: mbrogan@mbc.web
Subject: RE: yes please

OK baby, I'm back. Another list of things I might not like about you. Well, none of that matters. Not where we are. I think your feet just need to be rubbed and kissed awhile. If you cry when you are happy, do you cry when making love?

I hope you NEVER let me go. You will need to explain protected but not rescued. If you needed either, I would have to do it. How many friends will you have giving me the once over? Please write. I need you so.

lbj

From: mbrogan@mbc.web
Sent: Wednesday, June 26, 2002 8:34 PM
To: JAZMAN@mbc.web
Subject: sweet dreams

This will be my good night email. Jack is content with the NBA draft that will go on all night, so I can wrap myself around you and fall into dream after the sun sinks into the horizon. I can see it from my window now. Pretty sunset. Are all the colors of the world more intense today? The rainbow, the sunset.

Do you think I will get used to sharing my being with you all day and all night? That's what it feels like. Both of us are in here.

I won't let you go Jake, how could I? I don't think I can explain the rescue/protect thing right now. I may be too tired. Or maybe I am just too happy and it doesn't matter anymore. Tonight is a good night for sleep. None of my worries matter. I am safe. With you.

Heavy sigh.

See you in dreamland,
mb

From: JAZMAN@mbc.web
Sent: Wednesday, June 26, 2002 9:12 PM
To: mbrogan@mbc.web
Subject: RE: sweet dreams

I had to think about it for a minute but I now understand
what you mean by getting used to sharing your being
with me. I will leave you some of your own space
occasionally, but I will miss you for that one minute a
day. I do hold you all day long in my heart. Might be
what keeps us on the same wavelength and in the same
spiritual space.

Today was intense. I read your words and can't stand
up for awhile or anyone could see the effect you have
on me. If you were in my office I could not stop myself
from taking you right there.

Yes, I love flying with you. I miss you when I know
you are asleep because I can't talk to you for several
hours. You are probably tired from the adrenaline and
hormones that our emotion creates for our bodies.

I think we would make excellent business partners. If I
could get anything done. Should we go into business
some day, that is, once we get the romance on a
schedule we can live with?

I can't stop thinking about holding you close and
kissing you all over. God, I want you. Instead, I will
send my loving thoughts your way and hope you
receive them in a dream.

Always yours,
lbj

From: mbrogan@mbc.web
Sent: Thursday, June 27, 2002 3:57 AM
To: JAZMAN@mbc.web
Subject: sweet dreams

Well, you sure did send those thoughts. Each time I
woke tonight, I could literally feel you holding me. I
could feel you kissing me. Even once I was fully
awake. I can't tell if it is a heart yearning or truly a
spiritual communion we have going on out there. Do
you feel it at all?

When I try to compare it to something, here is what I
think. When I astral travel, I just know that the beings
are there. I know their shape, know their voice. It is a
knowing, not a seeing or hearing. But when I
remember it, I see and hear in my memory.

I don't know if that makes sense, but it is all that I have
to compare. For the first time, I knew you were in my
arms. The thing is, my body could actually feel you,
kind of an invisible pressure. I could almost hear you
breathe. More than just a knowing. Your spirit had a
physical presence.

I can't tell if it is real. Certainly feels that way. I do
know that I am not getting enough REM because I am
tired and headachy so much. I am going to have to stop
looking for you constantly at night and find a balance of
mind here.

I am thinking we are just right for every kind of
partnership. The more I hear your voice, the more
deeply I get into us, I know it. I used to only
fly with people in my dreams. This day and night
flying is incredible.

Fortune clues everywhere. The day I stopped holding
back on what I might do when I first see you, my

horoscope told me that it was important to express the emotion I was feeling. That good things would happen. What happened was much better than just good wasn't it.? Glad I took that leap of faith.

I tried to call tonight after finally losing the feeling of you in my arms. About 11:15 here. Your outgoing voice mail message said you were unavailable. I rolled over and said out loud, "He feels so available. He's available." and fell back to dream.

Do you know how I can slow down the release of hormones and adrenaline in my body. It would be nice to have a little more control there. I would not be so conspicuous.

I thought of another place that I find in my readings over and over and feel that attraction. I really can't explain that anymore. New York City. Greenwich, Soho. Actually, since I started on my book, I have wanted to get to San Francisco to look up a book store founded by the writer, Lawrence Ferlinghetti. Would be nice to go with you so that if any past life weirdness happened, you would be my anchor.

You are beginning to feel like my anchor. Is that weird? Everything changing, all the new feeling, it all comes back to you.

Well, it is getting easier to explore my feeling without holding back, have you noticed? But you are not getting a lot of physical detail. Just a lot of spiritual detail. Do you mind? I seem to be stuck there trying to figure this out.

I sat in my new favorite chair here, the one that I sit in to write YOU emails, for the longest time last night just staring out the window. Thinking things through. I don't turn on the TV or radio much anymore so that I can think things through. So much thinking and

feeling. And so much you. Tell me it's real again.
When I hear the words in your voice, all that doubt and
confusion melt away.

Kissing you,

mb

From: mbrogan@mbc.web
Sent: Thursday, June 27, 2002 7:26 AM
To: JAZMAN@mbc.web
Subject: sweet dreams

For the first time all week, I was hitting the snooze
button. When I finally did open my eyes, a gorgeous
sunrise was just beginning. I put my pillow on the
window sill and watched it unfold. Breath taking.

I wanted to get both my morning emails to you from
home. My boss will be there this morning so I will
probably be popping in and out of availability.

I have been thinking of a way to describe my Jake place
inside to you. I know I go there too much and need to
begin taking better care of myself. Start finding
balance.

But as I fall asleep, I imagine your voice. I guess that is
my way of calling you out. You always show up. Very
reliable. It only takes a little while and there you are
with me. I think it is the place that we first sat on the
beach. It is a place where we can create any scenery we
want. But we normally don't. Just us holding each
other in space.

It is not like a dream. My dreams are like movie screen
pictures. In my Jake place, like places of meditation,
there is no screen. Only space- dark like outer space.
But inner space. And light and color appear to create
form but are not a reflection on any surface. they just

give us the form to recognize and remember. Our place to be together for now.

After watching the sunrise, I showered, went down for coffee, sat in my recliner cross-legged, and conjured you up again. Slipped easily into the Jake place. I noticed my pulse and breathing slow, like in transcendental meditation. Same calming effect.

But when I woke up from the Jake place and felt you with me, just like last night when we were in my room. It was as if you followed me back. Not your body, but your spirit. I could feel your warmth, your breath. Christ, I think I could even smell you. And I could feel you moving in my arms. Just could not see or hear you physically.

Whether it was my heart of our spirits creating that experience, it was UN FUCKING believable.

Just wanted you to know.

Smile for me today,

mb

From: JAZMAN@mbc.web
Sent: Thursday, June 27, 2002 9:15 AM
To: mbrogan@mbc.web
Subject: intense communication

Good morning Molly. And thank you for your gifts. Spiritual. Emotional. Your words. Your thoughts. Your intentions. Your attention. They all fill me in a way that makes this world better than ever for me. We are truly connected. I want it that way always. My affinity soars for you when I read your words. Thank you for being who you are and caring about me.

You have such a remarkably high awareness of spiritual beingness. I envy that. I wish I could join you. Maybe some day. Need to enhance my perceptions. I call exteriorization what you call astral travel. When we are outside our bodies, we use our spiritual perceptions. But we are nowhere near native state so these need to be rehabilitated. Your lifelong meditating seems to have sharpened these perceptions. My theta reaches you beyond my awareness. But it is real. With the intensity of emotion that I feel, I am sure it is real. It is certainly possible. Believe what you know. Don't invalidate it. Just another reason for a night at the beach (smile.)

In that regard I have purchased a small, private jet. I know it sounds crazy but I will need to come to Chicago more frequently now, and will save quite a bit of time this way, avoiding public airports. Will you find us a beach? I'll look at my schedule today and we can arrange for some time together.

You know what you know. I find you amazing. We are now connected in a way that neither has experienced in a very long time. It is beautiful. And I do hold you in my own way. The feeling transfers to your body because that is how we have learned to understand it. We can be in each other's arms, although physically apart. Amazing that I can talk to you about this and you get it.

I miss you madly. And want to kiss you physically. I will do whatever it takes to make this work, baby.

lbj

From: mbrogan@mbc.web
Sent: Thursday, June 27, 2002 3:03 PM
To: JAZMAN@mbc.web
Subject: leaving work

Sorry I have been out of touch today. My boss was in the building. Went from meeting to meeting. Gave the hand to the complainers. Problem solved our crisis that developed because they rolled out multi-product installations without planning a way to bill for them or route them to the techs. Had lunch with a contractor to talk about a job offer.
Trained another Contract Labor Administrator on using the tracking spreadsheets that I use to calculate cost per connect as invoices come in. Crazy fucking day.

Missed you terribly. And everything you bring to me. Kissed you passionately and often in my head.

Can you call so that I can be with you tonight?

You mentioned planning for a weekend together. Look on the Augustana web page to find the fall football schedule. You will be looking at my weekends through Thanksgiving. I could break away for a night to a close by getaway while Jack is home this summer. But he won't be with me much longer and I hate to leave him alone too much. Afterward, you are welcome to spend weekends at my place. We will have it all to ourselves (heaven.)

It is amazing that today you tell me you now have a plane to make it easier to find your way to me. Here is why.
While having lunch today in Lake Forest I ran into a retired business associate who at one time held the position of President of the Chicago cable market. He offered me his beach house for some quiet time to write while he is in Europe. So unexpectedly, he gave me the keys to his beach house right there! I've been to his

home several times over the past few years. It sits on a lakeside bluff with a cobblestone stairway down to a secluded white sand beach with a bungalow.

I came back to work beaming, having pulled in the perfect spot for us, only to find that you have found your way to me! If you land at the Waukegan airport, I will pick you up and we can head there.

Now I need to run to one last meeting. To make up for my absence, here is a poem I have been working on for you:

Forever

When
Did we begin
Our free fall
Into heaven
Into eachother
Into the place
Where our spirits reside
And call to us
Each moment?

It seems just yesterday
Or an eternity
That we said hello
That familiar echo
That instantly brought
Us here again
Together again
Even though
We remain
Miles apart.

Never before
Have I known
Someone
So completely.

Never have I
Felt so deeply.
Not in this life
Did I expect
To fly to such heights
To open so wide
To see so clearly
The possibility of us.

Time becomes
Irrelevant
Because each moment
You are with me
And in me
Filling emotion
To the brim
Changing the future
Changing my viewpoint
Changing awareness
Forever.

Please don't ever leave.
I can't go back.
Can't un-know
What I now know.
It is true
Two can be one
Now and forever
In each thought
And each moment.
Connection
Can be so clear
So pure
And so strong
That it can last
Forever
And bring forever
To our finite lives
To our days and nights
To our touch

And our words
And our love.

Yours,
mb

From: JAZMAN@mbc.web
Sent: Thursday, June 27, 2002 6:54 PM
To: mbrogan@mbc.web
Subject: RE: leaving work

Tonight? You are with me always, baby. More than
you know. I can't stop thinking about you for a minute
or two. Must have checked my email 50 times today.
But now I know why you weren't writing. Got some
work done, didn't you? Good work too.

I know better what you mean when you say you can't
explain what happens to you when you call me baby. It
happens to me when I read one of your poems. Oh,
baby. I do love you.

I am looking at both of our schedules for the next few
months and suddenly panicked because we will just not
have much time together. Right now one long weekend
together would be heaven. But how long can that go
on? I am having a hard time not being near you now
and we haven't planned our first weekend together.

What I think I need to do is get my wife and kids to
move out here. Then when I am in Chicago, I can be
yours exclusively and not have to divide myself
between you and the kids. Then I can bring you out
here sometimes. How does seeing each other every two
or three weeks sound for awhile? Sooner or later, that
won't be enough time together and we will need to
make some decisions.

I know it sounds premature, but it is on my mind as I try to plan here.

Back to work. Miss you.
Jake

From: mbrogan@mbc.web
Sent: Thursday, June 27, 2002 7:35 PM
To: JAZMAN@mbc.web
Subject: panic

OK, now would be the right time to rescue me. I don't understand and I'm scared. It feels like I am missing something.

What I see is us. In the future. Weekends for a little while, then us always. Is that what you see?

It is hard to let go of you with a phone call now. I can't imagine having to let you go from my arms over a long time. And I guess it is time for perfect honesty here. I was thinking more of me coming out there to you. Permanently. I don't understand your plan, or why you would want your ex out there. So I must be missing parts of your planning.

Help please,
mb

From: JAZMAN@mbc.web
Sent: Thursday, June 27, 2002 7:44 PM
To: mbrogan@mbc.web
Subject: RE: panic

Molly, I am so sorry. I did not mean to disturb you. I didn't see that coming. I thought it was important for you to stay near your children. Well, that is what I was so loudly hinting at, getting you out here with me for good. I just did not know it would be possible soon.

Let me be blunt. I want you with me always. How is that? I am crazy about you and want to marry you. My divorce will take a little time is all. But then I want us to go all the way with this.

I was trying to think of a way to have my children closer to me. I don't think that will be possible without their mom moving here. I miss them terribly.

I am going to call you now so that we can talk this through.

Forever yours,

lbj

From: mbrogan@mbc.web
Sent: Thursday, June 27, 2002 8:43 PM
To: JAZMAN@mbc.web
Subject: panic over

OK, settle down. Tonight, and for good this time. That's what I see. I do see marriage as the logical conclusion. Better get that out now before it has to pop out like this. I will work harder at not holding back. Just as I was walking upstairs in tears you called on the phone. Your timing is exquisite, dear.

I am not sure how we jumped from having not even planned our first meeting, to planning our lives together. But I can do that. It is there inside already. Transparency isn't always easy is it?

I suddenly though you were not intending to divorce, but to stay married and have your family there. That would leave me here, and you visiting I don't have that in me, love. Now I know what it would feel like to lose you. Let's not do that again, OK? So much for ferocious independence.

Here, I am trying to settle down this constant state of spiritual peaking (not too successfully.) I guess I can plan settling down with you at the same time. Why not. No sweat. Well actually, a lot of sweat seems to be part of the peaking. But I will have that settled down soon. Until I see you. Maybe we should schedule our first date at the Abbe in Lake Geneva. They have great steam rooms and my condition will go unnoticed.

Oh my god, how will I ever sleep tonight. Do you have more planned for us while I sleep? Will you follow me out of the Jake place and into my bed like last night? I did know after last night that waiting wasn't really an option.

It won't be hard for me to settle things here. The hard part will be establishing myself there and turning Jack toward our plan. Who knows, if Jamie crashes and burns soon, he may join us. He always had a thing for UCLA.

Don't hint anymore. Let's just talk about it all. And hold eachother real tight, OK?

mb

From: JAZMAN@mbc.web
Sent: Thursday, June 27, 2002 9:05 PM
To: mbrogan@mbc.web
Subject: settle down

Thanks for sending your words so quickly. We need to make love at least a dozen times. What are you doing Friday night? (smile)

What started this whole thing was the fact that I did not think that leaving Chi was an option for you so soon. But I have to say, that being separated from the kids is not easy. That is why I would like to get my children out here. I really miss them. Distance can really change the relationships.

As long as we handle the issues as soon as they come up, like we did tonight, we will be fine. This is actually a very good sign that we will make it, don't you think? It isn't going to be easy, but it is up to us to make it work.

What about Jamie? What would need to occur to get him out here?

I think about you every minute. Love is amazing isn't it? Can you call me before you go to bed, baby? I need to hear your voice again.

Loving you always,

lbj

From: JAZMAN@mcb.web
Sent: Thursday, June 28, 2002 9:24 AM
To: mbrogan@mbc.web
Subject: missing you

Good morning Baby.
Your spiritual awareness is rare. I have not met anyone else like you. It was very late last night that I could finally give you all of my attention. When I sleep, I don't remember all that happens. But while awake, I feel our connection like a softness all around me, very loving.

Yes, we got here very quickly, with much conceptual exchange, verbal and spiritual communication. We probably communicate more than most married couples during any given day. The addition of your voice to our connection deeply enhanced what we already have.
This is cool. Your voice is like no other. It takes me to places I have never been.

Are you too analytical? Never. What happened last night was the result of my failure to be direct. I should have just said what I was feeling. That I want you with me everyday forever. When we spoke last night I realized that you are willing to do whatever it takes to make that happen. Much more than I was hoping for. You are so much more than I ever imagined love could be. And I suspect it will be even more intense in time.

When I took the calendar out and looked at all the possible time we could have together living so far apart, it just wasn't enough. I did not mean to upset you. Sorry. We just need to continue to make this work until the time that we are living our lives together.

I actually need you now. I realized what a massive loss it would be not to have you in my life. It seems we are beginning in the middle. Who said we have to be normal?
Time to get ready for the day, love of my life.

lbj

From: mbrogan@mbc.web
Sent: Friday, June 28, 2002 9:51 AM
To: JAZMAN@mcb.web
Subject: more

More intense? I really have to find a way for my body to handle this better. When you mention ecstasy last night it gave me an idea. I think I have some reading material there. I will go looking for clues this weekend.

My body's reaction does feel like ecstasy. Constant flush, slow, passive movement and thoughts, no appetite Expanded awareness. Blown wide open without the orgasm. Or constant spiritual orgasm. I wonder if we were really meant to walk around like this all day.

When I fell in love with you, this is where I landed.
Amazing.

Love you.
mb

From: JAZMAN@mcb.web
Sent: Thursday, June 28, 2002 11:22 AM
To: mbrogan@mbc.web
Subject: RE: more

We are going to handle this and be happier than we
have ever been. More direct? A little better?

Can't stay online, but I'll be back soon sweetheart.

lbj

From: mbrogan@mbc.web
Sent: Friday, June 28, 2002 2:04 PM
To: JAZMAN@mcb.web
Subject: fun lunch

I'm back darlin'. Here's what I learned: it is much
easier to have no appetite around guys. Those girls
made me send my small Cesar salad back and ask for a
box for my small salad with ranch. I nibbled though.
Guess those extra pounds won't be a problem for long.

Sitting on the river was beautiful. Last summer I found
a spot south of 120 on Riverside Dr., here in McHenry
where two branches of the river come together. Nice
long pier. Lots of trees. I may start refusing those
lunches and go relax next week. Watched the world go
by for an hour. I love rivers. They carry my spirit
farther.

One of my coworkers busted me in the bathroom about
my lack of appetite. Asked if I was pregnant. I think I

am going to lay low this weekend. And come up with a really good explanation for this.

Can you call at lunch? Or am I a brat?

mb

From: JAZMAN@mcb.web
Sent: Thursday, June 28, 2002 4:56 PM
To: mbrogan@mbc.web
Subject: sleep now

The conversation at lunch was inspired. Sitting in the park, under a tree, talking to you - I may have to spend each lunch hour that way from now on. I was glad to hear you will be napping after work. I worry that our pillow talk cuts into your sleep time. And given your accelerated body functions, you need to take good care of yourself now. Eat when you can, take your vitamins, especially the Bs, naps and lots of water. For me, my love.

Since we have 30 years to catch up on, I don't know if we ever can catch up on the lovemaking in store for us. Sure will be nice to try! I think about that way too much lately. And it is all your fault, beautiful. I was doing all right until you seduced all my defenses from me. Now, I can't wait for our nights together.

You may be home by now so I hope you get this before dreamland. It was so good to hear your voice today. So hard to let go. I am here, when you wake up.

Love,

lbj

From: mbrogan@mbc.web
Sent: Friday, June 28, 2002 6:36 PM
To: JAZMAN@mcb.web
Subject: rested now

Over there, it may seem that I am the seductress. But
from here, it is all the Jake I have always known. We
are pulling eachother out, with a force stronger than
either of realize. Now THAT will be fun to discover.

When we are finally together, and I have stopped crying
from the happiness, I suspect our spirits will show us
exactly what to do. What we do all night long now, in
spirit.

I need to reach Meg now. But will check in afterward.
Just wanted to kiss you first:

Anticipation

I know
It is impossible
For us
To be
In the same space
Always.

The anticipation
In between
Is amazing.

Sometimes,
When you are gone,
I can actually
Feel you with me.
Your sweet mouth
On my mouth,
Your hand
On the side of my head
Caressing

While we kiss.

My body feels it
As if you are here.
With me,
Loving me,
Always,
In all ways.

You fill me,
My heart,
My soul,
My life.
Like color
Fills a painting
Or words
Fill a poem
Or two
Free spirits
Fill their love.

Love,
mb

From: JAZMAN@mcb.web
Sent: Thursday, June 28, 2002 6:36 PM
To: mbrogan@mbc.web
Subject: sleep now

It is past 6:30 for you and you are either still asleep or
about to have an orgasm thinking about me. Which
would that be, my love? Your poem takes me to your
Jake place instantly. And we fulfill all of your desires.
Because they are also mine. Naturally. I am still here,
apart from you, needing your touch desperately, feeling
you flowing to me now. It is wonderful to feel your
affinity near me. Write when you can.

lbj

From: JAZMAN@mcb.web
Sent: Thursday, June 28, 2002 6:36 PM
To: mbrogan@mbc.web
Subject: sleep now

My god, we were writing at the same time! You are a seductress! And I love it.

lbj

From: mbrogan@mbc.web
Sent: Friday, June 28, 2002 7:35 PM
To: JAZMAN@mcb.web
Subject: sigh

OK. Meg is fine. She sounds like she is breathing well and her spirits are up. whew. When I spoke to her yesterday morning, her lungs were hurting her so much she suspected that she should be going back into the hospital. Her doctor prescribed steroids to open things up and it seems to be working. She had a guest, so I told her I would catch up with her tomorrow.

I have enough people here that have already guessed the reason for my "condition" that will keep me busy all weekend. I wonder if I can retrieve my email at their homes. I will be excusing myself to go to the bathroom and they will find me in their computer rooms, in the dark, pounding furiously away at the keys to touch you again.

My goal this weekend is to get a grip. Whatever trick there is to discover, I WILL discover them. The bio feedback really does help. But not in a crowd. I really have to be able to concentrate. This is really hard! Well, I haven't shied away from difficulty before. Here, I seem to be irresistibly drawn to the challenge. And you. All of you.

Touch me, - mb

From: JAZMAN@mcb.web
Sent: Thursday, June 28, 2002 7: 44 PM
To: mbrogan@mbc.web
Subject: RE: sigh

I am glad that Meg is feeling better. The other night you said will wait to be with me before you have your first martini? I would prefer to be with you if you are drinking, but not used to it. That way, I can enjoy the fall out. I imagine THAT would be fun. Maybe we should make our first trip to Vegas and drink those martini's on the way. So by the time we get there, you will be willing to go straight to the alter with me.

You need to get a grip? It feels like your grip is all over me 24/7. I can't function without checking my email every 5 minutes.
Thinking of you always,

lbj

From: mbrogan@mbc.web
Sent: Friday, June 28, 2002 7:53 PM
To: JAZMAN@mcb.web
Subject: sunset

Well, if you have to get back to work, I will try to give you a kiss here that will be waiting for you when you return.

The sun is beginning to set out my window. I would be content just to sit here and watch it until darkness falls over the room. Thinking about you. Thoughts with no organization. Not planning, just experiencing. You. I do that more and more. Sigh.
When I marry you, I don't want anything between us. It will be clean and clear. The most poignant moment in our deep and rich time together. And we will go on to have so many more poignant moments that we will recognize eachother instantly forevermore. We will

have years to discover eachother on every level. How did I possibly live differently before this?

Well, I won't be releasing my grip on you, so if that is what it is going to take to change my physical condition, then I will just learn to live with it. Invest in ice bags, major heavy duty antiperspirant and learn to live with half the productivity I once had. Surrender. Completely. My love.

mb

From: JAZMAN@mcb.web
Sent: Thursday, June 28, 2002 8:07 PM
To: mbrogan@mbc.web
Subject: RE: sigh

It sounds wonderful over there, especially those beautiful eyes of yours. And your thoughts, so loving.

Are you sure you want to marry me? I think about it often. Can't imagine anyone else. It is frightening sometimes, what is happening to us. But I don't want to change it. You make me feel like no one has ever done before. You are in me, and all around me. And I love having you here. What a being you are! I want you so much in my life, it is hard to wait. I love you so much already it is hard to handle sometimes.

I will call you in a little while my love.

Loving you,

lbj

From: mbrogan@mbc.web
Sent: Friday, June 28, 2002 10:05 PM
To: JAZMAN@mcb.web
Subject: RE: sigh

I am very sure of you. And think about us together
constantly. In the car, on the job, with friends, alone,
but mostly at night when I am trying hardest to reach
you. Which is where I am headed now.

Are you feeling fear or indecision? I got a little of that
from your words today. Will that change our vision?
Do we need to clear it up, or is it natural? I am not
feeling that at all.

Is everything that we need to do to get to where we
want to be overwhelming you? Or is it just the
magnitude of emotion? Both are very real.

Planning and persistence can help with the first.
Communication will help with the second. I love that
you are such a great communicator.

Be direct, blunt or whatever you need to be to reach out
to me. Whatever it is, we can handle it together.
Without that clarity, we may not find the way to
eachother. If we allow our indecision, hesitation or fear
to remain between us, it may create insurmountable
barriers. Don't you think? I just think clarity is so
important. It takes effort. But ultimately saves effort.
And can save relationship. The more clarity, the closer
we are, the more depth we have, the more rapture, the
farther our spirits can fly. Do you know what I mean?

With love,

mb

From: mbrogan@mbc.web
Sent: Saturday, June 29, 2002 10:05 AM
To: JAZMAN@mcb.web
Subject: silent morning

You must have overslept like me and needed to jump
into your busy day. Mine has been busy already too.

Here is what I have learned so far: Stay out of public
between 8:30-9:30 AM. Were you reading my email
around 9? I was convinced of this because as I was
picking out potatoes at the grocery store, I became
flooded with you and all of the symptoms that come
with our ecstasy. I also learned that it is not easy to
shop in the throws of ecstasy. I may have Jack do the
grocery shopping for the rest of the summer. God I
hope it doesn't happen at the butchers!

I picked up a book off of my shelf called "Ecstasy, A
Way of Knowing," that I purchased in college (still had
the University Book Store sticker) but didn't read. I
must have been preparing for you even back then. I am
surprised it survived the library book donation purges
over the years.

When you said the word ecstasy the other night, there
in the dark during pillow talk, this book immediately
came to mind. I knew just where it was on the book
shelf, turned on the light and began reading. I think we
are on to something here. Might be helpful to achieve
balance. All of the psychological and some of the
physical symptoms are certainly described in this book.
I will let you know more after reading in the sun later.

Well, when I came down was breathing normally in the
grocery store again, who was in front of me in the
grocery store but my Uncle Marvin. This is significant
because when you were telling me on the phone the
story of your dad's passing last night, I was relating it to
my experience of my Aunt Mary's passing last March.

She came to me in a dream the night before I got the call telling me that she had passed away. She wanted to know what would happen to her, and asked me to watch over her husband and children. In the dream, I knew exactly what to say to comfort her. Now, I don't really remember what I said. More just the emotion of the dream, and her questions. Anyway, this completed my wonderful morning. I told him that I would call and we would meet for dinner Wed. with Jack.

I am still feeling the hyper-arousal and my mind is racing. I have so much to tell you and never enough time. I know that you have a busy day today so I will just tell you again, that I love you with all my heart. Every bit.

Let's think of a good lottery number. With all the ability between us, we should come up with a winner. Then you could marry me for my money.

mb

From: JAZMAN@mcb.web
Sent: Saturday, June 29, 2002 11:13 AM
To: mbrogan@mbc.web
Subject: RE: sunset

Two lovely letters waiting for me this morning. Thank you.

Do I sound like I have fear and indecision? I may worry a little that you won't always feel about me as you do now. That I may lose you. That you might change your mind. It is almost like this is too good to be true. I did not know that I could feel so strongly about someone (and visa versa) without having seen them in 30 years. But I pursue it because it may well be true. It certainly feels like it is.

I am not at all overwhelmed about all we have to do to make this real. Just overpowered with emotion. But it is wonderful.

I appreciate the offer, but I am going to marry you for all the right reasons. And do everything in my power to make you happier than you have ever been. Or ever thought you could be.

We'll have many years together so we can plan our next lives together. Next time, we can experience having children and raising them as partners. I will be honored to have children with you. They will be fine people with clear minds because we will guide them. And we will make sure they can achieve their goals.

I'm completely in love - lbj

From: JAZMAN@mcb.web
Sent: Saturday, June 29, 2002 11:24 AM
To: mbrogan@mbc.web
Subject: RE: sunset

It was a leap of faith for both us. And yes, we can wait awhile (until next Saturday) to talk about next life together. Although, I did want to mention that it's okay if you want to wait 5 or 10 years after me. I might want to play around a bit between. Or maybe I'll just hang around and take care of you until the time comes. We could be The Ghost and Mrs. Muir. I would have to do that for a while so I could tell you exactly where I was gonna be growing up again, once I made my decision. But you better not wig out on me and head to Paris or somewhere! I would track you down eventually. You know that.

Did I tell you how much I love you lately? It's a whole fucking lot, okay? My fear is pretty light now. Just too much to lose, I suppose. I don't want us to lose what we're feeling. Your certainty level about us is comforting. I'm realizing how aware you are and it is really turning me on in a major way. Suddenly, what it takes to turn me on has taken on an entirely new dimension.

I should have found you in '80. Sorry about that. We just have to learn from our mistakes and not regret the past. It's the future that matters, my love.

Get that lottery ticket.

Love you big time,
lbj

From: mbrogan@mbc.web
Sent: Saturday, June 29, 2002 1:32 PM
To: JAZMAN@mcb.web
Subject: forever

Well, I am going to make some calls, hop in the shower (coming?) and then head out so that I can get to the Health Food Store before it closes.

One of the things that this books talks about is that people who feel frequent episodes of ecstasy also feel episodes of great despair. Well, I have had plenty of those for the past 10+ years so we should be good for awhile. A reason for it all. I had my doubts that I would find one. Totally worth it.

Your going first: That would mean more profound despair.

The book also links ecstasy to madness, theorizing that people without a coherent social connectedness or strong personality could become unstable. No problem. All of the feedback that I have gotten so far tells me I am up for this, big time. Done my work there.

I guess I will need to invent lots of different ways to say I love you so that it doesn't begin to bore you or seem insincere. The sound of your voice when you say it out loud is all it takes to convince me. The whisper - biorhythm time.

Forever yours, my love,
mb

From: JAZMAN@mcb.web
Sent: Saturday, June 29, 2002 2:22 PM
To: mbrogan@mbc.web
Subject: RE: forever

Hi baby. Don't go believing that you need to have moments of despair to have moments of ecstasy. I'm gonna do all I can to prevent that or at least get you out of it quickly if it turns on. Just need to be with you if and when it happens.

Would love to shower with you, but the hopping part could be a problem. Don't you ever hit your head? Do you do it on one foot or both? If it's that much fun you'll have to teach me. Sexually, I would love to kiss you forever in the shower and do other pleasurable things to you, but I prefer the main event in a bed, on a beach, carpeted floor, couch, grass, almost anywhere soft.

Showers, like back seats of cars, are a bit too cramped and tend to "cramp my style". I am willing to learn though. I am willing to learn anything you want to teach me. I'm a good student.

You've already have expressed your affinity in many ways besides I love you. Those three words are pretty much the ultimate statement, conceptually. I haven't said that in a very long time and haven't felt it nearly like I do now. This is a new love, purely from this being to you as a being. It's how it should be, with our physical / sexual attraction towards each other based on our spiritual love. Love based on physical appearance is temporary at best. This is the real thing. I know it. I love it. And I am so into you, baby, that I can hardly hold myself back. Saying I love you is saying a whole lot from me, just so you know. You finally helped me fully understand it by getting me to feel it. And it feels damn good!

Having said all that, you should know that I really do want to spend forever with you. This is an honest appraisal of how I feel about us. I know you're good for me, you'll be good to me, and I have this burning desire to make you happy. I'm so glad you waited and didn't start something else these last seven years. Thank you. Thank you. Thank you. And guess what? I love you.

Jake

From: mbrogan@mbc.web
Sent: Sunday, June 30, 2002 6:00 AM
To: JAZMAN@mcb.web
Subject: forever

How could I have forgotten this message last night when we spoke on the phone? I must be dopey. I am still feeling a bit dopey but woke up with a thought that I just HAD to get to you. I was very tired last night for pillow talk after that low level headache turned into a full blown problem at the end of the day. Had to take some medicine.

The Buddhists believe that it is desire that keeps us attached to the wheel of life and coming back for more lives. I had often thought that I might not have enough desire to come back. I did not know what real desire was until now. I could keep coming back for you for at least a million years. No, more, definitely more.

My despair is behind me. I don't dwell on it for a minute. My certainty of you leads me to know, if that is what led me here, I would choose to feel it again. I know some people think that we choose what happens in our lives. I thought that was crazy, until now. If I needed all the shit before to bring me here to you, then at least it has real meaning. You have given everything about me so much meaning. Thank you.

About 15 minutes after hanging up I became SO plugged in. That treatment does work! Even if it is your spirit playing doctor. Headache gone. Now I am plugged into 220 service. Heavy duty plug. More plugged than ever. It lasted all night. It is still occurring. Now, I better make coffee because I can't think or type now. I need a little walk. Either that, or just sit and let us wash over me for a long, long time. I may do both.

That helped. So happy to see that Jack put a new jug of water in the fridge for me. I walked downstairs for water last night holding my head with both hands. Let out a cry of desperation after I discovered the jug was dry. Asked him as I climbed back up stairs to PLEASE put a full jug in the fridge for me. He has been so good to me the past few days. Giving me time and distance I need. Always helping and being there. His timing has been real good, he is usually in the shower (like last night) before you call. He has always been tuned into me. Kinda freaky when he was little. Reading my thoughts kinds of things. I call him psychic boy from time to time. I don't think he understands his abilities at all. He is so conservative...I wonder if he will. You will love him.

OK, you and love in the same sentence. Neck burning now. You exceeded expectation on task number 2 last night. You were SO there I can't seem to come down. For the first morning, the feeling of you makes me have to stop typing the emails. Sometimes the ecstasy washes over me and my body becomes very slow, almost completely passive.

OK, coherency returned. For now.

Here is the quote from my little book:

"sex is likely to trigger ecstasy only in such circumstances where it takes place in an ongoing relationship in which both partners are constantly opening up their personalities to each other. Once can perceive the fundamental structure of the universe lurking in the body of the other, and in particular in that body's capacity to be linked with one's own only in the context of an expanding relationship and in the leisurely and elegant giving and taking of bodies."

They must not know this applies to the giving and taking of spirits also. I think this must be what is happening.

As far as useful tools to help me manage I did find one. Really just a reference. Will follow up in Boarders bookstore tomorrow.

When Donna was deciding what drink would best calm me down, she asked if Yoga would help. This stunned me, because I don't think that Donna recognizes Yoga as anything more than a exercise and form of relaxation technique. I did not expect that from her. I did tell her that I was thinking of going to the river next week and doing some relaxation at lunch time. That made her happy.

Donna is sensitive but does not know it. She gives me clues without knowing it. Like you did when you mentioned ecstasy. Or when you called me baby. I am always looking for clues. And some of my strongest affinities are reliable sources. You may be the only one that realizes it.

Anyway - rambling now - This book has a dandy little chart of ecstatic experience diagramed 180 degrees, with mystical rapture (that's me) on one end and a particular form of Yoga (Samadhi) on the other. It also mentions Zen Satori in between them, about 110 degrees on the chart, closer to the Yoga which is noted as "tranquil." I thought I would look those up, give them a try and see if they can provide balance without interfering.

There is my plan. I will spend early next week at Borders instead of the river. I feel so much better with a plan. I suspect we have that in common, along with so much else in the universe now.

Here it comes. Coffee time.

Interesting question: what was happening in your life around 2/4/02?

God, I love you. With every breath. Which are very heavy this morning with all of the electricity, all of you washing over me. Eternity with you is what I see. So clearly. Were we really throwing around ideas for weddings and honeymoons? Two months ago, I would have called anyone crazy that suggest that I would be here. But it is so right. All right. You make it all right for me. You fulfill your burning desire to make me happy by having it. And giving it your everything. It is working. You do, in all
ways. Heavy sigh.

Last night you asked about numerology. I really don't know much about it. For me, it is like tarot or astrology. If I have access that costs nothing, I will look at it and see if it makes sense. Sometimes the readings contradict eachother. Like reading horoscopes on different web sites. Goes to the sensitivity of the reader or reliability of the software. Just looking for those clues.

In numerology, they take the numbers of your birthday. They run an analysis and give you back certain numbers that have meaning in certain areas of life. For example, a birth number gives an idea of potentiality at birth. Hearts desire and idea of where your heart will take you in life (ours is both 6.) Destiny, an idea of destiny potential.

Well, it is a good thing that it's Sunday. I have poured out a novelette. Now, I will try to work off this hyper-arousal that you give me after dancing with you all night in spirit.. Constant, until the next wave of you. I look forward to that. My love.

mb

From: JAZMAN@mcb.web
Sent: Sunday, June 30, 2002   6:30 AM
To: mbrogan@mbc.web
Subject: RE: forever

Hi baby. I have been sitting here smiling since reading your beautiful letter. You are so phenomenal. Last night you said that you think we make choices about who we will be before we are born. I am still thinking about those long legs. Did you really choose to have them this time for me? Mmmmmm.

I suppose the Buddhists have a point. I think you need desire to play the game. Certainly to play it well. By game, I mean anything with goals, freedoms and barriers. The dwindling spiral that beings are in make this the only game in town for most.

I am glad to be a part in rehabilitating your desire. This means that I have accomplished one step in my purpose to make your life as joyful as it can be. I am starting to see clearly how choosing the right partner in life is the most important decision one can make. Again, better late than never. And it isn't too late. I think about the

25 years we missed together, but maybe we had to go through that to get here. Were we ready for each other then? Maybe separate experiences were simply the prerequisites. It was about fifteen minutes after we hung up last night that I began to get into you, my love.

Your book quote was interesting. I have never felt this way before so I am not sure that I have ever "made love" before. Afterwards, I don't think I'll let you go all night. My love for you is so strong. It will be hard to let go.

February 4. Was it a Monday? Not sure. Either in Chicago or San Francisco. I know that doesn't tell you much. Why, honey? What were you doing?

Woke up this morning with a stiff neck and shoulder pain. Am having a bit of trouble getting around because of the pain. Can't remember when this happened to me last. May need to find a chiropractor tomorrow. Will need to take it easy today. But that will give me more time to think of you. My favorite past time.

Yes, last night we talked about marriage ceremonies and honeymoons. Why? Because we both have high certainty that we are heading right there. Because we know we want to spend our lives together. And because marrying someone shows that the search is totally over.

With growing love,

lbj

From: mbrogan@mbc.web
Sent: Sunday, June 30, 2002 7:57 AM
To: JAZMAN@mcb.web
Subject: hmmmmmm

Sounds like that long leg choice will finally pay off big time. (Smile and giggle)

By the time we are finally, completely and totally together, I will teach you that the only real game in town is love. Good student.

I think the book quote was speaking to the difference between making love and having sex. But the book missed the point that spiritual love making, without the body, can also bring rapture. I am living proof of that. All night long our spirits make love. All day long I feel the rapture. Thank you.

Hanging on tight all night. hmmmmmmm

Well, Jack's car is blocking the garage. I hate to wake him. Once we have breakfast, I will go get our ticket. I have been working on coming up with a good number all morning in my Jake place. I have a new way to get there. Slow dancing with you. Smile.

Then I might go see Meg, after catching up on some relationships over the phone. I hope to have dinner with Jack tonight. I haven't seen him much this week.

But before then I think I will find you in the Jake place and give you a back rub. And lots of love to go with it.

Then I have to start getting my head in the game for the coming week. Last week seems a life time ago.

All my love,

mb

From: JAZMAN@mcb.web
Sent: Sunday, June 30, 2002   9:00 AM
To: mbrogan@mbc.web
Subject: RE: hmmmmmm

I don't think too many people experience spiritual love
making. Or falling in love spiritually first, with the
physical coming afterward. I wonder if this is how it
used to be, when people waited for sex until marriage.
If they felt the desire for eachother before hand, it
might propel their spirits.

My shoulder began to feel better around noon. Were
you rubbing it? (smile)

Christ, I am so in love right now I can't get you out of
my mind at all. Do you feel me over there?
Jake

From: mbrogan@mbc.web
Sent: Sunday, June 30, 2002 10:32 AM
To: JAZMAN@mcb.web
Subject: hmmmmmm

Completely

From: JAZMAN@mcb.web
Sent: Sunday, June 30, 2002   10:32 AM
To: mbrogan@mbc.web
Subject: RE: hmmmmmm

Would you call me now love?

From: JAZMAN@mcb.web
Sent: Sunday, June 30, 2002   11:22 AM
To: mbrogan@mbc.web
Subject: number

I m glad we spoke and came up with a number for you
to play. And a plan to meet over the July 4 holiday. I

can't stay away from you anymore. Let's meet at one of the clubs. The Sheffield club has a dance floor. The Michigan Av. Club has private little tables where we can stare into each other's eyes and cuddle for hours. I don't know what who will be playing, but it really doesn't matter does it?

I have you pictured in my mind in your summer dress. Sitting looking out your window, your dress wrapped and tucked around your legs. Those beautiful legs. What is it you do to me? This is so intense. I love you so. My shoulder is feeling better. Your meditations helped I think. We are amazing.

lbj

From: JAZMAN@mcb.web
Sent: Sunday, June 30, 2002   12:00 PM
To: mbrogan@mbc.web
Subject: hmmmmmm

What are you doing over there? How does that dress stay tucked? Here comes that irrepressible smile. I think this started with the thought of those long legs of yours. Have you decided where we will first meet? I really need to touch you right now.

I can almost feel you rubbing my shoulder. Along with this intense excitement and love that I feel for you. You are in my space now, aren't you?

Did you realize that we were emailing at the same time again when I asked you to call? More smiles.

Jake

From: mbrogan@mbc.web
Sent: Sunday, June 30, 2002 12:12 PM
To: JAZMAN@mcb.web
Subject: our numbers

Ran out to get the lottery ticket and stopped at Meg's.
She had an allergic reaction to an antibiotic. Is mostly
sleeping the past couple of days because of the
antihistamines. Boo. It was lovely to lie around and
talk to her for awhile.

OK, psychic man, we will see if your numbers are
lucky. I would like nothing better than to bring 83M to
the table here. I will tell you right now that besides
creating a home, I will not have many ideas on what to
do with that, aside from creating trust funds for our 4
children. I will leave that up to you.

Well, maybe I would like to show you my long legs,
and the way they stick out of my tucked dresses and
curl up under me when I sit and think of you, so far
away. Yea, I would like that better.

Dresses are my favorite thing to wear in the summer.
Lots of freedom and comfort. What do you like to
wear? You don't wear anything in the Jake place.

Whatever dresses I buy from now on will have to pass
the "removability" test. Can it be removed in one
motion, two…although that long, slow zip all the way
down the back might be so nice.

I have been taking a few minutes once an hour to close
my eyes and work on your shoulder. In my mind, I
hear you say "Hi Baby" and am instantly drawn to you.
I crawl right inside of you and work on your muscles
and bones. Kiss you inside and out.

When we first meet, I would like to dance with you.
Can we dance very slowly, no matter what music is

playing? Very slowly, just barely touching, for hours.
Oh man, I need a cold shower now.

When we meet, we will have ten seconds from the time
I stop crying from the happiness to the time we will
have to find some privacy. Better plan for that!
Although I may cry awhile and that could buy us some
time, at least a walk to the car. Where you might just
have to hold and kiss me awhile.

There is no end to the depth is there?   mb

From: JAZMAN@mcb.web
Sent: Sunday, June 30, 2002   6:27 PM
To: mbrogan@mbc.web
Subject: my number

I wear everything from jeans to tuxedos (or nothing at
all.) I will wear whatever pleases you, except dresses.
Those are for you to wear and me to remove. Your legs
won't be curled beneath you for long. Are you seducing
me? Think you have my number? That it will only
take 10 seconds? Well, you are right, and I love it.
Where will we honeymoon, my perfect wife to be?

My shoulder is completely healed. Amazing, since
there was so much pain and restriction of motion this
morning.

I love you,

Jake

From: JAZMAN@mcb.web
Sent: Sunday, June 30, 2002   7:44 PM
To: mbrogan@mbc.web
Subject: asleep early?

My love is deep; the more I give to thee,
The more I have, for both are infinite. - WS

A little Romeo and Juliet for you, my love. I can't believe that you inspired me to pick up Shakespeare again. The witch in you. Transforms me.

I think you fell asleep early. I will call for pillow talk. I love it when you are so sleep and talking from dreamland. So direct, so soft, so sensuous. I wish I was there with you. To hear the rhythm of your breathing. And match it with my own. There, with you completely.

Whew, - did you feel that? You must have me in your Jake place. I will be in your space in awhile to comfort you my love. I am loving you every moment of my day.

Love my baby,

lbj

M ONTH THREE

From: mbrogan@mbc.web
Sent: Monday, July 1, 2002 6:00 AM
To: JAZMAN@mbc.web
Subject: Good Morning

Good morning love. I am very sleepy and running late.
Our pillow talk was marvelous. When did we end the
conversation? Is conversation the right word?
Communion sounds closer. The thought of me sending
you those rushes got my heart pumping this morning. I
so want you to feel me the way I feel you. I will need
to keep working on that. Will you stay open always? It
is almost as if you read all of my thoughts and emotions
now. From so far away. How will it be when we are
together? What are your travel plans?

Need to run love,

Molly Brogan Jacobs

From: JAZMAN@mbc.web
Sent: Monday, July 1, 2002 9:06 AM
To: mbrogan@mbc.web
Subject: RE: Good Morning

Travel plans: Flight leaves SF tomorrow night around
7. I will return Monday the 8th. I am not sure how
much I will be near a computer in between my love.

This, will indeed be a test. Because this morning, I am already all worked up over you. I won't be able to set my schedule until I am in Chicago and test the climate there. I would like to make some headway in divorce proceedings. All will depend on her reaction.

I also have some work to do at the clubs that I have been putting of and can't any longer. Can we play it by ear? I will call and write when I can.

I really want to see and hold you. It is hard to believe that it may be possible just a few days away. I live for that moment.

I love you every moment,

lbj

From: mbrogan@mbc.web
Sent: Monday, July 1, 2002 6:54 PM
To: JAZMAN@mbc.web
Subject: the quiet

I am sorry for the day long quiet love. Our lunch time phone call filled that in nicely. Your voice is so soothing to me. Brings me right where I need to be. Comforted, in your arms, and in your heart.

I have been holding something back today because I just don't know how to tell you. I now think that the only thing to do is just come out with it. Please know that I give this with love. And don't understand it completely, but know it is important to give.

Last night, during healing meditations, I got a glimpse of what it might be like for you this weekend. Vivid and powerful. Visually, it was empty (no bodies), unfamiliar (to me) surroundings. But there were beings there. I did not know any but you. There was a profound sense of loss, fear and uncertainty. Which created an overwhelming sense of compassion in me. I knew for certain this was where you would be this weekend. That this was your family. Those were not your feelings. Maybe your children's. I don't know.

It was an unusual glimpse for me. Future time glimpses usually come to me in dreams. This was while I was awake. And very powerful.

Be gentle, my love. Give everyone the time they need to accept change. My wish is to help you see this through with the complete compassion that you have given it so far. There are many endings that can be written. Take time to explore options without a sense of urgency. It will be important for all of us.

There, I said it. I hope that was OK. Sometimes it is confusing to me, what should be said, how it will be received. But then when you respond, you are always so completely open with me, I wonder what my confusion was about in the first place. I love you.

Yours,
mbj

From: JAZMAN@mbc.web
Sent: Tuesday, July 2, 2002 8:08 AM
To: mbrogan@mbc.web
Subject: RE: the morning

I just had to call last night after reading your wonderful email, instead of answering with a reply. Our connection is so rare. I am beginning to rely much more on our phone calls, on hearing your voice. I sometimes need it desperately. Like last night. You answer the phone immediately for pillow talk. With the most warm and welcoming hello I have ever heard in my life. Draws me right into you. Melts me. Your voice is like no other.

Thanks for telling me your thoughts and advice. More than that, thanks for offering your patience in all of this. I do feel urgency. I want this to end so I can begin with you. It is time. I think the long delay was necessary to keep me available for you. Kept me from getting involved in something much less than us. Everything seems so much less.

I do have concerns about my children. My son is old enough to understand that his parent's relationship is a toxic one and should end. Has given me encouragement to start over several times. But my daughter is still young enough to feel the sting of divorce, whatever the circumstance. It is her I worry about most of all. My love for you is very strong and will help me.

I love you very much. Your sweet voice last night made my sleep serene, deep and satisfying. Thank you for being you.

I get goose bumps when I think of our future together. I love US. We must make this go right. You are who I need to be with and fully connected to. I become so much better and will continue to if you are the one with me. You are the only solution that makes sense.

Loving you deeply as always,

Jake

From: mbrogan@mbc.web
Sent: Tuesday, July 2, 2002 9:24 AM
To: JAZMAN@mbc.web
Subject: morning rapture

No wonder I have been feeling the bodily effects of rapture all morning. The happiness of it actually brought me to tears. Your love reaches me completely.

Takes me into rapture instantly. I guess I will just have to get used to living like this. Integrate it into my life.

"Do you not now me? – and her voice was soft
As love, and full of confidence it sounded.
Do you not recognize the one who oft
Gave healing balm to you when sorest wounded?
Ah, well you know her now, with whom forever
Your heart aspiring longs at one to be!
Did I not see your tears, your heart's endeavor?
Even as a boy you craved for me."
Goethe

I hope you get this kiss before you leave for work. Have read but not processed your beautiful email. It took me somewhere, farther, in love with you. I do love you so.

Low productivity, high rapture is the forecast for the day. Will be going out for drinks with Amy about 3:30 PM. Short business meeting into happy hour. Rebel girls. I will send you mischief later this morning. Can you call on your way to the airport?

My love,

mbj

From: JAZMAN@mbc.web
Sent: Tuesday, July 2, 2002 9: 33 AM
To: mbrogan@mbc.web
Subject: RE: morning rapture

You cried this morning baby? So wish I was there to hold you and dry those tears.

Drinks with Amy today? You will probably be buzzed by 2:00 PM my time. Which I could be a fly on the wall there!

This is amazing. I got in and out of the shower so fast this morning, hoping there would be something from you before I went to work. And there you were, concerned with getting something to me before work. We are one, baby.

God, I want to spend my nights with you in my arms so badly. Want to hold you for hours on end while we experience eachother spiritually. Romancing on and off as our connection turns us on beyond self control.

Loving you more every day - can you tell?

Jake

From: mbrogan@mbc.web
Sent: Tuesday, July 2, 2002 11:22 AM
To: JAZMAN@mbc.web
Subject: finding you

Well, mischief making has been delayed because I need an accomplice. So I will tell you my 2/2/02 (wow-hearts desire number) story about when I think I called for you.

I remembered this last week. My alarm went off in the morning and a song came on called "In The Arms of the Angels." It brought back this experience that I had forgotten.

On Saturday, 2/2/02, while dusting (I have since organized the National Alliance of Women Against Dusting) I stood up from sitting on the floor and my back went out. I had never had back pain like this before. Excruciating. I laid down on the bed to see if it would pass. No. Called the Chiropractor. Walked to the car like a really old person and drove there. He did what he could but told me to call my medical doctor. On the way home, that song, "In the Arms of the Angels was playing." Those angels must have gotten me home because I knew I should not have been driving.

When I got home I called Meg and asked her to help me think of what to do next. She put me on hold and had Hank send the paramedics. It was a busy day at Lake Forest Emergency and I laid on the table from 9-4 before a nurse came in to ask how I was doing.

They might have forgotten about me because I was so quiet. I left my body about 9:15 to handle the intense pain by hearing that song in my head, and ended up in a place with about twelve familiar beings. I asked them to tell me what makes life worth living. And told them that I wanted to go with them. I thought I was ready. They circled around me and made a kind of soothing harmony that I can't otherwise describe. I was lying down and they moved their hands underneath me and took all the pain away.

I don't know what was communicated exactly, but right before the nurse came in at 4 I knew that there was a reason for living that I had yet to experience and that everything was going to be all right. I was crying when the nurse came in and back in the painful body. Big fat shot of meds after that.

After a short stay and a lot more meds, a little rehab the back is fine. I can't believe that I forgot that until now.

I think I was calling you out. And came back in tears of happiness. In spite of the pain. Then after lots of meds, I forgot about it.

I love you.

mbj

From: JAZMAN@mbc.web
Sent: Tuesday, July 2, 2002 12:01 PM
To: mbrogan@mbc.web
Subject: RE: finding you

That was quite a story. It did have all of the elements
needed to petition the universe. I was a bit disturbed
that you were ready to go, before convinced to stay.
But glad to hear you were given a reason to stay. And
glad to hear that I am the answer to that petition. I
formed a similar postulate. Someone basically happy
that could share my views. Baby, you are so much
more than I ever hoped for.

Everything you do and say hits me, and makes me fall
farther into love with you. I hope, when you see me,
you feel the same. I will be calling you soon, baby.
Half hour or so. Can't wait to hear your voice. Can't
wait to change those initials to mbj. I am actually ready
for that. I love you so.

lbj

From: mbrogan@mbc.web
Sent: Tuesday, July 2, 2002 12:10 PM
To: JAZMAN@mbc.web
Subject: RE: finding you

I know the MOST beautiful things about you already.
Everything else will just be frosting on the cake. Lay
your worries down, my love.

mbj

From: mbrogan@mbc.web
Sent: Tuesday, July 2, 2002 3:00 PM
To: JAZMAN@mbc.web
Subject: mbj home

Well, you are hard at work trying to focus after a day of strong and lengthy connection between us. It is sweet, isn't it?

I will be heading home soon, so you will have more time to give the rest of the world for awhile. I cooled down considerably after our lunch over the phone. God, we seem so natural now, don't we? In voice and work. I can't imagine life without you. Wouldn't want to.

I love you Jake.

Molly

From: JAZMAN@mbc.web
Sent: Tuesday, July 2, 2002 5:07 PM
To: mbrogan@mbc.web
Subject: RE: mbj home

Yes, it is now very natural, together with you. Like we've known each other for a very, very long time (smile.)

Will you meet me at the club over the holiday? I need so much to hold you in my arms. Will you dance with me, my love?

Getting ready to leave for the airport, but wanted to let you know that I will be calling. And I really love you a lot, baby. I am going to be so close for a few days, yet out of reach. It really bothers me that we will not be able to talk and write the way we do now. But I need to be focusing on working things out at home. Reach an agreement with her. Tell my children that their parents will be divorcing. One of life's tough moments. I will look at it like a necessary medical treatment required for health.

It will be difficult not to be in touch with you. It's been building every day for so long and I can see I am addicted to it. I am completely into you, fully in love and happy. I am postulating permanency with you. The future looks full of happiness with us together. Pure joy as we go through life and handle all its challenges. That is just how I see it. You are the one of a kind love that I won't find again, that makes this lifetime really worth living. I love you.

lbj

From: JAZMAN@mbc.web
Sent: Tuesday, July 2, 2002 5:16 PM
To: mbrogan@mbc.web
Subject: here and there

I had to write one more time. Are we going to make this go right and take this all the way to the alter? The way I feel right now, I could fly into town and meet you at the justice of the peace. If I was legal, I would certainly do it now. The certainty is there. Do you know your ring size? I want to have them ready so that when the love rushes over us, we can take it all the way. Are you willing to let me select the diamonds, or do you want to be part of that? You make me happy - so happy. I'll be in touch in all ways, baby.

lbj

From: mbrogan@mbc.web
Sent: Tuesday, July 2, 2002 5:25 PM
To: JAZMAN@mbc.web
Subject: here and there at once

I was working on a poem, and started to cry inexplicably just BEFORE your email arrived. I was confused for a minute, until I heard the little mail delivery sound. Why am I crying? - OK, now I know. Christ Jake, I feel your feelings AS you are feeling them. I have never been this clear and constant about anyone. Bit here or there, sometimes months or years between glimpses. With you it is so constant. So real. I am sure that is why I feel such rapture.

This is amazing.

mbj

From: mbrogan@mbc.web
Sent: Friday, July 6, 2002 5:01 AM
To: JAZMAN@mbc.web
Subject: mbj home

Have you gotten used to my yes please:

Meet me tomorrow: yes please
Reinvent your life for me: yes please
Realize our potential with me: yes please
Fly farther than anyone has flown with me: yes please
Feel more than ever with me: yes please
Live more than you thought possible with me: yes please

Jake, Jake, Jake. Love, throughout all of me, for you. Churning, growing, splendid.

Haven't slept since talking to you tonight. Went outside awhile and looked at the stars. Tried to imagine all that you could show me up there. Star gazing with you would be heaven. What do I feel when I think about it? Just a deep, solid, clear feeling of what is to come.

Watched the trees move with the soft, fragrant, early morning summer wind. Moving in rhythm, without resistance. Just like me. The sound of their leaves moving sang to me. Sang of a bright and endless future. With you. All ways. God, I love you. It is hard to believe that I could ever love you more than I do now. But I am sure that I will. Much, much more. The sound of the future calling us out.

I lay back down and listen for your heart beat from time to time. Listen to extreme calm. Listen to complete faith in us. Happiness gets me up and walks me to a window. To watch the world awhile. Serene in my love for you. It is hard to believe that I will be seeing you tomorrow.

The sky is turning the color of lapis. Pink beginning to wake the sky in the east. A day of rebirth. Born into you. Completely.

My love,
mbj

From: JAZMAN@mbc.web
Sent: Monday, July 8, 2002   8:15 PM
To: mbrogan@mbc.web
Subject: back home

I'm back baby. Although it is hard to know that I am so far away from your arms, your embrace, your kiss. I can't stop thinking about our dance. And how I feel when I am holding you as we move together in rhythm. Will you call me tonight?

Jake

From: JAZMAN@mbc.web
Sent: Monday, July 8, 2002 9:03 PM
To: mbrogan@mbc.web
Subject: back home

So, sexy, where are you? Sleeping already?

Write me!!!!!!! Please? I miss you!

lbj

From: JAZMAN@mbc.web
Sent: Monday, July 8, 2002 9:21 PM
To: mbrogan@mbc.web
Subject: searching

Well, I'm assuming you're sound asleep, dreaming
away, keeping your beautiful spirit to yourself tonight.
I am exhausted myself. Trying to get back into our
"zone." Writing to you seems to be the best way under
the circumstances. Holding you would be even better.
I wonder what you are dreaming about. Can you feel
me at all? I'm flowing my affinity your way hoping to
wake you and get you to call me. I love you and miss
you in an uncomfortable way. You are very special.
More than you know. But I know.

Until tomorrow baby,

Jake

From: mbrogan@mbc.web
Sent: Tuesday, July 9, 2002 5:01 AM
To: JAZMAN@mbc.web
Subject: morning love

Good morning my love. You did send a slew of
messages! I was so happy to see the times on those
emails. I checked my mail several times last night

before I finally went to bed. OUR timing was on. The mbc server was messing us up again.

And your last message - "do you feel me at all? I was hoping you would wake and call me." Powerful stuff. Actually, I did awaken before the thunder began. Made sure my phone was in my hand. Wondered how far along in your day you were, what you were doing, if you would call. Needing the silence to end and you to begin. Then the booming thunder. It pushed me into action, to you. Thank goodness. Now I understand your reaction to my call. Oh, I love you. Mmmmmmmmmmm

Maybe my feelings of uncertainty did cloud my recognition of your affinity for awhile before I called. You are right. I do feel uncertainty now, but don't know why. Came to me after our dance, actually. Without reason. Because that dance was heaven. As were your kisses. Sometimes, I don't know if I am actually feeling you, or just my wishful feelings I guess. Talking to you vanquishes all of my uncertainty. You do know that don't you? Your voice, the way you hear me completely, YOU. Remove all barriers, obstacles to what flows between us. So real, and clear, and FUCKING amazing! We are so lucky, you and I. And I am so happy to be back into us completely. The separation is difficult.

But we do have the rest of the world to settle around us. You will need to give so much more time to your personal life than you have in the past couple of years. I am sorry your divorce is proving to be more difficult than you anticipated. And even more sorry that your children did not take the news of your divorce well. I don't know why, but I thought you were much farther along in this process...

Jamie reacted the way that Grace did when we told him his dad and I were divorcing. It was a bit easier for me because my children were told in our counselor's office. He kept a lid on the emotion and facilitated the process. Jamie cried and cried. It must have been Grace's emotion that I felt in my glimpse. I think it will get easier. Just keep communicating with her.

I do understand and I am with you EVERY step of the way. I want to get better at feeling you with me without the words and voice. I do feel it. But without validation sometimes I doubt what I know. Could be part of my uncertainty. Why do I do that? Can you help me work on that? Get real close, hold me tight...show me the way. Lord, I love you.

And not just because that torso plugged in feeling has returned. But because you bring the soul on fire feeling to my life. So much more than I ever dreamed possible. You hear me and hold me, while I discover my self through you. Does that come naturally to you? Do you do it on purpose? Is it just part of your impeccable integrity, or something you learned along the way? Whatever it is about you, it is now my greatest treasure. My morning kiss to you. (It may just go on all day. One of those days our spirits can't get out of bed.) So here is a poem for you. To thank you for our beautiful dance:

Forever

When
Did we begin
Our free fall
Into heaven
Into eachother
Into the place
Where our spirits reside
And call to us
Each moment?

It seems just yesterday

Or an eternity
That we said hello
That familiar echo
That instantly brought
Us here again
Together again
Even though
We remain
Miles apart.

Never before
Have I known
Someone
So completely
Never have I
Felt so deeply.
Not in this life
Did I expect
To fly to such heights
To open so wide
To see so clearly
The possibility of us.

Time becomes
Irrelevant
Because each moment
You are with me
And in me
Filling emotion
To the brim
Changing the future
Changing my viewpoint
Changing awareness
Forever.

Please don't ever leave.
I can't go back.
Can't un-know
What I now know.
It is true,

Two can be one
Now and forever
In each thought
And each moment.
Connection
Can be so clear
So pure
And so strong
That it can last
Forever
And bring forever
To our finite lives
To our days and nights
To our touch
And our words
And our love.

Loving you more,

Molly

From: JAZMAN@mbc.web
Sent: Tuesday, July 9, 2002   11:01 AM
To: mbrogan@mbc.web
Subject: search over

Good morning sweetness. Thank you for your beautiful
words. This time I cried. I don't ever remember crying
with happiness. But as I read your poem, tears came to
my eyes. Thank you for the joy.

Amazing that you woke for me to call last night.
Again, thank you. Did you get enough sleep, honey?

We do have an incredible connection. I fully realized it
while we danced. When we are apart, I can feel you
and reach you with my spirit. I send my affinity to you
on that flow and you can sense it. This is not just me,
it's both of us. You have an antenna that picks up my
signal, baby. An ability you have that others would

hardly understand at all. I am not sure how this developed exactly, but know that it is natural. Just so rare. In time, this could get quite intense. But we will have to assume ownership for what we create here. You are an extremely aware and very able spiritual being.

The world around us. Yes, there are situations to deal with. Getting to where we want to be will take time and effort. I need your positive thoughts and strong intention behind me, and your decision that all has been worked out. Postulates work best when the end result is postulated rather than "it's going to happen." We want to bring it to the present. Not keep it somewhere out in the future, always chasing it.

We have responsibilities and challenges that we have created for ourselves in this life. Changing our lives to what we now want will take some doing. We have many other factors in both our lives that need to be aligned with what we want together. It will take effort, but very doable.

I miss you. I love you.

Jake

From: mbrogan@mbc.web
Sent: Tuesday, July 9, 2002 9:03 PM
To: JAZMAN@mbc.web
Subject: breathtaking

Thank you Jake, for the orchids that were delivered to my office this afternoon. So many, so fragrant, so beautiful and thoughtful.

This evening's sunset was breathtaking. Like our love. The sky had sporadic dark, billowy clouds but the horizon was clear. As the sun broke, brilliant pinks and oranges all over the clouds to the west, north and south. Could not take my eyes off of it. Like trying to take my attention from us. Just can't do it Captain. Don't have the power.

When I am in your arms I am whole. I don't believe I have ever been whole before you took me into your arms. Our nights at the beach are in my heart. I return there often. I love you.

You have some difficult days ahead. I want so to hold you, and give you all that I can to help you along. So I will work as hard as I can to make sure that I continue to hold you in spirit. Tightly enough that you can feel me every minute. Feel the strength of my love for you. Feel our certainty. Our possibility. Our potential. So great. So real.

Tomorrow, down by the river, I will take us to my healing place. Together, we will gain strength. And happiness. And love. And power. To make all things possible through us. My love.

I want to be there in the morning to kiss you passionately. So that our passion can give us power. Then kiss you tenderly before slowly releasing you to the world. Releasing all but the spirit I continuously hold in my heart. Forever. The forever us.

What will we discover today Jake? Discover together. Everyday, something new, through our incredible love. I feel that today holds something amazing for us. More us, together, my darling.

Totally yours,

mb

From: JAZMAN@mbc.web
Sent: Wednesday, July 10, 2002   8:41 AM
To: mbrogan@mbc.web
Subject: search over

Good morning darling. I am still a little sleepy. Jet lag.
I could use some of that healing today. Please do take
me with you. My love will flow like the river.
Unstoppable.

The way I feel today, nothing would be too difficult for
us to handle together. I get that from you. Being in
your space and feeling the affection that you have for
me. It feels so good to have that for you, too. I believe
we actually need each other now, not just want. I know
I do. A few more hurdles to jump and we will be
getting our needs met once and for all. I love you so.
Does it feel right to you, too? Soon, baby, soon.

Jake

From: mbrogan@mbc.web
Sent: Wednesday, July 10, 2002   9:03 AM
To: JAZMAN@mbc.web
Subject: first thoughts

Woke this morning in the middle of an REM cycle. The
overriding thought was of you. The intention of the
dream was to get to you. But the random images and
symbols used as the means were interesting, puzzling.

I was trying to get to you. In some kind of store, next
to one of my dream homes in South Deer Park. Outside
the store was a river. I really wanted to float up that
river. But there was a phone call for me inside the
store. A man, telling me that I should take the Bronco
parked outside and run fire drills with a group of people
waiting for me to begin. I knew that if I did that, I
could get to you. But I really wanted to float up that

river instead. And I wasn't sure if you would be waiting for me up the river.

Wrestling with my uncertainty in my dreams I suppose. Trying to find the best way to you. It reminded me of the dream journal sequences in Remember Me that represented the characters letters to God. Her prayers in story form. My prayer is to find you up the river.

Falling asleep with you was much easier. I was already all wrapped up in you from pillow talk. I just let my mind turn toward you, and kiss....I took sometime this morning to think of you with love, to imagine you with endless energy and joy. I see you in your perfection.

Good mornin' love,

mb

From: JAZMAN@mbc.web
Sent: Wednesday, July 10, 2002 9:30 AM
To: mbrogan@mbc.web
Subject: RE: first thoughts

Hi honey. The fog here is beginning to lift as I gaze out the window and think about you.

How are you today? What did you wear today? I want to be waiting for you when you get home from work so that I can remove those clothes and kiss you all over. It is hard to wait for our time to begin.

I can tell that I will be staring at your pictures a lot today. I want to touch you so badly. To take all of your uncertainty away. Assure you that I will always be yours, in every way. My last visit home was not all I hoped it would be in terms of the divorce. But I will work on that with steadfast resolve. And do everything I can to get an agreement as quickly as possible. So that we can be together soon. Christ, I need that.

I am thinking of flying back to Chi for a long weekend on the 25th. Can we spend some time together? I don't have the details yet. But need you desperately. It will be my first opportunity to take time off here. Shall we dance again? I am thinking every other weekend is reasonable for now. Leaving you will be tough, but knowing that our next time together is only 11 days away will ease the pain.

Loving you, sweetness and light,

Jake

From: mbrogan@mbc.web
Sent: Wednesday, July 10, 2002 1:02 PM
To: JAZMAN@mbc.web
Subject: healing

Well, my plans for you are also beginning to gel. I have to prepare to have more of you in my life. Find that perfect nightgown. The one I won't be wearing much. Create a room for us in my home. Looking forward to that. Been hibernating in the little comfort zone I created with the best parts of my past. Will need to create something that takes us into the future.

Then I need to think clearly about what to say to my children. After Jack leaves for school, you should have your won set of keys to my place. Home when you need it to be. I will need to prepare the path for that. Don't want anyone to be surprised by a chance encounter.

I was restless by lunch time, so I cut out and took us to my healing place. The thought of dancing with you again, mmmmmm. My answer: yes, please.

Before I called for you I called on my guide and asked what about me needed healing. He simply answered

YOU. Then I asked if you would heal when with me.
And he answered "YOU will heal him." So simple.

It is amazing. And energizing. And powerful. We
were in the healing place, and more this time.
Whenever I asked for help, we became more.

While you hold me, light swirls within us, between our
hearts and heads. It is the light within us and between
us. And the light of the universe. All connected. So
healing.

I feel so peaceful now. I want you to feel that too. I
want to hold you here. I love you.

Yours,

mb

From: JAZMAN@mbc.web
Sent: Wednesday, July 10, 2002   2:01 PM
To: mbrogan@mbc.web
Subject: RE: whatever

You are amazing. I do feel the peace you generate for
us. No wonder I want so much to hold you again for a
dance.

I am thinking, we have wasted so much of this life
apart. Let's set our postulates now to spend the next life
together. Reasonable request?

A key to your place! This is really happening isn't it?
Sometimes it seems too good to be true.

Pillow talk will be much better in person. That is, if we
have any energy left to talk. Sometimes, everything you
say creates desire for you. Then again, words may not
be necessary at that point. I am totally in love with you.
lbj

From: mbrogan@mbc.web
Sent: Wednesday, July 10, 2002 6:33 PM
To: JAZMAN@mbc.web
Subject: pure, unadulterated love

Me, say things? Like how, if I were next to you right
now, all I would need to do is get real close, plant my
lips firmly on your neck in that lovely ridge right
beneath your jaw, under your ear. And move upward
with kisses, whispering I love you in-between them.
Until I reach that ear. Then a kiss and another whisper.

You mean like that?

Thank you, Jake, for the beautiful emerald pendant. It
was delivered today and Jack was home to accept
delivery. Even the packaging was beautiful – gold –
like your golden heart.

The phone just rang. It's you! You are so funny. I love
you.

mb

From: mbrogan@mbc.web
Sent: Wednesday, July 10, 2002 8:31 PM
To: JAZMAN@mbc.web
Subject: pure, unadulterated love

Well, we just said good bye on the phone, for now.
Thought it would be a good time to compose my
nightly lullaby for you. The sun is sitting on the
horizon. Lighting up the stratus clouds that stretch
across the sky like watercolor. Lending only light yet,
not color. But that will come with the sun's setting. A
very romantic time of evening. The sky turning color
moment to moment. A hush descending on the world.
The time of day I can wrap you around me. And no one
will interrupt. Or deter.

How did we get here at all? How did we get here so quickly? I am not sure. Something about both of us. One of us could not have done it alone. Something about the time being right for us. It must not have been before, because we kept passing each other.

I remembered you when I saw your name on the high school web page. You were a tender, intriguing memory. What made you post it there? I was looking for stories of long lost friends. Stories that may help me understand human nature. Stories that continue friendships. I never imagined that I would find what we have. Here, there or anywhere.

What made you keep writing to me? Over the years, I have had many correspondents. Some sporadic, some consistent for a short time, then fizzle out. What made you so consistent? What kept you going the distance?

Somewhere along the line, the voice in your letters became a daily sustenance for me. A necessity. And when a letter did not arrive, a hole occurred. That was only filled when finally, I got mail. I suppose that was when I knew we had something special.

Then the day I heard your voice. That was the day I knew we had something extraordinary. I still cannot accurately describe what your voice does to me - my body- my being. But it happened the first time I heard you. And it continues to happen, every time.

Sometimes it might seem like I am not listening. But really, I am listening completely. Caught in the moment. In the sound of your voice. In the way it propels my spirit into eternity while my body continues to listen for more. That spiritual orgasm that occurs so frequently, daily, hourly. But when you are speaking, sometimes moment after moment.

I have stopped trying to explain that to myself. And allowed myself to just experience. To explore the experience. And allow it to grow. And discover myself through it. Through you. I think we are healing each other. And renewing each other. And discovering eachother. And deeply, completely loving each other.

How did we get here so quickly? Neither resists. We allow our instincts to guide us. We follow our intuition. And the depth of our spirits guides us, as we discover the fundamental structures of the universe, together. We would not be so far if we weren't such strong spirits. Or if we did not recognize each other. Or if we allowed the world to slow us down. But we followed each other. And our faith. And here we are. In FUCKING credible isn't it? Love is so much more than I ever thought it could be. Thank you for showing me.

Your final love,
mb

PS I have decided that if you want to marry me twice so that we can make it the best 2 out of 3, I will say yes again. And again. And again...

From: JAZMAN@mbc.web
Sent: Thursday, July 11, 2002 9:11 AM
To: mbrogan@mbc.web
Subject: spiritual reaching

Thank you for the beautiful communication. Had two cups of coffee reading, and re-reading it. If I were next to you, I would ask you to tell me again and again. And let your voice send me to where it always does. Heaven.

I posted my name on that web page so people that wanted to reach me could. I kept writing because you interested me and liked it. It became an emptiness when we didn't write, like on the weekends. The affinity grew and grew. I asked myself "Who IS this being?" The high school memories were there, but somewhat vague, and I kept asking that question. Then our connection became a necessity for me. I began to miss you more and more. Not telling you exactly how I felt was bothersome. Then all of a sudden, we were there, in our own world together. And before I knew it, I was saying I love you. Pretty intense ride I have to say. There WAS no resistance from either of us. No pulling back. Just going with the flow that never stopped.

Yes, inFUCKINGcredible. I think the way our affinity grew was unique, but more natural because it was spiritual first. We were forced to reach out with our spirits because we could not be together physically. And we have both worked in this life to strengthen our spirituality. So we were able. Spirits are forever, and I think we now feel some of the eternity between us. It makes US intense. Gives us passion. We came along at a time of need for each other, and seemed to do everything right to grow this enormous, loving relationship.

What are the odds of this happening? Like the lottery probably. We won our own spiritual lottery.

Jake

From: mbrogan@mbc.web
Sent: Thursday, July 11, 2002 10:11 AM
To: JAZMAN@mbc.web
Subject: us

So you signed on to the high school web page to be found and I logged on to find you. A good match there! And yes, I have been thinking about you inside me, kissing me passionately. I only think about that every

1-5 minutes so chances are good I am thinking about it when you are. So get OVER here.

I love you MUCH more today. Just so you know. By the way, we called each other out. Both of us. But if you insist on giving me all the credit.....

I am heading downtown soon and will not be home until after dinnertime. But if we miss pillow talk tonight, you will have one whacked out baby on your hands by morning. The risk is yours. But know this, those parts of you that are revealed in the early morning hours of pillow talk I cannot live without for long. Sigh. Too true.

Loving you every minute,

mb

From: JAZMAN@mbc.web
Sent: Friday, July 12, 2002 3:00 AM
To: mbrogan@mbc.web
Subject: RE: us

Just finished our long, wonderful pillow talk. We can talk the night away, can't we? Hope you are dreaming happy dreams right now. I can't quite sleep yet and need to write to you. Never, have I had the need to touch someone so often, so tenderly.

When I'm all alone and you're unavailable, it is almost painful sometimes. Life needs to become simpler. We should just be able to be together without interference or concerns about others. But we love too, so I guess our time will come later. In the meantime, we will just make the best of what we have.

I know this email has a lower tone. Sorry. I'm tired and I'm not. I can't get you off my mind as I think of you lying there alone with those clothes on you described, wanting to be near you to just listen to your heart beat and hold you. You are my Molly. Thank you.

I love you,

Jake

From: mbrogan@mbc.web
Sent: Saturday, July 13, 2002 10:11 AM
To: JAZMAN@mbc.web
Subject: RE: us

Good morning my love. I was VERY deep into sleep. Really needed it. Missed you, although you were in every dream. But best of all, when I woke, your spirit was all over me. First, kissing my neck passionately. Then my mouth. Then, inside me. What a way to begin the day. Did you plan that? I will be so deeply into you all day now. A wonderful peace has become me. God, Jake, how the hell do you do this? Please, don't ever stop.

The "missing you" part of us is really beginning to affect me. Knowing that you were alone, needing me, and I couldn't physically touch you - or that you think I am unavailable - great yearning. Yearning on every level. With a touch of sadness. The first bit of sadness to hit me I suppose. I want so much to hold you.

Making the best of what we have won't do for long. Making what we have into the best for us will need to unfold daily, quickly like the rest of us. Because our need for eachother seems to be growing just as quickly. Our need to be together more and more. We need to stay one step ahead of the pain, yearning and sadness. And ride the love, happiness and rapture right into each others arms. I am not sure how we will do that. But follow our instincts, just as we have until now. They have been our best guide.

You being horny for me. I do love that. And not just because of the idea that I can turn you on sexually, but because it is part of the passion that sweeps over us, through us - the most visible part.

Here is a secret for you. It is the thought of the incredible strength of our passion that is the real turn on. Not only the overwhelming sex drive that has overcome us, but the spiritual propulsion. The continual revelation of each other's soul. The opening of our characters to each other, for each other - the compassion and the passion - on every level. The way you turn me on in entirety.

It is the passion on every level that I love. And the most amazing part, the part that keeps US growing so quickly, so deeply, so incredibly, is the integration of the levels. We do not open one level here, one there. Turn each other on physically one moment, spiritually the next. Each turn on, each moment of growth, each opening to the other is done on every level simultaneously. When we open to each other, when we turn toward each other, when we reveal ourselves, it is with body, heart, mind, spirit, soul all at once. I know that this is the true power of our passion. This is what makes our intimacy so rare and so deep. Our love has consilience. As we express it, as we experience it, as it frees us from the mystery and illusion by showing us the truth.

That is what we do. We do it together. And together, it comes naturally. I do so love you. God, I love you.

And what convinces me that we are eternal? The fact that it is the physical passion that we have the hardest time managing. The rest comes so naturally, without resistance. This tells me that we are so deeply connected that it may take multiple lifetimes to understand the depth of US. This convinces me that

you are the one. And makes me unequivocally willing
to do whatever it takes to join my life with yours. We
are just right. That's all.

Today, is already better than yesterday. Thanks to you
my love,

mb

From: JAZMAN@mbc.web
Sent: Saturday, July 13, 2002   12:00 PM
To: mbrogan@mbc.web
Subject: RE: us

Molly Brogan. Wonderful name. Incredible being.
Very aware and able. Beautiful and sensuous to the
max. Loving. What are you doing tonight? I would
like to dine you, undress you and then please you all
night long. Would you like that too, baby?

Christ, I need this to move forward.

I am still smiling with compassion about what you told
me last night during pillow talk. When you talk to
people about spirituality, you watch for the first
indication of blankness, and then know the limits of
their understanding. Was it hard for you, honey? All
those years with such high awareness yourself, and not
having people to talk to about it? Continuing to try to
find someone who could understand you and what life
is really based on? I feel for you. And love you.

I realized this morning that my sleeping habits have
changed too! We both go to sleep earlier, to enjoy
pillow talk. And wake up earlier, to read and compose
our morning emails. I spend so much time thinking
about you and gazing out the window in the morning.
Postulating our future. Basking in the light of your
love. Listening to the birds and the calmness. Reading
your words and becoming sexually aroused (every

time!) Observing my affinity for you soar. Very nice.
I look forward to each morning now.

Right now, I only want to say that I care deeply for you.
Can't seem to think about much else. I admire you so
much. Admiration is such a large part of the love I feel.
Is that real to you? You are so special and I don't think
you fully get that. But you are - more than you know.
And I am just so into you, baby.

Forever yours,

Jake

From: mbrogan@mbc.web
Sent: Saturday, July 13, 2002 6:06 PM
To: JAZMAN@mbc.web
Subject: RE: us

Took a cat nap. Awoke in my Jake place, totally
energized. Surrounded by you. But unsure about why.
Thought the only thing to do was to get up and
compose an email.

Not sure about content. Only sure of intent. My love
for you. Pure intention. Hoping to get your attention.
To lift your spirit and carry you through the day. In a
way that my body can't because it is not there. But I am
there. With you. Always.

Sue wanted to know how I could be so sure of you so
soon. She is the only friend that I have, beside you, that
would understand how connected we are spiritually. So
I tried to explain to her just how my spirit lives with
yours on a daily basis. How we experience the same
moments spiritually, from 1745 miles away. I found
myself crying while explaining. Because of the beauty
of what we have. Her extreme smile told me that she
understood completely. And is in as much awe of it as
I am.

I tried to explain, but I am not sure that you understand how completely connected we are. I am not sure that I even understand it. The rapture, the clairvoyance, the healing that I experience when hooked into you. I think I am just beginning to be able to articulate it. And struggle to find language and form so that I can communicate what I experience.

I tried to explain the way I know when you are reading my words, or I know when you are upset. The way I felt your hunger last night before you told me you were getting something to eat. The way I sometimes see a bit of what you are seeing. Silly things. Out the windshield. The computer screen. People walking by. I can't really explain it because it is all so new. I have never lived like this before. Have not yet had a chance to integrate it all into my life. Let alone explain it. To myself or anyone else. Could it be that my intention and your attention and visa versa are completely together during these moments? And that becomes my experience? Not really clairvoyance but a merging of two into one? Or maybe that is what clairvoyance is all about.

It is like the DeJaVu Vu. A solid glimpse. On every level. Some lasting longer that others. But all ways about you. In real time.

I know that you don't experience all of this the way I do. And I think that because I experience us in this way, I have no fear about giving myself over to it completely. Not really of even losing it. Because I will never lose what we have experienced. And am so much more already because of you. And so sure that our future is real. It is up to us to make it real. But I feel us doing that on every level. Now, and forever. I know it.

Well, this has been more of a hypnotic writing than any

of my other emails. I hope it isn't too far out there or redundant. Straight from the heart, and all other regions inside. Straight from us. How I love you, Jake.

Touch me love,

mb

From: JAZMAN@mbc.web
Sent: Saturday, July 13, 2002 8:40 PM
To: mbrogan@mbc.web
Subject: RE: us

Thanks honey, for giving me the reality of what's happening. Not far out at all, once you've lived it a little. Not too many people would understand a connection like ours. Most people believe they are only bodies, that their spirits are something that goes to heaven with no real power for them here on earth. Only people fully connected to their spirit can experience what we do. I love you.

Spiritual orgasms. We have already had some. But only in the early stage of what I believe will be massive ones, where we take each other to heights we haven't known since (?)

Yes, I am in love. The fact that we consider this stuff proves that. I will call a little later for PT.
Jake

From: mbrogan@mbc.web
Sent: Sunday, July 14, 2002 5:34 AM
To: JAZMAN@mbc.web
Subject: morning love

This morning, I sat outside and watched the sun come up. The air is already thick with Ozone. The human noise of the world is louder, that wa wa. More air conditioners probably. And the birds seem quieter.

Probably planning one of those laid back days. Like a Sunday, when we just cuddle all day and watch the Comedy Channel. Let's have one of those someday.

It struck me suddenly, that you have given me a place in this world. I don't think that I have ever felt that before. My children gave me a sense of purpose certainly. But that began to fade as their independence increased. My work (especially the writing) gives me a means of expression. Relationships, a feeling of connectedness and a mirror. But I have never felt that feeling of having a place. A very secure, permanent feeling. I suppose that "place" is by your side, where ever that may be. But I have such certainty that is where I belong. A first and final home.

Do you think it is possible that I just never gave my heart completely before? Always loved with reservation? It must be true, because although I have always felt myself to be a "centered" person who knows herself well, I never really felt this sense of having a place before. Or a willingness to place myself within anyone else, like this before.

Maybe it is like you say, I have finally put myself in your space completely. Knowing, that is where I belong. I do not know how you made me feel safe and protected enough. You can consider that a lifetime achievement. But you did, so quickly too. How do you do that? Do you do it on purpose?

And here I am. In my place with you. Together with you. What a blessing we are. How I love you. Much more today than even last night when we spoke. Because I have now realized that I have a place in this world. (Extreme smile.) And managed to discover myself through you this morning before my eyes lost their early morning blur. God, I love you. So lucky to have found you. So lucky that you'll have me. So finally, really alive. And in love. Marvelous.

Had a voice mail yesterday from a friend from high
school that is in town. My friend Sandy. Cheerleader
and homecoming queen. We were very different. She
is outgoing and very bright. I wondered, sometimes,
why she liked me. She has a brother, Tom, who was in
the same class. I may have even been closer to Tom in
high school. I remember him as a very witty guy. Lots
of long talks in study hall.

Anyway, Sandy is in town and is going to stop by
today. Have not seen her since 1977 or somewhere
around there. Should be fun to catch up. Looking
forward to another wonderful day as Jake's girl. Just so
right.

Love,
Molly

From: JAZMAN@mbc.web
Sent: Sunday, July 14, 2002   8:40 AM
To: mbrogan@mbc.web
Subject: RE: morning love

Here's my take on it, sweetness. Somehow you seem to
have this ability to duplicate my wavelength. You trust
me because you can pick up my thoughts and
beingness, not just hear my words. Not the exact
concepts necessarily, but my emotions, intentions,
feelings. You just simply know things about me. Like
you have an antenna that's tuned into my frequency.
And for reasons only you can determine, you like
tuning in. There is something very unique between us,
something that's way above the human norm on this
planet. You can tell that I have these intense feelings
towards you and you can feel me trying to get into your
space as a being. You felt that early on as we wrote to
each other. I don't think you knew what to do with it
back then (smile). Obviously you liked it after a while,

but you had your reservations and uncertainties. Eventually, you must have decided that the upside in terms of potential happiness and joy was worth more than whatever potential risk you perceived. As you lowered all defenses, your ability to reach into me increased.

It's hard to express feelings like this in normal terms because available terms get used for lesser things than what we are actually feeling. "Love" is the best we have to communicate the concept. So we use it a lot. You're able to put some real oomph behind it with your communication talents so I can really get it.

How did I do it and was it on purpose? I have no idea. I mean as I started having feelings for you I hoped you would have affinity for me too. I certainly didn't expect this from either of us! I didn't know "this" even existed out there. I am certainly in uncharted waters with you. It's just this pure admiration I constantly feel for you and everything about you. And you're so CUTE in so many ways. And the love just roars inside of me.

Actually, I would like to ask you the same question. How did YOU do this, baby? We are in the same boat, going down river. Drifting with the current of US.

mb's Jake

From: JAZMAN@mbc.web
Sent: Sunday, July 14, 2002 2:10 PM
To: mbrogan@mbc.web
Subject: RE: morning love

Thanks again for making me hard again this morning. Interesting how my feeling such high affinity results in that. No blunt sexuality needed, just your loving words expressed so well, and I'm "at ready". Fascinating. Never before, but happens every day now.

I could not wait to hear from you before writing again. I have so much to say it pours out. I imagine you are with Sandy (I do remember Sandy and Tom. Do they remember me?) now. I envy her. She can see you. And touch you. And hear your voice.

Yes, the "so right" factor is amazing. Almost too good to be true, but I did say almost. Maybe we both just deserve this kind of a relationship finally.
I'm sure you do, sometimes wonder if I really do or just got lucky. Then there's the old saying about life being full of opportunities and it's simply a matter of acting on them. Real love is such an intense feeling, isn't it? Such happiness, such a high. I don't want to be crude, but these love hard-ons are brand new for me. A totally new experience. Didn't even realize that could happen before you arrived in my life. People do such weird things to get excited and all they need is love. Then again, this kind of love is a bit rare, don't you think? It gets so intense sometimes. I mean it's always there, but those spikes are something else. Don't ever want it to change unless it's more. God - just had another major spike.

What happens to me when you think of me? Part of you comes into my space. It's that wavelength - you match mine somehow and part of you is with me and vice versa. Can you understand this? It's what it is. It's the wavelength - happens to some twins occasionally. But Molly, as I write this I am getting an uncomfortable feeling. Like you are terribly unhappy or in some kind of danger. Whew. That was like changing the channel from a love story to an action adventure movie. Are you all right?

I love to validate your knowingness, your beingness. I get a bit sad thinking of all those years you experienced

without someone to really understand you, but now you've got me. And I've got you. And I love you and care about you
soooooo much. Sometimes, I wonder if I deserve you.

There it is again - a feeling that is beginning to nag and seem very real. I am going to call you love.

Jake

From: JAZMAN@mbc.web
Sent: Sunday, July 14, 2002   4:17 PM
To: mbrogan@mbc.web
Subject: please call

Molly I am very worried. The feeling that something bad is happening is not going away. I can't reach you at home or on your cell. Please call asap.

lbj

From: mbrogan@mbc.web
Sent: Monday, July 15, 2002 5:34 AM
To: JAZMAN@mbc.web
Subject: so sorry

Do you deserve me? Certainly, yes. There is no one else in the world for me. I am convinced of that. I will convince you too.

Oh Jake. I don't think I fully understood your concern until this morning, when I read your three emails. You regained your composure so quickly last night when I finally called you around ten. I am so sorry that I forgot to take my cell phone with me. I guess this is the first time either of us has been inaccessible without planning for it. I mean, when you go home, I know that I won't be hearing from you. But this was different. And your feelings...how amazing. Even though the danger was not mine, you picked it up from me. I wonder if anyone else would believe this.

And I am so glad to have someone to talk to about it. I have had dreams before that cause concern for friends or family. I call them, they say "that's amazing. That actually happened." But getting glimpses while with someone is new for me. I don't know how to tell Sandy about my glimpses. I think I need to get more of her story to understand what I am seeing. She will be in town all week. Next weekend is a family reunion at her sisters. They have invited me. Hopefully by then I will have this all figured out. And find a way to tell her my worry without sounding like a freak. She is VERY religious. Irish Catholic, like Meg.

I am not sure that I would even have known how to tell you! The impressions that I was getting when she took my hand from time to time were so vivid. I could see her ex husband. Feel his violent intentions. Feel her fear, and her daughters' fear. I hope things become clearer to me before she leaves town. I do think I should say something.

Thank you love, for staying so close. For helping me through the rough times WHILE they happen. Your love is unbelievable. But I believe it. And I believe in you. With all my heart.

And - I will really try to remember my cell phone.

Yesterday morning, Meg asked me how much I talk to you about my divorce. She was not surprised that it was very little. I do not talk to anyone about it really. When you asked me if anyone had ever hit me last night, it threw me a bit. I didn't want to lay all of that on you last night, especially after working you into such a frenzy with my thoughtlessness. But I had to be honest. Do you still love me?

Meg wants you to know that if you feel I am not forthcoming enough about my past (the way she often does…she always has to drag things out of me) that she will be glad to fill you in. She was smiling the rebel girl smile when she said it. She could certainly give you the full flavor of my history the past 10 years. And give it her own, humorous spin, I am sure. Let me know if you want her number.

We seem to be the same in our lack of need to relive our past marital troubles. I like that. But you are still going through the worst part. And I want you to know I am always here for you. Because I feel I was not able to do such a great job in my own situation, I am not sure how much I can help. But I can certainly help process. I am good at that (if you haven't noticed.) And I am always here for you Jake.

We.., maybe I did the best I could do during my divorce. The outcome was just not what I would have wanted. Peace and kindness just not possible between us. When one person wants war, how can the other avoid it? How do you not engage the stalker as he makes all the moves? I probably need to give myself a break there. I would have done anything to turn the circumstance from war to peace.

I love you Jake. More than I can say. Your long legged baby,

Molly

From: JAZMAN@mbc.web
Sent: Monday, July 15, 2002   4:26 PM
To: mbrogan@mbc.web
Subject: a kiss

Loved your letter and would say so much more if I had the time. Our lunch time phone conversation will need to carry me through to pillow talk. Have to drive up to

Mendocino County to meet with a client. But will be back in time to wake you for pillow talk. Will you be ready to receive me?

You know, I am REALLY happy that you love me. Thanks for telling me and thanks for feeling that way. And most of all, thanks for being you.

I love you, baby. Can't wait to talk again.

Jake

From: mbrogan@mbc.web
Sent: Monday, July 15, 2002 8:58 PM
To: JAZMAN@mbc.web
Subject: kiss good night

I have to warn you. Once I start kissing you, I just don't know if I will be able to stop. I think about your kisses constantly. How they feel. How they make the rest of my body feel. How they give my spirit flight and put me outside of myself instantly. What a struggle it was to think of the rest of the people in your club, when you kissed me as we danced. I don't want the kissing to stop once it starts again. What do you think of that?

As I fall asleep, I think of your kisses. As I calm myself into meditation, I think of your kisses. As soon as we find each other in the healing place, kissing. When I loose my focus at work, I think of your kisses. On the way to work, I am kissing you. On the way home from work. Same. In the shower, kissing you. Between each breath, a passionate kiss. God, I love you. And your kisses.

Someday, I will not have to live without them. I live for that day.

My love,
mb

From: mbrogan@mbc.web
Sent: Tuesday, July 16, 2002 5:52 AM
To: JAZMAN@mbc.web
Subject: sleepy girl

Sorry love. Overslept after talking all night, loving all
night. I will reach out from the office.

From: JAZMAN@mbc.web
Sent: Tuesday, July 16, 2002 9:21 AM
To: mbrogan@mbc.web
Subject: right here

Good morning. I am really tired too. But will wake up
as I think about you.

Last night was rough. I am sorry to dump all of that on
you. I guess I have been worrying about it for quite
awhile. When my ex called and went off on me it all
came to the forefront. I have so much to deal with
regarding my children. Grace is a major concern. Mike
is handling it much better, but beginning to take on his
mother's anger. I think she has created a rift between
me and my children. I think they feel sympathy for her
and aren't happy with this ending because she is so
upset. Mike used to say things like "How could you be
married to her," or "When are you going to get a
divorce?" But now that they see her so upset and I
think they are seeing it differently. I have to get them
to see my viewpoint without making her look bad. That
will be difficult because they hear her daily. I only see
them from time to time.

How do I get my daughter to see that her life and
relationships with her parents won't be much different
than it is now? We were very close up until the past
couple of years. And even then, when home, we
enjoyed each other's company. I worry that will
change.

So when you asked about spending the night together next time I am in town, I wondered about what they would think about us. Would they wonder where I am staying? I have slept on the couch for the past couple of years while in town, but I was there in the house. On the other hand, she has been screaming that I am no longer welcome in the house so I may have to spend the night elsewhere.

If that happens I would really want you with me because I will be concerned about the scene at the house the next day. I will need your advice and steadiness. I will not want to be alone. But is this how our first night together should be? Thrown in the middle of my crisis at home? I feel badly about that too.

These are my thoughts and concerns. If she wasn't so freaked out and ready to fight it would be much easier. Hard to believe that after all this time, she still can't let go. I did not anticipate this. She is showing an evil streak and it is effecting my children. Her never ending attempts to get me to change my mind have turned into hate. It's pretty bad. I have never been hated and am not sure how to deal with it.

Having said all that, I feel better. Explaining it to you helped me to look at it. I was bothered by it, but hadn't looked at it fully. I hope this isn't too upsetting to you. I am worried about that now too. But who else can I talk to about all this? I want you to be my best friend, too. That's just how it has to be. But I didn't expect to be the first one with a crisis.

I love you so much, Jake

From: mbrogan@mbc.web
Sent: Tuesday, July 16, 2002 10:02 AM
To: JAZMAN@mbc.web
Subject: right here too

Glad to see you thinking this through so clearly. And I completely understand. I have been intensely hated before (my ex reacted the same way), and had my kids (and everyone else possible) used against me. It is difficult. But don't take it personally. We will get through it together. I am happy to be your best friend. So very happy.

It was a toss of the coin on who would have the first crisis wasn't it? Sorry it had to be you, but glad that I have some experience to draw on. Please give me every opportunity to provide comfort to you. It is what I want to do more than anything. Don't worry about me. I have lived it already. And am proof that you will get through it. And we can hold on to eachother through it.

And this means (and I really like this) that maybe I CAN BE THE DOCTOR NEXT WEEK. I would like nothing better than to find provide some sexual healing at the Lake Forest beach house hideaway. We won't have to talk at all.

Turn to me when you need to. I am here for you through this in any way that you need me to be. You are doing fine. It is not easy for anyone.

I have meetings for the rest of the day and am meeting Sandy for dinner. If you pick up anything weird, not to worry. I am still working on this thing with her. I will try to drop a line in between, but may need to catch up with you at pillow talk.

Until then, something to carry you through the day when I can't be with you:

Touch Me

You touch me in ways
I never thought possible.
I wonder
If you understand
What you do
Or how you do it.
Or is it simply
The natural result
Of your sweet love.

You touch my heart
And open feeling
Of such power
And magnitude
That it washes away
All doubt and fear
Leaving a peace
That seems contagious
To all around me.

You touch my body
And create a passion
That instantly draws
Our world
Into the moment
And this moment
Becomes every moment
And the only moment
Endlessly.

You touch my spirit
And we begin
Our flight
To the realm
Where all is possible
Through our love.
Where we explore
Possibility

With new dimension
Healing each other.
Healing our world.
Expanding our love
Farther into forever.

You touch my soul
And awaken it
To the depths of our
Experience together.
You clarify
Who I am
Who I was
And who I will be
Through your touch.
Through our love,
My love.

I love you,

Molly

From: JAZMAN@mbc.web
Sent: Tuesday, July 16, 2002 2:10 PM
To: mbrogan@mbc.web
Subject: RE: right here too

Your response to all that I just dumped on you was
VERY welcome. Thank you. And the sexual healing
will be most welcome. Your presence, even more so.
God, I love you.

I printed out your poem so that I can take it with me
today. And read it whenever I need to feel your
comfort. I can't tell you how much your poetry means
to me. It makes me want to take you in my arms and
never let go. I love you Molly.

I don't know why I didn't look at this until last night.
Just cruising along, thinking everything would be fine.
Until I took a closer look and looked at the risk.
Freaky. But no matter what, I feel like I will have you.
And that is a real comfort, baby.

Just spent an hour on the phone with my mom
explaining things. Well, at least that's done.

I will be all tied up (Hmmmmmm) until later tonight
too. Have fun with Sandy and give her my best.

Love,

Jake

From: mbrogan@mbc.web
Sent: Tuesday, July 16, 2002 3:00 PM
To: JAZMAN@mbc.web
Subject: right here too

Well my dear,

Our busy day has kept you from me. But you may be
encouraged to know that down by the river, you were
ALL over me in spirit. It was quite lovely.

Then I did some transcendental meditations. Stayed
inside myself and left my thoughts behind. There is a
total awareness of my surroundings that comes with
that. The river bank made that especially lovely.

Very strange day. My friend called from Vegas to
touch base. He can't wait for us to do a Vegas weekend
so that he can see me and meet you. Maybe we can
work that in during football season when there isn't a
game.

His company was awarded the RFP for
telecommunications in the new Washington DC

conference center. After he told me this there was a short silence on the line because we had been discussing (before you) my taking a position with him to get that going. A little strange. Not too. He is glad that I am so happy.

Dinner with Sandy was again interesting. When she touches my hand, which she is in the habit of doing for some reason, I get very clear impressions of pain and violence. I am not sure yet how to process them, of they are of her past or future. I don't really have enough experience here to know what to do. So I suppose I will try some different meditations and spend a bit more time with her to clarify. I just don't want to sound like some kind of nut if it turns out that I need to caution her. I wish I knew someone else that has these experiences.

Well, as you can see, none of the highlights of my day involve my job here. But I did manage complete everything on my desk AND write a few additional chapters on the book. Both of our days have been whirlwind. Sorry mine was so much more enjoyable. Hope you find comfort in the fact that a big part of that enjoyment was YOU. As always.
I love you,
mb

From: mbrogan@mbc.web
Sent: Wednesday, July 17, 2002 6:00 AM
To: JAZMAN@mbc.web
Subject: late morning

Sorry sweetheart. Running so late this morning. Had the MOST wonderful dreams of you. Inspired by pillow talk last night. I swear, you could be reading the phone book and that voice of yours would send me into rapture. Why is that?

As soon as I dropped the phone from my hand last night your spirit came rushing in. Passionately, completely. When I tried to let my body feel it also, I began to lose the spirit so I had to stop. And learn how to respond with my sprit. Oh my god Jake, it was so amazing. And so much more real than it has ever been. My body can actually feel your warmth and caress. Do you feel any of that? I can still feel it. It is real, isn't it Jake?

It will be a very intense, exciting day. Full of rapture and spikes and rushes of all kinds. I know it. And know, above all else, that I love you.
mb

From: JAZMAN@mbc.web
Sent: Wednesday, July 17, 2002 9:21 AM
To: mbrogan@mbc.web
Subject: RE: late morning

Yes, it's real baby. You and I make it real, together. We have to keep creating what we have already created. That's all. Just continue to put it there every day, forever. It is easy for us because the match is made in heaven. And we are doing it without romance! When that finally begins, it will get pretty intense. And the memories…

I know you wonder about us. Our interrelated pasts and how we got together this time. I love you very much, and have for a very long time. So here we are, in 2002, in this high tech society, playing the game and now finally together. It is time to make the most of it.

Does that make it more real to you, baby? Does what I'm saying have an effect deep inside you somewhere that your can feel, but can't fully see yet? Don't be surprised if you begin to get glimpses of our other times together. When the time comes, we will talk about it all night at the beach. You know, I will always love you.
Jake

From: mbrogan@mbc.web
Sent: Wednesday, July 17, 2002 3:00 PM
To: JAZMAN@mbc.web
Subject: echo

I have read your email several times throughout this
busy day. I am forever yours. That is just right. Isn't
it? It is amazing that you love me. God knows how I
love you.

mb

From: mbrogan@mbc.web
Sent: Wednesday, July 17, 2002 8:07 PM
To: JAZMAN@mbc.web
Subject: echo

Well, I have missed you today. The world kept us very
busy. Down by the river at lunch, I found you in the
Jake place. Quite lovely. Also did more transcendental
meditating. I think it helps keeps a balance.

Took a walk across the street after dinner. Laid down
for awhile on the grass under a tree. Watched the tree
stirring in the wind against the blue sky and tiny white
clouds. The wind would pick up, and the branches
would swing in all directions. Creating a lovely sound
as the leaves brushed up against each other. Then the
wind would die. And all would quiet. Until the next
gust. I watched for quite awhile in fascination. And
remembered how I used to do that for hours as a child.
Just pondering the world. Watching the sky and
everything in it.

Read a little, Shakespeare's Romeo and Juliet. Now my
eyes are tired. Think I will watch the sunset until it is
dark, and then look for you in my dreams.

Take care of yourself for me. I love you,
mb

From: JAZMAN@mbc.web
Sent: Thursday, July 18, 2002   8:43 AM
To: mbrogan@mbc.web
Subject: so quiet

Hey - I am alive! I missed you yesterday too. Our
client base is growing by leaps and bounds. So many
people lost a large chunk of their net worth in the stock
market in the past couple of years. Word of mouth
about our company's ability to create profitable
portfolios is beginning to keep us very busy.

Sounds like you had a mellow day. The only thing
missing would have been my embrace from time to
time, had I been there (smile.) I would have loved to
deliver that for you. Will have to rely on other
deliveries to show you how much you mean to me.

I'm tired and in love. Didn't sleep much last night,
tonight should be better. I want to be with you so
badly. I wish these obstacles were already out of the
way. I can't imagine wanting to do anything more than
laying next to you, and holding you... an occasional
kiss and wherever it leads us...

Thinking of you baby,

Jake

From: mbrogan@mbc.web
Sent: Thursday, July 18, 2002   10:05 AM
To: JAZMAN@mbc.web
Subject: loving expressions

I was running late again this morning so could not send
my usual morning email. As soon as I dropped the
phone from my hand after pillow talk, your spirit came
rushing in again. Passionately, completely. I have
learned to respond with my spirit instead of my body so
that our love making can last. My god Jake, it is so

amazing. Do you feel it? So much more real than it has ever been. I can still feel it.

Then, as I opened the door to my little office, the scent of orchids hit me like a wonderful surprise. Filling my office with orchids was an amazing gesture. I am sure I will be the talk of the company for quite some time. So very extravagant, which is not necessary. But so sweet, and greatly appreciated. I love you.

It will be a very intense, exciting day full of rapture and spikes and rushes of all kinds. I know it.

And know, above all else, that I love you.

mb

From: JAZMAN@mbc.web
Sent: Thursday, July 18, 2002 8:52 PM
To: mbrogan@mbc.web
Subject: RE: loving expressions

Can you call now?

From: mbrogan@mbc.web
Sent: Friday, July 19, 2002 5:55 AM
To: JAZMAN@mbc.web
Subject: morning comfort

Good morning my love. I took you to my healing place last night. Had to ask for help to hold you there. That is how I could tell that you were still upset. In many ways that you could not communicate last night. Which is fine. You talk when you can. And in the mean time, I will use everything I have to hold you. And comfort you. And create a place of empowerment for you. That place is my arms.

I think I even caught some glimpses of your dreams as you fell to sleep in my arms, in the healing place. And my hope for you is that you were able to work some things through for your self in dream so that today is more peaceful. Please carry my love with you from the moment you awaken, until you fall asleep again tonight. And reach out to touch me whenever you need to. I would love nothing more than to touch you today.

Your ex obviously intends to make this complicated and filled with conflict for you. All I can advise is that you do your best not to contribute to the complications and conflict. Don't take the bait. Just work the process. Don't take it personally. And keep communicating encouragement to your children. You will all get through it.

I am getting a bit better at handling our connection at times when you are upset. I am better able to check my doubt and worry and draw on my faith and the certainty of our love. It is like a skill set. I know when I feel like that, what to do to gain strength and bring power to the connection. Experience is helping me handle this better. The strength of my character provides the tools for processing. And our love increases the connection in time and duration and strength. All so amazing.

You wrote to me once, in May, "why do you worry so?" It was a poignant question that gave me insight into myself and has not left me. I do worry when we are connected and you are upset. But because of this question, am able to check that worry, and use higher level perceptions to process what I am experiencing. You help me in more ways than you will ever know. This is just one. A significant one.

I have much internal work to do this weekend. And a lot of work to do on the book. And a lot of spiritual energy to give to my relationships. But look forward most of all, to your voice, and your touch, and your love. I just don't see how I could ever live without it now. I don't know how I ever did before. You are splendid. And I am fortunate to have you here, so close, so completely within me. Thank you, for everything that you have done to get us here. God, I love you so.

I told Jack last night that I want him to meet you before he goes to school. I told him that I love you, and that this may just last (gentling him into it). And that I hope that you will be able to come to a game or two. So I would like you to meet him before hand. I don't know if this is logistically possible for us, but I wanted to put that out there verbally for him. He took it very well. He had a look in his eyes of such love and happiness, and gave me a big hug. And then he stayed very close to me in the kitchen while I finished cooking dinner, just talking about the day. At one point, I rested my head on his shoulder while we stood side by side. He moved toward me with a little hug. I am sure he will be fine with us. He is happy for me. When the time is right, your children will get there too. Because they will see the joy in you. And they love you. Don't lose sight of that in the difficult weeks to come. Have faith. Everything will be all right. In time. My love.

All yours,
mb

From: JAZMAN@mbc.web
Sent: Friday, July 19, 2002   8:52 AM
To: mbrogan@mbc.web
Subject: RE: morning comfort

Good morning, my Molly. Great news on Jack. Very cool.

Thanks for last night on the phone. And your loving words this morning. The best and the worst of life happening to me at once. Thank god for you. Your love brought me up a few notches immediately. I thought about not asking you to call, about leaving you

alone for the night because of all the unhappy stuff I am
going through. But I am so glad we talk. We get closer
every time I reach for you. Amazing.

I understand now that I need you in my life. I am not
used to needing someone, but I feel that with you and
don't seem to mind it. I like it really, it bonds us
together, doesn't it? Different than wanting you,
although I feel that always too. Last night's call was
very important to me. It wasn't as up as our other
phone conversations but so needed for me. You were
completely effective. Well done, by true and only love.
I love being loved by you. And hope I don't fail to
meet your expectations. I want this to work so badly
but know I am not perfect. And worry that I don't
deserve your love. I feel such admiration for you that I
feel just plain lucky. Then I remind myself that you
feel the same for me and I know that we are perfect for
each other - that neither will be happy without the
other. I am already happier with you than with anyone
in my past - other than you. My certainty level keeps
growing, even when I think it has maxed out.

It is harder to be apart from you now. These stressful
times actually bring us closer together. There is a good
indicator. I need you more and more and the love I feel
is totally out of control.
Less than a week now, and I will be in your arms. I
will come straight from the airport. I do have some
business and need time with my kids over the weekend
but want every spare minute spent with you. Our good
luck that Jack will be out of town with his dad. Do you
think this was meant to be? I do. Can you handle that?

Your, Jake

From: mbrogan@mbc.web
Sent: Friday, July 19, 2002 9:06 AM
To: JAZMAN@mbc.web
Subject: RE: morning comfort

I feel exactly the same. And can handle that asap

 lbj

From: JAZMAN@mbc.web
Sent: Friday, July 19, 2002   9:33 AM
To: mbrogan@mbc.web
Subject: RE: morning comfort

Just went outside to call you (because I love you so
fucking much) and my phone can't hold the charge
because of the dense fog this morning. If it doesn't
clear up before I leave for work I will just call you on
the land line.

I feel absolutely addicted to your love this morning.
And soooo happy that you love me. Thank you so
much. I can't get over the emotional rush to think of
anything else to say other than how much I love you
and miss you. And I want to share my entire life with
you. There isn't anyone else that would do. Can you
handle that?

On my way to work now. We can talk a lot today if
you like. I am totally in love.

lbj

From: mbrogan@mbc.web
Sent: Friday, July 19, 2002 6:00 PM
To: JAZMAN@mbc.web
Subject: weekend itinerary

I wonder how many minutes we spent on the phone
today: your lunch, my lunch, coffee breaks, on the way

home from work, after work (for me.) Your words, your laugh, your love fill me to the brim and keep that smile on my face.

I know that you are with your client (how I envy him.) Thought I would take this moment to get you my weekend schedule. Tomorrow morning I will spend with Meg. She has read my book and has some feedback. I am excited to hear it because she knows more about the details of my divorce than anyone. I am not sure I could have gotten through it without her.

Thank you Jake, for expressing your love for me in so many ways today. The beautifully bound books were delivered after work. The gift took my breath away. The complete works of Shakespeare bound in leather and gold. It was all heart felt and made me incredibly happy. You are so good to me and good for me and just plain good. And I love you. With all my heart. With every breath, every moment. I am alive, because you are finally with me.

In your arms,

mb

From: JAZMAN@mbc.web
Sent: Friday, July 19, 2002 10:41 PM
To: mbrogan@mbc.web
Subject: sweet dreams

Hello my Molly. Such the loving one. I look out past the trees and mountains onto the pink horizon and wish you were here with me to watch the sunset, together as one. I'm lonely and you are so needed and wanted. Soon we will be living together in the same space, together as happy as we can be. A complete reality. I need to hug you very soon. And it gets harder to be away from you as it gets closer to the time when I can hold you in my arms.

I love you. Just wanted to say that. I always will. I always have. I will never find another you, but if needed some day in the distant future, then I will find you again.

I hope your morning tomorrow is a happy one. It feels good to write to you again, to tell you my feelings, to know you are perfect for me, to be in love so deeply. Take care of yourself, baby. I am all yours.

Jake

From: mbrogan@mbc.web
Sent: Saturday, July 20, 2002 5:10 AM
To: JAZMAN@mbc.web
Subject: RE: sweet dreams

Oh Jake, I love you. Your email brought me to tears of joy this morning. Good way to start the day. Crying in my coffee.

I need to get an early start. Have quite a bit of housework to do before beginning my busy day. Jack will be going over to his dad's when he finally gets up.

I will get as far as I can here and then it is off to Meg's to go over the book. Her feedback should be good. She knows most of the story already, having lived it with me.

I should have my cell phone with me most of the time. If not, don't fret. I will get to you asap, my love.

I feel myself quieting. Still processing this thing with Sandy and having difficulty articulating. Please be patient with me for the next few days my love. Something is brewing. A change maybe. Or a calling. Or an inspiration. I will tell you when I can.

I think I understand the phrase "under my skin," finally.
I feel you within my skin. And with each thought of
you, my skin and the rest of me surge. I love you much
more than I can say. Much more than anyone can see
in my smile. Much more than I ever thought possible.

Sweet dreams to you, love. mb

From: JAZMAN@mbc.web
Sent: Saturday, July 20, 2002   10:05 PM
To: mbrogan@mbc.web
Subject: where are you?

Are you okay? Everything is going to voice mail -
home, cell. What's happening? I don't know if you're
sleeping and don't hear the phone or what. It feels like
you are very upset. I am VERY worried. Please make
contact.

From: JAZMAN@mbc.web
Sent: Sunday, July 21, 2002   1:23 AM
To: mbrogan@mbc.web
Subject: where are you?

It is almost one thirty and I just took a little peek at
some of you photos and got excited. Pillow talk tonight
was fantastic. Do you know we were on the phone for
over two hours? I am again, sorry that I forgot about
your thing with Sandy tonight. I felt your pain and
flipped. I, also, need to get a handle on this. I have so
much affinity for you. Am always wondering what
you're up to in your day to day life. Admiring how
you've handled all the crap you've had to deal with. I
could kick myself for not finding you earlier and
making your life better than it has been. And mine too,
for that matter. You are a fascinating individual and I
love to talk to you, look at you, think about you, love
you, everything and anything that involves you. I love
that we have this special thing with each other. I am
sooooooo happy that we fell in love so easily - both

ways. I want so badly to help you be happier than you've ever dreamed of. I love you, Molly. So much. We belong together forever.

Jake

From: mbrogan@mbc.web
Sent: Sunday, July 20, 2002 8:16 AM
To: JAZMAN@mbc.web
Subject: me and you

OK, crying now. Happier than I have ever been. More who I am than I have ever been. Closer to God than I have ever been. More alive than I have ever been. And certainly, more in love than I have ever been. Because of you. Thank you Jake. I love you so.

I am back to waking before sun rise. The weight of what I needed to do was exhausting. THANK YOU for seeing me through with that rare and wonderful unconditional support that only you have given me. You are such a blessing.

I will make my best effort to make sure that I don't worry you like I did last night. I can't believe that I did not miss my cell phone all day, forgetting it at home like that. I was so stressed and confused about what I was doing. Driven by faith and instinct really. Following blindly. But I will think about what happened and look for the lessons that will lighten that load and make the next experience easier on both of us. Two Sandy experiences without a cell phone – there must be something there.

I got to Sandy's late. We walked her daughter down to my house so that she could go to the gym with Jack. On the way back the MOST vivid and powerful telepathic glimpse for her overtook me and I could do nothing but share it with her, as it happened. At one point, I had to ask her to stop responding and let me continue so that I would not lose the message. I was crying, she was crying. I surely hope that she does not think I am a crack pot. I am not sure what I would think if the roles were reversed. Before this week, I have not seen her in about 25 years! And I hope it helps her with her decisions going forward. The danger I felt for her was so real. Afterward, we talked about possible paths for her to avoid the scene that I saw. God, I hope it helps. I still feel deeply connected to her and her brother. They are both wonderful people.

I am just so unsure about what I am doing here. Do I relax and allow it to just happen? Do I pay closer attention for clues that I would miss if I didn't? Do I talk about it, can I talk about it, or is it better to process quietly so as not to interfere with the process? Or maybe it isn't possible to process beyond the learning afterward. Maybe all I can know is within the experience itself. I have much to learn. But Jake, I am the luckiest person in the world because I found you. And you are so willing and understanding and loving. I am convinced that none of this would be possible without you. All of this is part of US. That you felt what you felt during my glimpse because you are an essential part of the process. It is the power of us. And we are just at the beginning.

I will spend the rest of my life convincing you that we both deserve this. And that I do not have one harmful intention toward you. That all of my doubts are self doubts. That creeps up about ME in times of anxiety. I might get angry at myself, but can't imagine being angry at you. And I will always turn to you, tell you what I am feeling if I can articulate. I promise you that I will not hold back. I KNOW that all of your intentions toward me are honest and loving. And that this is part of the strength of our connection. And why our match flows to and from heaven. And I thank god that I found you. You are a man of honorable intention. Great depth. Great compassion. And passion.(smile) So rare in this world. I am the lucky one.

I am not sure that I was able to make the result of this mistake better than things would have been had I not made the mistake. Which is what I like to do. I want so badly to make it up to you. Somehow. To simply tell you that you mean everything to me doesn't seem enough. But it is true. All things for me are now through you. It gives me great strength. And ability to "do" great things. And love with unimaginable depth. And tremendous happiness. I hope this morning kiss of passion begins to make up for any distress I may have caused. And am happy that our connection is stronger. That what flows between us has intensified. Become clear. More clean. Our love more vivid than ever.

Today, again, we are much better than ever. Thank you Jake.

Completely yours,
mb

From: JAZMAN@mbc.web
Sent: Sunday, July 21, 2002 11:04 AM
To: mbrogan@mbc.web
Subject: RE: me and you

Wow. What passion with words. Amazing. Got me "ready" in a hurry, honey Like intense foreplay. Whew. Now what am I supposed to do with this? It feels like it will last until I see you Thursday! What will happen when we see each other? I have imagined it so many times, so many different ways. So hard to wait as the time approaches.

Last night was SO intense. The not knowing what was happening with you was unbearable for me. Another interesting phenomena. I think I am just addicted to you, and have a hard time not knowing that you're OK and that we're OK. It's called maximum caring. But something "turned on." An impression from you or an earlier experience. There was some heavy worry for me as I felt something wrong in your space, but didn't know what. Then, what a relief when I knew you were OK. I have to learn to relax when you are MIA, but don't know if I ever will. I know you have a life outside of us, and that is fine. I just need to know you are OK, and be able to communicate with you if I feel something wrong. I am just so fucking in love and so far away.

But again, the worry and difficult experience convince me that we must be together. That WE are meant to be. So there. You keep reeling me in more and more, don't you baby? Fascinating that you do that by just being yourself.

Today, we begin at a higher level than yesterday, although that is hard to believe. We both feel the same increases in love at the same time, don't we? I am SO ready for a future with you. It is hard to wait. But we are close to the end of our separation now. I want to lie down with you and hold you for hours on end. And kiss you all over. And squeeze you so hard. And make you so happy. I love you Molly.

Jake

From: JAZMAN@mbc.web
Sent: Sunday, July 21, 2002 11:13 AM
To: mbrogan@mbc.web
Subject: RE: me and you

Just one more question, baby. Do you understand how perfect you are for me? I don't know if you realize that yet. It is important that you do because it is so true. There never has been anyone for me but you.

lbj

From: mbrogan@mbc.web
Sent: Sunday, July 21, 2002 1:23 PM
To: JAZMAN@mbc.web
Subject: RE: me and you

good morning love,

My love for you is suddenly rushing in. typing is
difficult. Breathing
rapid. God, I love you.

Spirit, not forsaking him,
Him you will cloud
Warm in the snow-whirl;
To warmth the Muses come,
Come the Graces.

Float around me, Muses
And you Graces!
Here is water, here is earth,
And the son of earth and water
Over whom I walk,
Godlike.

You are pure, like water's heart,
You are pure, like earth's marrow,
Round me you float and I
Float over water, over earth,
Godlike.
 - Goethe

The sun was up before I was. Rare and needed.
Hopefully, my sleepy Sunday morning caught me up
for the week. Because I have a lot of connecting to do
with you. Lot's of thoughtful emails to write. Lots of
phone conversations. Lots of meditating and spiritual
love making. Sigh.

Do I realize how perfect I am for you? I better realize
how perfect you are for me. And thank God each day

because you are now in my life. I certainly know your love for me. And the knowing brings implicit trust and growing affinity.

You will need to show me how perfect I am for you. And you do. By the reliability of your communication. By your complete, immediate responsiveness. With the way you listen so intently and hear with such understanding. By the way you enjoy sharing each day with me. By the unfolding of your love for me. By your need to join your life with mine. With your unconditional support. And the way you love every part of me. By the way that you continue to give me the best parts of you, every day, sometimes as soon as you discover them.

And you will, by the way that you look at me. By the light in your eyes that is only for me. By the smile you will smile whenever you see me. By the way you stand by me, touch me, protect me. By the way you make love to me.

And in all of these ways, I will show you, how perfect you are for me. My love.

All ways yours,
mbj

From: mbrogan@mbc.web
Sent: Monday, July 22, 2002 6:00 AM
To: JAZMAN@mbc.web
Subject: your love around me

Still sleepy this morning and running late, love. But I awoke, feeling your love wrapped around me like a comforter. Your comfort around me like a deep, unending kiss. I love you so Jake.

Can you call on the way to work? I have no meetings this morning and need desperately to hear your voice.

Had some very interesting dreams last night. In them, I looked very different than I do now, and so did you. But it was clearly us, living very differently in each dream. Same love, different settings. Fascinating really.

Call when you can love.

mb

From: mbrogan@mbc.web
Sent: Monday, July 22, 2002 3:30 PM
To: JAZMAN@mbc.web
Subject: daily lessons

Well, it is almost time to go home. I feel very quiet today. Quiet and extremely happy because of your maximum caring. Thank you.

I am beginning to get used to the idea that there is someone who understands me. An incredible feeling really. Something I did not think I could have in this lifetime. The wonderful part, is that you know and understand me without my having to communicate. Our communication is just something we do to continue the flow, to bring each other joy, to surprise eachother and to realize eachother. To allow our love to unfold and the world to open to us. So rare. Such a blessing.

I can be patient. Knowing that your love awaits me. The greatest reward I have ever known. I love you so much. And feel your arms around me constantly. Here is what I learned today:

I love your voice much more today than yesterday. Don't go swimming in a chlorinated pool after having an eye exam. The doctor says I may look like I have been on a bender for about a week, even with eye drops. (Had an eye exam Saturday morning before spending the morning/early afternoon in Meg's pool

Saturday.) It has been 10-15 years since I shopped for pretty sleep wear. I like it. Patience still is not easy for me, even after all these years. I could not live without our pillow talk. Let's not test that, ever. It keeps me going. And keeps me sane.

Bye for now love,
mbj

From: JAZMAN@mbc.web
Sent: Monday, July 22, 2002   8:34 PM
To: mbrogan@mbc.web
Subject: your amazing love

Thank you my love, for everything that you give to me. Your words bring me to a level of love I never dreamed existed. I am afraid that I don't deserve you. You are so amazing. Your warmth, your words, your caring and insight.

I am sorry that I have not been communicative. Our phone calls are getting me through. Meeting after meeting, I am thinking of you with every breath I take.

My X has been calling constantly. Occasionally I pick up because I worry that something has happened to the kids. But nothing has. Except that they have to deal with her raving. She has been fighting quite a bit with the Mike. And saying things to upset Grace. I can't imagine what it is like for them right now.

I will need to go there Friday and pick up my things. I am sure it will be ugly. But Thursday will be just for us. The calm before the storm. The time for us that nothing can effect. Nothing can touch.

As wonderful as this weekend will be with you, it will be difficult at home. Although the family has known that Friday I will be leaving the house for good, except to come back as a visitor, the knowing does not seem to make it easier. And she is getting crazier as the time approaches.

I will be glad when this has settled down and my Chi weekends are filled with you, and laying in your arms. And my home there is with you. Heaven, until I step out of the door.

Shall we go to the club this weekend? I will call and see who is booked. A long, slow dance and a little champagne will do us good. Is there anything else you would like to do while I am town? I would do anything with you. Although we may need to slip away into some private corner repeatedly. I am not sure if I will be able to keep my lips off you. You are exquisite.

I love that you are dreaming of different lifetimes together. Someday, we can tour them together. I will teach you how to go into a meditative state and review our past lives. It will be interesting to see how our viewpoints differ in lifetimes that we share. By doing it together, we can better determine our considerations and recurring patterns across lifetimes. We can get past the difficult lessons by understanding them. I love that you actually get this. Should we go to the beach for this long talk?

I will be tied up until pillow talk, baby. But then, I am all yours.

Jake

From: mbrogan@mbc.web
Sent: Tuesday, July 23, 2002 5:10 AM
To: JAZMAN@mbc.web
Subject: spiritual lessons

As the time approaches that you will be in my arms, my spirit soars higher and higher. As we grow closer, my spirit is blown wide open. I love it, as I love you. Did you know relationship should be like this? I think I sensed it, sensed all that love should be. But never dreamed that it was tied to awareness like this. Never understood the power of two. No wonder there is so much depression at the loss of great love. To have this, and then be without it, is unimaginable for me right now. Let's not ever test that Jake. This is for real, right? This is forever, isn't it? It certainly feels that way.

Well, so far I have had intuitive dreams of us on a beach, us in Europe before the Renaissance, and us as Western Europe nobility. All so different. We look different, feel differently about eachother, live differently. This is all so interesting. Please tell me more about how to explore this.

I don't know if I have had dreams like this before. But I think our love gives me a heightened ability for glimpses of others and into myself. All quite amazing. I had all but stopped thinking about any of this stuff before you came into my life. Content to live like others do, tied to this time with little depth.

I love you Jake, all ways.

mbj

From: JAZMAN@mbc.web
Sent: Tuesday, July 23, 2002 9:33 AM
To: mbrogan@mbc.web
Subject: RE: spiritual lessons

You are the most unique woman I have known. Do you realize that? Well, you are. And I love you for that and may other qualities. You are everything a man could hope for. Lucky for me that not many other guys have realized it or I would might not be the lucky one. I wish I had opened my eyes a little wider 30 years ago.

I am going to call you in a few minutes, baby. I love you very deeply.

Your, Jake

From: mbrogan@mbc.web
Sent: Tuesday, July 23, 2002 6:54 PM
To: JAZMAN@mbc.web
Subject: busy day

Sorry that there were no emails today, love. Jack just left for the gym so I finally have a minute to myself. Our phone calls got me through the day. Without our morning and lunch talks, and of course, pillow talk, I would be lost.

The routing supervisor went on emergency medical leave to have a triple by-pass today. I have been told that I will be taking over her responsibilities. Today was spent scrambling and trying to figure out the details of that job. Nine people route and check in roughly 1200 jobs in the North Chicago market daily. And the work HAS to get done. The next 8-10 weeks will be hectic juggle both jobs.

After our lunch talk I had to close the door and feel your love wash over me. I closed my eyes and felt wave after wave of your love wash over me. Hearing your voice echoing in my heart. Feeling your love all through me. Coursing through me like the blood in my veins. My pulse/your love = my life. God, I love you.

I found one of my old poems, written in '96 – I've decided to use it as a prelude for, and possibly the name of, my book:

Remember Me

Remember me
Near the long day's end

When moonlight
Initiates your heart
To the journey of your soul.

Remember me clearly
As I stand, paused,
Listening for your soft entreat.
Waiting to offer a touch of kindness.
Understanding what you have to offer
Of your mind, emotion and being.

As our spirits fly
In parting dance
I will wrap you in comfort
And keep you close
Until you next
Remember me.

I was loving you even then, Jake.

mbj

From: JAZMAN@mbc.web
Sent: Wednesday, July 24, 2002 9:24 AM
To: mbrogan@mbc.web
Subject: RE: busy day

Wow, baby. You wrote that back then? A beautiful
poem that really communicates to me. My God honey,
that was very nice. Interesting, that I made my final
decision to end my marriage in 1996, when you wrote
your poem. Too bad I wasn't more open for you, but I
didn't feel ready to leave my kids at that time. I wish
we could get a do over and have children together. You
and I together with half the parenting job would've done
an absolutely marvelous job. Well, there's always next
time, right? And I will be totally honored to be the man
that fathers you children, my love. Absolutely honored.
We'll pull in some really able beings and have a joyous
time raising them in their new lives. And when the

time comes, we'll help them remember their pasts so they can understand what's really happening. False ideas never helped anyone. Our kids will know the truth and be so much better for it.

I will call you on the way to work, so I can tell you how great you are and that you are the best woman in the universe for me. I love you and it's a very pure, clean love. That's the best kind, baby. I just didn't know what it was before.

Jake
From: mbrogan@mbc.web
Sent: Wednesday, July 24, 2002 10:50 AM
To: JAZMAN@mbc.web
Subject: RE: busy day

Looks like another crazy day here. Got called into work very early with a routing problem. But I wanted to tell you how much your call and letter meant to me this morning. Your voice, sends me straight into a soothing, fully loved state of mind.

I know the waiting has been difficult. But when our time comes (tomorrow!) all of the pieces will be in place. It will be perfect because of the waiting. And worth the wait. Mostly because of you, my love. You have been much stronger than I have in making sure that everything is done in the proper time. And that strength is part of why I love you so. Your strength, intelligence, wisdom, creativity, understanding, gentleness, passion, compassion. Our values and morals are in tune. Our world view, for the most part, in line. Our dreams and visions forming. Our desires and passion for each other growing. MUCH more today than yesterday. And all of our touching today, will lead to more tomorrow.

With you all ways,
mbj

From: JAZMAN@mbc.web
Sent: Wednesday, July 24, 2002 11:22 PM
To: mbrogan@mbc.web
Subject: RE: busy day

I hope you are home. You may be asleep. I should
have sent you a couple of letters so that you could read
them while you were up.

I want to hold you and feel you right now. Can you feel
me moving into your space? Sharing it. Holding you.
Loving you. Oh, I do love you.

Time to wake you for pillow talk.

Only yours,
Jake

From: JAZMAN@mbc.web
Sent: Thursday, July 25, 2002 10:32 AM
To: mbrogan@mbc.web
Subject: coming to you

Am leaving for the airport. But wanted you to know
before I leave, that I love you very much Molly. And
look forward to showing you in every possible way
soon.
I will call you on the way to the airport. Molly, you are
everything to me.

I will be at your place shortly after you get home from
work. Should I rent a van, in case we can't make it too
far down the road before we need to make out?

The waiting will soon be over.

All my love,

Jake

From: JAZMAN@mbc.web
Sent: Tuesday, July 30, 2002 10:32 PM
To: mbrogan@mbc.web
Subject: holding you

Just got in and settled. Want so much to be holding you right now. I was so glad to be there with you when Meg got the call to come in for her transplant yesterday. Did she realize what she interrupted when she called at 5:30 AM? Actually, any time she called from Sunday to Monday would have caught us in the same way. Christ, I can't get enough of you. Please tell me the latest on her recovery. Has she regained consciousness? Is it normal to keep her on an epidermal for so long? Were there complications in the surgery?

You know her, so you can keep in touch. It was an amazing experience to be with you during her "visitation" to you while she was in surgery. I was glad to be able to help you both. You got a little worked up for a couple of minutes. Operations often result in exteriorization and release from suffering. People become aware of options they didn't know they had. She needs to be reminded of all the reasons to stay with us for now. But in the end, it is her decision. My guess is, she associated being out of her body with death and became anxious. The fact that she pulled your spirit to her is a sign of how close you two are, and the strength of your spirits. She probably intuitively knew that you are aware enough to help her when she needed it.

Just keep helping her with your prayers. Whatever you do, it works, baby. Believe me.

Staying with you in your home feels so right. There is such peace there. You have created a real sanctuary from the chaos in the world. Even for me, when things were so crazy after leaving her home. Her "fax machine sounding" (as you so aptly put it) emotions

bled over into me and I was so upset until I stepped into
your home, and into your waiting arms. And then, once
again, the world was all right. God, Molly, life with
you will be so rich and so full of love. I can hardly wait
until we are in one home permanently. The fact that we
managed to have such a rich and loving weekend in the
midst of all the crisis just confirms my belief that we
are so right for each other. And together, we can
handle anything. Do you feel that honey?

Our one night out this weekend was amazing. I hope
you didn't mind staying in so much. I just can't get
enough of you. Need to feel every part of you. To
show you how much I love you. Do you think I will
ever want to go out again? Of course I will. I must
really be missing you already. Fear grips me when I
think that you may not always feel the way you now do
for me. Now that you have shown me what love can
be, how could I ever live without you?

I needed a night out after having to leave the kids with
her. I felt so bad for them. I was able to speak to each
of them privately and they told me they understood.
But their faces when I left.... And Grace really fell
apart when we told her we were divorcing. I hope she
can forgive me.

Friday was a horrible day. But then came our night out.
The contrasting high and the low of that day was
amazing. Our dance at the club, I will never forget that
either. The band just happened to be there, but I could
not have picked a better one. That little trio seemed to
be improvising to suit our romantic mood, didn't it?
Christ, I love dancing with you, sweetheart.

Well, by now, you should be surrounded by some of
your favorite flowers. I wonder if you have discovered
the gift that I left. I know I should not try to be so
clever, but I didn't want to give you a chance to return
it right away. When I saw it, I knew that you should

wear it. Diamonds and emeralds will heighten our spiritual connection. My love will flow more freely to you, if that is possible. I just wanted some guarantees that will continue. I need to find you while so far away, and hold you the only way I can. I hope you will agree to wear it. I love you so, and want you to remember that always.

I was shocked when you gave me a set of keys to your place. I loved the Lapis pendant, an extraordinary piece. So that was your mission to the Renaissance Fair, wasn't it? I wondered at the time… When you told me the stone would help keep us close I almost fell out of bed. Because, as you can see, I planned to use just that line with your bracelet! We are on the same wavelength, honey. And I love it.

Yours,
Jake

From: mbrogan@mbc.web
Sent: Wednesday, July 31, 2002 5:01 AM
To: JAZMAN@mbc.web
Subject: RE: holding you

As I begin this email, your whisper "I love you" echoed in my head, and my heart, right down to my soul (and my sex) and now my fingers are not working too well, and my skin is hot, and I love you so. God, so much, it is hard to stay in my body, even when awake. Your love propels me in so many ways. Thank you.

I have been sending reassurance to Meg all night, all morning and will keep doing so. When she comes around, she will be in so much discomfort. She will need all of hers and everyone else's' strength to hold on to her healing intentions. I said thank you prayers again this morning. My heart would have broken had I lost her…thank God that did not happen!

Meg's sister told me that one of the lungs was very disintegrated and difficult to remove. This is why the operation took so long and why she is being kept so sedated. It was not SOP. The condition of her old lungs complicated the procedure. Looks like I will be praying for several days more.

I also, am very glad you were here with me when I got the call from Meg and experienced what I did during her surgery. I have never been whisked away in spirit like that before while awake. Sitting in my home with you and being in the operating room with her at the same time was an incredible experience. I was just beginning to understand what was happening when suddenly, anxiety rose in me like a sink filling with water, Meg's anxiety. So odd, to be able to see all of the details of the operating room. And to see Meg out of her body, looking like she was ready to go out for the night. But she was really ready to leave this life. I said everything I could to her to convince her to choose life. I hope that I helped her. I hope that I did the right things. Then, I am not sure what you said, but while you were talking to me it was as if someone pulled the plug in that sink and the anxiety drained just as quickly as it rose. Meg re-entered her body on the operating table and I returned to you.

This experience was more amazing than the one with Sandy. But it had the same feeling of being in two places at once, yet totally connected to all of life. I really think it has something to do with my love for you: the power of US. I was never this sensitive before, love.

I got an email from Sandy this morning telling me that her attorney will be meeting with her X to try to settle things between them without court action. She promised to let me know how it goes. That tells me that she heard me (smile.) Hopefully, she doesn't think me a lunatic.

I certainly did feel your passionate kisses last night. I could tell you were sending them while awake, because I felt us fall asleep together. Probably why I dreamt so profoundly. I am the luckiest woman I know, because you love me. I only want to become your partner for the rest of my life. I can say this so easily because I know your tenderness. And know that you want what is best for me. And that because of this, my life with you will include all that is necessary for my happiness. You will make sure of it. I know it. And will make sure that it is an exchange of abundance between us. This creates the implicit trust necessary for our spiritual flight. That happened so quickly between us. But you make sure we create it every day. I love you for that, Jake. For showing me all that love can be - and because you are who you are. The man I love entirely.

I cannot thank you enough for (all of) the roses and the beautiful bracelet. Again, it is too much, but I do appreciate your generosity, and everything else about you. You are so thoughtful. I often touch it while meditating. I am sure it brings us closer, love. Thank you. I am uneasy accepting expensive gifts. You seem to give them so freely. Much admiration. I am sure there is a lesson in accepting love in here for me. You are wonderful to teach it to me.

Hold me close love,
mbj

From: JAZMAN@mbc.web
Sent: Wednesday, July 31, 2002 9:06 AM
To: mbrogan@mbc.web
Subject: RE: holding you

If only I could hold you close right now, I would be a very happy guy. I am with you baby, in more ways than you know. And about those passionate kisses…mmmm. I really need some of those right now.

We will start with those and see where they take us. Your clothes may not stay on for long. Those kisses sound too good.

Your words are so soothing and arousing at the same time. I don't have the words to describe the way you make me feel, to be loved by you the way you do. It is beautiful and calming. The strong sexual urges are clean and pure because they are based on love. I love it and I love you.

Well, I am overwhelmed with love right now. I will shoot this over to you now, my only real love, the one I so belong with. The one that I can never get enough of – ever.

I will call on the way to the office.

Lovin' you baby,

Jake

From: mbrogan@mbc.web
Sent: Wednesday, July 31, 2002 1:05 PM
To: JAZMAN@mbc.web
Subject: RE: holding you

Hi sweetheart. Went down to the river for lunch and dreamt of you as the world drifted past.

Had an email from Viv when I returned from lunch! She sent me pictures of her wedding last month to Shane. She seems gloriously happy. She has barely changed since high school, hasn't she? She is still so beautiful. I am past Greek because of her. Can we make plans for a weekend in New York? I would love to see her.

I am still reworking some of Remember Me. The Mary Margaret character is tricky to develop since she is so close to my own character, but has many dimensions to her that cannot be of me. Certainly one of the missing pieces of the character is that true love never found her. And while she had experiences of awareness, she did not understand them. Or integrate them. I thought the poem might bring the beginning and the end full circle. The book will leave my past behind.

Would you like to read the book when it is finished? Let me know what you think. I think I love you. With all my heart. For ever. And ever.

Your baby, mbj

From: JAZMAN@mbc.web
Sent: Wednesday, July 31, 2002 4:11 PM
To: mbrogan@mbc.web
Subject: RE: holding you

Hi baby. So Viv got married again. Yes, she is still very pretty. They make a good looking couple. I would love to see them at some point. Actually, I would like to meet all of your friends. You seem so close to all of them. Must be a good reason for that.

Last weekend was so nice with you. The passionate kisses, some soft, some more aggressive, mmmm, you do it to me, baby. And you know it, don't you? We will have a lot of that. Our time is closing. And your warm wetness, I can't get it off of my mind.

I was so worked up there, and she called again. She has been calling constantly, but won't let me speak to the children. I am very worried about Grace. She sent me a hostile email. Well, I am not sure if she actually sent it, or if her mom is running a game. It is so hard not to be able to reach them. Mike's cell phone is off for some reason. I will call the wireless provider tomorrow and see what the story is. She pays all of the bills so I would not be surprised if she had it turned off. I will need to take over the bills. God, it is hard to be so far from the kids and so worried about them.

Well, as I read this over, I can see it took a major nose dive. No longer the romantic love letter it started as. I do love you baby. It really helps to be able to talk to you about this. You have been through it, and made it. I so admire you for that.

I am coming into town next Saturday morning but have to leave Sunday night. I have been told I can't stay at her house anymore. Would you like some company? (smile) Will Jack be home? Is the beach house ready?

How is Meg?

Jake

From: mbrogan@mbc.web
Sent: Wednesday, July 31, 2002 7:44 PM
To: JAZMAN@mbc.web
Subject: RE: holding you

Your timing is impeccable. Jack will be out of town with his brother at a weekend football camp Saturday and Sunday. How do you do it? It always works out so well.

You have the keys…this is your home now. Don't worry sweetheart. This will work out. I love having you here. Jack leaves for school early, I think the weekend after next, because of the Augustana football camp. I will get specific dates for you. Actually, I would love for him to meet you before he leaves for school. If you do come to one of his games, you shouldn't be a stranger.

Jake, I hope you understand. This is you home now too. That is the way it has to be. The transition may be a little rough. But when your kids are ready, you are more than welcome to bring them here to spend time with you. I would be glad to take down my family pictures and redecorate a bit so that is a more neutral environment for all of our children. Sounds like your X does not intend to make it easy for any of you. But you will all get through this, love.

Meg is still sedated with epidermal medication. I am told that will continue for at least a week. That sounds so extreme, but so does a complicated double lung transplant. Her vital signs are all strong. I continue my prayers for her healing. I envision her as a body of light, and see the color of each of her chakras intensifying in color. I see her heart expanding and becoming the center of her entire energy so that she has the courage needed to maintain her commitment to life.

What we have is so right. The strength of our love will get us through. And in time, our children will understand the depth of love and respect between us. And begin to smile our unending smile with us - the smile that comes from our love.

Forever yours,

mbj

M ONTH FOUR

From: JAZMAN@mbc.web
Sent: Thursday, August 1, 2002 1:05 AM
To: mbrogan@mbc.web
Subject: RE: holding you

You did it again! Your words in this letter, your voice
during pillow talk, your spirit that is always with me,
actively loving me. God, I am so in love. Your are so
perfect. We are so perfect.

You are right. We do have a great relationship, the best
for me certainly, and it is way beyond what most people
can comprehend. Just want to be with you, live with
you, and create with you in all ways. It will be so much
greater once we have each other in our arms and are
fully sharing our lives. This intense, love based
sexuality is so heavy for me sometimes. My desire for
you is almost more than I can deal with. But I have so
far. If it was only physical, it would be so easy to turn
off. Clearly, it is soooooo much more than physical.
Two more days and I can show you what I mean.

I love you, baby.

Jake

From: JAZMAN@mbc.web
Sent: Thursday, August 1, 2002 1:32 AM
To: mbrogan@mbc.web
Subject: RE: holding you

I enjoyed our pillow talk. I enjoy your beingness. I
love you more than I can say. I really, really want you
with me so badly that it is difficult to deal with
sometimes. Does that make sense? You have the
ability to make me so happy and use it so well. I want
to be with you forever. I need to be with you forever.
You are the one and only, baby.

Jake

From: mbrogan@mbc.web
Sent: Thursday, August 1, 2002 5:28 AM
To: JAZMAN@mbc.web
Subject: RE: holding you

Trouble sleeping, sweetheart? Your emails are so
endearing. They filled me with rapture this morning.
Can you feel it? As if we did not stop making love all
night long. Again. Is that what kept you awake?

You are my one and only too. That thought makes me
immeasurable happy. You make me so happy. Thank
you. Jack just got up, so early. I will write again when
I can from the office.

I love you.
Molly

From: JAZMAN@mbc.web
Sent: Thursday, August 1, 2002 8:34 AM
To: mbrogan@mbc.web
Subject: RE: holding you

Slept in a bit after a restless night. Yes, holding you in spirit all night got me through. The softness, the warmth, you are incredible.

She called this morning to scream at me. But did let me talk to Grace, who was so cold and obviously unhappy. I am in such pain because I cannot help her. I feel so far away and helpless.

The ex will really get wild when I turn Mike's cell phone on today. I told her I planned to do it. I refuse to play her games.

Need to run baby. Have a hectic day ahead. Loving you always.
Jake

From: mbrogan@mbc.web
Sent: Thursday, August 1, 2002 7:26 PM
To: JAZMAN@mbc.web
Subject: a moment

We have both had days that kept us away from each other, haven't we? Seemed so odd, to not hear your voice or read your words for hours on end.

Hopped around town and picked up a few things for a gift basket for Meg's homecoming. An angel of courage. A journal. A silver finish bookmark engraved with a quote by Edith Warton "There are two ways of spreading light: to be the candle or the mirror that reflects it." Small box of note cards and stationary. A book called Hugs for Friends. A beautiful rose quartz and silver rosary. Luckily, the summer sales were going on in all the shops so it was fun and painless.

I also made her one of the poems in a frame that I make. I had a stained glass frame on hand. Bordered the following poem with stencils and ink:

The Road of Life
I expect to
Pass through this world but once.
Any good therefore
That I can do
Or any kindness that I can show
Any fellow creature
Let me do it now...
For I shall not
Pass this way again.

It was the saying on the mass card at her father's funeral. I put the mass card that I kept in a frame that she gave me for my birthday and keep on my dresser. She has always liked it. Now, she has one of her own.

So, I think I am ready to pay her a visit when she is stronger. She is still sedated. Her sister thinks that will end this weekend. They are unsure about a release date. Keep a good thought...

I wanted so many times today to look at your sweet face and tell you that I love you. God, I love you.

Yours,

mbj

From: mbrogan@mbc.web
Sent: Friday, August 2, 2002 5:01 AM
To: JAZMAN@mbc.web
Subject: missed you

Missed you for pillow talk last night. That is a first, isn't it? You were right, a hectic day for you! I hope you felt my love there with you.

Call today if you can. I miss you.

mbj

From: mbrogan@mbc.web
Sent: Friday, August 2, 2002 3:03 PM
To: JAZMAN@mbc.web
Subject: missing you

Crazy day at work. So many routing problems. Our talk at lunch was most welcome.

I am sorry things are so difficult for Grace, but glad that she is communicating to you, even if she is just saying what your X is telling her to say. Your response will put her at ease, and that is much needed.

Your X seems to be upset that you are not staying at her house anymore even though she has forbidden it. The anger and betrayal may be intensifying. And knowing you, that will be difficult. I must say, I thought you two were well beyond the kind of attachment that her emotions are indicating.

I know this. The mystical Jews, and many other religions, consider forgiveness the highest, most excellent human quality. And there can be no trust or forgiveness without betrayal. This may be Grace's initiation into forgiveness. How could she experience great forgiveness without betrayal? Given time, she WILL find her way back. You are her father. And believe me, every girl needs her father. Sooner or later, she will find her way back. And learn many lessons in trust and forgiveness on the way. With patience and guidance, those lessons could be your gift to her.

You may just need to give it time for emotions to cool. This thing will have to run its course. These emotions, although a bit intense, are typical. It is VERY hard to be on the receiving end.

However you decided to handle the end of your marriage, I will support you. I suppose that means even if you decide to return to the marriage for Grace's sake. I didn't mean to upset you when I told you that I had a glimpse of that the other night. Maybe it was just a fearful fantasy. Right or wrong, that is your decision, dear. And I love you enough to know that you will search your soul and do what you believe is the best. And I believe in you. And hold you with an open hand. With patience. And understanding. What is best for you, is best for me.

I do wish that you would let me hold you. I can help. I won't judge. And although I did freak out a bit when I thought you were thinking of returning to the marriage, I will survive whatever comes, as long as we face it together, honestly and clearly. No hiding.
Molly

From: mbrogan@mbc.web
Sent: Saturday, August 3, 2002 12:12 AM
To: JAZMAN@mbc.web
Subject: new morning

Good Morning Sweetheart,

I know you are leaving very early for the airport and wanted to have a little something for you in your mailbox before you shut your computer down for the weekend. I hope you had a good night's sleep. My dreams were not the usual good work that I have, more conflict and unpleasantness than normal. My worry I suppose.

My wish for you is this, that you have a much better day today. When your day begins to slide, I am here for you. And will send all that theta your way to remind you that you are loved completely. That, according to natural law, you have acted on value, done the right thing. In order to show your children the importance of love. And then when love is missing in a relationship, it has run its course. It is essential to the soul to move on, and continue to move toward love and growth. Your children will learn just how to conduct themselves during difficult times by watching you now. Let all that negativity roll off of you. Keep your perspective. Act on value. Keep smiling.

Most of all, please remember, that every minute of every day, someone out there believes that everything about you is worth loving completely. Remember that you are entirely loved. And that you now have someone who was willing to wait a very long time to find you, and begin living soul to soul.

A kiss for you,

Molly

From: JAZMAN@mbc.web
Sent: Monday, August 5, 2002 8:34 AM
To: mbrogan@mbc.web
Subject: A new day

Thanks for that late night/early morning pillow talk after I got home. We were getting into it at the end there, weren't we baby? A little sexual playfulness can help more than just physical pain.

How is Meg? Have you heard anything?

I feel guilty for having so many emails from you and not answering them. Our phone calls at the end of the week saved me. What a time I have had the past several days. I felt my ex's evil intentions toward me all weekend and Grace's resentment toward me. I have so many business deadlines looming and am falling

behind schedule. But there is one constant for me –
you. I am so sorry I did not get to see you this trip.
You are my stability these days and I really need you.
Getting a divorce attorney is a priority. If I can get an
appointment, I will come in next weekend. I need to
see you and stay for a night or two. Or ten. Or forever.
I wish I could take you away from everything for
awhile. No cell phones, nothing but us.

I will remember you forever. And plan to BE with you
forever. About the possibility of my going back to her –
negative. But thanks for saying you would support my
decision. It would not be that though. I will say that
while I was holding Grace and drying her tears, I was
feeling regret – but I could not go back to the marriage.

My back is killing me today. I haven't been in pain for
a long time. It probably comes from the high stress
level. I think I will lie down and call you.

Love you, baby -- Jake

From: mbrogan@mbc.web
Sent: Monday, August 5, 2002 9:30 AM
To: JAZMAN@mbc.web
Subject: RE: new morning

No guilt necessary. I knew you were having a hard
time. The hard part for me is that I want to comfort
you, and I am so far away. But even if I were there,
you would need to turn to me. Can't really connect
until then.

Evil intentions, interesting way to put it. I think the
best way to process them is to recognize them and ask
yourself: do I have any part in this? If the answer is no,
let it roll off. If the answer is yes, self-examination and
possibly correction is necessary. It is hard NOT to
react emotionally, but necessary for your peace of
mind. You are not responsible for someone else's

negative emotions or intentions, unless they are mirroring something in you that requires your attention.

You may want to gel your plans to meet with an attorney while they still have time in their schedule. If you wait too long, you might not be able to get the appointment you need.

Grace's resentment, might just be a product of immaturity and being placed in the middle. Give her time. If she gets frantic with it, pull back and give her a little space. Let her responses dictate your efforts. But don't give up. Just stay sweet and consistent (in other words, you.)

Happy to know your intention is to be with me forever. Beginning with a man still in the midst of an ending is uncharted territory for me. Your reassurance is most appreciated.

Please do lie down and call me AMAP. We will get that back feeling better, and lots of other things. I will find you in our sacred place and kiss you gently – touch you heart to heart – crawl inside and message your back – infuse your back with my love and bring the earth and sky together to heal you. I love you Jake. We need to re-establish your peace. Let's keep working on that.

With you all ways,

Molly

From: mbrogan@mbc.web
Sent: Monday, August 5, 2002 2:58 PM
To: JAZMAN@mbc.web
Subject: RE: new morning

Your love just washed over me. Were you thinking of me? My love for you is brighter than our star, deeper than all of our lives together. MUCH wider than the smile on my face when I think of you. God, I love you Jake.

Meg is somewhat more lucid now that they have taken her off the epidermal. They have her on a morphine drip, so much that she is not making sense. She calls me often, thinking she is calling her husband or someone else. It is that connection between us, and I find it comforting. She is having a rough time, but moving along in the recovery. Still no date for release from the hospital.

I will keep you posted.
Molly

From: JAZMAN@mbc.web
Sent: Monday, August 5, 2002 6:00 PM
To: mbrogan@mbc.web
Subject: Hi

Hi baby, and thanks for all of that theta work. My back is so much better. You are amazing. I know that you are not getting the attention you deserve, but I am trying. I should be making love with you right now. Instead, I am swamped at work with a dozen new clients, dodging calls from her to avoid her bad temper – when all the time I am thinking of you. I will call soon. We are going to be very happy together, wait and see.

Love,
Jake

From: mbrogan@mbc.web
Sent: Tuesday, August 6, 2002 5:01 AM
To: JAZMAN@mbc.web
Subject: RE: Hi

Don't worry about me. Although I was a bit worried about you yesterday when you were silent until pillow talk. Thanks for being so consistent with that. I have become so dependent on it. I wake up for it, whether the phone rings or not. Because you are important to me. And I am here for you when it becomes our time. In the mean time, passionate spiritual kisses here and there. Just for you. I am happy with you now. And will be always. So here is a gift for you:

Through you

Every moment
Of each day
You are with me
In voice
In spirit
In the way that your love
Colors all that I see
Harmonizes all that I hear
Adds a touch of ecstasy
To all that I feel
Every moment.

Each moment
I feel you
In every part of me
In each breath that I take
Each expression of me
Each smile
Each movement
Each sound
And each silence.
You are here
In all ways
Within me.

It is so.
I am reborn
Into you,
Through you.
From now on

All of me
Can only become
Real
Through you,
My love.
Always,
Through you.

Love,

Molly

From: JAZMAN@mbc.web
Sent: Tuesday, August 6, 2002 8:25 AM
To: mbrogan@mbc.web
Subject: RE: Hi

Good morning baby. The first thing I want to say to
you is that I love you. God, do I ever. And although it
is so natural and you are so familiar, it still amazes me
sometimes. Thank you for your beautiful words. I am
honored that they are for me.

My back is completely healed today. Thanks, for
whatever you did. And thanks for being you. I need
you in so many ways. I want you in so many more. I
don't ever want you to get enough of me. I can see this
is going to be another wild emotional day. If you were
here, and we could, I would be looking for the nearest
justice of the peace. I feel so ready for that with you.
The complete opposite of what I just got out of. I did
learn a lot from that one though. What I need and want,
what I really need to offer you, the concept of
exchanging in abundance, each taking 100%
responsibility for the other, and more. Then throw in
this active love life we are going to have and I just
don't know what to say. We will have the ideal
relationship. Almost is now but we don't see each
other enough, soon to be remedied. But I will
appreciate our time together much more, and appreciate

you much more when that time arrives. Our base is becoming so strong because we're building it that way, you and me. We'll have our hurdles, but together we can overcome whatever is waiting for us.
Love - Jake

From: mbrogan@mbc.web
Sent: Tuesday, August 6, 2002 10:23 AM
To: JAZMAN@mbc.web
Subject: healing together

Your words...well, I had to shut my office door after reading them. This morning, before my first yawn, I found you. Kissed you many times. Wrapped myself around you. And took you with me to Meg. I needed your strength. Thank you so much. Whenever I began to lose focus in the healing meditation, you gave me strength with your voice or spiritual touch, or just your presence next to me, always with me. Until, together, we left her to rest. You are so wonderful for me. Thank you.

She is increasingly uncomfortable. I will need to call her sister today to make sure she is not having complications. May just be the natural progression of things as they move her from one anesthetic to another. But she is down. I try to keep her working on a future vision, and all she will be able to do when she is healed. I reminded her that leaving her body relieves her physical pain. But she is still not comfortable with that. So I associated it with the Lord's prayer. That comforted her and relaxed her. I may keep doing that. I am just trying anything to raise her spirit.

Worked on your back before I left you to your dreams. I was hoping you would wake up with less discomfort. Don't know if the relief came from the job that I did on your lap or your back. Both probably. I enjoy them both. Because I love you. Christ, I love you more than words can say, Jake. And, I am thinking good thoughts for your children, to bring them to you.

Woke up with a headache today. Not excruciating, but very nagging. Took something right away to keep it at bay. Remembered something too. Vague, visual, emotional, having many levels. I was somewhere in Western Europe. I had strawberry blonde hair. Female. Great emotional pain. And physical pain. And struggle – for survival maybe. Lots of green – trees, grass, hills. A very dark home. Physically and in the psychic sense. That is all I can put into words. For now. Not enough to keep the head ache away I guess.

Well, I am going to print copies of my book today so that my (friends) editors can read and tell me what they think. Let me know when you can free up a weekend to read it. I will be glad to autograph your copy (smile.)

I am yours. Completely in every moment,

Molly

From: JAZMAN@mbc.web
Sent: Tuesday, August 6, 2002 7:44 PM
To: mbrogan@mbc.web
Subject: RE: healing together

I know that I haven't been around much today baby. Short phone conversations, no emails. Let me make it up to you with passionate kisses tonight after pillow talk. God, I love meeting you spiritually. But love being with you more.

It is shaping up to look like I will be in Chi the next three weekends, maybe more. The clubs need attention. She is screaming at me and I really need to see my kids. And I need to set up an appointment with an attorney. Could you stand to see me that much? Maybe my company will help you get over missing Jack so much, now that he has left for college. It would certainly help me get over missing you so much. And I do baby, every minute.

I've never loved like this before. Just wanted to tell you that.

Forever yours,

Jake

From: mbrogan@mbc.web
Sent: Wednesday, August 7, 2002 4:56 AM
To: JAZMAN@mbc.web
Subject: healing together, loving eachother

Oh Jake, during my healing meditation with Meg this morning I burst into tears. Your spirit held me while I cried awhile. It is as if her spirit is weak. Is that possible. Before and after, OUR healing was wonderful. But I don't know how to help Meg. I love you so, Jake. Do I say that too much? It feels like I can't say it enough.

I also did the same meditations while I was falling asleep last night. You were holding me, we were with Meg, and then the fax machine noise kicked in. That unbearable screeching that forced me to let go of you. I stayed with Meg alone awhile before waking. Did your X call you? That has happened before to me while I was with your spirit, and the noise came up because she called you.

Still want to be in your arms,
Molly

From: JAZMAN@mbc.web
Sent: Wednesday, August 7, 2002   9:06 AM
To: mbrogan@mbc.web
Subject: RE: healing together, loving eachother

No baby, you don't say it too much. Use me as you
need to. I am glad to give what strength I can. I have
so much more to say about Jack, Western Europe, and
your book. But it is hard to get past my emotion for
you. Today is already an intense emotional day. The
affection is of such magnitude. I always feel it and it's
always love, but today, it is so intense, at a continuous
spike level. I can't even imagine what will happen
when we can finally live together. But I do love it so.
We need to take a tour of our pasts together soon, my
only love, and also get on with our future together. I
love you so much, baby.

Yes, she called. But don't worry about it. I can handle
it. You are amazing, do you know that? So perceptive,
and sensitive. Do you think that's why I love you so?
It goes deeper than just the past experiences. I know I
admire you a great deal, I feel incredibly close to you,
most of my thought processes either start or end with
you, and I can't imagine not being with you. You know
I am in love with you, don't you baby?

Yours,
Jake

From: mbrogan@mbc.web
Sent: Wednesday, August 7, 2002 11:13 AM
To: JAZMAN@mbc.web
Subject: why

Do you realize that each day this week your morning
call is made as you are arriving at the office? You used
to call as you were leaving the house. That was just an
observation. It is almost as if you call when you have
little time to talk. Too many other calls?

The depth of our love is astounding isn't it? I thought that I had loved with depth before. And I suppose, compared to all that I saw around me, I did. But it was nothing like this. I just had no idea. Could it be the exchange of abundance? I intuitively knew that's how it should be and that is how I always gave. But never got in return. How could depth involving the spirit and soul be attained otherwise? When I think about how much my inner life has been enriched by the depth of our intimacy, it makes me certain that I cannot go back to loving any other way. I love you dearly.

Molly

From: JAZMAN@mbc.web
Sent: Wednesday, August 7, 2002 3:03 PM
To: mbrogan@mbc.web
Subject: RE: why

Yes honey. She has been calling every morning, as if she knows that we talk to each other then. My cell bills go to the Chi office. I need to make sure she isn't gaming here. It will be all right, honey. This is just a rough spot.

That was one incredible statement, my love. Makes me realize again, how lucky I am to have you and love you. Finally getting what I really need and want in this area of life. I want to make sure you get the same. I know I have some work to do for that, and that I have been preoccupied lately. I promise to make it up to you because I love you very, very deeply and want to be with you forever.

I realize that I miss my connection with my children. They don't call anymore. Spoke to my mother today. She asked if I was going to bail on my family financially. Guess my X put that idea into her head. I am beginning to worry about all of my family relationships. It brings real sadness. It has nothing to do with you. You are my stability. I can usually push away sadness but this was different. Something turned in her and I haven't spotted what. When I do and say it to someone it should turn off. That is how it works.

But you are my perfect angel and I know that even when I am down. I will be in this weekend and we will regain our peace. I do love you so and I know that I made you feel bad today when I called so late in the morning. I need us to get into full force soon. We will talk more tonight, my love.

Jake

From: mbrogan@mbc.web
Sent: Wednesday, August 7, 2002 8:43 PM
To: JAZMAN@mbc.web
Subject: good night

Well dear, the day is ending. I missed you so today. We missed pillow talk last night. Can you call tonight? I missed you, yet feel so incredibly happy, a constant state of ecstasy. Do you think it has to do with all the time we spend together in spirit?

Spoke to Meg today. She was more coherent but not ready for visitors. Her family is so large, the traffic through her room now is probably overwhelming. She sounds so weak. And her spirit is still very weak, almost feels broken. I am worried. And wonder if I am reading it accurately. When I visit her in spirit, she always welcomes the comfort. She no longer wants to leave her body with me, so I slip inside her and pull in the loving energy that is all around her. I hope it helps. I think I will wait until she is home to visit her.

Are you coming this weekend? Have you made your plans? Anyway, I have so much to say to you. I feel you all through me. Not just your voice, or your sex, but YOU, and where we go together. My love, the love of my life. I feel for all that you are going through. I asked you before if you were sure you are ready for us. I won't ask again. But I can see that you are having a difficult time blending endings and beginnings. I wish I could help you.

Stay close love - Molly

From: JAZMAN@mbc.web
Sent: Thursday, August 8, 2002   8:07 AM
To: mbrogan@mbc.web
Subject: good morning

Hi there. I am so glad we had our pillow talk last night. You have a lot of good advice for me. Well, I am very horny for you today and I actually see that as an indicator now. Weird, but it seems like a kind of barometer of how I'm doing. Enturbulation of my theta seems to kill that at first, then as we communicate, it comes back. Often so much that it interferes with my ability to function. Right now I'm in a heavy sex mood where you're concerned and if I were there you would be handled (smile.) Can't wait until Saturday. I will be there Saturday morning about 8. Will you be ready? My flight out is Sunday night. I am sorry this stay couldn't be longer.

It sounds like you are doing just fine with Meg. Don't invalidate your knowingness, honey. Keep doing what you know is right. Well, I'll be calling you after a few business calls. I'm loving you as intensely as always, missing you, needing you, can't wait for our time together. Not in the best mood, but not too bad, considering. I rally want to kiss those long legs from top to bottom, baby. I love you very much, honey.

Jake

From: mbrogan@mbc.web
Sent: Thursday, August 8, 2002 5:10 PM
To: JAZMAN@mbc.web
Subject: worldly barriers

Well darlin,

Have not heard from you since this morning. I am
assuming that the damn world is still getting in our
way. Things seem to be heating up for you.
Please explain Enturbulation. Fabulous word. I
imagine it means a blocking of spiritual energy that
comes from a psychological disturbance or avoiding.
Keeping things clear between us will be important
always. Especially as our time together waxes and
wanes.

I am kissing you constantly in my mind. The fact that
our spirits are preoccupied won't change that, love. I do
get a flash of your spirit from time to time, especially
when I imagine going crazy on your neck. Or when I
whisper "I love you" in your ear between kisses. And
when the tongue wrestling begins, look out! You are
with me instantly. God I love you. But you are not as
available as you once were. Can you feel that?

Don't let the world drive you too crazy. Some of it is
simply small stuff.

Missing you,
Molly

From: JAZMAN@mbc.web
Sent: Thursday, August 8, 2002   10:05 PM
To: mbrogan@mbc.web
Subject: RE: worldly barriers

My future sex slave (and visa versa),

Enturbulation has to do with theta, the energy particular to a spiritual being. Enturbulated theta is like the inside of a tornado. The opposite would be free theta. An upset person, or a person upsetting others is enturbulated. Some people are almost always enturbulated and annoying to be near. Others are more quietly and covertly enturbulated. Theta is Entheta when it is enturbulated. MEST (matter, energy, space and time,) is enmest when enturbulated, such as after a bombing or just a messy house. Enturbulated MEST can enturbulate a spiritual being. And enturbulated being has less free theta available. Free theta creates, entheta destroys.

Call you later.
Jake

From: mbrogan@mbc.web
Sent: Friday, August 9, 2002 5:10 AM
To: JAZMAN@mbc.web
Subject: good morning

Your explanation of enturbulation is fascinating. Especially the people "causing others to be upset" part. Is there some way to prevent others from upsetting us? Some kind of higher level perception process? That is what gets me through some otherwise ugly meetings! You already help me develop more energy, or free theta as you call it, than anyone else in this life time. And you have helped me understand how to use it better than anyone. Sounds like we have much to discover together, and the rest of our lives to discover it (smile.)

Getting past this next hurdle of beginning our physical lives together will be a great relief. It will make us so less abstract, more real. Although I like ALL of our levels, along with the fact that we have already discovered so many of the deeper ones. Yes, we seem to have the potential here to create a great deal in our lives together. A sacred promise, with unlimited possibility. Like a great novel, inspired, and waiting to be written.

To let you know, Meg was released from the hospital today and is recovering at her in-laws home in Winnetka. Peaceful and quiet with all the help she needs. I will go deliver her gift basket early next week if all goes well.

Touch me - Molly

From: JAZMAN@mbc.web
Sent: Friday, August 9, 2002   10:05 PM
To: mbrogan@mbc.web
Subject: RE: worldly barriers

The world got in the way again, baby. I will be so glad to be in your arms tomorrow morning. Looking forward to lots of romance, foreplay, kissing, being inside you.

Yes, there are methods of limiting the amount of enturbulation others can cause in us. One way is called "flattening buttons." We are enturbulated when some button is pushed. If the button doesn't exist, it can't be pushed. Eliminating them takes self analysis and removal of very deep imprints. How that is done will need a long night on the beach baby. Are you ready for that? I am, although I don't think we will have time for it this weekend. Soon, baby, soon.

Good news about Meg. Release from the hospital is a huge step forward. She has my thoughts and good intentions.

Can we go to the beach house and cuddle and talk for hours? I haven't had time to check the weather there. I hope it cooperates. I have so much to say to you. It runs through my mind constantly. I have such a need to make the conversation real.

I will call you when I land,

Jake

From: mbrogan@mbc.web
Sent: Sunday, August 11, 2002 8:43 PM
To: JAZMAN@mbc.web
Subject: traveling safely

I know you are on the plane back to SF. Travel safely love. I can still feel you in my arms, the way you were Saturday morning, so loving and peaceful. After that, it seemed the world got in the way again, even though you were here with me.

Saturday morning, when you told me my eyes were the color of lapis, I looked deep into yours and my awareness blew wide open, losing all physical boundaries. As I looked at you, your appearance changed. Your face became more familiar. As if it were a composite of many faces that I have loved. I felt so deeply connected to you.

At that moment I was convinced that we have shared lives in which we have experienced great love. And together done great things because together, we have an enormous amount of spiritual power that can be used to turn the world to good.

The state of awareness is something that usually happens to me during a meditation or dream, but not normally while I am awake. I wonder if there are people that always live like that. How wonderful it would be.

I am not sure what was going on with you the rest of the weekend, after you returned from seeing your kids. Problems that drove you deep inside yourself, away from me, even though, I was there touching you. Very

different than anything that has passed between us
before.

I did not know how to tell you this while you were here
this weekend. While you were visiting your kids, I got
a glimpse of you. Your X and children there, emotional
turmoil and conflict. I clearly got the message that you
changed your mind and were intending to separate from
me to appease your daughter. I was emotionally
detached while it was occurring. But it has continued
to disturb me since. Did your X confront you about us?

Please know that I am here for you in any way that you
need me to be. I hold you close to me every moment.
Sometimes, when I can't feel you close, my spirit will
say, "Jake," and yours always responds "I'm here
baby." I swear my ears can actually hear you.

I did a lot of praying for Meg this morning. I can't talk
to her in my meditations like I was able to before. But I
can see her sleeping. She is hooked up to the IV at
home with morphine running through it. Sleeping a lot.
But she calls me occasionally, usually confused. She
did tell me she missed me. So I meditate more for her
healing, pulling in all of the love that surrounds her. If
nothing else, it is like a prayer from the depths of my
soul. That is always positive.

I love you Jake, with everything I have in me.
Including the smile on my face that pops up at the mere
thought of you. Thanks for those smiles. And
everything else you give me, love.

Molly

From: mbrogan@mbc.web
Sent: Monday, August12, 2002 9:33 AM
To: JAZMAN@mbc.web
Subject: so true

I found these words for you, written by Emily
Dickinson:

"I have no life but this,
to lead it here;
Nor any death, but lest
Dispelled from there;

Nor tie to earths to come,
Nor action new,
Except through this extent,
The realm of you"

I love you Jake.

Molly

From: JAZMAN@mbc.web
Sent: Monday, August 12, 2002 2:04 PM
To: mbrogan@mbc.web
Subject: RE: so true

I love you Molly. I slept late so could not send a
morning email.

Your experience Saturday morning was fascinating.
We have shared many lives together. When you begin
to remember them, we can talk more about them. We
will have that conversation on the beach soon.

I love the poem you sent. Thank you. You are so
amazing. I actually did think about putting us on hold
for a split second. Grace was so upset it took a great
deal of effort to calm her. My X was contributing to it,
instead of helping. It was very ugly. I am sorry, Molly,

but I did not know how to talk about it. I am very worried about my daughter and what effect the divorce will have on our relationship. But I WILL NOT stay in the marriage.

I had no idea that you felt badly about anything Saturday night and Sunday. You were a total comfort to me. I want so to protect you from all the ugliness. But I guess you have seen your share of it too. I should have known you had an insight. You are remarkable that way.

My love for you is so strong that it gets out of control sometimes. Like now, I am working to suppress intense sexual feelings for you and would like, more than anything, just to hold you right now. I think my feelings for you are stronger. If you don't agree, you will have to convince me otherwise. In person would be preferable. The urge for you is so intense that it's almost a problem.

I will call you soon so I can again reassure you. I love reassuring you. And I have this other intense urge to be your husband someday (smile.) Do I stand a chance?

Jake

From: mbrogan@mbc.web
Sent: Monday, August12, 2002 3:03 PM
To: JAZMAN@mbc.web
Subject: RE: so true

Your email immediately sent me into rapture. Difficult to get my fingers to type. Oh, love.

I have an advantage over you with the sexual tension problem. I have suggested this to you, but probably not clearly enough. Our spiritual love making sometimes brings a physical orgasm for me. I don't understand how it happens, but it does. So I do get release from time to time.

I will marry you in a heartbeat. I do marry you, with every heartbeat.

But I still need your reassurance (smile.)

mbj

From: JAZMAN@mbc.web
Sent: Monday, August 12, 2002 7:44 PM
To: mbrogan@mbc.web
Subject: so much

I miss you so much more than normal today. Your voice on the phone this afternoon was very soothing. A peace instantly fills me when I hear you on the line. But afterward, the missing returned, unusually strong today. I wonder if something happened last night, like a dream that I lost you somehow and now I'm grasping you closer into my space so it won't really happen. It is so heavy. I hope you always love me like you do now. It almost freaks me out sometimes. And I love you so much, baby. Do you really get it? It is a little tough to work.

I'll be calling you for pillow talk (and some day, doing other things to you as well, my love.)

Kissing you, my forever love.

Jake

From: mbrogan@mbc.web
Sent: Tuesday, August13, 2002 5:55 AM
To: JAZMAN@mbc.web
Subject: achy morning

Pillow talk was wonderful last night. I hear your voice
and it is almost as if you are here next to me. But I
woke this morning with a powerful headache. Phooey.

I had very heady dreams last night, as if I was working
on an abandonment issue. But, I was not aware of
having one! I could not resolve it in my dreams. I
probably would not have remembered the dream if you
hadn't asked about it when you called.

I love the way you felt my hesitation to tell you my
dream last night, but created the safe space for complete
disclosure. The dream was so vivid – standing outside
my parent's home in Northbrook with Christmas trees
all around. Having the dream character hold me while I
cried with abandon. Hearing the comforting tone in his
voice when I said "I thought he was the one," and he
said "so did I."

This dream reminded me of the abandonment dream in
Remember Me – the character's prayer for wholeness.
She is running through a house of mirrors. Her emotion
is only felt in the mirror. Her true self turns a blind eye
to the external drama to find her God. She looks away.

Yet in my dream last night, I knew I was not looking
away, but embracing and releasing the emotion of
feeling abandon. So interesting.

You help me in so many ways. Do you know that?
You will find me in the bookstore at lunchtime
exploring this dream. Lately, in the bookstore, there
will be one book that stands out for me on the shelf
somehow. It looks almost as if there is a light around it.
When I settle into a chair and open it, I find that I have

opened to a page that is telling me what I am looking for. It's an amazing process really and one that I don't bother questioning.

Do you tell me you love me too often? No you don't, not at all. Do I think about your love too often? Only if that means constantly. And since I am thinking about your love constantly, I can't possibly have you confirm that enough. When you do, it sends a current through my core, entirely. I live for those currents. Until I have you in my arms again. And they increase in ways I cannot yet imagine.

So interesting to hear you read my poems last night on the phone. You are right. I felt as if you wrote them for me. We wrote them for each other. An unexpected bonus that makes me love you more and more. It will always, be only more, Jake. You seem to know how to make that happen. I can't imagine that changing, unless, for some unexpected reason, you turn away from me. That is what it will take. I will not be the one to turn. Great certainty tells me so.

But go ahead and freak out. And then run to me. I will be waiting to soothe you and reassure you. And provide that sexual healing that I have waiting for you.

Always for you,

Molly

From: JAZMAN@mbc.web
Sent: Tuesday, August 13, 2002 9:24 AM
To: mbrogan@mbc.web
Subject: RE: achy morning

Good morning Molly. Sounds like another missed opportunity to test the pain relief theory. I love you. When we are finally together, do you think three treatments a day will be adequate? We'll have to see.

God, I love you and want you so desperately. I feel bad when you're in pain and want to help any way I can. That would really be something if the theory were true!

We are so madly in love, aren't we? For me, my love for you is well beyond a love level necessary to spend my life with you. I can honestly say that I don't think I can find anyone that could make me happier than you can and do. I don't see anything I would like to change in you except for that occasional pain you feel. As long as what we both consider are the important things are in good shape, then we will be fine. We communicate extremely well with each other. We validate each other, grant each other our own beingnesses and allow the other to have our own life activities. We are clearly sexually aroused by each other and we're both much happier being together than not. I just don't know of I can keep up with you sexually (smile.) I'm in love, and very much so. Can't help it.

Jake

From: mbrogan@mbc.web
Sent: Tuesday, August 13, 2002 2:13 PM
To: JAZMAN@mbc.web
Subject: RE: achy morning

Here is what I learned at lunch today. Psychologists believe:

A person generally develops an abandonment issue because of an incomplete bond with their mom or dad. Carl Jung, in his theory of individuation would say that an abandonment issue would illustrate a neglected or suppressed peculiarity of the individual development. This individual would not have integrated all necessary factors into their beingness.
People with abandonment issues usually have trouble feeling separate or alone. I don't have the indicators of

a person like that. I take way too much alone time and love it. But maybe I am so into feeling one with you and all of the ecstasy it creates, I am reluctant to leave that for any period of separation. And maybe, during this beginning period for us, that is OK.

The dream's a mystery. Could it have been a foreshadowing? I get those kinds of dreams sometimes. Guess only time will tell.

Well, anyway, lunch was interesting. The air was fresh. And I thought about you constantly, because right now, for me, it all comes back to you, Jake. I love you so.

Hope you are smiling and thoroughly aroused today when no one is looking (smile.)

All de love all de time,

Molly

From: mbrogan@mbc.web
Sent: Wednesday, August 14, 2002 5:55 AM
To: JAZMAN@mbc.web
Subject: sunrise

There is a marvelous strip of pink across the horizon, waiting to pull up the sun in a few moments. Like a ribbon, intertwining heaven and earth.

I called you back last night to tell you again that I love you. Left a voice mail message for you.

Running a bit late this morning. Very sleepy, but the headache is finally gone. Had a hard time getting back to sleep last night after all that happened. Lots to think about.

My insight into your daughter right before she called you and replayed it had a profound effect on me.

Especially since she repeated my words exactly. The fact that she interrupted our call just when my premonition was eerie. I am glad, however, that you were able to work things out with her.

I heard the concern in your voice last night, especially when you wanted to hear me say that I love you. So I will need to say that a gazillion times in as many ways today. And I will, because I do. And I see you working on maintaining our intimacy while struggling with the end of your marriage.

I will confess that I never imagined you to be as enmeshed in your marriage as you now seem to be. When you told me that you had been living in California and separated for two years after legal divorce through your church, I imagined more distance between you. I imagined that your family had accepted the reality of divorce for everything but the financial separation.

I feel your angst. Know that all your intentions are loving ones. And that your desire is to clarify. And I love you immensely for all those reasons, and more.

Do you know your travel plans for the weekend?

Love with all my heart,
Molly

From: JAZMAN@mbc.web
Sent: Wednesday, August 14, 2002 9:24 AM
To: mbrogan@mbc.web
Subject: RE: sunrise

I have been listening to your voice mail message over and over. Is that weird? I am very addicted to you and your love. I couldn't ask for more affection and care than you provide. I really do want you in my life forever. This little problem I'm having will sort itself out soon, baby.

The inexperience with this level of emotion leaves me so vulnerable. Not hearing any response to my first "I love you" last night actually bothered me. You were silent, not even your usual mmmmmm. I thought you weren't in the mood to say something at the moment, which would be OK, honey. It just wakes me up to how much I care about you, how intense this is for me, and how desperately I want this to work and last and last and last. Vulnerable is an understatement. The wanting for you in all ways is of such great magnitude. You are the only woman for me. I know that. But sometimes I feel it leaves me in a very weak position – something I am completely unprepared for, but will have to deal with.

I am not done but have to run. Can't call on the way to work because I have a call to return to the kids. But I will talk to you later, my love.

I love you more than you know. Please don't check out any other guys while I am gone. You are taken, forever.

Jake

From: mbrogan@mbc.web
Sent: Wednesday, August 14, 2002 3:12 PM
To: JAZMAN@mbc.web
Subject: crisis

Oh sweetheart, I wasn't withholding after you told me you loved me. I simply didn't hear it. I must have been switching the phone from ear to ear or something. I do remember the sound of your voice when you asked me to say it. I then realized that the conversation had gone on MUCH longer than usual without my having said it.

I feel badly. And need you to know that it was not intentional. I don't do that. Withhold or manipulate like that. Now, I am glad you asked me to say it. I would not have realized your feelings otherwise. If you were here, I would go crazy on you and (probably cry the whole time) try to make it up to you.

I do love you Jake. With everything in me. I love you.

Our conversation this morning about what is happening with your kids did set me back. I am truly sorry for your X's instability and the effect it is having on your children. Do you think her outbursts are an intentional means of control through fear? It is common in dividing families. Worrying about your children in that situation is natural. Your rational response to the situation will be important for them. I have reserved emotion or judgment until I know more. I mention that just to let you know I am not getting "weird" about it. The emotion that I choose is love for you. Still, completely. Just more calmly. Does that make sense?

I do look forward to talking it through more. Is that difficult for you? This may be one of those things about me that might bother you. My need for clarity. Not everyone can handle it. For me, it is important to continue living each moment consciously. Without clarity, I get stuck in my ego. It becomes much harder to observe and choose thoughts and feelings. That is the way I formulate response AND perception, staying clear. Not everyone can live like that. Not everyone can live WITH that. I hope it doesn't become a burden for you. I have seen that happen.

My wish for you is a much, MUCH better day today. But if that doesn't happen, then I am here for you, baby. Always, in all ways that you need me to be.

Spoke to Meg earlier. She is feeling much stronger and I am going to deliver the basket tomorrow at dinner time.

Touch me, Molly

From: JAZMAN@mbc.web
Sent: Wednesday, August 14, 2002 8:07 PM
To: mbrogan@mbc.web
Subject: you

I love you.

From: mbrogan@mbc.web
Sent: Wednesday, August 14, 2002 8:43 PM
To: JAZMAN@mbc.web
Subject: RE: you

I love you too. But are we dancing around something?

From: JAZMAN@mbc.web
Sent: Thursday, August 15, 2002 9:06 AM
To: mbrogan@mbc.web
Subject: you

Sorry I missed pillow talk last night, honey. I have so much going on and I still don't know how I am going to handle this weekend. Mike is meeting me at the airport Saturday morning so that we can talk about the situation. I will make my plans after getting a better understanding of the situation from him. I am sorry I can't be more specific with you about weekend plans.

So I should start to tell you some thoughts of mine now. My ex apparently hates me. Just can't understand how I could come to the decision that I did, even though it was made so long ago. I think telling the children brought it all to the surface for her. She doesn't want the children and me to get along and expects most of my income to go to her. She is constantly in touch with my family, complaining about how I am abandoning them and all kinds of other stuff. She tells the kids that I don't want them and that I suck as a father. Like I am divorcing them too. The daily brainwashing is upsetting to some degree. I know it effects Grace terribly. Mike is older, and understands the situation better.

I am done with her and have been for years. In her current state of mind, I am worried about what further damage she will attempt to do my relationships if she found out that I have fallen in love with someone else – or that I am even dating. She is currently my enemy and basically has my loved ones as "hostages" in a sense. My kids may also look down on me if they knew I was with someone already. It is basically a public relations issue, because I feel that you are the best woman I could possibly be with. Whatever happiness I feel is due to you. If I have to take a whole lot of enturbulation from all sides to be with you, I will. Having you with me is well worth it. But long term, it is better to bring you into my life, as far as they're concerned, a little later. Even though there is nothing wrong with what's happening between us. Everything is right about us.

I am trying to keep a bad situation from getting worse. I need to get her agreement on this to prevent a blood bath. I want to do something legal that eliminates the potential for criticism, but I don't and refuse to wait some long time. It's just not right and I can't hang on much longer.

I don't feel I am saying all I want to say but it is a start. I love you forever and ever.

Jake

From: JAZMAN@mbc.web
Sent: Thursday, August 15, 2002 10:23 PM
To: mbrogan@mbc.web
Subject: Hi, baby

I wonder if you are asleep yet. Pillow talk soon, baby.

No emails from you today. That may be a first! Too
busy telling all those other guys no thank you? We did
have more phone time today. And I enjoyed your
viewpoints. It's time to end this fiasco with less
concern over the consequences. Your encouragement
to keep the big picture in mind was needed. Thanks.

To be honest, baby, I am a bit nervous about this
weekend. With all of the negativity in my life there is a
fear that I may lose what we have. Do you have that at
all, or is it just me with the insecurity?

Thanks for your wisdom on the phone today. I love
you.

Jake

From: mbrogan@mbc.web
Sent: Friday, August 16, 2002 5:01 AM
To: JAZMAN@mbc.web
Subject: RE: Hi, baby

The sun is coming up much later now. Soon, I will be
waking up in the dark until the time changes. I won't
be able to write to you while the sun is rising. So my
morning emails will be all about anticipation, waiting
for the moment, and all the memory work going on
during that. Now that I think of it, it might be a good
time to work on those feelings of disappointment that I
have when you are expected, but don't arrive. It seems
to becoming a pattern with you. Communicating a
change in plans seems simple enough – what's
happening?

Do we have clashing buttons here? Mine with broken promises, yours with fear of her violent reactions. If something comes up just call and let me know. I have more to do than time to do it, and would appreciate being set free to do something else if you cannot arrive. I love the fact that we both bring with us experience, wisdom and language that help us deal with these life problems. It gives us the opportunity to share, blend processes, pick best practices, and support each other through spiritual restoration. And resolve life conflict. And expand our love.

How rare what we have here, such great possibility. I love you Jake. Your openness and receptiveness to look at what is happening to us. Do you know how much comfort and reassurance that gives me? As long as that continues, I think we have a good shot here.

It seems that we both come from marriages where we were controlled through fear. That simply means we have a vast amount of experience to help each other through it.

The process we engaged in yesterday will be an important part of our foundation. Can you handle that? As time goes on, we will improve our ability to clarify what lies between us, to retain the big picture viewpoint, to meet each other beyond our egos, release and transform negative emotion, recreate ourselves, heighten our awareness. And, as time goes on, will create many more process that will deepen our bond.

The fact that you naturally and willingly do this makes me fall in love with you all over again every moment this morning. Christ, I love you.

This is exactly the stuff that makes us so rare. Affirms and creates our affinity. Gives us the HUGE spiritual reality that we share.

Let's not stop talking about your fear and my problem with broken promises. When we first began telling each other that we love eachother, I asked you not to take me anywhere that wasn't real. That is still important to the utmost. Our continued effort, the exchange of abundance, our clear understanding of ourselves and eachother will continue to make it real each day.

If we cannot get together because of your problems with your ex, I will understand completely. Give your children the attention they deserve. But don't leave me waiting again without the courtesy of a phone call. I will busy myself helping Meg's family with her recovery. I might see her children this weekend. And, if she feels strong enough, I will see Meg again also.

I may even take off and go see Jack at Auggie if you think you will be tied up all weekend. Stay in the little bed and breakfast I always stay in. Get him out for some decent food. Let me know your plans asap, love.

Molly

From: JAZMAN@mbc.web
Sent: Friday, August 16, 2002 8:17 AM
To: mbrogan@mbc.web
Subject: RE: Hi, baby

Good morning, my love. I see you were up early. Thank you for writing me all that beautiful theta. You are loving and understanding and so desirable.

I don't know if a broken promise would classify as a button. It is natural have a reaction of unhappiness when a promise is broken. But it depends on the magnitude of the promise. If you promised to marry me and then broke that promise, much unhappiness. But if you promised to make burgers for dinner and make chicken instead, I would be fine. To be upset with you in that case would indicate a button either about broken promises or about chicken.

The concept of a promise should not be taken lightly. Using the word loosely can be a mistake. Want to, probably, will do all I can, those are probably better words to use unless we really know what we're doing in a given situation. But if a promise ever does get broken, the other needs to make it right with the other one somehow. Make it up to her. Do something that makes it not so important that the other thing didn't happen, so it balances out.

My fear of her reaction only has to do with my relationships with my family, not with my ex.
And the fact that I can tell you all of this amazes me! It's like I'm writing my thought process down and they go where they go.

Jake

From: mbrogan@mbc.web
Sent: Friday, August 16, 2002 9:06 AM
To: JAZMAN@mbc.web
Subject: RE: Hi, baby

I read what you have to say about broken promises several times now. I will say this: that I think we should take your family's needs into account before we make weekend plans. Not leave it up in the air any more. "Probably" and "will do all I can" may work on occasion, but as a rule would prevent me from planning my time in other ways. And make me feel as if I am not a priority. Especially since I am having a hard time understanding what prevents us from spending our nights together when you are in Chi. What are the barriers? Your fear of her reaction doesn't make sense to me given the length of time you have been separated and the fact that you told the children that you would be divorcing weeks ago. Why is where you stay an issue? Why do they HAVE to know? If you are feeling that much pressure while your are in Chicago, why don't we meet in NY next weekend? We could spend some time with Viv. I would love that.

I do know that I lived with the fear of my X's reaction for many years. Still do to a certain extent because he continues to be unpredictable and make public scenes from time to time. But I established my privacy before the divorce and some things are just none of his business. I am at the point now that he has one all the damage that he can and if things heat up again, I will just move and remove myself from the possibility of his reaction.

Your children are her primary weapons against you. Your family members are others. This is not uncommon with a bitter spouse. Are you worried that I may become one if she finds out about me? You need to honestly ask yourself how many of your actions are based on fear of her reactions. As you look back with that question in focus, you may see things differently in retrospect. I know I did. She has all the indicators of someone who controls through fear. She is causing fear that the divorce will be damaging or impossible for you. Fear of financial ruin or at least, difficulty. Fear of losing your children, the respect of your friends and family, the possibility of any future happiness. Fear of how she will react if she doesn't know where you are.

Do you honestly think that after a two year separation, the people who love you would not want to see you in love and happy again? What is true is that your children will figure out who is behaving responsibly and who is raging. Unless you stoop to her level and begin behaving in the same way, they will see her reactions for what they are. They are both old enough to do that. If you behave honorably and continue to remind them that you love them, will always be there for them (a phone call away) and that they will always be a part of your life, when things cool down, they will find you again. Right now, the way she is acting, there may be some punishment associated with communicating with you or moving toward you. A rise in conflict, or some passive/aggressive treatment afterward. You can't stop that. All you can do is continue to act with honor, be true to yourself, and keep the lines of communication with your loved ones open. EVERYONE will figure it out sooner or later. She will only reveal herself through her actions.

You might consider telling your children when you come into town again that you will be staying with friends. And because of all the conflict, you would rather not tell them where or with whom, so that the people you are staying with are not put in the middle of any ugliness. My bet is they will accept it without question. Can you get on with your life if you don't draw those boundaries? And if you choose not to create the boundaries, you need to ask yourself if you are really ready and willing to move on with your life. Well, enough from me on that. What are your thoughts?

I know this: that I love you with my WHOLE heart because we can examine our problems like this. And do so with love and intelligence and spirit and 100% investment
in eachother. Part of, as you say, putting it out there for eachother each day. Another good reason for me to love you more the next moment than I do in this.

Jake, if you need a cooling period between us, TELL ME! I will understand and agree. But don't tell me you love me and want to be with me, and then pull back in all these other ways. It isn't fair to either of us and seems almost like self sabotage!

Touch me - Molly

From: JAZMAN@mbc.web
Sent: Friday, August 16, 2002 9:33 AM
To: mbrogan@mbc.web
Subject: RE: Hi, baby

Thank you for giving the scene some sanity. Guess I am feeling a little blackmailed by the X. She has such a terrible effect on my loved ones. They are so vulnerable to her attacks on me. I know she hurts them and it is hard to know that is happening. Grace is who I worry about most. Our relationship has already changed, she is very distant now. When I told her about the divorce she really lost it, and hasn't been the same since. A little more time and distance, a legal filing and it will deactivate to some degree.

You are my future, and I need to meet your needs somehow so I don't threaten that. Losing you would be even worse. I love my children and I love you. My future lies with you and our time together needs to grow on a gradient scale, more and more until we are sharing the same address. It fills me with happiness just thinking about that. I can't wait to be able to kiss and hug you every day. To gaze into your beautiful eyes for hours.

Oh baby, I know I went off the track a bit here, but I couldn't help it. I love you with everything I've got. I don't think I could possible love more, but there's always tomorrow and the next few weekends, the rest of the year and the rest of our lives.

Thank you for the wisdom today. I love you.

Jake

From: mbrogan@mbc.web
Sent: Friday, August 16, 2002 10:05 AM
To: JAZMAN@mbc.web
Subject: RE: Hi, baby

Jake,

If you need to take more time to settle things in your
life before we meet again, then take it. It will not be a
threat to me in any way. I will be fine traveling to
Auggie this weekend and NY next on my own. You
have the keys to the townhouse. Use them when you
need a refuge. I am sorry if I caused you to feel that
you might lose me if you don't give me your time
immediately.

From my end, I just did not understand your saying we
"might" get together and then it not happening. I want
that to stop. Please don't feel that you need to tell me it
might happen to satisfy some need in me. You don't. I
can wait. I have lots to do with my time. I just need to
know what is real. Uncertainty gets in our way, not
delay.

But I do want you to ask yourself just how long YOU
are willing to live with delay. At what point will it be
the right time? You waited two years to file, waiting
for the right time that did not come. Your waiting did
not prevent or deactivate her reaction.

You are not going to lose me because you need to give
your children and your divorce time. But we will
continue to struggle here unless we can clarify what,
exactly, we are doing. And that struggle will create
your feeling that you may lose me, and my feeling that I
am not a priority, or that this may not ever happen.
And these negative feelings will get in the way of the
growth of our relationship.

Let's stop talking about what we want and need. And start determining what WILL happen. To continue to talk about want and need creates the want and need and keeps us stuck there. Does that make sense? But maybe you need us stuck there, so you have time to sort out your life. Somehow, being stuck there is swerving you. It keeps us there. Let's figure this out. Can we? Because being stuck in want and need is doing us harm. I think we will be better off with a more realistic picture of what is happening, what will happen and a plan to get us from what is to what will happen. Does that make sense?

I do love you. And very much want us to get past this in a way that serves us both. And serves Grace. Who seems to be the most vulnerable person in this scenario.

Our first few weekends together here were lovely. Now, when you come to Chi, your family consumes your time. And when we are together, your mind is on them. Why don't we meet somewhere else for a weekend? I could come to SF. We could go to NY, or Ireland, like we talked about. I think we should consider that.

Talk to me,
Molly

From: JAZMAN@mbc.web
Sent: Friday, August 16, 2002 12:21 PM
To: mbrogan@mbc.web
Subject: RE: Hi, baby

Hold on baby! I can't come to Chicago and not see you. I am only concerned about spending the entire night or nights with you and the effect it might have when she is questioning my every move. Then again, it might be worth it.

I spoke to a couple of friends today who told me it might be worse there than I suspected. She is really losing it. I do need to see my kids and try to sort this out. But I will definitely make time to see you, my love. I LOVE you, and can't wait to see you when I am there. What did I say to make you think that?

I am going to try calling you in a few minutes before my next meeting.

Loving you, baby.

Jake

From: mbrogan@mbc.web
Sent: Friday, August 16, 2002 2:04 PM
To: JAZMAN@mbc.web
Subject: RE: Hi, baby

Well, I've read this email again and still need to reserve emotion and thought. I am just not sure what to think of all of this. I feel much empathy for your children. Mine went through similar emotional trials. But somewhere, and I don't know exactly where or how, we moved from you having the key to my place and staying with me when you are in Chi, to you not being able to spend a night with me because of fear of her reaction. You have been separated for two years and told the children that you are divorcing weeks ago – why is she concerned about where you stay? And why do you fear her reaction? Illinois is a no fault divorce state. I don't think you have anything to fear legally.

Anyway, I will be glad to see you tomorrow whatever the circumstance. I do think that I will take off Sunday morning, have Sunday dinner with Jack and spend the night in Rock Island. I just gave notice at work that I will be taking Monday off. A leisurely ride back to Chicago Monday afternoon will give me time to collect my thoughts. I can stop at all of my favorite places and make a day of it.

Call when you can sweetheart,

Molly

From: JAZMAN@mbc.web
Sent: Monday, August 19, 2002 8: 17 AM
To: mbrogan@mbc.web
Subject: home safe

I know you are probably still on the road back home but I wanted to write you to tell you how much I love you. I woke up very early this morning and watched a storm roll in. It made me feel loving and sexy, which of course, made me think of you.

I am having a massive urge to make love with you. Massive. I wonder where you are and what you are thinking. Are you thinking about making love too? I really need to take you down right now, and keep you there for hours. Kiss every spot, some longer than others. I am just so into you and need to express it. You are the most sensuous, desirable creature I have known. We're perfect for each other and I love you very, very much.

Your Jake

From: mbrogan@mbc.web
Sent: Monday, August 19, 2002 7:08 PM
To: JAZMAN@mbc.web
Subject: the wind and the river

Hello love,

I feel like it is a brand new day, although I had lunch on the riverside on the way home from Rock Island. The wind was stirring now and again. My friend, the wind, who shows up from time to time. She lets me know she is with me by stirring trees with a particular sound at a time when I feel no wind. Or with the wind on my face as I emerge from inside to outside. The wind feels like a kiss, and I then feel her presence within me.

Sometimes she is telling me that something wonderful is about to happen. And sure enough it does, usually that same day. Sometimes she is warning me of impending danger. That is when I proceed with caution and watch something happening, like a car accident, in front of me, that might have included me had I not been on my guard.

Is it strange, this knowing of an invisible spirit? I've never expressed this to anyone before. I met her as a child. I spend a great deal of my time between the ages of 7-16 in the forest near my parent's home. I suppose children are more open to such things. I always welcomed her. She kept me company when I was alone. Warned me if I needed to run home. Sometimes, when I felt her warning, I could not get my friends to believe me. Until a surly looking stranger appeared and then we all ran like hell.

Today, she was comforting me. It was a warm, loving feeling that surrounded me. But a bit surprising as I was not feeling in need of comfort at the time. I was just getting ready to meditate. Instead, we watched the river and the world go by together. Speaking to eachother without words, the way best friends do.

I really did not want the lunch to end. But it did, and I continued my journey home. Thinking about the contractor ass that needs kicking when I return to work tomorrow. And you.

All my love,
mb

From: mbrogan@mbc.web
Sent: Monday, August 19, 2002 11:31 PM
To: JAZMAN@mbc.web
Subject: RE: home safe

Hi Darling,

After I hung up from pillow talk your spirit came rushing in and washed over me. Your words "it will be alright, baby," echo like a mantra. I moved from extreme happiness to something of a much higher order. My body seems to be having trouble handling it. My mind is very quiet. My hands are not working well on the keyboard. Feels like passivity from rapture. Except the rapture is not ending. It doesn't come and go. It stays. And goes on and on. Making it difficult to focus, communicate or do anything.

Lots of heavy sighs. Breaks in motion while I try to quiet my body down to meet my mind. It is like my mind and spirit are racing and my body can't keep up. And only in the quiet can they meet. Is that too much love? Is that possible?

Christ, are you feeling this way too? Dreaming tonight will be exquisite, if I can get there. I may not be making a bit of fucking sense here, so I will sign off.

All rapture, no sense.

Molly

From: JAZMAN@mbc.web
Sent: Tuesday, August 20, 2002 8: 17 AM
To: mbrogan@mbc.web
Subject: RE: home safe

Good morning, lovely one. I don't know exactly what to say, but I'm thinking about it. Maybe you just need me to make love to you a few dozen times. I can't tell if you like how you feel or not. Too much love, don't think so. I do know that my love for you is quite intense today.

No email this morning, baby? Running late to work? It felt like emptiness in my heart, instead of my mailbox. I missed your morning words to start my day although your story of your trip was wonderful.

I am sorry that we only had our time on Saturday. It seemed like just a moment. It seemed eternal. A passionate time warp that I return to again and again in my mind. And my emotions spike each time I return.

Can you call this morning? I have this need to hear your voice, honey.

I love you,
Jake

From: mbrogan@mbc.web
Sent: Tuesday, August 20, 2002 3:30 PM
To: JAZMAN@mbc.web
Subject: lbj and mbj home

I look forward to the day when I can go home from work to find you there. When we finally call the same place home. When we find our home together. I will love that day.

I may take a little nap when I get home today and see if that helps the slight headache that has developed. I am so completely detached from the concrete. In two places simultaneously, in body and out. This is actually a familiar state of mind to me. My objective state of mind, self reflective. But today, I feel more detached from the body. My spirit is in some incredibly abstract level that I have little experience in. Not comfortable, because I don't understand it well. I keep rubbing my head to try to clear my mind. It is as if the senses of the spirit are hyperaware. A quickening. Makes me wonder if something is about to happen. I keep trying to find reason or purpose for it. Maybe just a new level of awareness that our love brings to me, and I need time to integrate it.

It is like my being is connected to my soul and aware of my entirety constantly. The lid is blown off my mind and spirit. The visual and the knowing are of everything in me. And sometimes, more frequently, parts of others. The sky is limitless and so am I. Until I was able to acclimate my body, the lightness was unbearable. But the serenity and the rapture were exquisite. Everyone around me felt it. And I began to welcome it. It locks me into forever every moment, as I open forward.

By the way, it is nice to have someone, finally, that understands this. Maybe this is my spirit preparing the way for the time when we can be together. And when we are together, all will become clear. Saturday went by so quickly, with such depth and intensity. I was fine Sunday and Monday until pillow talk. Our talk was all about the spirit. And my spirit rose with each word. And afterward, when your spirit rushed in and made love to me – well I haven't been the same since. What are our spirits trying to teach us? Where are they trying to lead us? My dreams forecast trouble for us. Our spirits forecast endless possibility. It's all such a puzzle in the midst of our increasing problems. I am resigned to let our love lead the way.

And I do love you.
Molly

From: mbrogan@mbc.web
Sent: Tuesday, August 20, 2002 7:54 PM
To: JAZMAN@mbc.web
Subject: late night thunder

I woke from my extended nap to the sound of thunder. It is pouring outside, the winds howling. Thunder is rolling across the sky. I felt such a need to get up and reach out to you. But am still very sleepy and headachy. I don't think I am feeling well physically. I tried to find your spirit but couldn't. It was the first time that you weren't there when I called. I wonder if something has happened. But need to return to sleep to escape the pain in my head.

Will you call tonight, love?

Molly

From: JAZMAN@mbc.web
Sent: Wednesday, August 21, 2002 8: 17 AM
To: mbrogan@mbc.web
Subject: RE: late night thunder

Thunder – wish I had been there to see and hear the action while I held you close. Maybe get a few kisses while we're enjoying it. Glass of wine, some deep conversation, some of your terrific cooking, you can create something so tasty out of almost nothing can't you? It's lonelier here now when I'm without you.

Thunder – the sound that lightening makes. I wonder why two words are used for the same thing, one for the sight and one for the sound? When you hear a car, you still call it a car.

I miss your loving ways and the peacefulness you bring when everything else is such chaos. I'm loving you baby, and hope you're feeling better.

I do understand why you want to go to New York without me next weekend. I wish I could go with but need time to straighten things out with my kids and X. She is really stirring things up now. I have an appointment with my attorney Saturday. The whole weekend is full and I wish it could be full of you instead. Give Viv my best.

Jake

From: mbrogan@mbc.web
Sent: Wednesday, August 21, 2002 9:06 AM
To: JAZMAN@mbc.web
Subject: morning floods

It's lonelier here now when I'm without you.

I know just what you mean. I feel the loneliness too. Have already been busted for it. Heard an "Oh no, where's that smile?" after entering the building. I miss you. Our mischievous verbal play. Your spirit over me, within me.

I did love your email though. I continue to analyze. Everywhere I turn, there is some material for what I am wondering. Viewpoints, ideas, opinions all seem to be related to us. Like angels trying to give me answers. Putting little pieces of the puzzle on my path for me. Extreme happiness has turned o peaceful quandary. But I suppose that is as it should be.

I know your spirit so much better than your character. I feel that your spirit has withdrawn, and I find myself looking to understand the man that you are today. Putting what I know together. Formulating questions and looking for answers. I suppose it helps me feel close to you. Helps ease the loneliness I feel. I can't feel you today like I have been feeling you for so long. It's like a door has been closed or a valve turned off.

We got almost four inches of rain last night. Lots of
lightening and thunder this morning. Will storm off
and on for the next day or so. The expressways are shut
down in many spots. Pretty much a mess. But I am
thinking of you.

Hesitation

You are so inviting
With your warm
Generous greeting
You bring me
Into you
With a rush of excitement
A kaleidoscope of ideas
A blanket of sweet words
That warms my soul
And comforts
Like parent's lap.
When I am
All locked in,
Completely yours,
You hesitate.
And ask me to wait
For the readiness
That you now reveal
Like a new game piece,
A sudden barrier.

So I agree
To wait again for you
While you resume seduction
Into the world of US.
You seem so certain
Of this world
And its possibility.
Until it is time
To make it real.

Then comes

The hesitation.
Is it self doubt?
Insufficient trust?
No room in our life?
No room in your heart?
What keeps our world
In the air, afloat
On our paper ship
That sails the course
Between fantasy
And reality?

And why do you hesitate
To reveal it?
Do you fear
Disagreement?
Harsh reaction?
Disappointment?

Have you forgotten
Who I am
And how I play?

Molly

From: JAZMAN@mbc.web
Sent: Wednesday, August 21, 2002 8: 16 PM
To: mbrogan@mbc.web
Subject: RE: morning floods

I hope you are all right with the flooding. Sorry I have
been out of touch today. Many crazy calls from home.
I can't tell if the kids are alright because I can't get
through to them.

I feel like I need someone to say it's morally OK to
begin another relationship now. Isn't that weird? But
I'm trying to analyze it and find that consideration in
my universe, stuck to me like a fly on fly paper. The
question I need to answer is: who is that someone?

That's my next search. Do we just need more time? I know I don't want us to be found out because it might ruin things for us in the future. Not sure how or why but that thought is there too. Is it somehow similar to something in the past? I'm not sure. Loving you is something I can't help, and there's nothing wrong with that. I'll keep evaluating it, eventually realizing exactly what needs to occur so that I don't feel this way anymore. I don't like it and want it to go away. I really enjoy loving you.

I'll be calling you soon, baby

Jake

From: JAZMAN@mbc.web
Sent: Thursday, August 22, 2002 8: 16 AM
To: mbrogan@mbc.web
Subject: RE: morning floods

Are you there? No answer for pillow talk. That was a first. Are you upset? Please call or send me something. I am concerned that my last email upset you.

Jake

From: mbrogan@mbc.web
Sent: Thursday, August 22, 2002 9:15 AM
To: JAZMAN@mbc.web
Subject: I'm here

I feel like I need someone to say it's morally OK to begin another relationship now. Isn't that weird? But I'm trying to analyze it and find that consideration in my universe, stuck to me like a fly on fly paper. The question I need to answer is: who is that someone? That's my next search.

I guess I have a couple of questions. Are you unsure of your own moral code, or mine? Or you unsure as to whether our moral codes match? Is now the time to be asking this question? Seems to me the time was a few of months ago. You asked me to marry you many weeks ago. Now you wonder about "beginning" our relationship?

I'm here at work Jake. Have been. Just don't know how much to put out there anymore. I feel the need to be careful. I don't know why, but it hurts. Like there is more you are not telling me. I guess I wonder if you still think I am the right person for you. I have the feeling you are beginning to doubt it. That you are pulling back for reasons other than those you are expressing. I want to know what's real. Whatever it is. Right now, I am not sure what's real. And I am not sure why. The withdrawal of your spirit was painful to me. But now, at least, I understand the abandonment premonition. Your words confirm it. I am sorry if that was blunt. It is what it is.

I do know I love you.
Molly

From: mbrogan@mbc.web
Sent: Thursday, August 22, 2002 3:57 PM
To: JAZMAN@mbc.web
Subject: FW: I'm here

Thanks for calling this morning after reading my email. I promised to send you something before going home for the day so here goes.

I know it's not me Jake. You have your reasons for pulling back. I believe that you don't know exactly what they are. But I do still have the feeling that you are not telling me everything. Looking away and hiding like this will most definitely limit us. Anyway, let me offer some observations.

It has been my experience that when people don't understand what they do, the cause is primal. Some of our deepest stuff.

If we want to know why someone has done something, we look at the effect of the action. In your case, you pulled back with the result of distance between us. So the question becomes, why did you need to put distance between us by unilaterally changing the dynamic of our relationship? Again, we look at the result. You gain control.

People generally feel the need for distance and control in a relationship because of fear of intimacy. That vulnerability you feel expresses this. Problems with your ex are understandable. The behaviors that create barriers for us are lack of honesty by not disclosing and creating expectations that are not fulfilled. Even those could be later clarified when changed, but aren't. Why?

I know I have a lot to learn about you. And probably have some missing pieces here. But give it some thought. I offer this with love, without judgment of any kind. My intention is only to help you through this. And get US back into loving, flowing relationship that is possible for us. If it is still possible for us. It will take two. I can't do this alone. Are you willing to do the analysis necessary? WE have much possibility. But realizing it will take effort from both of us. It won't just happen by itself. It won't just happen while we wait. And it won't happen if one of us doesn't intend for it to happen. I would like to know, if your intentions toward me have changed.

And I know this. What we are looking at is the stuff that causes people who aren't paying attention, to let it slip away. I love you too much not to keep trying.

Think about it Jake. And call when you can.

My flight leaves early tomorrow morning. The time apart might do us some good. I am glad I will be spending it with Viv. We have seen eachother through a few broken hearts.
Molly

From: mbrogan@mbc.web
Sent: Thursday, August 22, 2002 3:57 PM
To: mbrogan@mbc.web
Subject: ghosting

No baby. No spiking. No rapture. Only the memories. As recent as last week.

I thought the opposite would happen. I thought, that when we were finally together, our love would grow, our spirituality would blow wide open. I would finally understand what I thought I knew. Did I know it? When our spirits aren't combined, I don't know for sure. No longer a part of my waking mind. I miss that. And you. And us.

mb

From: mbrogan@mbc.web
Sent: Thursday, August 22, 2002 8:07 PM
To: mbrogan@mbc.web
Subject: ghosting2

My ghosting experience. Designed to survive this terrible separation of spirit from you I now feel. And continues now.

I am writing you, and sending it to myself. You see, I just have to be able to speak to you, to reach for you. You took me there, Jake. Told me it would be fine, that you would not take me anywhere that wasn't real. Well, here I am. And it isn't real, or I would be talking to you now, instead of your ghost.

I wonder if you will feel this. My heart breaking as I write. My withdrawal of spirit as I try to survive. Last week you felt every emotional spike. You seemed to know just when I needed you. Was reaching for you. We had an amazing connection of spirit. I don't know what is happening between us anymore. But I do know this. I have fallen completely in love with you. And now, the withdrawal is breaking my heart.

Our spirits were ready. But we were not. How can life be so cruel? My responsibility is, I suppose, that I wanted so desperately to believe. I took you at your word: that you were ready for me. But you aren't, are you love? I suppose that I should have known better. What did I miss?

I will do my best to get us both through this with our hearts in tact. Hearts can break, and continue to love. I just don't know if our hearts can continue to beat as one, as they have been. Enabling our spirits to take flight into our souls, into the parts of life that are more real that reality, the parts that require great faith. I suppose, if that finally ends, I will continue to breathe. Sometimes, I doubt that. I am hoping that careful preparation up to the point where I can no longer feel your spirit with me will allow my breath to continue, my life to continue. But hope needs to be accompanied by action and faith. Will I still believe in love?
I told myself that I deserved a relationship that met my needs, not just my partners - one where I did not feel so alone. And now I do feel so alone. I worry that is exactly what I have stumbled on to here: another relationship that leaves me alone. For the first time since I fell in love with you, I cannot feel you in spirit. And I am living my life alone again. Parallel to yours. Not joined to yours. Should that have happened? Is it natural that our spirits separate from time to time? Something I need to learn to live with? Is it individuation? A moving toward interdependency? Or

is it, as I fear, the beginning of something between us that we cannot remove? It feels like the last. Because my heart is breaking.

For the first time I am not certain, because you have changed your position. Things have changed. You say they haven't. But I suspect they have. And dread the point of realization. And the choices I will be left with. Those fate defining choices.

I want to run to you, not away from you. Run away from the war zone and into the safety of your arms. I am not sure they are open to me. Why?

I can give you the space you need now, to clarify your life. If that is what you need. Somehow, I suspect that what needs clarifying is internal, not external. If you can get through it, will things be the same for us afterward? Will it change you? Will your feelings for me change? I'm scared Jake. And know you cannot rescue me. But want that desperately, with all my breaking heart.

Yours,

Molly

From: mbrogan@mbc.web
Sent: Friday, August 23, 2002 3:03 AM
To: mbrogan@mbc.web
Subject: ghosting3

Morning used to be our best time love. The time when our spirits soared, our desire spiked, the time of our best communication. My meditation guides tell me to wait. I will wait, and hope it all returns. What if it doesn't?

I don't understand the changes in us. Have you discovered that you need an escape hatch? You have begun the control dance. I don't know how to follow.

Don't know if I can. May not have it in me. My heart breaks at the thought of it.

You say you have pulled back because of considerations. I have given that much thought and cannot see me anywhere in those considerations. This alarms me, because I followed you all the way into love. I did lead sometimes while you followed. But I don't recall you resisting, until now. Now you pulled far back. Without warning, without discussion. without my consideration. Is this the control dance? Were we out of control? I did not see that.

But I will wait to see what your next steps are. Will you notice that I am not dancing with you? You haven't so far! This only gives you the illusion of control, love. But gives us (now) different viewpoints. Far enough apart that our connection is constricted. Not enough room for our spirits to fly. Christ, I miss that, the flight of our spirits.

I worry. That given enough distance, I will begin to feel as if we were just a story I was writing in my heart. That we never really existed, except for in me. A lovely story that my spirit believed out of desperate need. And from believing took flight into uncharted waters. I still know those waters. And can swim them alone. But remember swimming with you in the Jake place. And long to be able to do that again. Were you really there? Or did I imagine you? You told me it was real. Were you only hoping out of your own need?

I have gained much from knowing you. But I miss the knowing. I expected it to grow and blossom into understanding. What prevents that? Will it last? There is a dread in my heart, that once your escape hatch is constructed, it will be used. Why else construct it?

I will wait. Until I can no longer endure the heartbreak. Until your hiding creates greater distance between us. I cannot say how long that will be. Everyone thinks that I am strong. I don't feel strong. But will do my best. Until I can not go on. Then, I will do my best to explain where we have taken me. Until then, I will do my best to tell you where I think we are headed. Without overwhelming you or increasing your burden. Because my broken heart is my burden, not yours. I followed you here. I led while you followed. It was a beautiful dance until last weekend. Now you dance alone, and don't notice. Will we dance again? I am ready love, as long as it is our dance, and not just yours.

Please convince me that you still love me. For the first time, I need that to go on. You used to feel my insecurity before I verbalized it. And lovingly give your reassurance before I needed to ask. I miss that. And I miss you, terribly. Miss the beauty and tenderness of our love.

We now put it out there for each other in small doses, cautiously. As we did in the very beginning. While we were getting to know each other. Testing each other. Giving a little, then pulling back to wait. No longer giving completely without thought of getting. Thus, we lose our depth, love. Is that truly what we want from us? If so, that has also changed. How did I miss that?

Please hear me,

mb

From: mbrogan@mbc.web
Sent: Monday, August 26, 2002 8:52 PM
To: JAZMAN@mbc.web
Subject: I'm back

Not sure if you are back yet. Never did get your travel plans for the weekend. Hope all went well for you. I missed you. And gave US much thought while in the big apple.

I think this: I have gained much from knowing you. But I miss the knowing. I expected it to grow and blossom into understanding. What prevents that? Will it last? There is a dread in my heart, that once your escape hatch is constructed, it will be used. Why else construct it?

I will wait. Until I can no longer endure the heartbreak. I cannot say how long that will be. Everyone thinks that I am strong. I don't feel strong. But will do my best. Until I can not go on. Then, I will do my best to explain where we have taken me. Until then, I will do my best to tell you where I think we are headed. Without overwhelming you or increasing your burden. Because my broken heart is my burden, not yours. I followed you here. I led while you followed. It was a beautiful dance until last weekend. Now you dance alone, and don't notice. Will we dance again? I am ready love, as long as it is our dance, and not just yours.

Please convince me that you still love me. For the first time, I need that to go on. You used to feel my insecurity before I verbalized it. And lovingly give your reassurance before I needed to ask. I miss that. And I miss you, terribly. Miss the beauty and tenderness of our love.

We now put it out there for each other in small doses, cautiously. As we did in the very beginning. While we were getting to know each other. Testing each other. Giving a little, then pulling back to wait. No longer giving completely without thought of getting. Thus, we lose our depth, love. Is that truly what we want from us? If so, that has also changed. How did I miss that?

Hear me love,

Molly

From: mbrogan@mbc.web
Sent: Monday, August 26, 2002 10:05 PM
To: mbrogan@mbc.web
Subject: ghosting4

Well, I did it. Put myself out there again. Now I am out there, alone again. Perhaps farther than I should be.

I took a chance and sent you some of 3ghosting, after not hearing from you today. I did appreciate that you opened to me a little last week. Offered some kind of explanation for pulling back. Not rational, but something. You did not respond to the challenge that I gave your offer. Do you understand your own moral code? Or do you question mine? Or do you question that I am the one? No response. Very different than before, when you would immediately take me in your arms, knowing I was in pain.

The pain gave me courage somehow. What do I have to lose? The pain? Your love? Do I have that? I have asked you to tell me honestly and gotten no response. So, I dared to send you 3ghosting. My best guess of our position here. Again no response. Disheartening. Again, no response to the fact that my heart is breaking. More steps in the control dance? Still don't see you are dancing alone? That I am just watching your Isabella Duncan primal dance of destructiveness.

We are each alone: you, in your dance, I in my watching place. This must be where you need us to be, apart. Is it the intimacy you fear? That is what I suspect. Would certainly explain the need to control. And the years with your X spent apart, dancing your dance.

I am not her, and you are not him. Why should it come out that way? Can we leave our past behind?

I suspect we are doing the best we can. Can we see our way through it? Can we hold each other? Or will this dance that creates distance prevent that? Will time make things clear? Or is that up to us?

Hear me love,
mb

From: mbrogan@mbc.web
Sent: Tuesday, August 27, 2002 9:06 AM
To: JAZMAN@mbc.web
Subject: say

Just wanted to say: I love you, with all my heart. Will love you my whole life long.

mb
From: mbrogan@mbc.web
Sent: Tuesday, August 27, 2002 9:33 AM
To: mbrogan@mbc.web
Subject: ghosting5

With every ghosting, I thought that I went farther. Then I sent you 3ghosting. How did I have the nerve to do that? Did I go too far? You don't respond to the challenges, so I guess I do.

Lately, I am always wondering. Not a good sign I suppose. Was it just a month ago that I was finding very good signs all over the place? Now, I see red flags. Am I perceptive, or neurotic? Saving myself from disaster, or ruining chances for happiness? A great big walking question mark. How did I get here, from such certainty?

You told me not to invalidate my knowingness. I tried to tell you what I know. But the silences between leave me to wonder. And sigh. Patience runs out. And only silence is comfortable. I wait in silence, for your silence to end.

I think I can make it through on my own. With a little finagling. Strategic alliances. Will I end in your arms? The happy ending of my dream? I so want that. And wonder. Have I gone too far? Can I be too analytical? Should I withhold what I know? Can I withhold it without invalidating it?

I remember my friend the wind spirit by the river. And the comfort that she gave to me, before I really needed it. Her foreshadowing of what to expect beyond the loss. Her prediction of my survival. Her faith in me, so much more than I have in myself right now.

You taught me to be sure of what I know. Why is that harder alone, than with you? I suppose because you no longer accept what I know. You avoid it. Hide from it. Will I be able to continue to do it alone? I learned much with you Jake. Many thanks. For all you have given me. The comfort of the wind spirit now makes sense. The dream with the Christmas trees, I guess that makes sense too.

Now, I am tired of wondering. Need to give it a rest. Good night,

Jake.

From: mbrogan@mbc.web
Sent: Friday, August 30, 2002 6:00 AM
To: JAZMAN@mbc.web
Subject: say

Last night, your voice was hypnotizing. I don't think you understand where the sight and sound of you sends me sometimes. I do love you so.
mb

From: JAZMAN@mbc.web
Sent: Friday, August 30, 2002 8: 43 AM
To: mbrogan@mbc.web
Subject:

It's Friday already. It doesn't feel like it. It was nice
hearing your voice last night too, baby. I hope it made
up for the lack of emails over the past couple of days.

I don't have any real plans for next weekend except that
I will be in Chicago. I need to find out what my kids
are up to and I need to see an old business associate at
some point. I think I will say I am staying with him if
anyone asks. I guess the first thing to do is check my
flight times and then talk to the X about the kid's
schedules.

Slept in a bit again. The extra sleep felt good though.
Thinking of you, as usual, when I woke. You make me

smile, Molly. Time to get ready to go. I will call on
the way to the airport

Love you a lot baby,

Jake

From: mbrogan@mbc.web
Sent: Friday, August 30, 2002 9:24 AM
To: mbrogan@mbc.web
Subject: 6ghosting

Here it is, Friday, and I am still ghosting, love. Guess I
am still pretty rusty at relationships. But I think I have
stumbled onto something here. Ghosting has really
helped me make it through the week. If things can't be
clear between us, at least I can keep them clear in my
head. Keeps me moving forward. I know you are still
stuck. You will just have to catch up when you can.

30, 20, 10 maybe even 5 years ago I would have stopped myself and not moved on until you were ready. That never really worked for me. And after all that I have learned during those sometimes, tumultuous years, it just doesn't feel right any more.

I have done the best I can this week to bring what keeps us from flowing together into the light. I can't do it alone. It took a lot for me to put it out there, to send you 3ghosting. Having still not gotten your response, I don't know if it had an effect. But you seem to still love me. And God knows I still love you. And although that leaves us back at start, it is a start.

I just don't have it in me to go through any more of the toxic dances. You will need to do them alone. The control dance. The bouncing in and out of intimacy dance. The close - distant dance. The avoidance dance. I will wait here for as long as I can to dance with you again. And hope that once you learn the steps of the dance of great love, the dance of depth, the dance of spiritual flight - that you will become more comfortable with them. And leave those other dance steps behind. Join me, forever, in our passionate dance. Have you forgotten it so soon?

It is my experience that one cannot leave the primal dances behind without insight. The need for those dances must be handled, love. I worry that you don't understand that. If you don't, you may continue to dance alone. You would be stuck there. While I kept moving forward. Eventually, the distance will prevent the flow of love, don't you think?

I am dreading this weekend. The distance, the disappointment, the unavailability that has cropped up lately with your visits. When will you come? How long will you stay? Does it matter anymore?

The guides say wait. I can wait. Until the heart break of the distance becomes unbearable. And I can only watch as you vanish, in the distance. Touch me love. Try to move. Can you? God, I hope so. God, help us.

Please hear me,

mb

M ONTH FIVE

From: JAZMAN@mbc.web
Sent: Monday, Sept. 2, 2002   9:51 AM
To: mbrogan@mbc.web
Subject:

I'm back. What are you doing over there sweetheart?
Kicking ass? Why don't you kick mine, or squeeze it?

I sure could use some of you biscuits and gravy right
now. Can't wait to taste your cooking again. Does a
candle light dinner sound good, baby?

I should stop writing and get on the phone with you.
What do you think about that?

Loving you,

Jake

From: mbrogan@mbc.web
Sent: Monday, Sept. 2, 2002   10:23 AM
To: mbrogan@mbc.web
Subject: 7ghosting

Here we are again. So quiet. We just never did get
back into our rhythm did we love? No spiking. No
rapture. I yearn. Every bit of me. Misses you. And
yearns for you.

Is this where we lose it Jake? Where you get all caught
up in your life and leave me behind because in
actuality, you were never ready to have me in your life?
Will I become the girl you left behind? I am feeling left
behind. And then - the obligatory phone call. Where
you talk about the superficial things on your mind. But
end the call with an "I love you, honey," or "baby," in a
voice that melts my heart. And keeps me waiting for
more. Or that fate defining choice to fall in my lap.

I suppose that I am stumbling across those fate defining
choices already. I feel the need to move on so strongly.
Sell or refinance. Share residence. Change jobs.
Change jobs out of state. I can't keep making the
choices to move toward you without doing so for long
love. My choices will begin to work against me. I
hope they haven't already.
We were like strangers this weekend, passing on the
street, compared to our time together last month. So
much difference, so quickly. Does your pain prevent
the intimacy, or something more? Something between
only us, that I did not see coming?

All that meaningful communication, I miss it, not the
wild, desire building stuff. Although I miss that too!
But the soul searching, the future building, the history
sharing. We have fallen into something polite. It
weighs heavily on me. Like the humid August air after
days of rain. But I keep going, because I love you so.

Hear me love, mb

From: mbrogan@mbc.web
Sent: Monday, September 2, 2002   10:32 AM
To: JAZMAN@mbc.web
Subject: phooey

We have gone from 12 to 2 emails a day. Don't you
miss the fun? I do.
mb

From: mbrogan@mbc.web
Sent: Tuesday, September 3, 2002 10:23 AM
To: mbrogan@mbc.web
Subject: 8ghosting

Here we are. Where is that, love? Love, a word you use less and less. Has it become obligatory? Is your caution part of your pulling back? Or have you already left me? Waiting for me to figure it out, and make the first move so that you don't have to be the one to turn away? If so, you probably hate the fact that I keep bringing your new position (away) into the light. With things clear, we would both know that you were the one to turn. Can't do that dance, love. But I can't stop you from avoiding either. Avoiding the discussion. Avoiding our depth. Avoiding my spirit.

The Mary Margaret character in Remember Me began a downward spiral of loss when her marriage ended. It was not within her character to process loss and keep herself in tact. With every loss, she lost a part of herself also. Parts lost to her shadow that would lunge back at her at the next loss, like uncontrollable compounded emotion that could not be contained or released. In the end, she not only lost hope, but herself and was left with only illusion.

I am not that character. And while I feel the pain of loss of you with every breath – with each breath I release you, and all that was possible between us. I release you with gratitude for all you have given me. Thanks for opening me and lifting my heart to new heights. I will always remember. While I feel the collapse, I also know the resurrection.

In my dream, the guide appeared in the middle of the Christmas Tree dream. After running to the front door, and finding a Christmas tree, I decided not to enter the house. Instead, I returned to the street and found the guide.

I said "there you are, I've been looking for you."

He said "I know," and put his arms around me.

As I began to cry I said, "I thought he was the one."

He said, "I know. So did I."

End of dream.
At the time of the dream, I thought I was working on an abandonment issue. Now I know, the dream warning me that you were leaving. I wish that I could remain in the arms of that guide, and continue to feel the comfort. I feel only heartbreak and loneliness.

We share so much spiritual reality. There is so much within our souls of each other. I know it as my awareness soars while looking at you. And your face takes on the familiarity of so many other lifetimes. Changes before my very eyes and I can feel, and I know those other lifetimes in the now. I am blown wide open in your presence. I thought that meant that we are for real. What if it doesn't? How do I know?

I suppose I will need to wait and see what happens in the near future. See if you will continue to drag your feet. See if you will continue to pull back and come up with more excuses. I suppose, I have nothing to lose by waiting. Wait or leave, seem to be my only options. While I wait, I can occasionally have what we share. Know what we know together. Until you pull back completely.

I choose to wait in the hopes of feeling that again. Knowing that again. Together we have great power. That is, when you allow the togetherness. For now, having that once in awhile seems to be preferable to never having it again.

But, I need to begin again to plan my life separate from yours. You have stopped planning a future together. So I will need to get on with mine. I can't wait forever to move on love. When I met you, I was planning to move out of town. If that move is not near you, it will need to be somewhere else.

I can't wait long to decide. I don't have the financial flexibility for that. And the universe isn't sending it to me. I can promise you this: that I will continue to do my best for as long as I can. Make all the moves here that I can, until it is time to move on. I hope that move will be into your arms. But remember: that hope needs action and faith to be meaningful. It cannot stand alone. I suppose the next step for me in my step back is to stop using the word love. Damn. I was so happy to use it again. It pours out of me each moment. But that only works when each moment is every moment, forever. When love exists in rapture. When it is real.

Now, it seems like forever since we have had that between us. It has actually only been a week since forever was part of our love. Why does it seem like forever, because I miss it so? I see myself in a place of pure being. The area of my heart is a spinning ball of light. My heart cries out for my soul mate. He steps out of the darkness and extends his arms as an invitation to dance. I step toward him and his arms embrace me. We slowly dance. A dance of deep desire. A dance of knowing. A pure dance of love.

I know you no longer hear me. Or if you do, you are avoiding me. But the ghosting is my way of trying to reach you. Of continuing to reach for you. Speak to you. Touch you.

Please hear me - mb

From: JAZMAN@mbc.web
Sent: Tuesday, September 3, 2002 5:01 PM
To: mbrogan@mbc.web
Subject:

I thought you were at Meg's. No? Was kinda waiting
for you to call me after you got done over there, but in
case you're not, I'll go outside and call you right now,
baby.

From: mbrogan@mbc.web
Sent: Sunday, September 3, 2002 7:53 PM
To: JAZMAN@mbc.web
Subject: nighty night

Well, I know it is early to write a good night email, but
since we are so FAR off on our correspondence timing,
I don't know if you will even look for this tonight.
And, since I am sitting here in my nighty, what better
time to write a nighty night email?
My day since I last spoke to you? Constant music,
cooked a dinner for Meg and her family (hope it tastes
as good as it looks,) rough draft of the synopsis of the
novel (this could take longer than I thought,) washed
the shower curtain (white) and changed the lining (now
blue,) vacuumed, read the chapter on marital
relationships in The Portable Jung while I rested my
glass of Rumple Mintz on the copy of Dianetics that
you so generously gave me (yes, I will admit that I am
probably self medicating this week with alcohol.)

Did I properly thank you for my gift? It is a beautiful
book. I noticed today when I took the cover off.
Leather bound, my favorite color for a book, burgundy
with gold lettering. I suppose smacking you with it was
somewhat ungrateful. You must know I love it. And
will always treasure it. Read a little each day. Let the
book fall open and tell me what I need to know. Leave
it on the bed always. Thank you Jake.

Just answered the phone (thought it might be you – why do I always hope it's you?) It was Sue, confirming coffee tomorrow morning, She is reading the manuscript and offering suggestions. Yep, I will be in the woods in the morning – then quickly home to pick up the food and the dog – then to Meg's for the afternoon. You will need to ding the cell to reach me.

Yours,
mb

From: mbrogan@mbc.web
Sent: Tuesday, September 3, 2002 8: 52 PM
To: JAZMAN@mbc.web
Subject: 9ghosting

Wrote a pretty good night email. Only used the word love once. So hard for me to ration. Had to keep backspacing and deleting. It pours out to you before I can catch it, love.

"And yet I wish for the thing I have:
My bounty is as boundless as the sea,
My love is deep; the more I give to thee,
The more I have, for both are infinite."

Will I ever be able to send you these words again? They ring true, yet cannot be given.

The horoscope that I read to you on the phone described the distance, and the needed patience. Did you understand that? Or did your heart freeze with your computer? The universe was speaking to us, love. Probably speaking to me through you. I am the one who needs patience. Actually, answered the questions I was asking my guide in my healing place before I was pulled out to call you. I was dialing the number before I was conscious again. Amazing. Whatever must you think of me - and my complex responses? Whatever do you feel for me? Hard to tell, beyond the superficial dialog. Yet I find myself living for that dialog. Your voice's sound, that brings the familiarity of distant lives to the present. That opens my soul and heart. I keep my spirit home as much as I can love, for your sake. But occasionally, I will confess, I cannot stop myself from finding you and going crazy on your neck. And when your tongue finds the deepest parts of my mouth, my spirit is satisfied for a moment. And the moment is eternal. But you don't feel it do you? Maybe you do, but need your distance. I can't tell.

I hate the waiting. But Jung thinks it is all part of marital relations. Which, when all is said and done, is what we have here. The most intimate relations between a man and woman. I won't settle for anything less than sacred, will you? Will you tell me if you decide you need something less? I suppose, if you wait long enough, you won't have to say it. I see through your eyes every day. I will know. When I can't wait any longer I will allow myself to see. And then, I will need to do what is right for both of us. Right now, I love US so much that I might not want to see it. Right now, it doesn't matter if it is there or not. I am content with your company in what ever form, in what ever time you give it. And will remain so. Until I can no longer wait for what I know is possible. Do you know what is possible? I thought you did. Now, I am not sure.

Well, your ghost has done me well again tonight. Two or three times a day, I pour my hear out to you from me now. So I will hold your ghost close. Because I can't hold you. Because I have to keep writing you. Reaching for you. Reaching to touch you, love. With and without words. I wish I understood the reason for where we are. But will remain...

Yours - mb

From: mbrogan@mbc.web
Sent: Wednesday, September 4, 2002 9: 51 PM
To: JAZMAN@mbc.web
Subject: ps

Wrote a pretty good night email. Only used the word
love once. So hard for me to ration. Had to keep
backspacing and deleting. It pours out to you before I
can catch it, love.
"And yet I wish for the thing I have:
My bounty is as boundless as the sea,
My love is deep; the more I give to thee,
The more I have, for both are infinite."

Fills my heart, but I know I should not send it.

The horoscope you read to me over the phone described
the distance, and the needed patience. Did you
understand that? Or did your heart freeze with your
computer? The universe was speaking to us, love.
Probably speaking to me through you. I am the one
who needs patience. Actually, answered the questions I
was asking my guide in my healing place before I was
pulled out to call you. I was dialing the number before
I was conscious again. Amazing. Whatever must you
think of me - and my complex responses? Whatever do
you feel for me? Hard to tell, beyond the superficial
dialog.

Yet I find myself living for that dialog. Your voice's
sound, that brings the familiarity of distant lives to the
present. That opens my soul and heart. I keep my spirit
home as much as I can love, for your sake. But
occasionally, I will confess, I cannot stop myself from
finding you and going crazy on your neck. And when
your tongue finds the deepest parts of my mouth, my
spirit is satisfied for a moment. And the moment is
eternal. But you don't feel it do you? Maybe you do,
but need your distance. I can't tell.

I hate the waiting. But Jung thinks it is all part of marital relations. Which, when all is said and done, is what we have here. The most intimate relations between a man and woman. I won't settle for anything less, will you? Will you tell me if you decide you need something less? I suppose, if you wait long enough, you won't have to say it. I see through your eyes every day. I will know. When I can't wait any longer I will allow myself to see.

I wish I understood the reason for where we are. But will remain...

Yours,

mb

Comes to Light

What happens to me
When I think that I know you,
And unexpectedly find
That I misunderstood
Your signals
And words
And intentions?

Something hidden
Comes to light.
I suddenly see it.
And it readjusts
My entire perception.
My place in the world.
Your place in my heart.

Emotion floods me.
And I pull back.
I observe myself,
And the emotion.
I want to be able to choose it.

Hope that it doesn't choose me.

I struggle to see that
It isn't my only choice.
That at least, I can not choose it.
And not worry
About where that non choice leaves me.
Embrace the nothingness
That may take its place.

Joy, love, happiness
Would be better.
I have become accustom
To those emotions.
Resting in your arms.
Secure in your love.
Until something hidden
Comes to light.

Will it take both of us
To sort this out?
Or will I need
To go it alone.
Individually.
I prefer sharing
But am prepared
To make the individual choice.
Without emotion.
Unless, that is what I choose.

From: JAZMAN@mbc.web
Sent: Thursday, September 5, 2002   9:33 AM
To: mbrogan@mbc.web
Subject: RE: nighty night

My reaction to what you have to say is interesting. I
feel as if being in your physical presence more and
more brings these considerations in on me. Almost like
live entities waking up and saying "Hold on." It sounds

like a warning that jumping the gun could be high risk with potentially dire consequences.

I enjoy being with you. I will enjoy it more when it feels fully safe and we can create together as we envision. All of those beautiful moments we have imagined together can actually become a reality. But I think my fear is related to hurting those that I have already hurt more by doing what I know is right. I think our relationship would pour salt on their open wounds.

There is no one that I can trust in regards to you, except you. Anyone that I talk to about you could potentially make things worse if they broke confidentiality. That is why I feel "hunted" when I am back there. It restricts my reach toward you.

Does this make any sense? This has nothing to do with anything about you, who you are and so forth. You are sooo special to me. I just didn't predict this would all turn on as the divorce got closer. Weird. And I can't help but love you.

Your artistic abilities amaze me. Your poem was well said. Know, that this will all be fine, baby. I have to get through this stage with as little emotional destruction on others as possible. Not easy, and impossible for there to be none.

Funny how I just sit here and think about you when I'm writing. I imagine happy times in many ways, the freedom to be, do, and have what we desire, moments of great pleasure, and general happiness.

I think about the time when we can begin spending all of our nights together. Sometimes I think about living back there again. Those I care most about are all there while I'm here. The same goes for you. Your kids, your friends, your family.

I am extremely aroused today at the thought of you. Now what do I do with that? If I were only alone with you, those eyes, thighs and cleavage…and the beingness that I love so.

I miss you,
Jake

From: mbrogan@mbc.web
Sent: Thursday, September 5, 2002 9: 33 PM
To: JAZMAN@mbc.web
Subject: here or there

What a crazy day. Sorry that after your beautiful email and phone call this morning, I was out of reach until now. You are not answering your cell so you are probably in a meeting. I did not discover that my cell was dead until a few minutes ago on the way home from Sue's. We had dinner together to continue yesterday's sunset discussion which I will now share with you.

I love you Jake. But get such mixed messages from you. Those messages that cannot be spoken are the most confounding. The ones that are spoken, I know, are the ones closest to your heart. But are they closest to our fate?

You are having increasing trouble spending time with me in Chicago, feeling hunted because of circumstances surrounding your family. Understood. You are now reluctant to have me move to SF because of your associations there who also know your family. Not understood. But it seems my understanding is not required there. Where is our place Jake? I feel great loss when I see that you no longer have a future vision for us.

Sue and I have been discussing the possibility of both of us moving to the New York area. She has family there, I have Viv and may be able to secure a position with US Cable, headquartered in New Jersey. More and more I feel that you need time to work through your family issues. And I have been quite honest about my intention to move out of the Chicago area after the holidays. Recently turning down the position in Washington DC seemed the right thing to do and I still feel it was. Where ever I go, I hope I can find you there, one way or another.

I had hoped to move West, toward you. Denver is another possibility since Sue also has family there and it is the home of the corporate offices of my current employers. But where ever I move, will be determined by job opportunity and relationships. Starting over near Sue is inviting, since we know each other so well. This will free you to settle affairs in Chicago without feeling hunted or feeling the need for secrecy. It will free me to develop my future. It will free us to be together in a place without chains. Everyone wins.

Yours always,
Molly

From: JAZMAN@mbc.web
Sent: Thursday, September 5, 2002   10:32 PM
To: mbrogan@mbc.web
Subject: RE: here or there

Your letter threw me off. When are you considering leaving there? I didn't know you disliked it there. Guess I don't fully understand the situation, but I thought you wanted to be close to Jack. And this talk with Sue. I don't get it. What's going on here? We may have talked about this before you read this.

Grace's birthday is tomorrow. Feels strange not being there. Mike is not answering his cell so I don't know if he has picked up her gift for me. Probably will wait until the last minute.

I need to get ready for bed and call you. I miss you honey, and wish that I was there, close to you.

Love always,
Jake

From: mbrogan@mbc.web
Sent: Friday, September 6, 2002 6:00 AM
To: JAZMAN@mbc.web
Subject: RE: here or there

Well, now I'M puzzled. I thought I stumbled on to an "everybody wins" option. And, I thought my intention to move from Chicago next year was clear from the beginning. Yes, let's discuss soon.

If you can, call before 9 – ding me. Otherwise, I will try to catch you after 10. If now, your lunch hour I suppose. Or, let me know your feelings in an email.

I am also puzzled about why you didn't bring it up until the end of the conversation last night. We talked for two hours Jake. I thought you hadn't read the email. We are throwing eachother off here aren't we? Interesting.

Love always,
Molly

From: JAZMAN@mbc.web
Sent: Friday, September 6, 2002 9:06 AM
To: mbrogan@mbc.web
Subject: RE: here or there

Hi. Hope your meeting isn't a total drag this morning. Hope my day isn't either. But, as the saying goes, life goes on, like it or not. Actually, we can control that, just sometimes it's easier than others.

So explain this option where everyone wins. You're in Colorado or somewhere with Sue and I am flying back and forth from SF to Chicago. Are we talking phone sex here? Are you talking about getting out of there while I get my shit together? I'm confused, but am willing to listen. If you say everybody wins then I must be missing something here. That's OK, it wouldn't be the first time.

OK. I am going to order flowers for Grace and try to track Mike down again. I miss you today, wondering what exactly you are doing while I write this. We'll be in touch soon and I'll feel a lot better when I understand. I was too damn tired last night to really get into it. Seemed too important a topic to deal with in that state of mind.
Love - Jake

From: mbrogan@mbc.web
Sent: Friday, September 6, 2002 3:30 PM
To: JAZMAN@mbc.web
Subject: OK there

I am so very glad we talked this thing through today. Here is what I learned:

Never buy olives at the liquor store. Much too pricey. What kind of olives do you like in your martini? Stuffed with pimento – or almonds – or blue cheese…there seems to be a variety out there. My first martini with you this weekend sounds lovely.

And:

Relationships are much harder without the clairvoyance. I feel like the Empath on the Starship Enterprise who lost her powers (Diana Troy?) Thank you for relieving my fear. I was encouraged to hear that our diminished spiritual connection does not mean diminished love between us. The fact that I no longer feel and KNOW your intentions as I have for so long is a mystery to me. But I will take it on faith when you tell me that your love for me is more real than ever.

I am sorry if I threw you for a loop. I just did not understand that you still see us living together in California after the holidays. We hadn't talked about that in quite some time and you seemed to be leaning toward moving back to Chicago. And you seemed to be having more and more difficulty spending time with me in Chicago, and reluctant for me to spend time with you in SF. I am not sure what Sue will think about your idea that she move to SF with me. But we can give it a shot.

Love is much easier when it is not dependent on language. When I saw what you saw, felt what you felt, I did not have to guess and was so certain of your love and my place in your life. But oh well, I guess you will just have to tell me you love me more, darn.

I am very excited that you are coming next weekend, in all ways. I was feeling that I had no place with you, the weekend connection is needed for both of us. And we have the WHOLE weekend together. No distractions, interruptions or intrusions. The beach house will be ready. Otherwise, let's just stay home and enjoy our time. Just the two of us. Let's take this time to begin plans for me to move to California. I will need to get out my resume asap, think about putting the townhouse on the market, and think about how to present this to my children. All this planning while laying in your arms, and in-between the plans, the passion...

I am glad that you will be able to spend Thursday with Grace and Mike. I will be home from work Friday sometime around 4. If you arrive before I do, help yourself to whatever you like in the fridge. I will make sure that you find some of your favorites. But don't start on those martinis without me. I want you in dancing shape when I arrive!

Thanks for the lunch conference call.

Love always,
Molly

From: mbrogan@mbc.web
Sent: Tuesday, September 17, 2002 5:10 PM
To: JAZMAN@mbc.web
Subject: Cried today

Hi Darlin. Cried today when I got home from work to find your beautiful orchids waiting for me on my doorstep. So many orchids and such variety. The colors are breathtaking. Thank you with all my heart.

I've missed the many phone calls and emails. But like you, am working furiously to catch up after exiting the world over the weekend. I carry our brief exit with me in my heart every moment, forever. Hard to believe I will see you again this weekend, so soon.

I can't stop thinking about our night on the beach. Will we have time to return there this weekend? I felt removed from time, as if we had been there many times before, eternally. That our love has been expressed on beaches throughout eternity. And that we were again, totally in touch with the best parts of our love.

I feel the certainty and possibility of US when you are with me. Not so much when you are gone anymore. I miss that. Call tonight for pillow talk if you can manage it. After we hang up, I would love to hold you all night long.

Molly

From: JAZMAN@mbc.web
Sent: Tuesday, September 17, 2002 6:01 PM
To: mbrogan@mbc.web
Subject: RE: cried today

I am glad you liked the flowers, honey. Although I'm
not sure what I feel about the crying. I much prefer
being the cause of your cries of ecstasy when I make
love to you. Here we go, I will be thinking of that
every minute now until I hear your voice tonight.

Your powers are fine, baby. It's mine that are lacking
now. You can't read without light. I think my family
situation is weighing heavily on me. It brings down my
tone. Maybe that is to be expected.

But my love for you is real. As I will show you, again,
this weekend, my love.

Until later my ideal scene,

Jake

From: mbrogan@mbc.web
Sent: Tuesday, September 17, 2002 7:44 PM
To: JAZMAN@mbc.web
Subject: busy girl

Hi Darlin,

My week has collapsed and this may be my only night
home. Tomorrow, I am having dinner at the lake with
Sue after a paddleboat ride at sunset. Thursday I
deliver dinner to Meg and her family, she still has little
strength and needs lots of help. Friday, Jamie's football
game and you (if that is still the plan.)

In between I will be preparing for you so don't be
surprised if I start cleaning during pillow talk.

Any meal suggestions? I will be grocery shopping on the way home tomorrow.

If my powers were fine, I would have been leaving that voice mail when you were typing this email!

I feel very close to you tonight. And have been smiling like crazy.

I do love you so,

Molly

From: JAZMAN@mbc.web
Sent: Tuesday, September 17, 2002 9:32 PM
To: mbrogan@mbc.web
Subject: Jake's girl

I am about to leave the office and wanted to write you one last email, even though I will be calling you as I crawl into bed tonight. I can't stop thinking about you, baby. The way you feel when I hold you, the smell of your hair, what you do when I caress your ear with my tongue, when I message the back of your thighs up and down as we make love, these memories are as real to me as the experiences themselves. As if you are right here with me each moment, and I live in two worlds at once. The day to day, and the real world with you.

The amazing thing is that I accomplished a hell of a lot tonight in the day to day world, while my heart and spirit were in the real world, making love to you. I am glad you feel it.

I feel good about US. You were right, I did take a step back to look at what I was doing and the sequence of it. I do not like the hunted feeling I had which had absolutely nothing to do with you. Just something which will go away once I deal with it. It will be better this time my love.

I am going to call you when I get home. I'm missing your voice, baby. Missing your lips and several other things about you. Be with you in a bit. Mmmmmmmmmmm...I'm right here with you, baby, Jake

From: mbrogan@mbc.web
Sent: Wednesday, September 18, 2002 6:00 AM
To: JAZMAN@mbc.web
Subject: phooey

Woke late after an incredible night with you last night. I thought the PT was splendid. But the spiritual love making afterward was unbelievable. The fact that your spirit can bring my body to orgasm leaves me speechless (and breathless.) I hope this happens to others, one of the true great joys in life.

I am running late this morning, and in my haste, dropped my cell phone in the toilet. Phooey. It will take a day or two to replace. So unless you can catch me at my work or home numbers, I will be out of reach. But I hope you will feel my enormous love for you all day. I will be thinking of you, and smiling for you. Eternally yours,

Molly

From: mbrogan@mbc.web
Sent: Wednesday, September 18, 2002 3:30 PM
To: JAZMAN@mbc.web
Subject: goin home soon honey

The phone calls at work today were a wonderful treat. I wonder if you will ever understand what your voice does to me, especially when you call me baby.

Talked to my printer about the way publishers want the manuscripts bound. They are going to research and get back to me tomorrow. Chicago or Revere screws – whatever they are. Gives me a little more time to finish the formatting.

Paid my annual call to Jamie's counselor who is a wonderful man. I requested him for Jack because I knew he could handle my X. He is the sophomore basketball coach, and a mountain of a man. But very soft spoken (off the court) and articulate. The boys respect him very much. Anyway, I let him know my read on Jamie and the family situation. I know he will call me if I am needed.

Hung up, closed my office door, and cried for 20 minutes all curled up in my chair. But I did it, it is now over. Hopefully, my X will not present any problems at the football game Friday. He has been known to try to start argument with me at the games. Anyway, enough of that. I look so forward to Friday after the game. I will be ready for your arrival. I will let you think about what that can mean. (smile) Pillow talk is going to be splendid.

Forever yours,
Molly

From: JAZMAN@mbc.web
Sent: Wednesday, September 18, 2002 8:42 PM
To: mbrogan@mbc.web
Subject: RE: goin home soon honey

Been working all day like crazy, breaking only to talk to you. Your voice re-energizes me, takes me out of my body and away from to rest of the world. Gives it all perspective so that I can continue.

Lots of difficult calls from the family too. Sounds like things are tough at home for the kids. I wish I could help them more. Mike says she is going a little crazy. Losing it, throwing things. She is really running me down to Grace and trying to alienate her from me. Her business partner called me today and told me that she has asked him to take a leave because of her inability to control her temper and emotions. Her business partner is an old friend and we talked a long time about getting her some help, for the sake of the kids. I am not sure if she will be willing. But maybe if enough people ask her the same thing. I have asked my mom for help with this too. She calls my mom to confide in her from time to time. I can't get a call through to Grace and she is not answering email. I can reach Mike on his cell and he thinks that she is not going to let me reach Grace out of spite. This is so hard on everyone.

Friday night I will arrive about 8:30 and come straight to you. I do need to try to see my kids. I hope you understand. Begin with a shot of your love, which should get me through the rest. I will need to leave after breakfast and head to the kids to see what I can do. I also have some business to clear up this weekend. But I will be there Sunday morning, and probably Monday night before I fly out Tuesday morning. Some time in-between may be possible for us, I am just not sure right now. I wish this weekend could be just ours, like last weekend. But life is pressing me to settle things so that we can be together for good, baby. I live for that day.

Gotta run. Love you.
Until PT,
Jake

From: mbrogan@mbc.web
Sent: Wednesday, September 18, 2002 9:32 PM
To: JAZMAN@mbc.web
Subject: sunset on the lake

It was lovely on the lake. Nice breeze. Sue paddled mostly. But the wind picked up and it took two of us to get back. I told Sue it was a sign that it was going to take both off us to find our course back home. She laughed.

We did talk about the bay area the whole time. She has her resistance, but I could tell she is thinking about it. Northern California will suit her. Organic. You will see what I mean when you meet her. But I told her about the mountains and the ocean view. And the advantages for a business near a major metropolitan area. And the University near by. We revisited the book store dream. She may or may not consider moving to the San Francisco area. It would be nice for me to have friends there.

Do you think you can close the deal? Or at least, more the negotiations along a bit? She was happy to hear that you would join us on Sunday. I was happy she did not completely discount the idea of moving to the SF area. I asked her to consider a trip out there later this fall.

I also finished the formatting on my manuscript. I can have it ready for the printer, who hopefully, will figure out what a Chicago screw is.

So all in all, a very productive evening. I am sorry that you are having a difficult time on the home front. I do know what if feels like to see your kids going through the pain of divorce and feeling the need to protect them from it. Is it difficult, blending endings with beginnings? I will have to make it up to you during PT. Call early, I will get into a VERY soothing place. Ready? I will imagine my lips all over your neck until then, love.

Molly

From: mbrogan@mbc.web
Sent: Thursday, September 19, 2002   8:25 AM
To: JAZMAN@mbc.web
Subject: hmmmmmmmmm

Did you enjoy my passionate views last night on
domestic violence, violent language and cultural
sensitivity? What did get me started? All about
respect. Serious lack of that in this country. I did not
hold back last night did I? I think your laughter drove
me on.

I will share with you that Jack's coping strategy is to
find it somewhat amusing, and accept it with kindness.
He will get a certain look on his face occasionally when
someone that is near us has hit a nerve in me related to
those particular topics. The look is "mom-be careful."
Especially if his friends are anywhere near. Just shakes
his had if I can't stop myself. I will say, in my own
defense, I have not alienated any of his friends. So I
guess they accept the whole package. Or maybe they
just don't want Jack to kick their ass.

I did hear your concern about the home front and your
need for a flexible agenda this weekend. I do want to
caution you that not showing up for coffee on Sunday,
or showing up too late to get to know Sue and talk
about a possible move would disappoint her. I don't
want to do that. She has been looking for direction for
the past year and a half since I reunited with her. Hope
has not been easy to come by since her husband passed
away (Jack's namesake.) Please be careful there, love.

Just let me know about the rest. I should have my new
cell phone today. I have much personal business to
attend today. I need to work on the synopsis of
Remember Me for some of the publishers. Need to
interview some realtors. Selling my townhouse will not
be hard.

I love sharing my days with you, whatever the distance between us. Don't know what I would do if I didn't hear from you for a whole day. Has that happened? I don't remember one. It would certainly be an empty day for me, my love. I am wondering how I would feel if you suddenly disappeared from my life, how I could go on? I suppose I would, I always do. Just don't know how, or in what form.

Tonight I deliver dinner to Meg's. I am worried about her impending surgery. She is so thin and weak already. And it just doesn't seem right that they already have to repair things so soon after the transplant. Meg is the one person in the past 10, long, ugly years since my divorce that I did not have to hold back from. She was always there in a crisis, calling me often before I called here. Her intuition is strong. She would always drop what she was doing and help me through. And visa versa. We both gave others such small doses of the trauma we experienced with violent, deranged X's, knowing all of it would burn anyone else out. But having each other got us through. Together, we learned the true meaning of friendship. And sharing your life. Of giving strength, and getting it from another. The bond is incredibly deep. I very well could have become the character in my book, had I not had Meg in my life. She has been closer to me than any of the women in my family, and has actually taken some of them on in my behalf. Always being angry for my when I didn't have it in me. I just don't know what I would do without her.

Well, this isn't turning out as planned. But I think I will send it anyway. I love you so, Jake.

I look so forward to being in your arms again.

Bright morning to you,

Molly

From: JAZMAN@mbc.web
Sent: Thursday, September 19, 2002   9:15 AM
To: mbrogan@mbc.web
Subject: RE: hmmmmmmmmmm

Good morning my love. I had a restless night and woke
up much too late so I can't write for long. But I did
read your letter and understand what you said about
Meg. I can see that losing her would be a huge loss.
It's a loss when you know the person is OK and is just
moving on, because you still lose them for an unknown
amount of time, certainly for the rest of this lifetime.
Recognizing them in the future is difficult because of
the new look and new things about them. It does help
to know they still exist and the basic being remains the
same. Hopefully, she will come through this somehow.

Talk soon honey,

Jake

From: JAZMAN@mbc.web
Sent: Thursday, September 19, 2002   3:12 PM
To: mbrogan@mbc.web
Subject: my love

It has been so good talking to you today, his morning
and throughout lunch. No one has a voice like yours,
so soothing to me, stirring up such powerful emotion.
God, I love you Molly.

I have been thinking about Meg, and I wonder, is she
connected to someone that makes nothing of her?
Jake

From: mbrogan@mbc.web
Sent: Thursday, September 19, 2002 3:57 PM
To: JAZMAN@mbc.web
Subject: RE: my love

If you mean by "makes nothing of her," does she have
an X like mine and yours, the answer is yes. They
married when she was 18. Is that important to her
continuity? I can certainly see how it might be.

I am on hold with Peg right now. She is squabbling
with an electrician while she is on her cell phone with
me. If she ever gets back on the line, I can finish the
conversation. She is excited about the prospect of Sue
and I moving to SF. She really wants Sue and I to
come out and stay with her for a weekend to get a feel
for the area. Sue and Peg were both bridesmaids for
me. I don't think they have seen each other since. Will
be tricky to schedule though. Peg's interior design
business takes her out of town a lot, she just got back
from Japan.

Well love, I am off soon. Made arrangements to drop
my manuscript at the printers this evening. Still don't
have my cell and I probably won't be home until after
9. Please try to make PT tonight. My interest is piqued
about "makes nothing of her."

Thanks for taking me along at lunch. For the life of me,
I don't know what we talked about. But that voice…it
echoes in my head (and heart) and gives me a certain
feeling. Like I should be kissing you… hearing your
voice calling me baby, how do you do that to me?

Molly

From: JAZMAN@mbc.web
Sent: Friday, September 20, 2002 9:06 AM
To: mbrogan@mbc.web
Subject: RE: my love

Good morning my love. Why does that word do things to you? I am not quite sure baby, but I like it! I am just hours away although I won't know my schedule until I touch base with my kids. I will see you tonight honey.

I need to finish packing now. I will be here for awhile, love, if you can call.

Jake

From: JAZMAN@mbc.web
Sent: Tuesday, September 24, 2002 9:33 PM
To: mbrogan@mbc.web
Subject: home

I'm finally home, honey. Tried to ding you on my way home from the airport with no response. Everything OK?

Thank you for your hospitality this weekend. I find such peace in your home. Such sanctuary.

I will try you again in a bit. Until then, sweet dreams.

Jake

From: JAZMAN@mbc.web
Sent: Wednesday, September 25, 2002 8:34 AM
To: mbrogan@mbc.web
Subject: feel better

So sorry you are not feeling well. Hope today is a better day. Call if you can at lunch. I will look for your emails as well. I am thinking about you.

From: JAZMAN@mbc.web
Sent: Friday, September 27, 2002   9:06 AM
To: mbrogan@mbc.web
Subject: the doctor

I was surprised and a bit concerned that there have been
no emails. This is so unlike you. Talk to me honey, is
everything OK? Are you still not feeling well? Have
you been to the doctor? I hope so if the headache is
still there. I miss you. When I talk to you or am with
you, there is a calming effect for a little while. I will
call soon.
Jake

From: JAZMAN@mbc.web
Sent: Saturday, September 28, 2002   10:14 AM
To: mbrogan@mbc.web
Subject:

Was it just a week ago that I was at your place? Seems
like a lifetime ago. It has been such a crazy week for
me. And still no emails from you.

My ex is very much a concern. Spent quite a bit of time
on the phone with her best friend trying to figure out
how to help her. She has discovered rectal bleeding
and is waiting to hear from the doctor about that. She
thinks it is cancer. She is too enturbulated to work.
She has gotten herself all wound up emotionally and is
affecting too many people negatively too often. I am
afraid to do anything that will cause her to freak out
even more, if that is possible. We are all trying to talk
her into some kind of treatment.

It is late now, and I haven't left for work. Need to get
moving today. Hope the physical stuff is over for you.
Catch you later.

Jake

From: mbrogan@mbc.web
Sent: Monday, September 30, 2002   3:57 PM
To: JAZMAN@mbc.web
Subject: RE:

OK finally back in business. It was very strange to
have that virus come on so quickly after you left my
place. I was so glad when the headache went away
over the weekend. I was truly ready to go in to the
hospital and let them poke and prod me for West Nile.
VERY glad it did not come to that.

I don't think I properly thanked you for the bracelet. It
was a bit disorienting, waking up after you had gone,
seeing the beautiful diamond bracelet on my arm, and
then realizing that I was so sick at the same time. But
as my week in bed dragged on, it brought me much
comfort. I could not feel you close and that was
disappointing. But you are right, that was probably the
illness. The bracelet was my anchor to you. Thank you
Jake, with all my heart.

Did not hear your ding last night. Woke up about
midnight, the time when you usually call for pillow
talk, and tossed and turned awhile. Finally got to sleep
with a heavy heart. Pillow talk was so sporadic last
week.

So here we are. Where is that exactly? We came from
a place of "love you very deeply," and "I am going to
marry you," to "thank you for the hospitality," and
"when I talk to you or am with you there is a calming
effect for a little while." I find the difference stunning,
don't you? You call when you are arriving somewhere
and have little time to talk. That seems so obligatory.

Our weekend together seems so long ago. From my
viewpoint, the distance between us grew as the
weekend progressed. Your arrival was the epitome of
our love in all its depth. And then the silence and

physical distance grew. Life came between us more and more.

I see that you are having trouble expressing yourself here. This also seems to be new. So either you are holding back, or have little left to express to me, which is it Jake?

If you are looking to back away completely, you can do so without explanation. Just tell me. There is no hook to let you off. As a friend, I can still have a calming effect. If that is what is left here, just tell me. I completely understand your fear surrounding your ex and your children. If you don't have it within you now to maintain our relationship while you deal with your family crisis, tell me directly. But know that whether you do or not, will tell us much about the strength of our relationship.

Whatever is between us needs to be REAL. We define the parameters, love or friendship. We both deserve that.

Call or write,

Molly

From: mbrogan@mbc.web
Sent: Monday, September 30, 2002   6:00 PM
To: mbrogan@mbc.web
Subject: ghosting 10

I didn't think that ghosting was going to be necessary anymore, but it is. I thought I was stronger. And that I could accept your absence in my heart and my life. But I can't get you out of my head. You are there constantly and I tell you everything. How the hell do I stop that? Well, if I can't stop it, I can at least relieve the pressure by ghosting.

Christ, I miss you. I can't admit that to anyone buy your ghost. Why? I have great friends who might understand. Isn't it OK if they worry a bit? I certainly worry about them. But they all seem to have their own full plates right now. And I have no one to turn to. I used to turn to you all day, every day. By phone, email, spirit. There is this HUGE hole in my life that even your ghost cannot fill.

I let myself cry over you for the first time yesterday. Over the loss of you. Yesterday, it occurred to me that if I did not allow myself to grieve, it would come back to me in other ways. So I now cry. But I feel angrier now. I thought grieving would relieve the pressure. It didn't. Now I am sad and angry. I felt much stronger before yesterday.

I know I need to pull back and formulate my responses more carefully. Today, my boss told me that my brutal honesty was welcome and not at all over the top or mean. Why did it feel brutal? Why does it all seem so raw? I know I probably helped him more today than ever, because I was not holding back or as diplomatic in my responses. Funny that he appreciated it. He may have thought I was cranky because I am still a bit sick. Well, at least it worked there. Can only hope it works tonight with Meg's family.

God, I wish that I could be telling you this. That I could hear your response, in that voice of yours. The one that blows my spirit wide open. I would know better then. I would probably see what is in store for Meg. Now I only feel it. Do I need you to see it too?

I found my guide in the middle of a dream. The guide wrapped his arms around me and I cried. "I thought he was the one," I said. "I know, I thought he was too," he said.

I would like to believe that meant that you are, and you will come back. It did not feel that way though.

Because I was crying, from the depths of my soul. To relieve the sense of loss. That was a month ago. Right before you began to step back.

You still can't talk about it. I don't blame you. You don't call, and that speaks volumes. Limit yourself to one email a day, if that. Limit us to the bare minimum. I would rather have the bare minimum than lose you completely. But you still take the maximum place in my heart. How do I reconcile that? Every minute of every day, that is my challenge. I would ask you for help. But I know you don't have it to give, love. I would ask you for love, but I am desperately afraid that you don't have that either. Much safer to ask your ghost. And guess at what the answer might be.

Before yesterday I told myself that you were not there for me when I needed you. Asked myself how I would ever be able to trust you again. Told myself you might be the kind of guy that withdraws love regularly, and that I could not love a guy like that. Those statements gave me strength. Do I stop grieving and start telling myself those things again?

I don't know what to do. I want so desperately to hear you say "It will be all right baby." But doubt seriously if I will ever hear you say those words again in this lifetime. Can we get it right in any lifetime Jake? We must - you seemed so excited a month ago. Hopefully, we will again. I will miss you terribly until then. There was never any other. I wonder now, if there will be. This is such a dark night of my soul. Hopefully, tomorrow, I will have more faith in myself.

Until then,

Molly

M ONTH SIX

From: mbrogan@mbc.web
Sent: Tuesday, October 1, 2002 5:01 AM
To: mbrogan@mbc.web
Subject: ghosting 11

 Have been up since two am, when the TV suddenly
went on. Last month, I would have called you, thinking
that you were reaching out to me. Last month, I would
have been right. I could always feel your reach. Until it
stopped.

I wonder if now, we look for email at the same time,
like we used to write and send them at the same time.
Are we both disappointed at the same time? Or are you
doing the sensible thing, and only looking in the
morning, when you are able to respond.

Are you looking at my picture, or listening to my voice
mails, the way I was last night on my front porch at 4
am? Thinking about the days and nights we sat there
together. Did you feel any of that? I suppose not. I
suppose you are completely closed off now. As your
actions tell me.

Your last phone call to me was only 5 days ago. It
seems like a life time. Sometimes, I cannot hear your
voice inside my head anymore. That scares me when I
am afraid to lose you. And reassures me when I know I

need to let go, and wrap myself in the comfort of forgetfulness.

You stopped calling after my email putting myself on the line and telling you that our relationship has changed. You never really did respond to my plea for clarity about US. You can only bring yourself to tell me where you are, alone. Which leaves me here, alone. And us, somewhere, obscured again.

Damn, I miss your love,
Molly

Can You

There are times
When you
Are hard to hold
In the place
Where our spirits meet
And love.
Times when we
Cannot be together
There.

Something or other
Obstructs
The flow of us.
Halts the dance
We dance inside.
Dims the connection
Needed to know us
Without physical touch.

What are those things
That keep us from eachother?
That provides resistance
To our love's current
That flows endlessly
Into forever?

Can we find them?
Reduce them?
Eliminate them?
Prevent them?

You accept them
As life's burden
And seem
Unwilling to self examine
Or analyze
The process.
Is it because
You cannot
Experience US inside
As I do?
You proclaim
That experience
As your goal
But will not plan
Your objectives
To obtain it.

So I begin to worry.
Do we share
This value
Of spiritual freedom,
Of love
In all
Its glorious depth,
In the flight
Of two as one?
Can you see this
As I do?
Or if not,
Are you willing
To follow my lead
And discover
The true intimacy
Of US together?

From: JAZMAN@mbc.web
Sent: Tuesday, October 1, 2002 9:15 AM
To: mbrogan@mbc.web
Subject: RE:

Good morning. I am a bit out of it, didn't sleep well.
Woke about 2 for a couple of hours. Set off the alarm
by opening the window and could not get back to sleep.

Today is an important day. We should know the results
of my ex's tests. I hope they aren't delayed. Life is
complicated enough without major health problems. I
worry about my kids.

I am really spaced out here. Keep making typos and
then have to correct them.
My ex returned to work, at least. I think I will call her
boss today and see how that is working out.

I miss you and your voice. I will call you. The phone
here at the house just rang after I said that. When I
answered, there was no one on the line. Was that you?
Very weird. How is Meg? Talk to you soon sweetheart.
Jake

From: mbrogan@mbc.web
Sent: Tuesday, October 1, 2002 2:12 PM
To: JAZMAN@mbc.web
Subject: RE:

Well, I have not heard from you so I am assuming that
you have not spoken to the doctor. Are you waiting to
hear from a doctor, or relying on what your ex is telling
you? Either way, I hope your anxiety is relieved soon.

I haven't had a chance to talk to Meg since yesterday.
She is still losing weight and they are contemplating a
follow up surgery of some sort. I know that she
minimizes her problems to everyone. I am deeply

worried about her. Am going to deliver dinner tonight so I will get a better feel for what is truly happening. Hopped around at lunch looking for birthday presents, since a few of those are coming up, both Jack and Jamie, Meg, Sue, some others.

Spoke to Sue today. We are having dinner together tomorrow. I am going to give her a signed manuscript. I think she will like it, she seemed to enjoy helping me edit it.

Is this day dragging by, or is it me, who has been up since the wee hours this morning. I think I will grab some invoices and go home. Don't forget to let me know what happens.

Molly

From: mbrogan@mbc.web
Sent: Wednesday, October 2, 2002 6:00 AM
To: mbrogan@mbc.web
Subject: ghosting 12

No email again this morning. When I realized it, I took off the bracelet. Tucked it away in its velvet box and buried it in underwear. I need to let go and find peace with it. We used to run like clock work. Now we just run.

I am beginning to wonder if you have given up. You did talk about people giving up the game when you were at my house. And then stepped so much farther back. Is that the sign of someone who gives up - when they throw love away? Lose their rhythm? Isolate? Allow life to overwhelm them into paralysis?

Then, I wonder more, if I am the one who has given up. Have I given up the game? Is that why everyone around me is giving up, one by one? Sue with her depression, then Meg now you? Just a reflection of my own deep, abiding decision? Christ, what a thought. All of the love, and enjoyable activity could be the morphine drip at the end!

Patience. I am getting so many mixed messages. Stories of relationships that survive rough waters. Stories about opposites living happily ever after. Stories about men returning to troubled marriages. Stories about giving up the game. It is certainly becoming difficult to listen to the angels. So much static, in and out, breaking up, fax noise.

Must be time to pull in a bit. I am no longer sure what to believe in. Nothing is making sense. Not even myself. Time to get quiet. To listen carefully to the silence. Will you find me, or lose me there?

Molly

From: JAZMAN@mbc.web
Sent: Wednesday, October 2, 2002 9:15 AM
To: mbrogan@mbc.web
Subject: RE:

Good morning. Another restless night. Was up again between 2-4. It will be another day of fatigue as I battle the stock market fluctuations.

There is so much going on in your life right now, with Meg's recovery, football season, and Sue getting back into the game. I have my stuff going on too. I wonder what the truth is with my ex. As time goes on, I question whether I am getting all of the data.

Have to hop into the shower. I will call you in awhile.

Jake

From: mbrogan@mbc.web
Sent: Wednesday, October 2, 2002 11:13 AM
To: JAZMAN@mbc.web
Subject: RE:

Sorry I missed your call. Caught up with the
contractors in routing issues.

Have a raging headache from out of body stuff last
night. I guess I should have known better. The good
news is that I have narrowed it down to particular
meditations that I can now avoid. Won't have to stop
everything. I will miss you there, though.

Had a brief conference call with Meg's sisters this
morning (she has an abundance of them.) I am deeply
worried about her medical setbacks.

Have you considered talking to a counselor yourself
about what is going on with your ex and children?
Maybe someone in the Church of Scientology could
help. I know that an objective perspective helped me
during the tough times. The constant chaos and crisis
(for you over the past few weeks) – the control with
fear – the pathology that I was feeding into without
knowing it. Counseling really opened my eyes to it and
how I was feeding into it. Or you can keep putting your
life on hold and wait for her to twig. I have been there
too.

Molly

From: JAZMAN@mbc.web
Sent: Thursday, October 3, 2002 9:06 AM
To: mbrogan@mbc.web
Subject: RE:

Good morning over there. I meant to call last night, but
passed out. I slept with my phone on all night and

woke at 4, tossed and turned. Finally gave up and got up.

Saw some friends from Deerfield last night. They don't work as many hours and are living large. Discouraging.

How was the conference call? How was your dinner? Hope the headache was gone by then. So certain meditations can be avoided and you don't have that problem? I would love to hear more about that.

Counseling – we have had some of that. It just convinced me that I did the right thing deciding to divorce her. But the divorce created some lower tones in her and my kids and is still somewhat hell for me. Just a different hell. I can't consider what makes others happy forever. I have been trying to take it on a gradient for the past couple of years, but think now that may have been a waste of time. I used to be so close to Grace. At least she is being a little more friendly now, but I miss the closeness to her. I can only imagine her suppressed emotion and it makes me sad when I think of how close we used to be. I guess I lose either way I go, but consider the relationship can be improved over time.

Anyway, here I am in something I don't need to be in right now. I'm pretty good at holding stuff away, but she is a tough one. Similar to your situation with Jamie, I am sure.

Haven't checked with the doctor. Don't even know who she is. Too much stress. Need to get out of work earlier, start taking lunch again. Can't stay away and can't sleep. Strange place.

I really hope you are doing all right. Will call you soon.

Jake.

From: mbrogan@mbc.web
Sent: Thursday, October 3, 2002 10:32 AM
To: JAZMAN@mbc.webSubject: RE:

Well, OK. More emails might be nice. We keep
missing each other by phone, but I can feel you
reaching for me. Let's see…

Dinner last night with Sue was great. Met a new friend,
it has been a long time since I did that. I think that
happened last night. Sue introduced me to a local shop
keeper, Anne, who kept doing the penetrating eye
search. I knew she was looking for confirmation of
affinity, I also felt it. Sometimes those feelings don't
pan out for me. Sometimes they do in a major way
(Meg.) Sometimes they take 30 years (you.) I wonder
if Anne is available for Sunday morning coffee.
Hmmmm.

The conference call with Meg's sisters was good. They
were very appreciative and seem to understand my
concerns for Meg's health and survival. I think they
understand now that their effort needs consolidation. I
heard from Meg last night at 10 PM.   (That is two
nights in a row isn't it?)

Anyway, it was the first time she asked about you in
quite some time. She was sorry to hear that things had
cooled for us. I let her know I was fine with it.

You think you are good at holding stuff away? You are
not as opaque as you think, dear. But that is probably
another guy/girl thing.

Tonight I am having dinner with Sue at a restaurant
along with some of her friends and family, including
Jack's (her husband's) sister.

Well, I guess that is it for now. Your turn - Molly

From: JAZMAN@mbc.web
Sent: Thursday, October 3, 2002 8: 34 PM
To: mbrogan@mbc.web
Subject: RE:

I can see that you are just fine. Handling one problem after another, going out and having fun. Enjoying life. Glad to hear the conference call went well. What do you think needs to happen for Meg to recover fully?

Still haven't gotten word on test results for my ex. I am very worried that the problem is cancer. She has the kids all worked up about it and I feel helpless from here. Looks like another long night at work. I will probably call you later if I am conscious.

Sweet dreams,

Jake

From: mbrogan@mbc.web
Sent: Friday, October 4, 2002 10:41 AM
To: JAZMAN@mbc.web
Subject: RE: ?

OMG (Oh my God!) NO – "Probably call you later if I am conscious," will more than likely GET YOUR ASS KICKED. Well, I will give it my best shot here, Jake. For now, I suggest, don't GO NEAR the mention of a phone call until you get millenniums closer to the sensitivities of a woman. I would really like to see you live much longer.

What did happen to that guy that knew just what to say and how to deliver? Exhausted, or no longer interested in the sensitivities of women?

Last night was great. I only had to threaten to kick ass once. Sue looked at me and laughed her best laugh.

Jack's sister, Eleanor, is VERY suburban. Dating the president of a Midwest area bank. She brought a stupid birthday crown for Sue to wear (yes, in the restaurant.) Sue was embarrassed and Ellie was insistent. I hid the crown on my knee under the table and Ellie actually looked under there for it! But when she asked the waitress if they would sing a song, well I had to do my thing. Sue does not like any of that but all she could do was blush.

Sue said, "Mary advocates for people."

I laughed and said, "sure I advocate, and I also kick ass."

Luckily, Ellie dropped the whole thing with a smile. What do I care, I haven't seen her in twenty years. May not see her again! Sue's friend Michelle, who I adore, opened up after that and made the night completely enjoyable. Sue and I plan to go downtown to her gallery (Atlas) and see the private showing of Grace Slick's artwork. Should be great people watching. It is always nice to see Michelle in her element.

You and your family are in my prayers. My read is that it will not turn out to be cancer. Probably a combination of hemorrhoids and drama. Afterward, some other crisis, MUCH WORSE, will arise. Do I sound cynical? Sorry. Meg reminded me that her X pulled the cancer ploy too. Right before a flimsy, half hearted attempt at suicide. She and I know much about being controlled by fear. Between the two of us, we have seen a great deal of it. YOUR fear allows. Otherwise, it is just someone else's nasty scene. She will run out of steam sooner or later.

Well, I am leaving town tonight and spending the weekend with Jack. You might not see this today so if I don't hear from you, I will catch up with you next week - Molly

Once

Once, for an eternal moment
I could reach for you with my heart
And find you, eagerly waiting
To touch me completely.

Once, and not so long ago
I could think of you
With total love
And you would answer
With a letter, or a phone call
Before the thought had ended.

Once, whenever fear gripped me
Making my need for you
Instant and absolute,
You knew it
And came to me immediately,
Before I could ask.

Once, you responded
To each of my entreats
Tenderly, entirely
So that our dance of passion
Traversed depths before unimagined
And since untouched.

Now, we are locked in five senses
Living like others do
Without those rare qualities
Of souls linked
And spirits in constant communion.

Here, I will revel in those five senses
Taking my fill of them every moment
Learning all I can of you through them,
The sweetness, the light,
The focal connection they provide
To awareness, as occasionally

They combine and blow the lid
From sensory constraints
That define us.
And our souls connect and open
Without needing the rest.

Because wherever you are
Is extreme sweetness for me
When I am there also.

From: JAZMAN@mbc.web
Sent: Saturday, October 5, 2002   8: 34 AM
To: mbrogan@mbc.web
Subject: Saturday

You're right. I didn't see this until the morning. So
good morning to you. Your letter makes it sound like
you had a blast at Sue's birthday. I could use that. I am
meeting some people from Chicago tonight, but will be
lucky to make it past 10. I have turned into such a dork
out here.

Did Sue ever put on the crown? Do you have pictures?
Can you send a picture of Meg?

Your poem, as always, is beautiful, like you. I
especially like the ending.

Cleaning people are here and I have to let them in. I
will call later today.

Kick ass,
Jake

From: mbrogan@mbc.web
Sent: Monday, October 7, 2002   10:41 AM
To: JAZMAN@mbc.web
Subject: OK

I will answer this now because I won't be in the office or near my computer after noon. But I will be home tonight (finally.) Need to catch up with myself

I got a shipment of books today, yea! I had to remember what I did with my spare time before Jake. And it occurred to me that I haven't read a novel since last May. So I ordered some new ones through my favorite 90% discount book place. Will help keep my mind off stuff during the waking hours. Drawing is only good for times when intensive thinking is needed. Somehow, drawing provides focus and intensity to thought. Been so long I forgot that.

Anyway, my life is filling back up. Finding my peace again. Thankfully.

Hope you have a great time with lots of laughs tonight. Shit, I think I had a glimpse of that. The laughing brought it back. Now the chills.

Jack is coming home this weekend, his bye week. (Puts my plans to explore job opportunities at UW Madison on hold.) Sue's oldest daughter is coming home from college too so we may be able to get these two together for the first time since they were 6 & 5. Can't wait to see how they respond to each other. I love them both completely. Held them both on their first day in the world. They both gave me that steady, loving, thoughtful gaze.

I found an interesting passage from Thomas Moore this morning, my favorite Jesuit/Psychologist/Theologian. I like him because he blows open the Catholic box:

""We could understand the arrival of a cool emotional temperature as a phlegmatic phase in the relationship, and we could 'ride' that emotion to wherever it is going to take us for whatever period of time." Sounds like what I am doing now, how about you? It goes on...

"A sometimes difficult yet important part of caring for the soul involves distinguishing carefully what is going on. It may take time, reflection, conversation, or even some form of therapy to discriminate the feeling and fantasies that are part of a cool cycle. Sometimes the emotion may be connected not only to the soul's own movement, but also to our reactions to that movement. A cold and distant air, different from the soul's own temperature, may develop as a quality of our relationship to the soul.

Another way of imagining numbing in a relationship is to remember that as the soul moves in its cycles, we may sense the transition periods as empty and arid. For the moment there may be no focus on clear theme. Relationships have their cycles too, and their transitions may be difficult to live through because they feel cool. When cooling of feelings seems to be part of the natural soul rhythms, we could honor them and even take their lead as we cultivate out lives. For example, we could learn something about ourselves and about our partners by entertaining the thoughts and images that arise out of our cool moods. We could notice where the feeling take us in memory, thought, and fantasy. We could trust that these images contain insight into our situation and might help give us grounding in a time of confusion.

Couples who sense flat and cool moods descending on them might ask each other not why this is happening, but what it is asking of them. Entering into numbness, they may find truths about their relationship and about themselves in the relationship that cannot be seen from an arid, enthusiastic life together. Numbness is not a path, a rather perverse way toward a deeper and possibly more honest participation in life. And paradoxically, there is a special kind of fertility available in places that are allowed to be exquisitely emptied of former growth and productivity.

The arrival of a flat tonality in life can perform an important service to the soul. By frustrating our attempts to live life as we imagine it best, the soul, so much more vast in perspective and potentiality, has a chance to insert itself. A flat mood, like a flattened piece of land, is something that can be built upon."
I found it fascinating., especially as I described our relationship as having "cooled" to Meg the other night before reading this.

Anyway – you are not a dork. You are just a guy that needs to take much better care of yourself. Which includes letting people in to love you. Taking your vitamins, a little exercise, a little diet change, and a lot more fun and laughing. Get on that, for God's sake Jake. Don't make me come out there and kick your ass. Take care - Molly

From: JAZMAN@mbc.web
Sent: Monday, October 7, 2002   11:04 AM
To: mbrogan@mbc.web
Subject: RE: OK

I looked for an email all weekend. I guess I forgot you were going to Augustana. Did you get my phone message?

I dreamt of you last night. Can't remember exactly, but woke up thinking of you and smiling.

When is Jack coming home exactly? You are looking for jobs in Madison? I think you should stay put, stay with the people that love you. I know first hand how hard it is to miss your kids.

Sue is a unique person, likable, someone to get close to, with high integrity. Like you, no wonder you are close. She will make someone very happy when she is back in the game. It is all in the decision. But making that decision sometimes means that opposing considerations be de-energized. Eliminated completely, or you will have a wobbly postulate.

Well, you are probably in your weekly staff meeting by now. I will ring you when I leave the office. I miss you.

Jake

From: mbrogan@mbc.web
Sent: Wednesday, October 9, 2002   5:44 AM
To: JAZMAN@mbc.web
Subject: ouch

We have been missing each other lately, haven't we. I don't think I realized it until I looked at your last email dated Monday!

Went with Sue to hear Peter sing and have dinner last night. How can three glasses of wine produce such a headache? Might have to take a snooze by the river at lunch time.

It was fun. Sue is getting closer to formulating a business plan that might work anywhere she decides to settle. We talked in length about my financial restructuring, and job search outside of the state. I need to decide if it would be better just to sell the townhouse now, and rent for a few months until I move out of state. In that case, I would realize more of my equity. I will need to decide next week when all of the good faith estimates from the refinancing companies will be in.

What holds me back from deciding is the fuzzy future plan. I hate moving so. And I have not done much of it at all in the past 30 years. But prior to that, moved around a great deal. Maybe I am just moving back to that state. It was a time of tremendous spiritual growth, like now. Do I keep more of my net worth, minimize the baggage, sell the house, become much more spontaneous with my life decisions and probably move around much more? Or continue to value the stability of a "home" and pay for it?

I may stop trying so hard to link my life to another's and just get used to the notion of moving on alone. That seems to be where I am headed. Sue is still not sure of anything. Her mind changes frequently. I'm ready to consider moving on alone, and all the possibilities that might bring. It feels comfortable. There is peace there.

Well, I am thinking myself into a stronger headache, so I will push this away for the rest of the day and resume the contemplation tomorrow. I suppose I should run some of this by Jack this weekend before I make any financial decisions.

Hope your day was a good one.

Yours,
mb

From: JAZMAN@mbc.web
Sent: Wednesday, October 9, 2002 6:00 PM
To: mbrogan@mbc.web
Subject: RE: ouch

Well, sorry about the headache. Other than oral sex, a nap, aspirin or Bloody M--- might take care of it. Judging from the time of your email and the time we hung up last night, only six hours of sleep might have had something to do with it.

Thanks for calling when you got home last night. You were in a good mood. I liked that. Mmmmm. And you have gotten Sue thinking about the future, good work on that. She's very cool, you know. She deserves some happiness again.

What are the costs to get a line of credit and how much interest do you save per month by paying off the credit cards? On 50K for each % point it's 41.67 per month, so your knocking out credit cards at a 10% higher rate, that's over $400 a month! Plus when you pay them in full after the closing the entire last month is interest free if the balances are for purchases. That can be hundreds more. Then the interest you do pay on the line is tax deductible so 7% becomes 5% with that 2% being a tax deduction. In a few months, this can add up. The variables are the amount of your debt to be paid and the closing costs. Renting can be as much or more than the mortgage payment when tax write offs are figured in. Property values are rising about .5% every month right now, which can also be taken into account if you keep your home. So, that is my analysis.

Tried to call you a few times today, but you must have been tied up in meetings.

I didn't know you were already sending out your resume to places other than Madison. I wonder why we did not talk about this last night. I will be calling you pretty soon, baby, and we can talk about it then.

Jake

From: mbrogan@mbc.web
Sent: Friday, October 11, 2002 5:35 AM
To: JAZMAN@mbc.web
Subject: interesting morning

Strange morning here. I had so many dreams last night about children. Lost children. Reading mail with children. Forts in the woods made by children. Don't know what I was working on. Think it had something to do with children? Woke up feeling hopeless and wondering why the hell those guides sent me back here last February after my back injury. It is hard to feel myself lately. Guess this is where the lessons in patience come in.

I am feeling very disconnected this morning. Odd feeling. Like something's coming. Or impending. I might be pushing away too much that I should be dealing with. Hmmmm.

Why am I looking to move? (I did not forget that I owe you an answer.) Last spring before we rekindled our affinity, I was generating opportunities anywhere in the country as I was feeling the need to move out of state. I have been getting advise to put as much distance between myself and my X as possible since I filed for divorce. Now that Jamie is living with his dad and not having much to do with me, and Jack away at college most of the time, it seems right.

I think I would like to end up out west. But as things keep changing for me, and the people around me keep changing their minds, it looks as if I will be on my own again. I had to ask myself – how far away from everything I know do I want to be, all on my own?

Ultimately, any move I make will depend on employment opportunities and people I know in the area

---

Right now I have gone back to generating as much opportunity as I can to see what comes up. Eventually, I will need to decide. Right now, the immediate decisions are financial and personal, not career. But I am preparing myself for a time when the career decisions will need to be made.

Was that more information than you needed? Seemed like a long explanation. I am a little out of it this morning. Is too much sleep possible?

Talked to Jack last night. He is driving home today because this weekend is his bye week. I get into this amazing place of peace whenever we speak. Anyway, I got him to commit to dinner with Sue and her eldest daughter Lauren Saturday. Lauren is coming home from school this weekend too (SIU.) These two kids have not seen each other since they were six or so. We have been trying to get them together for many months, but they are never around at the same time. Sue wants to go to a Karaoke place because Lauren loves to sing. That will be fine with Jack, who would much rather stay in the background and give her the spotlight. Should be fun.

Anyway, enough about me. How did your day go? Did you work long and hard again? Did you smile today Jake? If not, smile once for me, please.

Molly

From: JAZMAN@mbc.web
Sent: Friday, October 11, 2002 9:06 AM
To: mbrogan@mbc.web
Subject: RE: interesting morning

You know sometimes dreams don't mean anything, just random pictures forming together presenting themselves as a little story. Dreaming of children is usually related to happiness. Thinking of happiness is a good thing, so is dreaming about it.

Molly, I would really like to see you stay in Gurnee until everything settles down. You care for so many people there. Same for me except I am out here trying to start a new life, wondering if I should be there. I miss my kids and there is not a lot of happiness with that big hole in my life. Getting away from the ex was good, but leaving them behind really sucks.

For you, I'm not sure that the grass will be greener somewhere else. More money is good, but is it required? There may be opportunities in Chicago with more money.

I am out of time already. I type too slow or think too much in between. I will call you later sweetheart.

Jake

From: mbrogan@mbc.web
Sent: Saturday, October 12, 2002 1:05 AM
To: JAZMAN@mbc.web
Subject: home

We are home now. All banged up and badly confused (Jack in body, me in spirit) but safely home.

Molly

From: JAZMAN@mbc.web
Sent: Saturday, October 12, 2002 9:06 AM
To: mbrogan@mbc.web
Subject: RE: home

I was so alarmed when I got your call yesterday and told me you were on your way to the emergency room because Jack had been in a car accident on the way home. Thank you for letting me know and for the follow up email. I will let you two rest and try to call later. I am so sorry Molly.

As I look over your last email, it seems as if you had a feeling that something was going to happen – your dreams about children, feeling of something impending, wondering why you are here. I feel for you, baby.

Concussions can be so unpredictable. Who do you have that can read the MRI information for you. I have a friend in Chicago that may be able to help.

I am coming to Chicago next weekend and hope to be able to see you in some form or another.

Jake

From: mbrogan@mbc.web
Sent: Thursday, October 17, 2002 2:04 PM
To: mbrogan@mbc.web
Subject: ghosting 13

So much loss lately. You, Meg, Jack, Jamie. I know that Jack will be fine, but the events of the weekend took me to a place where I had to face the fact that he could be taken from me at any moment. Everyone can be taken from me at any moment. I can be taken at any moment. When our soul mates are so much a part of who we are - how can that not be painful? How do we go on in tact? Those attachments...

The fact is that I am in transition. Is it me, or just midlife? Children gone, friends moving on, love lost. I am so tired of being alone. I do everything I can think of internally to bring someone to me. It doesn't happen.

"I thought he was the one."

"So did I."

I am having a crisis of faith that is difficult to work through. Time passes. I meditate more. Ask the guides. Do everything I can. No results. Everything and nothing changes. Everything - more and more loss. Nothing - the heart I most desire is still obscured. I struggle to remain above the emotional reaction. I can't say that I am winning that fight. How do you do it?

You seem there, and not there. Interested and distant. Not there when I need you most. You are avoiding my need. Is it destructive? Then I should let it go. I haven't figured out how. Part of the fight.

Christ, there are moments when ALL I want is for you to hold me again. But know, that you probably never will. The waste of potential is painful. Why? We were so close. The spiritual reality was so deep and so real. What did we do wrong?

Your email after Jacks accident seemed so sincere. And then you vanish. Are you not able to face difficulty? Upset about something I did or did not do? I will not know unless you expose it. And am so tired from the events of the week that I do not have the energy to pursue your feelings. As I drove Jack back to school yesterday at his insistence, every thing in me did not want to let him go. He is still so banged up. His headaches are painful, I can tell. What a Spartan, to continue on without complaint.

I keep thinking that a good night's sleep will improve the reality. It doesn't. So every morning I pray for the strength to make it through another day like yesterday. And pray that no more loss comes my way. I honestly don't think I can take more. I am not sure I am going to make it through what I have. Until I meditate, and slip into that place above opposition. Back and forth. If I could become a hermit, and meditate always, only come back when I need to sustain the body - I could do it then. Where do I sign up?

Would you miss me? You disappeared again when I needed you most. Do we have a pattern developing here? I do not need to be alone in another relationship. I do not need another guy running the other way when times are tough. I suppose, if that is the way it is, it is for the best.

Well, I will go looking for answers again tonight. And carry on tomorrow. What else can I do? continue to self audit. I guess it has worked so far. Seems to be taking so long. Long, long time (we always go back to Without a Word.) Round and round.

And where are you Jake? Here I am, back to ghosting. Whatever works…

From: JAZMAN@mbc.web
Sent: Saturday, October 19, 2002   11:04 AM
To: mbrogan@mbc.web
Subject: hi

I am writing you from the club during my first free moment so far. Things are very crazy for me this weekend and it does not look like we will be able to get together. Hope all is well and Jack is OK. Will he play next weekend?

Jake

From: mbrogan@mbc.web
Sent: Monday, October 21, 2002   11: 22 AM
To: JAZMAN@mbc.web
Subject: reconnect

Seems like so long since we talked last, I forgot where we were. Can you take a moment Jake, and tell me what I am to you now? I may be different than I was when last we were completely connected, so much has happened it seems. Jack's accident really shook to the core. I am examining my attachments, all of my reactions, every part of me.

Jack's coach has found us a Neurologist near school and Jack will be seeing him regularly. His MRI showed an irregularity in an artery of the brain, so he is out for the season. Just as well, as his headaches are persistent. Spoke to the Dean, who has informed his teachers to give him more time to complete work, but he is not asking for it. Still getting As on everything, the hard way. He is one tough bird. It is a great school, and a strong support system sprung up immediately, thanks to the marvelous head coach of the football team. I am very grateful Jack chose Augustana.

As for me, I got out for awhile with Sue last night. We went to see Peter play with his full band, the same country swing music my X and I danced to for years before the kids came along. Actually did a bit of dancing with old friends who made me laugh quite a bit. Helps redirect attention and move on fast, as you would say.

Tonight, I will pack up the manuscripts to ship off to the publishing houses. Keep a good thought for me.

Hope your weekend is all you need it to be.

Molly

From: mbrogan@mbc.web
Sent: Thursday, October 24, 2002   2:04 PM
To: mbrogan@mbc.web
Subject: ghosting 14

If only to break the spell of 13ghosting. Have not indulged myself in awhile. Lucky 13 brought no such luck.

Your spirit has a hold on me and I cannot break free. So I have asked you to tell me what you feel for me. You have not been able to do so since you left my arms, so many weeks ago. I don't know why. But don't think I can go on like this without letting you go. I need you to tell me it is time. That you no longer feel the way you said you once did. Eternally mine. That promise had so much depth. And took with it, so much meaning. Hard not to give up the ghost. Living with your ghost would then be so much easier.

I would like to create a fabulous ending. Write our story, based on our correspondence. I hope you will allow me this. You, of course, will have editorial and revenue rights. I will change your identity and mine to suit our needs. It is a marvelous story. And I know that I could sweep a reader away, the way I was swept away. And leave them satisfied in one way or another at the end. And my hope is, that this would also provide an ending for us that will leave us able to let go and love again. I am far from there now.

All of the other plans that I have concocted to allow me an ending, I don't have the heart for. Brief flings, life as a biker bitch....when it comes down to it, there would not be enough of me in them. But a good book...now that is me. Thoroughly me. I think that I could then say goodbye. And leave us something concrete to live on. Like a child, or a love - neither of which we were able to create together this time around. Would a good story suffice? We have so much power together, I can't imagine it not spawning a life of it's own, our story.

Maybe after drenching myself in your spirit day after day through this book, it will finally reach the saturation point and release me. I have done everything I can think of that won't diminish me further, to let you go. But I may need to be completely diminished to let you go. Because you are in me to the core. Maybe, by

becoming this character, I can annihilate myself, and
then recreate and let go.

Think about it. The risk is low. The rewards could be
great.
mb

From: mbrogan@mbc.web
Sent: Sunday, October 27, 2002 11: 31 AM
To: JAZMAN@mbc.web
Subject: a good idea

Your spirit has a hold on me and I cannot break free. So
I will again ask you to tell me what you feel for me.
You have not been able to do so since you left my arms,
so many weeks ago. I don't know why. But don't think I
can go on like this without letting you go. I need you to
tell me it is time. That you no longer feel the way you
said you once did. Eternally mine. That promise had so
much depth. And took with it, so much meaning. Hard
not to give up the ghost. Living with your ghost would
then be so much easier.

I would like to create a fabulous ending. Write our
story, based on our correspondence. I hope you will
allow me this. You, of course, will have editorial and
revenue rights. I will change your identity and mine to
suit our needs. It is a marvelous story. And I know that
I could sweep a reader away, the way I was swept
away. And leave them satisfied in one way or another at
the end. And my hope is, that this would also provide
an ending for us that will leave us able to let go and
love again. I am far from there now.

All of the other plans that I have concocted to allow me
an ending, I don't have the heart for. Brief flings, life as
a biker bitch....when it comes down to it, there would
not be enough of me in them. But a good book...now
that is me. Thoroughly me. I think that I could then say
goodbye. And leave us something concrete to live on.

Like a child, or a love - neither of which we were able to create together this time around. Would a good story suffice? We have so much power together, I can't imagine it not spawning a life of it's own, our story.

Maybe after drenching myself in your spirit day after day through this book, it will finally reach the saturation point and release me. I have done everything I can think of that won't diminish me further, to let you go. But I may need to be completely diminished to let you go. Because you are in me to the core. Maybe, by becoming this character, I can annihilate myself, and then recreate and let go.

Think about it. The risk is low. The rewards could be great.

mb

From: mbrogan@mbc.web
Sent: Wednesday, October 30, 2002 2:22 PM
To: mbrogan@mbc.web
Subject: ghosting 15

Silence. Your silence. My call said "please call me. We need to talk. Or if you don't I will know it is because you don't want to talk to me again. One way or another, I guess I will know."

My email told you that I need to hear you say that you are no longer mine. Not saying it is just as emphatic. Your silence says more that your words probably could. Your words have pacified until now. Your silence abandons. Have you chosen martinis over me?

But I can now move on. Erase your voice. Take all evidence of you from my computers. I now know it is final. Accepting the finality will be the next step.

You will not give permission for me to write our story.

Can I write it anyway? Probably. I will just have to write it over entirely. Erase your words, like your voice or your presence on my screen. Rewrite you. There could be some relief in that. I could use some relief from you. I hold you with an open hand little bird, and whisper, "fly away now."

I will get over you. Writing our story should keep me busy through the holidays. After that, who knows. Until then, I have renewed determination to get over you. Because your silence makes nothing of me. And I have had enough of that to last eternity.

mb

From: mbrogan@mbc.web
Sent: Wednesday, October 30, 2002 11:22 PM
To: mbrogan@mbc.web
Subject: ghosting 16

Lots of ghosting today. Probably why I feel like a ghost. Unreal, empty,
unheard.

I am having trouble coming up with something to say to you that is void of anger. I guess I am angry. Moving right along in my grief. I guess that is a good sign. It feels so bad.

It will be a good day when I finally have no urge to reach out to you. To send an email. Or hear your voice. Or find your spirit. Can you stop finding mine when I am calling for someone? It might help.

Last night when your spirit came to me, I asked you to hold your passion. To sit with me quietly. I let my love light shine, quietly. Until I lost you. I can not continue to
receive your passion and let you go. I need to stop. I need to move on. And so do you. If you didn't, you

would have told me by now.

I have been asking you to tell me what you feel for me
for weeks now with no
response. Time to let go. Let me go. Please. God help
me.

M
ONTH SEVEN

From: mbrogan@mbc.web
Sent: Monday, November 4, 2002 4:20 AM
To: mbrogan@mbc.web
Subject: ghosting 17

As I gather the material for our story, I see that as our passion gathered strength, there was no mention of your marriage as a barrier. No mention that you would not be able to love me while you created your ending. Only a crescendo of attraction and affinity and discovery of spirit. Sheer passion. For both of us.

In the beginning, I encouraged you to take your time, never thinking that it would mean that we could not be together. That you would stop expressing your love. That you could not come to me. There was no hint of that. The opposite. Much talk of needing to spend days and nights together very soon. What happened? How did that become impossible? What did I miss? I did not see that coming. Did everything I could think of to stop it.
But back you stepped, farther and farther. Out of my control, just like falling in love with you was out of control. Was it just as inevitable? What was I missing? What did I not see? I wish I knew.

I should have stopped myself when you told me you were not yet divorced. But had I done so, I would never have discovered how to call you out. How to receive you and all of your love each night. How, when connected to you, life opened up to me within each instant. And my rapture blossomed. With my love. It all seemed so perfect. What made it fall apart? I wish I knew.

Reviewing all of the material helps me to understand why I am having such a hard time letting go. The depth and breath of this love was incredible. It budded, blossomed and withered so quickly, so intensely.

I wonder if there is a flower that blossoms at night and withers with the light of day. With a life span of one night. Note to self, call the botanical gardens. The perfect title to our story. Gone so quickly.

I had a co worker look at me today and ask if I was down. He said "don't worry, he still loves you." I wanted to believe that the universe was speaking to me. But I can't let myself think that way anymore. It brings so much pain. I surrender.

I miss you so. And wonder, how you were able to disregard me so easily. How can you not feel this emptiness? Have you forgotten those things you said? I will never know. Because you will not tell me. No response. Ties severed.

I did the best I could to be honest and still stay near. Both were not possible. Sorry. For both of us.

From: mbrogan@mbc.web
Sent: Thursday, November 7, 2002   6:00 PM
To: mbrogan@mbc.web
Subject: ghosting 18

1+8=9, my destiny number. I thought mine was you, Jake. How was I so wrong? And how do I get past the feeling that you are? And where do I go from here? I wanted so much to believe. Still do want it but don't dare.

I keep asking the guides for help. Go to the healing
places with others, Jack, Meg, Sue. You taught me that
I could heal. You showed me those places inside.
Today at the river I asked the guides to surround me,
and heal me. Help call someone to love out. I was
afraid you would show up. Was that you? I asked him
not to let go, like you did. He said he wouldn't. But then
again, so did you. In the same place.

You explained it away as a wobbly postulate, n your
inevitable indirect fashion. You did not let go of
postulates from your marriage. They got in the way.
Interesting way to tell me you changed your mind. You
kept telling me you were ready for me. If you were,
would we be here now?

I want to believe that there is someone out there,
looking for me, listening as I call for him. So I keep
calling. Calling and calling.

God, help me be heard.

I would like to think that I can take what I learned from
you and make the next love better with it. I want to
believe there will be a next love. That the guides can
help me. And heal me. But I would rather they take me
next time. Because I feel that I am left with so little
meaning. And so little possibility. And the harder I try
to make sense of it all, the more I lose the will to go on.
God, help me.

I wonder if you ever think of me. If you have taken me
off of your computer. Thrown away all the things that I
gave you to keep you close. Our Shakespeare prelude
quote, the lapis stone, my poetry. Have you thrown
it away with my love, because it was inconvenient to
keep it? You say you don't allow yourself to feel bad.
That you just redirect attention and stay positive.

Did it feel good to turn away?

I will never know because you won't talk to me. And
your silence tells me that I have heard the last of you.
So, my knowing has ended where you are concerned.
Why does it also feel like I will never know love again.

Because I don't want to? Because I have given up? Or is
it some karmic dept, this loneliness? God, please help
me.

From: mbrogan@mbc.web
Sent: Saturday, November 9, 2002   11: 22 AM
To: JAZMAN@mbc.web
Subject: killing frost

We had a killing frost here last night. The perfect time
for you to not answer my phone calls. The universe
does have it'' poetry doesn't it?

I wonder if something has happened. Did she find out
about us? Was I something you could not defend? I
will never know. Because you do not answer my calls.
Because your silence makes nothing of me. I am now,
nothing to you. From everything to nothing so quickly.
Nothing to everything to nothing so quickly.

An amazing ride. I have learned much. And will learn
more without you as I write my story. Yes, I will write
of us without you. I will rewrite you. It will be the
story of a powerful spiritual communion. Of the birth
and death of love, of self discovery and loss.

By rewriting you, I have more flexibility to create the
story line and symbolic structure. I can add meaning.
There is therapy there!

I don't have an ending yet. Maybe you will be kind as
you exit, helping me through the ordeal. You might

give me what I need to survive, your words, your arms, your comfort.

But it will be MY story, not the story of US. Not our story. Your silence tells me to let that story go.

Jake, I will respect your need for distance, expressed very loudly by your silence. I will speak to you only through my story now.

Goodbye love,
Molly

From: JAZMAN@mbc.web
Sent: Saturday, November 9, 2002 7: 44 PM
To: mbrogan@mbc.web
Subject: RE: killing frost

Molly, I have no intention of not writing or talking to you. My life has been so chaotic lately. I am spending more time in Chicago trying to settle things there and see my children, and then things pile up here. It used to take a couple of days to catch up after a trip. Now it can take a week, and sometimes that is just in time for another trip. I know it seems like I have disappeared and I am sorry.

I just wanted to get this to you for now. I will write again later. How are you?

Jake

From: mbrogan@mbc.web
Sent: Wednesday, November 13, 2002 5:10 AM
To: JAZMAN@mbc.web
Subject: RE: killing frost

Thanks for telling me what intentions you don't have. Would you mind taking a moment to explain what intentions you do have?

I will be off line for several days. I sold the townhouse (in a week!) and am in the process of moving. I will try to catch up with you afterward.

Take care,

Molly

From: mbrogan@mbc.web
Sent: Wednesday, November 13, 2002 6:00 AM
To: mbrogan@mbc.web
Subject: ghosting 19

Well dear,

I tried to call and you did not pick up. why did I try to call. Everything about you tells me you are finished. Everything but your spirit. Your spirit is wounded. And I hold you and shine the light. But know it is not the same. And ask you not to kiss me. Until you can make it real. That is it, isn't it? As I predicted, you are locked into your marriage. You may not have gone back to her in your heart. But you are locked in until she agrees to let you go. To assuage your guilt. She is not going to let you go. There is too much fear in her. I tried to tell you. I've had my glimpses. And know, she will not agree. Her fear consumes her. And she controls you with fear.

I am guessing, that you cannot bring yourself to tell me. Cannot allow yourself the sound of my voice. Your spirit tells me that you still care. And as you taught me, I will not invalidate my knowingness. So, I know you are taking the easy way out. Easy for you. You can assuage your guilt about her by waiting for her agreement. If you don't release me, you can assuage your guilt about me - and tell yourself that I walked away. Is that what it is all about? Avoiding guilt?

Maybe my Catholic upbringing makes me comfortable with guilt. And prevents me from understanding. What happened to taking 100% responsibility for the other? Does that not include my emotions after you walk away? does that not include telling me it is over? What prevents you from talking this through to the end? And why does it have to end? Why can't we transform ourselves from lovers to friends?

I wonder if something has happened. Did she find out about us? Does she hold something over you? Is it money? Did she buy you back?

I will never know. Because you do not answer my calls. Because your silence makes nothing of me. I am now, nothing to you. From everything to nothing so quickly. Nothing to everything to nothing so quickly.

An amazing ride. I have learned much. And will learn more without you as I write our story. Yes, I will write our story without you. I will rewrite you. And you will be much, much better in the new version.

I have learned so much about faith from you. Maybe in the book, we will continue as friends. Your will come back and continue to teach me as I fall in love again. You will be happy for me. You might even provide the connection. Offer some decency.

Maybe what I need to do with this book is completely diminish you, and then move on. Recreate you, as a way of calling out the spirit I truly need, my real soul mate. The one who is ready, and will not turn away.

Well, by diminishing you, I diminish me - and visa versa. Because, we were one. The one I cannot let go of. So I continue to ghost. So I begin our story. And when I finish writing our story, and let go - I will be able to start again.   I may be starting again now. Your silence releases me. My writing releases me. I close many more doors each day. Much the way that many doors sprung open each day as we were falling in love. Thank god, I have found those release mechanisms.

Today I will move to Sue's for a few months to end the insufferable loneliness. I can fill in the time, but need human contact to get over the last of you. This holiday season will be full of people, activity, laughter and love. Sue and I both deserve that. It will give me the strength to move on afterward. I wonder if you will even care, or if the move will mean the end of our connection. Time will tell.

From: mbrogan@mbc.web
Sent: Wednesday, November 13, 2002 8:44 AM
To: mbrogan@mbc.web
Subject: ghosting 20

Well love, I am still ghosting. Sent you my goodbye email and there you
were! With "no intention" of never writing or speaking to me again.
Well that did peak my interest, in spite of your cat and mouse game. So I
could not resist sending an email asking you to let you know what your
intentions are when you can spare the time.

And that is what it boils down to isn't it dear? Time and effort. Neither
of which you have to offer me. So sad really. To throw all of that
possibility away. Your choice of course. Your theta tells me differently.
But it often does. I still have trouble resisting. But I still need it to
be real.

Until then,
mb

Slipping Away

As sure as I felt
The affinity
And the attraction
That brought you
Farther into me
Than anyone
Has ever been,
I now feel
You slipping away.

Just as I could
Do nothing to stop
My free-fall into love,
It seems
I cannot stop you
From walking away.

What I cannot fathom
Is why.
But know
That is
The taboo question,
The place
Between us
That you will not
Acknowledge.

I do what I can
To hold on
To what remains,
And stop
My breaking heart
From crying out
To your deaf ears,
And drive you
Further into hiding.

But how can I stop

My heart from howling
For what could be,
And what was
So many times
Between us?

You know
It is real
In our hearts
And our spirits,
Yet walk away
From our lives
Together,
While I shake
My head
In disbelief.
I only hope
That disbelief
And heartbreak
Does not make me
An unbeliever
In love
Forever.

From: mbrogan@mbc.web
Sent: Wednesday, November 13, 2002   7:44 PM
To: mbrogan@mbc.web
Subject: ghosting 21

"Feel my weakness getting stronger with each moment
passing day."

With each poem, each ghosting, each connection with
others, the pain subsides. The emptiness is filled. As I
move on fast - sorting, packing, relocating, and letting
go - I heal.

I will leave behind many memories in my home of 5
years. Most of all, you. My hopes and dreams of our
love. How it could have been a beautiful home

for us. Now that US will never be, it is time to go.

Your silence makes it easier. I guess you have heard me loud and clear in my poems and emails. Telling you that when you ignore the fact that we are ending, it makes it easier for me to move on. To let go.

Sometimes I think I am past the pain that comes when I realize you don't care enough about our ending to feel about it, or share your feelings. At least that pain now comes and goes, and is no longer constant and paralyzing.

I won't say that I am happy, or over you, or ready to believe in love again. But I am once again able to find joy daily. And stir the deep currents of my soul, calling out my future. I come out of the meditations smiling. There is healing there!

I wonder if eventually, your spirit will tell me to stop speaking to you, to go

away. Or just turn away completely, finally lost in your silence. The ending is still not written, is it Jake?

We will have to wait and see.
mb

From: mbrogan@mbc.web
Sent: Thursday, November 14, 2002   7:26 AM
To: mbrogan@mbc.web
Subject: ghosting 22

Interesting dream while I was waking. I was running away from security. The security guard caught me, and held me in his arms, looking me squarely in the eyes, as if to really see me. I swore to him that my locker was in the next hallway, although he insisted it was somewhere else.

I took him to my locker and tried to open the combination lock. The first couple of times, it would not open, and I began to cry. The third try, it opened. I pulled out a photograph of pills, and me, and you. I said, here is the trouble that I was in.

He asked if I knew, that after leaving me with my trouble, you moved on to someone else. Someone who is now using the pills and selling the pills. I told him that I knew nothing of what happened to you after leaving. But that when you were with me, you made me feel complete, alive, loved. End of dream.

Maybe it was all of your talk about the desire addiction. How I became an addiction out of control to you. It seemed you could not see past desire to the awareness it was creating. Caught up in the feelings, the pills, the moment. Not linking to the eternity through your awareness to make intimacy comfortable. To make the dance tantric. To connect our current lives to all our lives, together. I kept telling you about the effort I was making to integrate the rapture into my daily life. To make it comfortable. The natural level of awareness. Was I too wrapped up in my new found telepathy and expanding awareness that I did not notice you struggling with this? Should I have pulled back then, until you caught up? I thought you were right there with me. I thought our connection was creating my exponential growth. I thought that meant you understood.

I wonder now, how much of what I said, you truly heard, or understood. You said you did. Had the language for your response down pat. Your scientology talking I suppose. Maybe you wanted to, and couldn't. Is this what scared you?

Is it true? Have you moved on to seduce someone new with the language and desire? Marketing it like an entrepreneur to close the deal? And feel the excitement therein? Was that your lesson here?

Staying in the beginning of our story to analyze the chemistry stops the pain of your absence. Halts the desire to reach for you. I was not feeling that in the beginning. My hope, is that given enough time in this stage of US, I will lose that need.

There is the trouble I am in. Finding every way I can to get over you. To stop missing you with all my heart. But not lose what we had. Who I became with you: more, better, complete.

From: mbrogan@mbc.web
Sent: Thursday, November 14, 2002 8:16 PM
To: mbrogan@mbc.web
Subject: ghosting 23

That place in my heart that belongs to you keeps calling me out. I try not to hear it. I don't know what to do with it. Ghost. Work on the book. The Jake poems. Meditate and try to calm the storm our spirits face, now that nothing is real between us.

In retrospect, I have done a pretty good job filling in the void that your love left in my life. But the job is not finished. I somehow need to make peace with your presence in my head and my heart. Expect you to be there from time to time. But not expect it to ever be real again. Burning that bridge will be the last thing I must do, I suppose. Your extended silence makes it inevitable.

And I still can't resist the love that your spirit gives me. Can I enjoy it without taking hope from it? That is the challenge I suppose. Will even your spirit move on some day and forget where to find mine? I hope not. Oops, more hope to let go of. Draught.

As you can see, I still struggle with laying hope to rest.
I suppose time and healing will allow it. Until then, my
ghost will write to you and send it across the universe
to myself. Do you remember when we felt eachother so
strongly, that we would write the same ideas at the
same time to eachother? Such validation of our spiritual
reality. Our possibility. Everything we could not make
real in the physical. True crime.

Fill the Void

I have already begun
To fill the void
Left when you withdrew your love.

Other spirits
Have replaced yours
While I meditate.
Spirits that show me ways
To substitute the love making
With other quests
In places where our spirits met.

Dreams of healing
Have replaced the erotic dreams
That we once shared.
They heal while rebuilding brick by brick
Areas of the soul washed out
By the flash flood of our desire.

Books have filled the hours
That we spent talking.
Sharing our beings
Exchanging emotion,
Expanding ourselves,
Nourishing our love.

Sleeping pills
Keep me sleeping
So that I do not watch

The hours tick by
While the phone does not ring.
There is no other way
To fill the infinite emptiness left
With the end of nightly pillow talk.

Quiet has replaced that silly laugh
That came and went
With the rush of our passion.
The laugh that expressed joy
And the excitement of deep abiding love
Found unexpectedly like a buried treasure.

A serious face
Replaces the goofy smile
That brought joy
To everyone around me.
A quiet, wry smile
Is now all
I can occasionally muster.

I will welcome
Forgetfulness
When its blessings
Cover me in comfort
And carry me on.
I pray each moment
That it comes very soon
To take away my pain.

From: mbrogan@mbc.web
Sent: Thursday, November 21, 2002   8:16 PM
To: mbrogan@mbc.web
Subject: ghosting 24

All revved up today. Like it used to be. With rapture.
Burning skin.
Rapid pulse. You all over me. It still makes me smile
love.

How can I feel this, and not you? I know that it comes
from your spirit in the same space as mine. Yet you do
not acknowledge it. A mystery. I could not feel this if
you were not feeling this too. Yet you stay in hiding.
Taking us spiraling downward. Losing communication,
reality, affinity. Losing US, love. How could it possibly
be that you do not feel the loss. No one could redirect
attention that cleanly. Anyone with a heart could
feel it.

I will allow myself the happiness today. Tell myself
that it reunites me with the possibility. If not you, then
someone who waits for me. Someone I will continue to
call for. Someone who will make it real this time.
Someone who will not hide. Like you.

I have had two offers of love today from unexpected
places. Makes me wonder if they can see my love lit up.
Neither is right, but it is tempting to accept what isn't
right just to replace your touch in my mind and heart.
So very tempting.

As I get settled into my new (temporary) home, I am
glad to leave behind all of the places where we did
touch. Moving on fast…

Smiling without you,
mb

From: mbrogan@mbc.web
Sent: Friday, November 22, 2002 1:14 PM
To: mbrogan@mbc.web
Subject: ghosting 25

Your spirit is strong Jake. I tried to resist. You have
been all over me all day. But at lunch, at the park, when
I opened my book to keep my mind focused and resist
you, there you were, standing outside the car. Waiting,
with your irresistible entreat. I had to receive you.

Well, the affinity is still incredibly strong. And although the communication is all thetan, it is real. On one level we still exist, stronger than ever apparently. Now what the hell am I supposed to do with that?

I will enjoy the glorious rapture and happiness you leave me with, Jake. Body opening to mind opening to spirit opening to soul. That incredible expansion of being that I have not felt since your leaving. How did you know I have been considering that lately? Trying to find the words for my book. Your spirit returned that to me. Thank you

From: JAZMAN@mbc.web
Sent: Saturday, November 23, 2002 11:31 AM
To: mbrogan@mbc.web
Subject: hi

I miss you. What's going on? My life sucks lately, but it ain't over till it's over. Someone knocked on my bedroom door this morning. I got up and opened it, but no one was there. Were you over here?

What are your plans?

Jake

From: mbrogan@mbc.web
Sent: Sunday, November 24, 2002 5:10 AM
To: JAZMAN@mbc.web
Subject: RE: hi

Yea, that was me, missing you. That is so funny because night before last, well, early in the morning, my TV went on without explanation. Scared the heck out of me. Actually, it has happened before but I thought it was you reaching for me. I am all moved into Sue's house. Jack is home now for a couple of weeks for Thanksgiving. His headaches finally ended but they kept him out of play all season. Sue's girls, Hillary and

Lauren will be here in a few days. The house will be full. It will fun to see our kids interact.

I have gotten a couple of job offers to consider. One in Denver, one in New York. Nothing from Madison yet.

Meg had a feeding tube surgically inserted and is on it 16 hrs. a day. She has talked me into joining a "women's spirituality group" with her that starts tomorrow night. Well why not, I like women and I like spirituality! She says she has changed since the transplant. And she has! I have not asked her what she remembers. This group might bring things out. It is really her first activity since the transplant in July. I am deeply worried about her.

Finally heard from Sandy yesterday. My future glimpse of her was so powerful. I was afraid to tell her, didn't want her to think me so weird, but felt obligated, the danger seemed so real. Nothing like it has happened to me since. She has settled things with her X amicably, through the attorneys. No court battle, no violence. Quite a relief. Made the telling very much worth the risk. A lesson there! Thank you Jake, you were such a big part of that.

I am taking Jamie out to dinner tonight and to Sue's afterward so he can see the new digs. Hopefully he will consider joining the fun this holiday season with all the kids around.

Future plans? Nothing far reaching really. Finish the book, find an agent after the holidays for the first one if a nibble doesn't come along in the mean time. Drum up possible employment options out of state for after the holidays. Might have a better idea of how the Comcast/AT&T merger will pan out after Thanksgiving.

Guess that's about it. Your turn - Molly

From: JAZMAN@mbc.web
Sent: Sunday, November 24, 2002 9:15 PM
To: mbrogan@mbc.web
Subject: RE: hi

It has been an extremely long day here at work. You're probably in bed by now, Huh? How did your day go? What are your plans for the holidays? What are we doing on this planet?

The wind is blowing out here. Luckily, there are no fires now. The windows are making eerie noises. Good night for cuddling, but really bad for going out.

Still miss the kids terribly. Grace just will be playing with the Lake Forest Symphony for New Year's Eve, so she has been busy practicing. Will have to wait to see if things will be calm enough for me to attend. Mike is busy with school and has been a big help in getting my messages to his sister.

I want you to be happier. What needs to change for that to happen?

Sleep well, dream well,

Jake

From: mbrogan@mbc.web
Sent: Tuesday, November 26, 2002 6:00 AM
To: JAZMAN@mbc.web
Subject: highs and lows

You are not the first person to suggest that I have been off recently. I was not sure of the reason until I got home from work yesterday and called Meg's house. Just a nagging sadness. Her daughter told me that she was taken to the hospital by ambulance because of pain in her lungs. If Hank determined that an ambulance was necessary, she must have needed whatever care they could give her on the way to the hospital immediately. I have not been able to reach anyone since.

The day itself was actually successful. I tried to lift the funk (remember that word) by a visit to the chiro and then the tanning bed after work. Makin' my own sunshine. Sue still asked me if I was OK when I got home.

During my last conversation with Meg, I told her that if she decides it is time for her to go, I might go with her. That way we could come back as twins! She laughed and was then thoughtful. I wanted to bring the thought into her awareness that it is a choice. That she will need to choose life. I am feeling at a loss.

In general, I don't think it is happiness that I lack. It is desire. What needs to happen to change that? I guess I need to look forward more. I have opened forward more, I know that. The feeling I used to have that I was not enough in my body, out too much is gone. Left in its place is – I can only describe it as – perpetual DeJaVu. Hard to articulate. But I think it means that I found the balance needed to integrate that awareness into my daily life. I know that I have opened myself to heightened awareness and love that.

I love the people in my life. Love writing. Love lots of little things that make up each day: baby's smiles, techs swearing, the sky as it turns to night. I continue to do my best every moment of every day and that won't change. I continue to forgive and treat everyone with respect and kindness. But somehow, if it all ended, it would be OK. I feel ready for that. And I am ready for it to continue. Either way, I am fine.

I hope that isn't alarming. Now I have a question for you. Did you turn away from me because of my unusual perceptions? Having never shared everything with anyone before, it occurred to me that was a possibility. I am wondering if I should say what I know or keep it to myself.

Molly

From: JAZMAN@mbc.web
Sent: Tuesday, November 26, 2002 9:15 AM
To: mbrogan@mbc.web
Subject: RE: highs and lows

Sounds like you think it is touch and go with Meg. But what's the idea about you being twins? You're not going anywhere, right?

If you can somehow show her what a spiritual being is, then the concept of death leading to a new life will make sense to her. Most people think they are their bodies and that they "have" a soul that goes somewhere after. Talk to her about the fact that her mind is a memory bank with all of her past recorded there. Have her close her eyes and pull up a picture of something and describe it to you. Then ask her what is looking at the picture. If she can grasp the concept that who looks at the pictures is her, she may understand the difference between her body, mind and spirit. I hope that is useful. But explain this twin thing more.

Jake

From: mbrogan@mbc.web
Sent: Thursday, November 28, 2002 7:44 AM
To: JAZMAN@mbc.web
Subject: thanks

I think Meg's postulate is wobbly, as you would say. She is very thin and very good at minimizing her symptoms to everyone around her, until a crisis occurs. I continue to pray for her.

The twin thing was just a way to get her to see that she will need to choose life to continue. But you sense there is something more there, and there is. I have always felt that I have a twin somewhere. Like someone is waiting somewhere for me that will complete me. Not a romantic thing really, although that would be a bonus, wouldn't it? I know I would make a great twin. Like an emptiness, waiting to be filled when my twin arrives. I suppose that is why I chose the analogy. For now, Jake, I choose life. Worry none. When the time comes and I no longer choose it – I do not fear it. My twin may be waiting!

So, why are we on the planet?
Molly

From: JAZMAN@mbc.web
Sent: Thursday, November 28, 2002 11:22 AM
To: mbrogan@mbc.web
Subject: RE: thanks

By the way, your unusual perceptions are not a negative trait at all, a complete positive. For someone else who had little understanding of what is really going on, I don't know. It is unreal to so many people.

Like you, I don't fear the end of this life. I know what it's all about. I don't fear the death cycle but hope the form is not difficult. The idea of being free of the body for awhile is exciting, saying goodbye to everyone whether they understand it or not. The loss of those I love will be a big negative, but I have found some kindred spirits this time who I know will be with me next. We go from life to life in groups.

Why do I think we are on the planet? I was hoping you would answer first. There are various possible answers to that age old question. We have been given the handicap of amnesia, like someone put us here in a trap. Maybe someone who didn't like us of feared us. If we chose to be here it must have been because it was the best choice available to us. Or we came for another purpose and ended up staying on some unplanned basis. Were we always here? I don't recall being a dinosaur. Now your turn. Why do you think we are on the planet?

Jake

From: mbrogan@mbc.web
Sent: Saturday, November 30, 2002   6:45 AM
To: JAZMAN@mbc.web
Subject: RE: thanks

How was your holiday, out there in wine country? I hope it was relaxing and peaceful.

Your interesting theory has echoes of LRon's fiction - earth as an alien penal colony theme. Are we being tested or punished by being here? I envisioned something more harmonious. With point and counterpoint. Rhythm and beat. Discord maybe, depending on the composer(s) But orchestrated by a higher design none the less. I see a touch of god at the core of all of us. Not a victim. Do you see life as a trap? Can you design your game with more freedom? Get agreements on the barriers before putting them into the game? Redesign goals with different purpose? Seems to me that no ancient enemy could prevent that.

I once asked you what made life worth living. Your answer was purpose and goals. The more I get to know you the more sense that makes. The Scientologist's definition on purpose in the game is: intention/counter intention; antagonists; problems. Your game seems full of those. Do you design your trap, or were you born with it as a result of some greater design?

But maybe we are answering two different questions. Why are we on this planet, and why are we living. I think I did answer you before. Self discovery, loving, growing, sharing, playing the game of our own design. Seems to me, if we were born knowing everything, we might not be as open to new experience. To change and resulting growth. Tell me what you think of that.

I have moved up tone a few notches in the last couple of days. I came home determined to go hear Peter sing, whatever I found waiting at home. His voice makes me happy. I got the chance to tell him that last time I went to hear him in Northbrook. Anyway, I came home to a house full of people with the same idea. Peter called Sue and warmed her up for me. Sue's daughter Lauren came home yesterday (gave me a huge hug as I walked in the door.) It is interesting to watch Lauren and Jack discover each other. He so reserved and quiet. She makes the effort, and then retreats. They are both great, and very different people.

Meg is back home and sounding less in pain (still some) and more exhausted. The doctors determined that a pocket of fluid (but not blood) formed in her right lung as the result of the biopsy. Rare. They predict that it will dissolve naturally in time but be painful for awhile. She will probably rest a lot this weekend. But I am glad for her that they sent her home. I think Jack is leaving for school in a few days. I will try to slip over to Meg's whenever he is at his dads.

How does your day look from the start here? Hope it is a good one.

Take Care,

mb

From: JAZMAN@mbc.web
Sent: Saturday, November 30, 2002   12:12 PM
To: mbrogan@mbc.web
Subject: RE: thanks

Thanksgiving was strange without my kids for the first
time. I spent it with friends from Glenview who are in
town. Actually, they have a home both places as well.
They would really like to meet you.

I think your very cool answer to our question had more
to do with why we are in the universe than on the
planet. I think it has to do with the joy we feel when
we are creating. We are like computers, creating
effects while recording it for history. As people move
down tone, creation turns into destruction, a low level
of creation.
Life is only a trap if we make it one. Underneath it all,
we make our own problems and solutions. It is always
interesting to watch someone who has a problem and
every solution won't work because of some
rationalization or another. People do things based on
postulates they aren't even aware they made previously.
It is interesting to watch someone who realizes that his
problem is based on a thought from long ago. I think I
need some auditing myself about now.

To answer your question, knowing everything prevents
the game from being played at all. Knowing too little
makes one ineffective and unhappy. False beliefs
create barriers, like believing you are a body, rather
than a spirit. In that case it is also easy to believe that
you are your emotions, and get caught up in anger and
pain. I still use anger when it is the correct emotion for
handling someone, but that is usually just acting.

I 'm glad Meg is home and her recovery is hopeful.
You are a wonderful person, perceptive, aware and
caring. It's been nice knowing you. I love having you
in my life. Are you happy? - Jake

M ONTH EIGHT

From: mbrogan@mbc.web
Sent: Monday, December 2, 2002   6:45 AM
To: JAZMAN@mbc.web
Subject: happy thoughts

"It's been nice knowing you" sounded so much like goodbye that I was glad to see it followed up with " I love having you in my life." Ultimately, we are probably saying goodbye every time we speak, not knowing what the future will bring.

I liked your thoughts on anger. For me, it is a signal that I need to process perception at a higher level. That my perception might be a lower level, in the ego, mechanical or low level emotion. I will then stop, and try to see things from a more creative, involving more of my spirit. The anger (or jealousy or other low level emotions) usually disappears. Been awhile since I have had to process anything other than sadness like this. Still working on the loss recovery. Those attachments.

You are right, sometimes anger can be used effectively to help someone change tones or move from a more destructive emotional level. Can be a show stopper, especially when unexpected and used effectively. But then, it is a choice. A kind of "act" because it is used consciously to create and affect. I only try this on children, or people who do not have enough emotional intelligence to understand the effect of their emotions on themselves and those around them. And I have found that becoming more calm, quiet and deliberate in my communication can have a better effect in most situations. But there are those people (like my X) who are in such emotional chaos at the time, it is the only resort. Even been awhile since I've had to use anger on him! I think it all boils down to formulating not only response, but perception at the highest possible level. Which takes much effort and concentration - until it becomes second nature. And even then, there can be lapse times (usually during crisis) or times when more effort is required.

What do you think of that?

Am I happy? I will be honest (again) and tell you that I miss being in love. There is an emptiness there that has not filled. But I do not regret taking the plunge. I am a much different person than I was last February.
The same, but so much more. An amazing year really. I love where I am inside and out.

Then there is the fact I remain in a place ready to say goodbye to everyone. Probably after the Meg scare last week and Jack's accident. Helps me appreciate everyone while I have them.

But I have my son close for a few more days. Jamie made the basketball team so I will try going to some of those games. Hopefully it won't get too weird with my X. Things are cruising along with Sue. It is good for me not to be alone so much and nice getting to know her girls so intimately. Happy to be growing with Meg. Our spirituality group is next week. Picked up writing my book again. Really missed it. MUCH that creates happiness. And when sadness or someone else's feelings sneak in, I know just what to do to move up tone. Go listen to Peter, etc.

Still have not gotten used to feeling with others. Often don't know who it is coming from, like last week when Meg was in pain. It all becomes so clear when I find out. I can then process it all, separate mine from theirs and do what I can with my spirit to help. I wish I knew someone who could guide me in that. But I seem to be doing OK with it on my own.

How about you. Are you happy?

Molly

From: JAZMAN@mbc.web
Sent: Monday, December 2, 2002 9:42 PM
To: mbrogan@mbc.web
Subject: RE: happy thoughts

I understand what you said. Thank you. Please watch the postulates on checking out. I need to, too. It's good that you're not resisting it because what we resist we often receive. I just don't think you should want it too soon. You're too young and have too much to offer other people to be leaving anytime soon.

Enjoy yourself and I'll check for you later.

Jake

From: mbrogan@mbc.web
Sent: Wednesday, December 4, 2002 5:55 AM
To: JAZMAN@mbc.web
Subject: not so happy thoughts

I had to read my email again to see what you saw. When I said that I was ready to say goodbye to everyone, I meant that I am ready to say goodbye because they are leaving my life. When Jack had his accident I thought a lot about what my life would be like without him, and what I wanted to say before he left. Likewise with Meg. I am glad for the opportunity to say a bit more to you too. But I just don't know when you will finally leave. Maybe I should keep some things to myself. I don't know. So I've been told.

Guess I did say too much. Well, can't delete after you press send---the best you can do is retreat a bit.

Molly

From: JAZMAN@mbc.web
Sent: Wednesday, December 4, 2002   9:06 AM
To: mbrogan@mbc.web
Subject: RE: not so happy thoughts

That one sentence in your last email had me worried about it even though I see that right after that you mentioned Jack and Meg. When I saw those words I guess I lost my concentration and thought you were thinking something else. Sorry for the misduplication.

Are you and Sue doing something together today? Are YOU happy today? It's a little lonely here.

Jake

From: mbrogan@mbc.web
Sent: Wednesday, December 4, 2002   11:13 AM
To: JAZMAN@mbc.web
Subject: RE: not so happy thoughts

Printed out all of the written pages of the book once I got my printer working (jostled around in the move I guess.) Organized things to begin work again. Three different notebooks (one a three inch binder full of emails) and many discs. Having not looked at it in a few weeks, I will need to review where I am before resuming. Just a review of the poems provides a great outline of the birth/death cycle of the love story. The morning just wasn't long enough.

I can see how the ongoing discussion about death and being ready/not fearing it can be confusing. And I am probably not articulating as clearly as I should. I make many internal adjustments that I don't have the words to describe. It all goes back to working on the no attachments/no aversions thing. Being ready for anyone to leave your life at any moment does not mean you wish it to happen. It means you accept the finality of life and the reality that other's postulates and choices are theirs. All you can do is accept them if you are not asked to agree with them before they are formulated. Not all elements of the game between people are also elements of their individual games, and visa versa. Although I think the stronger the relationship, the more agreements between them. Am I rambling?

Anyway, being ready, for me, also means telling people what they mean to me while they are near. Not taking any of the shared joy for granted. Not missing opportunities to express and cultivate love. But loving with an open hand and being prepared to let go when the time comes. Sue and I had coffee this morning before she and Lauren began their day together. She came into the living room, looking so sleepy this morning, ready to process a Jack (her late husband) dream. Again, just not enough time to spend on it before she had to get ready for her day.

I am feeling much happiness, among other feelings today. Had a wonderful meditation as the book was printing. My room has a marvelous window seat that I stuffed with pillows. I watched the trees blow in the wind and the clouds travel across the sky before I slipped into a wonderful place of joy and expansion with my eyes closed.

Take care,

Molly

From: JAZMAN@mbc.web
Sent: Thursday, December 5, 2002 9:33 AM
To: mbrogan@mbc.web
Subject:

I was talking to my friends about you again last night.
They would like to meet you. For that matter, I would
like to see you again myself.

Jake
From: mbrogan@mbc.web
Sent: Friday, December 6, 2002 6:00 AM
To: JAZMAN@mbc.web
Subject: RE:

This is a big change. What brought this on?

From: JAZMAN@mbc.web
Sent: Friday, December 6, 2002 9:15 AM
To: mbrogan@mbc.web
Subject: RE:

I was just talking to my friends out here about how
wonderful you are and how you found me and that we
spent some time together. I didn't tell them everything.
Is that bad? I hope I didn't upset you.

From: mbrogan@mbc.web
Sent: Sunday, December 8, 2002 5:10 AM
To: JAZMAN@mbc.web
Subject: RE:

I'm not upset. Just a bit confused. I thought you did not
talk to other people about me, so that was a change.
And I REALLY don't want to be the cause of any
family problems. But you know that I have told all of
my friends about you, so why would you talking about
me be upsetting? I hope that doesn't offend you. I just
don't think that things have cooled much in your
marriage.

Quite honestly, I had resigned myself to the thought of never seeing you again. I felt that was your intention toward me. Has this changed? Was I inaccurate?

From: JAZMAN@mbc.web
Sent: Monday, December 9, 2002   9:15 AM
To: mbrogan@mbc.web
Subject: RE:

Hi, I'm fine. Just terribly busy. Am just now getting a chance to answer you. We were talking about my friends and how I would explain your presence in my life. Meeting them is just a nice idea. We don't have to set a date for it or anything.

From: mbrogan@mbc.web
Sent: Monday, December 9, 2002   10:14 AM
To: JAZMAN@mbc.web
Subject: RE:

How bout if we meet in Vegas for a weekend to discuss my meeting your friends?

From: JAZMAN@mbc.web
Sent: Monday, December 9, 2002   11: 31 AM
To: mbrogan@mbc.web
Subject: RE:

WOW that sounds like fun. I didn't know you liked Vegas. I have only been there for conventions. Where do you like to stay? I think we might have fun when you kick my ass in Vegas.

From: mbrogan@mbc.web
Sent: Monday, December 9, 2002 5:55 PM
To: JAZMAN@mbc.web
Subject: RE:

I would be glad to kick your ass in Vegas. I have to leave shortly for my women's group. Meg is amazing. She still can't swallow from the surgery, but is determined to attend this group. I am with her, wherever she needs me to be. I really like this group. The first meeting last month was exciting - some very aware, highly energetic women.

Take Care,

Molly

From: JAZMAN@mbc.web
Sent: Tuesday, December 10, 2002 11: 31 AM
To: mbrogan@mbc.web
Subject: RE:

I'm glad to hear that Meg is up and around. Tell me more about the women in this group. It sounds fascinating.

Give me some time to consider a date for our Vegas meeting. Things are very hectic for me right now, with the legal mess of my marriage,.. She is still upsetting the kids a great deal. The attorney that she hired will not come to agreement on anything. The holidays coming and the busy season at the clubs. But there is nothing I would like more. Have a client here to see me. Gotta run.

Take care,
Jake

From: mbrogan@mbc.web
Sent: Tuesday, December 10, 2002   2:04 PM
To: mbrogan@mbc.web
Subject: ghosting 26

Christ, Jake. You got me again didn't you. Hooked me right in and then stepped back. Where do you think this will lead you? Is it just a reluctance to let go? Does the flirtation fill the lonely spaces for you, and nothing more? You seem to be able to let go and commit on every level but the heart. I don't know how to help you, other than to hold you with an open hand.

Love's Alchemy

Where do I begin
To turn down the fire
To remove the necessity
To let go of the need
In the love I feel for you?

I have never before
Tried so hard
To turn such passionate love,
Into the love of friendship.
A friendship that will last,
Because I don't want
To lose you forever,
But know
That you no longer have room
In your life
For my complete love.

There must be a way
To stop my mind
From turning to you
To stop the emotion
Before it sweeps me away
Into desire
And soulful yearning.

I am determined, love
To find that way.

I check each response
Before I offer it to you.
Comparing it to one
I would offer a friend
Making sure
It remains
Within those boundaries.

No easy chore,
Because not so long ago
Your love took me to places
Before uncharted.
Into rapture
And dances of the spirit
Where we reveled
In eachother
For such a short time,
But no longer share.

And while so much of me
Wants that back,
I resign myself
To offering only
The love of a friend
Of the inner circle.
One that I can tell
The most private secrets
Of my spirit's journey.

Each time I reach for you
With my heart
And you do not respond
This task becomes easier
My love simmers down.

Each time experience
Calls for sharing

With a partner
Or Soul Mate
And you are not there,
The alchemy ignites
And the transformation
Of our love
Becomes more complete.

Each time you tell me
That the way to me
Is impossible for you,
You make it much easier
For me to accept our fate.
The fate that you defined
By not choosing us.

My hope is
That when my work is done,
And our love has undergone
The necessary alchemy,
And quantum changes
Create our new boundaries,
We will find a way
To remain close friends
Through all of the trials
That life brings.
Because you are still
Essential to me
And always will be.

From: JAZMAN@mbc.web
Sent: Thursday, December 12, 2002 5:01 AM
To: mbrogan@mbc.web
Subject: RE:

Hi. I'm back. Now, what about Vegas?

From: mbrogan@mbc.web
Sent: Friday, December 13, 2002 5:55 PM
To: JAZMAN@mbc.web
Subject: amazing day

Today was an amazing day. An associate appeared in
my office suggesting that I submit a manuscript of
Remember Me to an agent (her mom.) Shortly after
that amazing visit I got a phone call from my friend
Paul, who actually hired me for the cable company
before he moved to Las Vegas, taking the Presidency of
a company out there. He had a job offer for me, in
Vegas! So interesting, after our banter about meeting in
Vegas. I agreed to go out there after the holidays and
explore this offer a bit more. Any ideas about questions
I should ask? I also received information about the
Comcast/AT&T merger. It will be finalized the first
quarter of next year. There is a mandated 15%
reduction in management. The severance packages
include 6 months salary and 18 months benefits. The
possibilities become more and more interesting…

What a day!

Molly

PS – I didn't tell you this to try to get you to go with
me. Actually, I don't think that would be a good idea.
I just thought it a weird coincidence that we were
talking about Vegas, then this!

From: JAZMAN@mbc.web
Sent: Friday, December 13, 2002 8: 52 PM
To: mbrogan@mbc.web
Subject: RE: amazing day

Wow this was quite a day for you. Will you be taking
that guy with you when you move?

I think you should find out how stable the company is and what the growth potential there is. What is your potential for advancement? Will he pay a signing bonus of moving expenses? Is he asking you for any personal reasons? I will think about more questions. What is the name of the company? I can do a little research for you.

I've had a long work day and still have a couple of hours here before I head home for frozen food. It just doesn't get better than this.

Jake

From: mbrogan@mbc.web
Sent: Sunday, December 15, 2002 5:37 AM
To: JAZMAN@mbc.web
Subject: that guy

Which guy are you talking about?

Paul's company is City Smart, owned by one of the country's largest and most stable cable properties. I love both Paul and his wife Kristine dearly. He is the best I have ever worked for and I am convinced that we have a sacred contract between us. I am happy at the thought of seeing that contract continue to unfold. I would be reporting directly to him in this, a marketing, position. He is still developing the job description.

You may remember that Paul called in July and offered me a position in Washington DC. At the time, I had committed to moving to SF with you after the holidays, and let him know I wasn't interested. But I like this offer better because I will be reporting to him and I would be moving to the southwest. I have had the time needed to fulfill my promise to Jack and Sue to help Sue move on. Things have a way of working out, don't they?

Personal reasons? Paul is one of those soulful friends that I have always known. His intentions are completely honorable and he is full of integrity. His professional success is due, in part, to his natural ability to surround himself with talented people that he can trust. He is very intuitive. We work well together because we honor that in each other.

You are right, I often don't do enough examining of personal reasons behind other's approach, although I think I am getting better at that before I respond. I would appreciate your further thoughts on this if you have the time.

I spent yesterday morning talking to Sue. Don't know how much time we will have for that once the kids get home for Christmas break. She is being very hard on herself. Has many fears. It was a great morning though, very deep. I think I have talked her into calling the woman who started the spirituality group (Meg's friend how has a local private practice as a psychologist.) A magical person, really. VERY good at the challenge. Also incredibly aware. She articulates so many of the things I experience and question, like saying what I know. I think she will be good for Sue - emotionally and spiritually. She has resisted counseling until now. But she is incredibly blocked and needs a leg up. I would love to see that happen for her. If any one can do it, it is Diana.

I got information on past life regression from Diana at our last women's group. I have some techniques that I can try on my own and referrals for counselors that can help (one woman studied with Brian Weiss.) Time to go looking for answers…

Then, I alternately slept and wrote all day and night. What a great day. I am really happy in this house. And am glad I followed my heart to get here. - Molly

---

From: JAZMAN@mbc.web
Sent: Sunday, December 15, 2002   12: 12 PM
To: mbrogan@mbc.web
Subject: RE: that guy

Tell me more about your group. Do others go exterior like you do? What does Meg think about all this? Do you think she is still postulating a trade-in?

Tell me more about your Vegas idea. That guy – he is hiding in my head. Once in awhile, he comes out to talk to you.

Jake

From: mbrogan@mbc.web
Sent: Monday, December 16, 2002   7:44 PM
To: JAZMAN@mbc.web
Subject: RE: that guy is hiding

That guy hiding in your head - he is in mine too! But he doesn't hide, and I talk to him constantly. Tried for awhile to get him out of there, then just embraced him again. Accepted the fact that he will be there eternally.

Now if we could get him out of our heads and into my arms....

Actually, you are right. A wealth of soul searching went into the Vegas idea. I just have not been sure whether or not to put it out there. But here is a bit of it.

I think, that whatever holds you back from finding your way to me is much like whatever keeps Meg locked in her illness. Risking it all, unable to move, losing ground daily. Don't you worry that once you are ready, your opportunities will be different? Or that you may never be ready, killing off what lies just beyond your reach? What choices have you made, that block the way to me? When all it would take is a plane ride to Vegas.

459

Between friendship and marriage there are many gradients and possibilities for relationship. What keeps you from letting love in? And if you do, what would keep you from maintaining intimacy? Intimacy is like awareness. It can grow or diminish. But it has no limit. What limits do you place on us? And why?

I don't ever have to meet your friends. I don't know them. They don't mean anything to me. You do. Why waste that?

On the other hand, cultivating friendship is not wasting that. If that is all you can agree to, then friendship it is. Like with Meg, my love is unconditional. What you need is what I will give. As long as what lays between us is honest.

Was that explanation better, or worse than the short version?

From: mbrogan@mbc.web
Sent: Thursday, December 19, 2002 7:08 PM
To: JAZMAN@mbc.web
Subject: skipping

We have done this in other lives before, haven't we? With you staying just out of reach. Why are we doing it over and over? Do you think we can figure it out this time? We haven't done it that way every time, have we? There are beautiful lifetimes between us when we seem to have gotten in right. Fascinating.

Had a long talk with Peg today. She is going through some tough times in her relationship with her intended in San Francisco. I have agreed to go out there and visit her in January for a week or so. I have vacation time to use up and haven't spend time with her in much too long. It will be great to spend some time on the shore with her, talking the night away. Just thought you should know. Didn't want it to come up later and catch you by surprise.

Molly

From: JAZMAN@mbc.web
Sent: Friday, December 20, 2002 12: 03 AM
To: mbrogan@mbc.web
Subject: RE: skipping

I'm not trying to hide. I just have had no time this week. I am still at work now, taking a break in a meeting with a client. Sorry. I hope you are doing OK. If I don't sleep to late tomorrow, I should have time to catch up with you.

Our CD needs a cleaning, some scratches removed without changing the music. It has played beautiful music, yes. Do you know what week you will be out here? What are your Christmas week plans?

Jake

From: mbrogan@mbc.web
Sent: Friday, December 20, 2002 5:28 AM
To: JAZMAN@mbc.web
Subject: scratch

I think I found the scratch. There is violence between us isn't there. That is something I never imagined.

From: JAZMAN@mbc.web
Sent: Friday, December 20, 2002 9:05 AM
To: mbrogan@mbc.web
Subject: RE: scratch

Do you actually do it – kick my ass? I need a time period and other details if you can. How much do you recall?

I am at work but will have more time to write today.

Jake

From: mbrogan@mbc.web
Sent: Friday, December 20, 2002 10:14 AM
To: JAZMAN@mbc.web
Subject: RE: scratch

Well, I know this. It was a lifetime before the "your highness" lifetime that we spoke of on the phone, because I have had some deep recalls of that lifetime, where our marriage was arranged, and I had a DeJaVu of this violent lifetime prior to that, that caused irrational fear of you in the "your highness" lifetime. Having that DeJaVu was interesting. It is interesting to me, that as you recounted the "your highness lifetime" you never mentioned my fear of you. Did you understand that in your recall?

I am not getting a lot of specific time period impressions. Just dress, room, emotion, faces, familiar beings. My best guess would be anywhere from 1200-1800. It is in a European rural setting, dark, hut like home. Dark in a psychic sense also. I had strawberry blond hair, was not heavy but solid framed. You had blond hair and a brown beard. Probably doesn't help you much. I don't want to go back there yet. But I do know that it created fear of you in other lifetimes. I don't know if I can do this with you in short emails. I have made some calls to find some local help in understanding my impressions.
You are always holding me tenderly before I am drawn into another lifetime. Thank you.
But I know this. I owe you an ass kicking. And this IS the lifetime to deliver it. And enjoy it. Really good that you are so willing. We can both enjoy it.

Molly

From: JAZMAN@mbc.web
Sent: Friday, December 20, 2002   10:23 AM
To: mbrogan@mbc.web
Subject: RE: scratch

You probably DO owe me a little ass kicking, but it's
not just a one way flow, Molly.

What people have done to others in previous lifetimes
is what actually causes the amnesia - an unwillingness
to accept responsibility for their transgressions. The
desire to "forget" these things also proves that people
are basically good. And the one life idea "solves"
having to take responsibility for their previous acts.
Interestingly enough, as people begin to confront these
past acts, they begin to remember more and more of
their own experiences - both good and bad. The false
ideas implanted in people's minds wouldn't be so
effective if there wasn't some level of agreement from
the being to go along with it. Making any sense?

I did not recall that you feared me when we became
betrothed in the first lifetime that you mention. It is
interesting that we each have our own viewpoints, and
they include our impressions and rationalizations. This
is the first time I have compared experiences with
anyone.

I don't recall the other life time you have described, but
as I read your description, I got a very real, sharp pain
in my head that tells me you are on track here.

As far as we go, there's a knowing feeling of having
had involvement together sometime in the past prior to
high school, right? Are you sure you really want to go
there? It's a mystery sandwich that might be hard to
digest.

Jake

From: mbrogan@mbc.web
Sent: Friday, December 20, 2002 12: 04 AM
To: JAZMAN@mbc.web
Subject: RE: scratch

So, now, you are going to kick my ass?

As I put the pieces together, it makes more and more
sense. And what I experience one day that makes me
wonder, is explained more the next, in a different
impression. Because I always begin in your arms, I
always find us in another life. I have found many. Some
puzzling. Some filled with ecstasy. The violence
startled me. I need to make peace with that. I did not
imagine that between us. But I am not blaming you for
it, if that is your concern. I realize that there is always
agreement on the deepest level. But I still get to kick
your ass, don't I?

There was also that impression where I experienced the
DeJaVu that was occurring during the past life
experience. Since I was seeing through (my) eyes, I
experienced the DeJaVu. It contained a knowing of this
life. So it would seem the knowing goes forward and
back. Nesting together in time through a single frame
of reference. Fascinating. REally cool. Like picture in a
picture. An infinite PIP experience. During this ultimate
big picture experience, I have such a sense of peace.
And a knowing that there is balance in experience – and
that it is all of god – not good nor bad, just purposeful.
The more experiences I have like this, the more
absolute trust I feel. Now, I go looking for the nesting
when I do past life meditations, instead of looking for
individual lives.

Your comment so long ago, about how interesting it is
that I have high awareness, but none of past lives - I am
discovering that some of my dreams were actually
glimpses. And certainly the DeJaVus. I have revisited
some of those places lately. The life with violence

between us - I have dreamt of it before. June or July this year I think. And then later again, maybe early September. I remember telling you about it. All very interesting in retrospect. Explains a lot of things I could not explain before. I made an appointment with this doctor that studied with Brain Weiss on Christmas Eve morning to ask my questions. More interesting stuff to come! I am excited about all of this, can you tell? Something, like the healing meditations, that I can enjoy my whole life long.

Too bad we can't do this together. Thanks for listening to the bits and pieces.

From: JAZMAN@mbc.web
Sent: Friday, December 20, 2002 1:33 PM
To: mbrogan@mbc.web
Subject: RE: scratch

I can think of better things to do with your ass instead of kicking it. I don't hold grudges.

The violence part is interesting. I'll have to look into that. It's always easier to confront pleasure moments than the other so they tend to surface
first. Especially when you're horny (smile). When you're ready to kick my ass, a little warning would be nice. Can you give me more details about these lives you recall?

I'd love to sit down and talk about all this one of these days. The DeJaVu especially - what you see. Need to make some time for that.

So what else is going on with you? How is Meg? I don't know why I feel so much for her, but I do, and hope she's doing much better.

From: mbrogan@mbc.web
Sent: Friday, December 20, 2002 2: 40 PM
To: JAZMAN@mbc.web
Subject: RE: scratch

Why do you feel for Meg? Because you and I are close enough to share experience on the deepest levels. I love that about you. Miss it terribly sometimes. But am VERY grateful for it. She may feel it for you too. She dreams about you from time to time. Called me up all concerned the other day because she dreamt that you went back to your wife. I think she just worries about me, having seen me through a few broken hearts. I assured her that even if her dream was prophetic, I would be just fine. Actually, the past life stuff is helping me make the final internal adjustments here. The ultimate big picture. Does really give this life perspective, doesn't it?

Why do I share all of this with you? And I wonder what my other friends would think if they knew. Do I share too much with you? Do you ever think, 'she's getting a little weird'?

The lifetime with violence was European, yes. That was the impression I had. I was not as slender, but not really fat. Red/strawberry blonde hair, long. It was a hard life. And the house was very dark and dreary.

But the lifetime that I feared you because of the violence in that lifetime, was nicer. Wealthier. I was wearing a very large, very uncomfortable ivory silk or satin dress with lace. This impression came on because I went into the meditation thinking about a reoccurring DeJaVu that I have always had. When I walk down a wide staircase, I am always drawn to the middle (when I am not too dizzy, which happens sometimes.) Then and incredibly strong DeJaVu comes on. Same one every time. I went into the meditation thinking about it because I wanted to explore it's origin.

As it began, I was walking down the staircase (wide, in the middle) on the arm of my brother, who was dressed formally and regally. Might have been military, not sure. We descended the staircase into a huge room filled with people. Beautiful room. Lots of portraits. Very ornate. A ballroom maybe. I took my place in a reception line next to my brother, feeling an overwhelming sense of duty. Not unhappiness, but not happiness. Duty, respect, I don't know.

After a couple of people passed in the line there you were. Bright and smiling. That beautiful face that I see sometimes now, when I look at you. And you always catch me and say "what are you thinking?" Looking right through me. But then the face from the violent lifetime popped into my mind. And while you were holding my hand and looking into my eyes, I fainted. I hope that makes some sense because I referenced three different life times there. This is a complicated process isn't it? The "I" that was observing knew that the face that popped into the past "I's" mind was from the other lifetime. But the "I" in the reception line did not understand her fear.

Anyway, I blacked out. And came to in an adjacent room with some attendants working on me. When my brother (who is actually my oldest brother in this life) saw that I regained consciousness, he left the room and the attendants got busy loosening my clothing (really uncomfortable stuff) and powdering me. That was when I had the DeJaVu triggered by the powder. Now this is really interesting. I use powder in the summer every day. I have often had the same DeJaVu. But while experiencing this past life, I recognized this current life of mine within the DeJaVu. Really amazing. It seems that DeJaVu opens to not only past, but future lives.

Well, when I had regained my senses in the regression - after the attendants had finished with me, I knew that I had to return to duty. I went back to the reception line and there you were waiting for me. You asked if I was feeling better and for a dance. I looked at my brother, a look that requested his protection. He nodded. Now that was interesting because he knew what I was asking with just a look. And I knew the answer contained in the nod. And I also knew that the dance with you was expected. Not something I could refuse, in spite of my fear.

My mother announced that the reception line would end so that I could be seated. It seemed that she controlled everything. Made all of my decisions. And always would. I accepted it as part of the duty. The interesting thing there is that I knew she was my mom in this life. But so opposite. Short, light hair, heavy set. In this life my mom was thin, tall, dark and made no decisions for me. Paid very little attention, really.

Anyway - I sat for a few moments next to my mother in these huge, uncomfortable chairs before you approached. Your face and smile were totally endearing. You had not the slightest idea why I should be afraid. And there was no apparent intention to you that should cause fear. It was all irrational past life stuff.

As we danced, you told me that I was beautiful. And that I felt familiar. As if you had known me in another life. I thought this was odd, not traditional thinking for the time, a new concept for me. But, in spite of my upbringing, could not stop myself from telling you that I feared you, but did not know why. You held me more tenderly. Told me that I had nothing to fear. As I looked in your eyes and saw your face, I knew you meant what you said.

And that was the end of the impression. Actually that was a few impressions of the same life put together. The first time, I didn't make it past fainting. Had the experience of the violent lifetime afterward. Then understood the fear in the final impression. Three separate meditations that took more than two hours each.

Well, how was that? Make any sense? There are others. I know why I feel the way I do when you say baby. And that dream of us on the beach...we lived on one and were gloriously happy.

What I really want to explore is why you stay just out of reach. But that might take awhile.

Molly

From: JAZMAN@mbc.web
Sent: Friday, December 20, 2002 1:33 PM
To: mbrogan@mbc.web
Subject: RE: scratch

No, you don't share too much with me. I love reading what you say and trying to follow your thought processes when you get deep.

Fascinating. The previous lifetime with violence is occluded to me, but that temporary pain in my head was real. I think I preferred the more affluent time and that just happens to be more accessible. Easy to see why that is. I really shouldn't be diving into my past too much on my own, but sometimes the "TV" just goes on and there it is. And if the show isn't good, there are always other channels to watch if they'll tune in.

We have been around for a very long time. To find the origin of the violence between us, go back much farther. I am glad to hear you will be getting help with it. You have had so many and such deep recalls without any help. Quite amazing. I know that earlier relationships can have an assortment of effects in present time. A
recognition of having known the other being is a beautiful thing. The fact that we have done each other

in at times to varying degrees is an interesting concept to ponder. The fact that all the details of both the good and the not so good are unknown have a tendency to create urges to react in certain ways that are not always logical or self determined. The earlier moments have a stronger impact than the later. They are more basic on the chain and addressing them has a more impacting effect on the present than addressing incidents closer to present time. Don't limit yourself to known history. Things that happened in recent lifetimes can have their basis in previous ones. It's very interesting that "dead" memories or pictures come back to "life" when enough things in the present are similar to that time. And even when they're turned on again we don't necessarily see them, but we sure do react to them in various and often unexpected ways. Anytime we're amazed at how we reacted to something, guess what?

Confronting all this is the trick. Being willing to confront anything, not just saying it. It's easy to say, but difficult to really assume that viewpoint fully. Then the mind only gives up what we can confront anyway. We've got it all rigged pretty well. The being's considerations, whether he or she knows what those considerations really are, is the key. Hard to explain, but those have to be gotten to the surface and viewed by the being. He made them and only he can change them - with a little help, of course.

You sound happy. Are you?

Jake

From: mbrogan@mbc.web
Sent: Friday, December 20, 2002   6:00 PM
To: JAZMAN@mbc.web
Subject: RE: scratch

Am I happy? I don't know. I miss you. I'm writing a part of the book that intensifies that. And the past life reviews probably add to my feelings of ambivalence.

Jack comes home tonight so that should help. I have been gathering materials for a stellar year of gingerbread house construction with the help of Sue's daughter Hillary. I am planning two evenings, one with the Gerken family and one with Meg and her children. Sue's girls will probably help with both. I have baked enough pieces for 22 houses, so there should be plenty for everyone to have and give away.

This house is already full of light and laughter with Sue's girls home. I am hoping that Jamie will join us once his brother arrives. It will certainly be the best Christmas in the past few.

Happy? I guess so, it is Christmas!

Molly

From: JAZMAN@mbc.web
Sent: Saturday, December 21, 2002   9:06 AM
To: mbrogan@mbc.web
Subject: Merry Christmas

I leave for Chicago tomorrow and will stay 6 days. I hope to be able to see you during that time. Will you be able to break free? I will call when I have a better idea of how my time will be scheduled.
By the way, is there a certain religion that you are into? Do you believe there is an architect of the universe?

Jake

From: mbrogan@mbc.web
Sent: Saturday, December 21, 2002   12:21 PM
To: JAZMAN@mbc.web
Subject: RE: Merry Christmas

Call when you can, I will have to see what I have going
on at the time. It is hard to say with the kids coming
and going. I would love to make time to see you if that
is possible for you.

What do I believe? That the kingdom of god is within
us, and all around us. In every word and every thought,
every tear and every ocean wave, every heartbeat and
every war, every star and every kiss, every love, all that
connects and the spaces between. The kingdom of god
is all that I AM. Our job is – to discover it. The
highest form of that discovery – creation. Don't you
think?

Much love,
Molly

From: JAZMAN@mbc.web
Sent: Monday, December 30, 2002   4:02 PM
To: mbrogan@mbc.web
Subject:

Will you be kicking ass and saying no thank you
tonight?

From: mbrogan@mbc.web
Sent: Monday, December 30, 2002   4:11 PM
To: JAZMAN@mbc.web
Subject: RE:

Only if you are around (smile)

From: JAZMAN@mbc.web
Sent: Monday, December 30, 2002 4:20 PM
To: mbrogan@mbc.web
Subject: RE:

Just checking. I am with the kids now, but might be able to break free later.

From: mbrogan@mbc.web
Sent: Monday, December 30, 2002 5:01 PM
To: JAZMAN@mbc.web
Subject: RE:

My only plans for tonight thus far are to meet Paul and his wife for cocktails at some point. They are in town to see their children for the holidays, and currently driving back from a short trip to Michigan to see friends. But I haven't heard from them yet, which is unlike Paul. And with the snow, I would have to say those plans are tentative.

From: JAZMAN@mbc.web
Sent: Monday, December 30, 2002 5:10 PM
To: mbrogan@mbc.web
Subject: RE:

Do you want to tell me where? I will catch up if I can. You might look up, and there I will be, sitting at the bar. You could come up and say hi, or pretend you don't see me. I don't want to interfere with anything.

From: mbrogan@mbc.web
Sent: Monday, December 30, 2002 6:00 PM
To: JAZMAN@mbc.web
Subject: RE:

Still have trouble committing, eh? But why would I do that to you? I wouldn't do that to anyone! Paul and I haven't discussed where we will meet. I just tried his cell phone but it went right to voice mail. They must be

driving somewhere out of range. I will let you know
when I find out more. You are welcome to join us.

From: JAZMAN@mbc.web
Sent: Monday, December 30, 2002 6:09 PM
To: mbrogan@mbc.web
Subject: RE:

Would you leave me a voice mail when you have the
details? I will be with the kids and not have email
access.

From: mbrogan@mbc.web
Sent: Monday, December 30, 2002 6:18 PM
To: JAZMAN@mbc.web
Subject: RE:

Sure

From: mbrogan@mbc.web
Sent: Tuesday, December 31, 2002 6:00 PM
To: JAZMAN@mbc.web
Subject: Very Happy New Year!

I have an evening full of joy planned. But you know
those plans....it should be interesting.

Hope yours is smooth sailing! A toast, in my heart with
you, for the New Year, and all the promise that it holds
for both of us.

Take care Jake.

M ONTH NINE

THE ENDING

From: mbrogan@mbc.web
Sent: Friday, January 3, 2003   6:18 PM
To: JAZMAN@mbc.web
Subject: new beginning

Well, I imagine you are home now, back to your old
routine of hiding. Or are you buried under a mountain
of work from being gone for so long? Not surprising
we were not able to connect over the holiday.

I have decided that I really do need to share my first
moment in 2003 with you. Because I have not stopped
aching from it, and need to let it go. If I can. I thought
at first that if I kept it to myself, it would retreat in
time. But now I am not so sure. I will not pretend to
understand what happened with the ending of US. And
while the big picture is helping me to accept it, I still do
not understand the reason for it. Or agree with it -
consciously, anyway. But need to accept it completely
(somehow) without agreement and reason. I am not
sure how to do this. And you seem unwilling or unable
to help as you avoid communicating about it directly.

I was outside, near a bonfire, surrounded by happy,
singing, dancing, embracing people. And at the stroke
of midnight, I remembered our star. The star we chose

for our own that warm night in August when you held me close and we wished for our future together.

My eyes were drawn to that brilliant star, and I could not take them off of it, even during the embraces and I love yous and happy new years. It was then my heart began to ache and has not stopped.

I have been mulling this over. The main character in Remember Me felt closest to someone to whom she wrote but never saw. Someone to whom she gave emotion, not exchanged it. I wrote the character like that, knowing it was unhealthy and destructive. I can not allow myself to become that character.

I think that I need to give US a rest. To get some emotional, and maybe spiritual, distance. To allow the people around me into my heart to occupy the places we once shared. The ones that I still reserve for you. Love is no longer leading the way. The ache tells me that.

I hope, after a rest, we can resume our conversation and our friendship. I would miss you terribly if we went our separate ways with no relationship. And hope to always be your pen pal, if you will have me. But for now, I need to stop looking for you. To open myself up more to those around me. And allow myself to heal. I hope you understand.

Since October, all of my emails that were directed to the heart of US caused you to shut down. I don't mean to do that. And if you would like to respond, please do. But it seems to me that the only agreement between us now is our pen pal arrangement. And if that is true, I do need to give it a rest for the time being and heal myself. I would like to let you go without losing my faith in love. I hope I can.

"Speak of me as I am; nothing extenuate,
Nor set down aught in malice: then, must you speak
Of one that lov'd not wisely but too well"
WS

From: JAZMAN@mbc.web
Sent: Friday, January 3, 2003 6:18 PM
To: mbrogan@mbc.web
Subject:

Just got settled back here. The holidays flew by and
now I am sitting in front of a mountain of work. It will
be long days here ahead until I head back to Chicago to
see Grace in her final concert of this series mid month.
I miss my kids already.

You must be getting ready for your trip to Vegas. This
might be a whole new life for you. Call me when you
are there, or maybe I will call you.

Jake

From: mbrogan@mbc.web
Sent: Tuesday, January 9, 2003 5:40 PM
To: JAZMAN@mbc.web
Subject: new agreements

My horoscope today suggested I make new agreements
with friends. Any suggestions?

I wanted to ask you something. I don't know if you
remember the lifetime that I do that involved violence
between us. Violence, in fact, seems to be a recurring
theme across lifetimes for me. A friend suggested to me
that reviewing some of my deaths may provide clues.
And I have learned some transformational meditations
to do during the past life review that may help me get
beyond this painful theme for good.

I saw myself die in your arms during that life time. We

were still young, you looked young anyway. I forgave
you while you held me. Very intense and interesting.

But it led me to think of all of the ways that I have
worked to get past the violence issue in this lifetime.
Creating a community partnership against youth
violence in Warren Township. Writing Remember Me
as a statement about family violence. Disengaging from
a somewhat violent marriage. My X helped me to
understand all of the levels of violence beyond physical
and sexual.

Anyway, you mentioned getting to the considerations of
the person in the past life time. I may have done that,
but how do I know? Can you tell me what you meant?

We had some great lives together. It is fun to trip
around in them. The more I do, the more perspective it
puts on everything else about me and my relationships.

Glad to hear you are going to enjoy your kids at the end
of the month, and they are doing so well. Keep up the
good work. Interesting that you will not be in SF when
I am this month. I guess that is the way it is for us now.

Molly

From: mbrogan@mbc.web
Sent: Tuesday, January 9, 2003   6:21 PM
To: mbrogan@mbc.web
Subject: ghosting 27

Well, I told myself I wouldn't do it, but here I am,
writing to you again. I just need validation Jake, even
if it is only from your ghost. I need to know you see it
as I do. I need to know it is over. I need to know that
you are not going to pop back into my life when you
think the time is right. I am just not sure what I would
do if you did.

As I move on, there is a part of me that wants you to tell me to stay. Would I? There is a part of me that wants you to take me in your arms and never let me go. And a part that doesn't, maybe the larger part because I know, that it wouldn't be long, before you would need to hide, and control, and leave.

More than anything, there is a part of me that wants to settle what remains in the deepest parts between us. What do these lives we share mean, with all their love and pain. Can we learn the lessons, and leave the pain behind? What will it take to do that?

I used to go searching for the most passionate lives that we shared. I used to trip through time to connect with our most intimate moments of love. Now I am drawn to the most difficult moments between us, looking for meaning and ways to transform the karma into love. It seems to me that forgiveness is the key to transformation. Will you help me here? Or will you go running as usual?

I seize upon the violence between us and bathe the scene in sapphire light, creating calm, transforming the horror to compassion. Then I rewrite the scene into one with a loving ending. The acts of transforming karma are a writer's dream actually. I write and rewrite the scene until peace is established within me. I hold the peace within my heart, unconditionally.

Molly

From: JAZMAN@mbc.web
Sent: Tuesday, January 9, 2003 8:10 PM
To: mbrogan@mbc.web
Subject: RE: new agreements

Hi Molly. So your horoscope said to make new agreements with friends. Interesting. I got your e-mail from the 3rd and didn't know what to do. Sounded like you wanted me to leave you alone. Well, I did that until now, and since you sent me this, here I am 6 days later.

I have no idea what happened to me a few months ago. I haven't figured it out at all so I can't really say anything that would make any sense. Too much stress certainly could have had something to do with it, but I've had stress before. We were very close and then something went haywire and I don't know what. Some day I will. I'm sorry it got that way. I was happy with how things were going and then....?? I am sorry if I hurt you, now or any time…

You may be moving very soon. How was your Vegas trip? Did you get a job offer? I really hope and have this feeling like what you're doing is going to be very cool for you. I've been thinking about how to get back to Chi more often. I miss my kids so much.

So tell me about these agreements. What are you thinking?

What is your flight schedule for SF? We might have some days here that overlap. I would like to see you.

Jake

From: mbrogan@mbc.web
Sent: Thursday, January 11, 2003 3:33 PM
To: JAZMAN@mbc.web
Subject: new agreements

Hi Jake,

I am not sure what I expected from you in response to my excitement about past life discoveries. I guess I was hoping you would share the experience. I was not expecting you, at this point, after so much disappointment and hesitation, to ask to see me.

Destiny is still calling us out. If it weren't, we wouldn't keep bumping into each other. But character defines fate. And fate can put a lid on destiny. Let's not let our egos stand in the way of what our souls call us to do. We do not need to be in love to fulfill our destiny together. We don't even have to be in the same physical space. But we do need real communication. Words in print or with voice. Not manipulation. No hiding or avoiding. We both do those. That is our egos getting in the way. Honesty is needed for us to unleash the power between us for the greater good. And that is what we are being called to do. To what end is for us to discover. Please carefully consider this.

Interesting how, in past life meditations, we recall things from our own perspective, somewhat oblivious to what's going on with another person right in the middle of everything during the same time and place. Yes, that is interesting, but given the way we communicate now, not surprising.

A friendship with you, going forward, will need to include honesty. How many times have you said "I would like to see you," and not followed through with the meeting? Let's stop that finally. I am doing my best to salvage some sort of friendly relationship with you, Jake. I won't go back to falling in love to be disappointed again. Can you remember our friendship in High School? Can we rediscover that spirit of mutual respect and enjoyment?
Molly

From: JAZMAN@mbc.web
Sent: Thursday, January 11, 2003 7:11 PM
To: mbrogan@mbc.web
Subject: RE: new agreements

Dear Molly,
I have thought a lot about what you've said since your email arrived. It has never been my intention to not see

you again. If you agree, I will leave your name at the Top of the Mark for whatever time and day you say, for however many people will be with you. I will arrange the evening and take care of everything. I just need to see you. Please. lbj

From: mbrogan@mbc.web
Sent: Thursday, January 18, 2003 6:03 AM
To: JAZMAN@mbc.web
Subject: new agreements

Hi Jake,

I just returned from a visit to Paul in Vegas, meeting many people there and seeing the sights. We are still negotiating his offer but it does feel right to be there. Something deep inside tells me that this move is the right one.

You are right, it won't be easy with the kids. But my kids are in a place now where they are ready for independence from me. They also know they can turn to me for support when needed. I think it will be good for them to see a bit of the west. This may not be forever, but for now, it feels right.

As for meeting you in San Francisco next week, I want to thank you for the gracious invitation. Peg tells me that the place you suggest is wonderful. But before I agree to meet you again, I need to see us in a place of honesty and support. A place that can develop trust between us. Quite frankly, Jake, you have left me high and dry so many times, I have come to expect that from you. I expect more from my friends. And I certainly expect more from the man I love.

Will you be my pen pal? Given our recent past, it is really all I can offer you. In the mean time, I have taken to meditation that allows me to cut the chords with you. No easy task, as the chords between us are massive. But cut them I will, as many times as necessary, until the exchange of energy between us is comfortable again.

Molly

From: JAZMAN@mbc.web
Sent: Thursday, January 18, 2003   9:00 AM
To: mbrogan@mbc.web
Subject: RE: new agreements

Hold on, baby, I have no intention of cutting chords with you or anything else. I think we should meet to talk this over. You say when and where. I really feel like moving for you will be a big mistake. Can we start over again in Chicago? I know I have not been there for you, but I am willing to change. I know we can do this if you will just try. I think I will try to call you now.

Jake

From: mbrogan@mbc.web
Sent: Sunday, January 21, 2003   5:13 AM
To: JAZMAN@mbc.web
Subject: is negotiating possible with you?

I carefully considered all that you said. I don't agree with you, although that is nothing new between us lately. We seem to have a serious lack of agreement, creating a chasm that is quickly becoming too vast and treacherous to navigate. I think it is time to tell you exactly what I am looking for in a love relationship. I think that once I do, we will both agree, it is not what we have here.

- First and foremost, honesty. Everything about me is about honesty. I don't want to guess or be kept in the dark. There are so many layers to complete honesty beyond telling the truth. I consider hiding, putting us off into the future without agreement, and being non responsive but a few of the ways our relationship has become dishonest.

- I will love a man whose love is not based on the needs of his ego, but the discovery of his spirit. Who will allow me to remind him of who he really is when he forgets. And who will do the same for me.

- I require psychological safety in a relationship. This means unconditional love forgiveness, no blame, no diminishment. This means agreement of terms, not manipulation. This means allowing our common will to align with divine will, not control.

- I expect a relationship where agreements are negotiated respectfully, and barriers are agreed upon.

- I expect the man I love to continuously reveal his intentions to me and not hold back. He must understand and practice full disclosure so that together, discovery and self discovery become possible. They are possible in a relationship that is transparent.

- I expect implicit trust and the freedom to allow it to grow.

- I am looking for a guy who understands himself well enough to respond, not react to my love. Who is able to empty his ideal vision and fill it with the real me. Who has the emotional intelligence to act with integrity on the basis of who he really is. Who does not get stuck in emotional quagmire. Who can experience and release emotion and not be confused by attachment to it.

- I expect my love to appreciate me totally, my best aspects and my shadow. Together, we can embrace shadow and turn fear to love. Together.

- I am looking for a man who is willing to grow and expand awareness, who is open to life and love. Who knows that true currency is of the spirit, and is willing to give freely to spirit, not buy what he owns with external "things." He must know that all he owns, all he holds sovereign, is of spirit. He must be willing to let go of the bonds that tie him to his fears, and limit him. The wealth in his heart will be manifest in his life because of how he loves with reverence and respect.

- I require a man who is willing to sustain love with depth, and who understands that he deserves it.

- I expect a relationship where we can both take care of body, mind and spirit in ways that include balance and generosity with self and others.

- I am looking for a guy who is willing to do whatever it takes to find his way to me. Who holds love as a primary value for himself. Because love is the primary energy force of the universe. To create is to love. And to love completely is the highest achievement possible.

It seems, also Jake, that friendship is not possible with you. You want this relationship on your terms, in your time, according to your needs. The funny thing is, if you had expressed that to me months ago, I probably would have agreed. Unfortunately, that is not how this unfolded.

I am infinitely grateful for what we have shared. Ultimately, once we are through this, I think we will both come to value all that has passed between us. I am a much different person for having known you. I appreciate and treasure all that you have given me. Perhaps, after all, that is the extent of our contract. The rest, is just the way our egos need finalize it according to our destiny and fate.

Goodbye Jake. And God bless.

Molly

From: mbrogan@mbc.web
Sent: Monday, January 27, 2003 2:34 AM
To: mbrogan@mbc.web
Subject: Final Ghosting

I went to the local college library this morning, to relax in the quiet and pour myself into my favorite authors. It was a bright sunny morning and I was up since sunrise enjoying the day as it unfolded like a new beginning. I got to the library before it opened and was wild with impatience, for some unknown reason, until a student opened the door for me.

I ran up the stairs two by two and headed for the rare book section, my favorite. After quickly perusing the shelves, I grabbed an old favorite, a first edition "The Art of Seeing," by Aldous Huxley, found my usual overstuffed chair that faced the windows and the lake, and settled in for the day. Half way through the book, I repeatedly lost my focus and finally closed my eyes to relax and explore the moment within darkness. Something unknown had me opening my eyes and turning around in my chair before I knew what I was doing. There behind me, looking at me, was a familiar stranger. Our eyes met instantly, and as long as our eyes quietly held eachother, I felt our affinity expand.

Finally, after what seemed like an eternity, he smiled and moved toward me. My heart began to beat madly and I am sure that my face flushed with anticipation. He sat next to me and said hello and I was left speechless. He gallantly stepped in as tears filled my eyes and mentioned that he had read "The Art of Seeing" many years ago, along with other books by the same author. His voice was slow, gentle and meticulous, pulling me back into the present and helping me gain my composure. His voice, his smile, his eyes, his kindness all drew me out and into him, as if he knew just what to do. As if he had done this with me many times before, and mastered all the little barriers my personality presented before ever meeting me.

He said, "Let those with eyes, see." I felt my heart space explode.

We talked until the library closed, about things like Huxley's Gratuitous Grace: his notion of cooperating with grace, not so much by will - as awareness. I feel as if I have accomplished that very thing today. That I have been graced, and cooperated. My reward is a new, powerful, deep connection that feels like love long lost. I know he feels it too. I could feel it in his kiss as we parted after watching the sunset on the riverside. The kiss expressed his honest intention, and all the other honest intentions I have known from him in the past, and have yet to rediscover.

I need to thank you Jake, for preparing me for this day. I was destine to learn this lesson from you. You showed me how to recognize deep affinity, and how to explore it to discover the honest intent behind it. Because unless the affinity is supported with an integrated personality and honest intention, it may not be fated to connect in this lifetime. I am now beyond an unhealthy relationship. I can now let go of those feelings of affinity that are fated for nowhere, because character defines fate. I am fine with it. Because of you, and all that loving you has given me, I can pass that by and keep going until the real thing comes along.

I will always love you for showing me how to know the difference between destiny and fate.

Who we are today dictated the terms of our relationship. There was SO much possibility between us because of all that we share spiritually. You taught me more about the spiritual possibility between two people than any person or experience in this life time. Our love took me higher than I have ever been, and showed me what love can be. Now, I must honor that by letting you go. Because of who we are, this love cannot be between us. But it can be for me with the right someone else. And I hope that you find it for yourself too. And I hope that love brings you many smiles, shows you more of who you really are everyday, opens you completely and brings you peace.

All ways yours,
Molly